Praise for Ja

White Knight

"I'd be a damsel in distress any day if this white knight was in the vicinity! Don't miss Reding's latest goodie."
—Catherine Coulter

"This is an exceptional book, one that ranks high in Ms. Reding's *White* quartet. Her development of plot is unique, and her characters are noteworthy. A truly wonderful tale."
—*Rendezvous*

White Magic

"A charmingly written, witty tale sure to please historical Regency aficionados."
—*Romantic Times*

"This very satisfying historical romance runs the gamut of emotions; it also leaves just enough unsaid to make you want to read the next book."
—*Rendezvous*

White Heather

"An exciting and passion-filled love story that has a cleverly and intricately twisted plotline."
—*Rendezvous*

"A fabulous story line. . . . This is a must-read for fans of historical romances."
—Harriet Klausner

"A magical Regency romance."
—*Painted Rock Reviews*

Continued on next page . . .

Stealing Heaven

"Heroes to die for, unforgettable courtships, and unique, entertaining plots make this a winning series."
—Rendezvous

Chasing Dreams

"A wonderful romance rich in detail . . . [a] fast-paced, pleasurable read."
—Romantic Times

Tempting Fate

"A breathtaking read . . . will remain with its readers long after they have closed the book."
—Rendezvous

"*Tempting Fate* keeps readers turning the pages. Strong characterizations and good plotting make this tale come alive."
—Romantic Times

"[*Tempting Fate*] gives you everything: a wonderful story, rousing adventure, and courageous characters you'll never forget . . . splendid."
—Catherine Coulter

White Mist

Jaclyn Reding

A SIGNET BOOK

SIGNET
Published by New American Library, a division of
Penguin Putnam Inc., 375 Hudson Street,
New York, New York 10014, U.S.A.
Penguin Books Ltd, 27 Wrights Lane,
London W8 5TZ, England
Penguin Books Australia Ltd,
Ringwood, Victoria, Australia
Penguin Books Canada Ltd, 10 Alcorn Avenue,
Toronto, Ontario, Canada M4V 3B2
Penguin Books (N.Z.) Ltd, 182–190 Wairau Road,
Auckland 10, New Zealand

Penguin Books Ltd, Registered Offices:
Harmondsworth, Middlesex, England

First published by Signet, an imprint of New American Library,
a division of Penguin Putnam Inc.

First Printing, November 2000
10 9 8 7 6 5 4 3 2 1

For my dad,
Fred Adamowicz,
the very truest of heroes . . .

We had a scare this past year.
Thanks for making it through
and sticking around.

After all, we still have
years of hockey games
to go to together.

As an author, I have the privilege of
meeting other authors whose work I
admire, and whose friendship I cherish.

Such wonderful ladies as Sandra Marton,
Allison Leigh, Susan King, Elizabeth Boyle,
Catherine Coulter, and Mary Jo Putney,
who have, all of them, touched my life
with their support and kindness.

I wish this small acknowledgment
could truly demonstrate how much I
appreciate them.

Prologue

Cha do dhùin doras nach d'fhosgail doras.
No door ever shut but another opened.

Life as she had known it had ended. It had happened the morning of 12 September 1820—and she had never seen it coming.

Lady Eleanor Wycliffe, heiress of the Westover dukedom—the most illustrious dukedom in all England, no less—had been raised as a good many gently bred young English ladies are. Her days had been filled with ease and comfort, with nothing more expected of her than to turn a neat stitch and conduct herself in a polite and agreeable manner.

Since before entering the schoolroom at Miss Effington's Exalted Academy for Ladies of Gentle Breeding she had been taught that her sole ambition in life was to marry well, entertain graciously, and do her best to provide that as yet unknown future husband with that as yet unborn, all-important male heir.

Sit up straight, miss.
You need to glide, dear, not stride.
Hold your fingers just so when you pour.

Indispensable words whispered to her by an assortment of elder females, words solely intended to send any lady between the ages of twelve and twenty-two into a state of abject fear of ending up alone, like So-and-So's sister or Lady Whoever's niece, those social pariahs known as—

—spinsters.

Shudder.

Eleanor, however, had had a marked advantage in it all.

Unlike those poor young girls whose marriages were arranged sometimes without much more than an introduction between the bride and bridegroom, (like her best school chum, Lady Amelia Barrington, who two years before had forever joined her life with that of her father's favorite whist partner), Eleanor had been told since the age of four that she would have the opportunity to choose her lifelong mate.

She had done her part during her first Season in society, searching for and then finding a man with whom she shared common interests, one who treated her kindly, and who could provide her a home and the same comforts to which she was accustomed.

Richard Hartley, the third Earl of Herrick was handsome, polite, and well spoken of amongst the best society. He enjoyed books and had an ear for music, as she did. He didn't purposely correct her when she pronounced a word differently than he, and he listened, truly listened, to the things she had to say. They would get on well together, and the best part of it was that Richard's country house, Herrick Manor, was but two miles from the Westover ducal estate in Wiltshire, making him, Eleanor believed, a most sensible choice.

How funny life was, she remembered thinking, that fate had brought them into one another's lives as far away as London when their families had been neighbors for generations. Eleanor had simply taken this as one more reason why they were meant to spend their lives together.

Christian, however, didn't seem to follow that logic.

Christian Wycliffe, Marquess Knighton, Eleanor's older brother and family patriarch since the death of their father two decades before, had been reluctant about the match from the start. But his reluctance, he assured her, was simply due to the fear that she had settled too soon, had chosen too quickly, this only her first Season "out" in society.

"Give yourself time, Nell," Christian had said to her when she'd first mentioned Richard to him as a prospective brother-in-law. "No need to rush headlong into something so soon."

But rushing headlong into things was a trait Eleanor seemed to excel in, like the time she had decided she'd rather not be left at home with her nursemaid whilst her mother and Christian had gone off to a ball. So with all the foolish bravado of a seven year old, she'd twisted herself into the small compartment hidden behind the seat inside the Knighton coach, thinking once they arrived, her mother would have no choice but to allow her to go. What Eleanor hadn't considered was the possibility that once she got herself into the compartment, after having been jostled about during the ride, it might not be so easy getting out. The result was that instead of attending the festivities, Eleanor's mother, Lady Frances, had spent the evening standing alongside the coach, anxiously twisting her handkerchief whilst Christian, the Knighton coachman, and several others had to nearly disassemble the carriage to free her.

Still, despite Christian's lack of enthusiasm, Eleanor had remained confident in her choice of Richard. After all, almost all of her acquaintances were already married, and the young man suited her well. They passed a good part of several months together, dancing, walking in the park (always under her mother's watchful eye, of course), heading toward that inevitable moment when Richard would make the offer for her hand. The society matrons nodded their beturbaned heads in approval and Eleanor waited patiently while every-

thing followed its proper course, just as it had been prophesized throughout her girlhood—

—until 12 September 1820, when Christian had revealed
to Eleanor exactly why the marriage could never, ever take
place.

For a day that would bring about upheaval to rival the
trembling of the earth, it had begun with a most deceptive
calm.

Eleanor had been visiting at Skynegal, the ancient castle
her brother shared with his wife, Grace, in the northwestern
Highlands of Scotland. It had been a chill morning, an icy
prelude to the coming autumn.

Eleanor had awoken early, just as the first light of the sun
was peeking over the eastern hills, shimmering on the iri-
descent frost that had dusted the heather-clad slopes beyond
the castle walls. Everything had seemed so *fine.*

She had taken breakfast alone in her room, relishing some
quiet time by the glowing warmth of the peat fire, tucked beneath the folds of a thick woolen blanket while reading and
even sewing a bit. She had thought to pass the whole of the
day in similarly peaceful pursuits, until shortly before midday, when a letter had arrived for her bearing the distinctive
heraldic seal of the Earl of Herrick.

Richard had written to her from a property his family
held in Yorkshire, and in the letter, just as Eleanor had long
anticipated, he had proposed their marriage with information about his London solicitor, Mr. Jeremiah Swire, who, if
she accepted, would see to the signing of the marital con-
tracts and other legal details.

Though not the romantic, bent-on-his knee, moonlight-
cast sort of proposal both she and Amelia B. had whispered
about as young girls, Eleanor had been teeming with excitement as she had gone immediately to search out Christian.

She had found him alone in his study.

After reading Richard's letter—twice—Christian sat quietly behind his desk, listening while Eleanor diligently attended to every argument she thought he'd bring forth and even some he had not thought of. She reminded her brother how his own marriage to Grace earlier that same year and even that of their parents had been arranged by their grandfather, the Duke of Westover. She contended that hers would have a far firmer foundation since she and Richard had spent time in each other's company and had chosen one another instead of having one another chosen for them.

Eleanor had been confident of her position, countering each reason Christian found against the match with another reason for it, and when Christian finally fell silent, Eleanor began to think she'd won him over.

She couldn't have been more mistaken.

"I'm sorry, Nell. A marriage to Herrick is simply impossible. There is nothing more to be said about it."

The Christian she'd faced at that singular moment had looked so suddenly different from the beloved brother she had always known. He had the same chestnut hair, a shade or two darker than her own, and their mother's striking pale blue eyes, but the brow above them had been creased deeply and the smile he'd always shown her was no more.

It wasn't until that moment that Eleanor had begun to truly worry.

"Why, Christian? Please just tell me why you are set so decidedly against Lord Herrick? Is it that you think him dishonorable? Is there something you have learned about him that I should be made aware of?"

"No," he replied on a bitter frown. "From everything I have seen and heard of him, Herrick is the gentleman he presents himself to be."

"Richard told me you didn't get on together as boys. He thought perhaps that might color him unfavorably in your eyes, but I would have thought—"

Christian shook his head. "This has nothing to do with any schoolyard scuffle, Nell."

"Then why, Christian? If I am telling you Lord Herrick is the man I wish to marry, why can you not give your blessing to it? Wasn't it you who always said I'd have my choice? Didn't you promise me that? Well, I've done my part. I've made my choice, and it is Richard."

Christian didn't answer her. He only stared at her, unmoving as well as, it would seem, unmoved.

Frustrated at his stoicism in the face of her future happiness, Eleanor challenged her brother as she had never done before. She sat upright in the chair, her hands tight around its arms, and said, "You leave me no choice, Christian. Since you cannot think beyond your own feelings to mine, I must tell you that I am prepared to meet Richard at Gretna Green if need be."

"No!"

It was the first time in her twenty years that Eleanor could ever remember Christian raising his voice to her. Not even when she'd ruined his favorite pair of riding boots by tromping about the hedge maze in the rain with them had he spoken sharply. Christian had always indulged her shamelessly, giving her virtually anything she'd ever asked, even filching three of her favorite lemon tarts from the kitchen when she was five years old, despite the fact that it had ruined her appetite for supper.

Thus his sudden outburst that morning had alarmed her. The words he spoke next, spoken in quiet contrast, had utterly staggered her.

"The reasons you cannot marry Herrick have nothing to

do with my personal feelings about him, Nell. You could not possibly understand. Faith, you weren't yet born when . . ."

Eleanor spent the next quarter hour sitting stone still as Christian poured out a grim tale that began by revealing that their father, Christopher Wycliffe, had not died of the sickness she had been told he had since she'd been old enough to ask. There had been no fever, no last gasp of breath uttered one chilling night long ago when she was yet a babe tucked away inside their mother's womb.

Instead, Christian went on, their father had died fighting for their mother's honor in a duel against the man with whom she had been having an illicit affair, the same man who quite possibly, nay, probably, was Eleanor's own true blood sire—

—the previous Earl of Herrick, William Hartley.

Richard's father.

Even now Eleanor could remember the utter helplessness of feeling that moment as if the very walls had been closing in around her. Her throat had grown tight, choking off any response she might have given, and her eyes had stung with impending tears. She'd shaken her head against her brother's terrible insinuations as if by doing so, she could somehow take them away.

"This is not true, Christian," she sobbed. "Richard told me his father died from a fall off a cliff when he'd been out riding early one morning. No one saw him, only his horse returned to the stable alone. His body was never found. Why are you doing this, Christian? Why are you making this up?"

Christian closed his eyes then, taking a heavy breath against long pent-up emotions. "I am not making this up, Nell. God, how I wish I was, for I have spent most of my life trying to keep you from ever having to hear these words." He looked at her, visibly torn. "I was there that night along with the duke. (Christian had never called their grandfather anything but "the duke.") I watched Lord Herrick fire upon our father. I saw him fall. I knelt beside him while he died. His pistol was lying there in the grass, yet cocked. I picked it up. I didn't know what I was doing. I only saw Lord Herrick walking away. I aimed for him. I—"

Christian stopped, shaking his head, unable to bring himself to speak the next words.

He didn't have to.

"Y—you killed him?"

"I swear to you, I don't even remember firing. I only saw him drop into the grass before everything fell into a blur. The next two weeks were a living nightmare. The duke concealed everything of that night, disposing of Lord Herrick's body, bribing the physician to attest that Father had died from an illness. He wanted to banish our mother, too, denounce her publicly as an adulteress, but I pleaded with him not to. I promised him that if he would spare her and the child she carried, if he would set aside the question of your paternity and go on as things had been, I would do whatever he asked of me. I would give up my life to him to direct as his heir. And I did."

Eleanor just stared at her brother, as she struggled to keep hold over her every breath. Her consciousness hummed. Her hands trembled.

A moment later, her consciousness cleared on a single realization.

"This? This is why you agreed to marry Grace without ever having seen her first? All those years I wondered why you were so adamant about allowing me to choose when you yourself seemed so unconcerned about who you'd take to wife. All along it was because you knew you had sacrificed your life to protect our mother and to keep anyone, including me, from knowing that I am a really nothing more than a *bastard*?"

Christian just stared at her, his expression frozen with the obvious pain of his regret. But was it regret that he had had to hurt her? Or regret that he had had to tell her the truth now after keeping it hidden all these many years?

If Eleanor had never met Richard, had never thought of becoming his wife, she would have likely spent the rest of her life oblivious to the truth, never knowing that she was not, in fact, Lady Eleanor Wycliffe, daughter to one of the most illustrious families in England. She would have never known she was actually a by-blow of an adulterous affair that had resulted in the murder of two men, one very likely her father in blood, the other her father on paper?

Everything she had ever known of her life had been a terrible charade. She had grown up believing that her mother and father had lived a fairy tale together before her father had been unjustly snatched away by death. She had believed it because it was what she had been told by the very people she should have been most able to trust.

She remembered thinking of a quote from Euripides' *Phrixus* about the gods visiting the sins of the fathers upon their children, and wondered if the gods punished *doubly* those children whose fathers *and mothers* had transgressed. If so, then she was surely damned for eternity, for what crueler fate than to have lived the whole of one's life in the role of someone who had never existed?

That night, while everyone else in the castle had been asleep, Eleanor had gone, stealing away under the protective cover of a moonless Highland night. She didn't think to tell anyone else where she was going. In truth, she didn't really know herself.

She'd taken fifty pounds she'd found in Christian's study

and had used it to traverse the Highlands, making it as far south as the tiny seaside town of Oban. It was there she sat now, sipping blackberry tea in the tiny back parlor of a thatched-roof inn along the main harbor-facing street. She was exhausted, her feet cramped in her slippers from the days of walking she had done, and nearly all the money she'd had was now gone. She could but think it laughable that once she settled her bill with the innkeeper, she would have just enough left to buy her a place on a packet boat that would take her right back up the coast to Skynegal. Back to the lies. Back to the betrayal.

Perhaps it was a sign. Perhaps she should have simply gone on with her life as she always had, blissfully ignorant, pouring tea with her fingers just so while pretending not to know the terrible truth of the past. Perhaps that was the person she was meant to be, the secretly illegitimate, blissfully naïve, *false* Westover heiress.

It was just as Eleanor was on the verge of asking the innkeeper's wife for direction to that north-going packet boat, that she happened to spot a notice hanging crookedly on the wall.

GOVERNESS NEEDED FOR A LASS OF NOBLE BIRTH, AGED EIGHT YEARS. INQUIRE AT DUNEVIN, ISLE OF TRELAY.

She read it again. And then a third time.

What followed was one of those occasions that come along once, maybe twice, in a person's lifetime. Some called it a crossroads, others a deciding moment. Whatever it was, Eleanor knew she suddenly had a choice. She could board that northbound packet boat and go back the way she'd come. She knew what awaited her should she go back. She would spend her life living out a lie, trying every day to conceal the truth of her bastardy while facing daily the pity in the eyes of those who knew.

Or she could take the other path, the untried one, precarious and perhaps even frightening, but on it, she just might find a journey to the truth. . . .

. . . the truth of just who Lady Eleanor Wycliffe really was.

Chapter One

Isle of Trelay in the Scottish Hebrides

He heard the gillie's lumbering approach a full minute before he appeared, huffing and puffing up the steep hillside slope after having made the nearly quarter-mile trek from the castle to get there.

"There's a visitor, laird." The man paused, bending at the waist in order to catch his breath. "A visitor come t' the castle t' see you."

Gabriel MacFeagh, Viscount Dunevin, barely lifted a brow at the man's arrival. Instead, he stood kneeling before what was once a plump peahen, now naught but a mess of feathers and bloody remains partially hidden beneath a covering of thick heath.

"Winter's nearing," he said more to himself than to the man beside him. "The creatures of the isle are on the hunt for the food stores they'll need to keep them through the icy months to come."

The smaller bite marks and lingering odor of musk, revealed it had been a polecat, a weasel-like varmint distinguished by a thieving dark mask of fur across its eyes. It was a nuisance they could not afford to ignore for even small lambs and other mammals had been known to fall victim to these nocturnal trespassers. From the looks of the peahen, or rather what remained of it, this one would soon be coming back.

Gabriel rose to his full six feet and a half, shaking his dark head as he dropped the hen carcass into a sack he'd brought with him in order to keep from attracting other predators this close to the castle.

"Looks as if that polecat was at the hens again last night, Fergus. This is the second one we've lost this week. Better tell MacNeill we'll be needing to set some traps."

As squat as his lord was tall, Fergus MacIan had been the viscount's personal manservant since his becoming laird some ten years earlier. Before that, he had served both Gabriel's brother and their father, having lived on the distant isle nearly all his life. Standing beside Gabriel now, conspicuous in his tartan suit and trews, he scratched his grizzled head beneath his Kilmarnock bonnet and nodded in agreement.

"Aye, we'd best be seeing to it afore much longer, laird. Tha' last time the beast took off four o' the chicks and still we couldna catch it, the filthy *messan*."

Gabriel turned, the hem of his kilt barely clearing the knee-deep blanket of gorse, heather, and sedge that covered the shaded hillside. He whistled for Cudu, his black beast of a deerhound who was poking his snout among the hollows and the marram at the foot of the hill, searching for a rabbit to make sport of.

"Thig a-nall an seo," Gabriel called to him in Gaelic, for it was the language the beast best responded to. He watched as the dog lifted its slender head in response and began ambling up the hillside to join him.

Above, Gabriel caught sight of a fulmar in the distance, soaring gracefully over the surface of the dark waters of the churning Atlantic to the west. The bird's narrow gray wings were a poetic silhouette against the banking afternoon sun, one that at this time of year offered very little light and even less warmth.

A bit off the shore, several herring boats had just started coming in for the night. Beyond that to the southwest, he could just make out the hazy hills of Donegal in Ireland, rising like distant islets on the outlying horizon.

Trelay had been home to the MacFeaghs for nearly four hundred years, but the clan had put down roots in the isles long, long before that; just when they had first come to the Hebrides, however, was a story lost to the drifting mists of time.

Ancient legend held that Trelay, "the Isle of the Exiled," as it was called, and its neighboring isles of Colonsay and Oronsay had been the first landing place of St. Columba after he'd been banished from his native Ireland. The saint had thought to settle here, to continue his Lord's work, but upon climbing one of its hillsides—perhaps even the same one Gabriel now stood upon—and seeing his beloved homeland outlined in the mists, he took himself off for the more northerly Iona, having vowed never to dwell within eyesight of his native soil. Before leaving, however, he'd established an ancient priory, the rocky ruins of which were still visible on the isle's western shore, a last remnant of a much holier age for this ill-fated isle.

"Who is it that awaits, Fergus?" Gabriel finally asked, scratching Cudu's wiry head as the dog trotted to a halt before him. Even standing on all fours, the beast's head hit Fergus at midchest. "Surely it isn't Clyne, my steward, come early to collect the rents? We've more than a fortnight afore Michaelmas."

Fergus shook his head, kicking a brogued foot through the heath. "Och, no, laird. 'Tis a lass it is who seeks to speak wit' ye."

"A lass?" Gabriel stopped. "Is she mad?"

Cudu whined at the suggestion.

Fergus simply grinned beneath his bushy gray beard.

"Nae, laird, she looks as if her mind is quite sound. Says she's come from Oban in answer to your notice for a governess for Miss Juliana."

A governess. Gabriel had all but forgotten about the advertisements he'd papered the mainland with nearly a year earlier when the last governess, Miss Bates, had unfortunately left his employ. She had been merely one in a steady stream of others, although he'd managed to keep her a six-month, longer than most.

It was a series of events that had fast become routine. While he might finally find someone willing to travel to the distant isle of Trelay, one of the remotest parts of Scotland, within months, sometimes weeks of their arrival, they would come to him with some sad tale of a sick aunt or helpless grandmother who suddenly needed their attention, requiring that they leave—immediately.

While in the beginning Gabriel had believed them, even paying one's transport all the way back to Edinburgh, he soon began to notice that with each successive departure, they all of them had that same look in their eyes.

By the time Miss Bates had taken her leave the year before, Gabriel had come to recognize that look as fear.

After Miss Bates, and despite inquiries made as far away as London and even France, Gabriel's efforts to secure his daughter a new governess had not received a single response. Word of the isle's tainted history had, it seemed, traversed international boundaries. He'd just about given up, resigning himself to the probability that his daughter would never know a world other than this foreboding, desolate place, when now, a stranger seemingly appears out of the very mists, offering a renewed glimmer of hope.

It was on that auspicious thought that Gabriel happened to glance down at his hands, stained with blood from the carcass of the peahen. An image of that same horrified expression his departed governesses had left him with flashed to his mind's eye. He turned to regard Fergus yet standing beside him.

"Ask Màiri to fix our guest some tea whilst I clean up. It wouldn't do for the lady to meet the Devil of Dunevin Castle even afore she's had the chance to unpack her baggage."

She was utterly surrounded by them.

Eleanor could feel their frozen gazes coming at her from all sides, watching her in silent study as she sat with her hands folded, gloved fingers laced tightly together in her lap. No matter where she looked, no matter how she tried to avoid them, they were there. If she closed her eyes, she could almost hear them, their tiny voices whispering to her on the flurry of the island wind—

Run. . . .

Get out now. . . .

Before it is too late . . .

Eleanor's eyes shot wide open.

A medley of assorted deer, wildcat, and furry pine marten, met her gaze, stuffed and mounted on gray stone walls that were unfinished and that rose a good twenty feet or more above her head. Nearby a rather fierce-looking claymore whose scratched and pitted blade had no doubt contended with more than its share of severed heads hung alongside a dagger that looked quite able to gut an ox.

Oh dear, she thought to herself. What in heaven had she just done?

Eleanor sat alone, her back lamppost straight, knees pressed tightly together, wondering not for the first time what could have possessed her to come there.

Perhaps she should have listened to the warnings of Mrs. MacIver, the innkeeper's wife in Oban, cautioning Eleanor not to leave the safety of the Scottish mainland for the remote and perpetually mist-ringed isle of Trelay.

'Twas the place haunted by lost souls, home of the Dark Viscount, Lord Dunevin—or as Mrs. MacIver had called him—*The Devil of Dunevin Castle.*

"He's the last of the MacFeagh and may they die wi' him," the woman had told her in a hushed and secretive voice as if she truly feared the man could somehow hear all the way to the Scottish mainland. "A clan branded by generations of unexplained deaths and deep-seated rumors of otherworldly worship. 'Twas said their kind held mystic powers. Sprung from a seal-woman, they were. Even the name, MacFeagh, had roots in the Gaelic *MacDhuibh-shith,* 'son of the dark fairy.' "

As if to lend credence to the woman's dire admonitions, when first within sight of the lonely isle, a sudden white mist had swelled thickly around the small single-sailed boat carrying her there. The notion of Charon's mythical ferry approaching the gates of Hades had come upon Eleanor so suddenly that she half expected to see the dog Cerberus with his three ferocious heads and snakelike tail standing guard at the bleak rocky shore.

Even the boatman Eleanor had hired with the last of her money to take her across the choppy waters of the Firth of Lorne had shaken his head when she'd stepped foot from his small smack, his brow tilted sadly as if he truly believed once she disembarked she would never be heard from again.

"Watch yerself there, lassie," he'd said, his eyes hinting that he meant more than just the step off the boat onto shore.

But then Highlanders were a well-known superstitious lot; Lady Eleanor Wycliffe was not.

Even now as she sat amongst the draft and must of the ancient keep, Eleanor assured herself that the room didn't really have the looks of the den of Satan. In fact, there wasn't a pitchfork or a puff of hellish smoke to be found. There were books tucked neatly in towering wall shelves, a worn carpet stretched across the stone floor, a broad battered desk with papers piled properly in one corner.

Behind her, a fire burned happily in a stone-framed hearth. No smell of brimstone filled the air, only salt and mustiness and age, and the earthy scent of the peat that the locals were even now drying on the moor to prepare for the coming winter. The wind didn't howl with the yawning terror of the underworld, but instead whistled through the battlements at the top of the castle's central tower, tugging playfully at the tartan curtains through the narrow open window beside her.

Indeed, the place presented itself as just what it was, a very ancient-looking tower fortress on a very remote Hebridean island off the Scottish western coast, and if she put aside all those many things she'd been told about the castle's owner, she could even begin to believe there was nothing for her to be nervous about.

Until a sound came from outside the door, like an approaching footstep, bringing Eleanor instantly upright.

He is coming.

Her bravado turned to instant ether as she wrapped her fingers tightly around the carved arms of the chair. What would she say when he arrived? *Good afternoon, my lord, yes, I've come to apply for the position of governess to your spawn—pardon me—child. And if you please, I would be ever so grateful if you would not sacrifice me to the nether reaches while I am in residence. . . .*

What if he was truly as terrifying as everyone said? Mrs. MacIver had told her the child couldn't speak, that her voice had been stolen away by her father in an effort to keep her from revealing the truth of his evil deeds. And what exactly, she wondered, had happened to the previous governess?

With a quick glance away from the dagger on the wall, Eleanor looked to the window, wondering how far was the drop should she need to flee.

"I've brung ya tae."

Eleanor jumped at the voice that came suddenly from behind her. She turned and drew a breath to calm herself when she found not the devilish viscount she had expected, but the wizened codger who had answered the castle door upon her arrival. She hadn't heard anyone come in.

The man could have stepped straight out of the pages of history dressed as he was in colorful tartan trews, his head covered by a feathered blue bonnet, his face blanketed from nose to chin by a thick grizzled beard. He was shorter than she, with the sort of permanently fierce expression brought on by squinting against the sharp winds of the isles. He reminded her of the engravings she'd once seen of battling Highland warriors, only instead of a claymore clasped in his hands, he bore a silver tea tray.

"His lairdship bids me to beg yer pardon. He'll be occupied a wee bit langer."

Without bothering to wait for her reply, the man dumped the tea tray unceremoniously upon the table beside her and turned away, leaving just as abruptly as he had come.

The ladies at Miss Effington's Academy would have been appalled.

Eleanor waited until he had closed the door behind him, and then a moment more, before she lifted the lid from the china teapot to peer cautiously inside. It certainly had the looks of tea, she thought, then sniffed the flowery brew. She had read once that arsenic carried a particularly almondlike scent. She eyed the small plate of biscuits beside the pot, giving the dusting of cinnamon and sugar atop them a most speculative study.

Her first thought, of course, was to leave the tray untouched, but then her stomach thought the better of it, undertaking a decisive rumble. It had been hours in making the crossing from the mainland; it was now nearing the close of day and she hadn't had a bite to eat since breakfast. Perhaps a few sips of tea and a nibble of biscuit would serve to settle the nervousness she felt. Besides, if she was to serve as governess here, she couldn't very well avoid taking meals in the household.

Throwing caution to the wind, Eleanor took up a biscuit and sank her teeth into it.

It was delicious, of course, as much as a biscuit could be delicious, and she finished that one and then another before the clock had passed another quarter hour. She left the third biscuit on the plate and, having finished her cup of tea, stood from the chair to poke about the room in hopes of easing her niggling apprehension.

She stopped to peer at one object or another that was set about the room—a globe that showed the placement of the constellations, a single-handed lantern clock engraved with dolphins—trying to glean something, anything about the sort of man the viscount might be.

She glanced thoughtfully at the titles that lined the bookshelves, more than a little impressed by the collection. Was he a well-read man, interested in a variety of topics? Or were these many volumes simply an assortment that had been accumulated through generations? The angling rod and pair of well-worn waterproof boots in the corner might lead one to think he enjoyed a pastime more suited to one blessed with patience. The size of the boots, however, hinted he was no small figure of a man.

Eleanor came to the window and paused a moment, gazing at the dramatic panorama below. In contrast to the bleakness of the rocky shore, the isle's midlands were stunningly lush and colorful, even at this late time of year, splashed with hues running one into the other like a kaleidoscope of watercolor paints.

Cattle of the darkest black she'd ever seen grazed lazily on the verdant machair overlooking the crude stone jetty that served as the isle's landing point, where she had first arrived not an hour before. Fleecy black-faced sheep peppered the rolling hillside behind them while along the distant coast she spied several small crofter's cottages, motley structures that resembled lopsided stacks of rock and stone topped by roofs made of thatch or green turf.

A dog barked a sudden deep baritone from below and she turned, catching sight not of the dog, but of a lone figure seated alone upon a boulder that faced out onto the sea. Something about the figure, the feeling of isolation on that windswept bluff, drew Eleanor's attention. A small brass telescope stood on the table beside her. Curious, she took a moment to bow her head to the eyepiece for a closer look.

The figure of a child, a girl, came slowly into focus through the glass. Dark hair, the color of a raven's wing, lifted on the gusting wind, blowing briskly about her face and eyes like tangled cobwebs, but the child seemed not to notice it. Nor did she seem to notice the small lamb standing beside her making a meal of the ribbon sash of her dress. She simply sat there, still as any standing stone, the feeling of loneliness about her so strong, so overpowering, it was as evident as the eerie mist that clung to the isle's shoreline.

There could be no doubt she was the viscount's daughter, Eleanor's potential charge.

"I am sorry to have kept you waiting so long."

Eleanor jerked away suddenly from the eyepiece, nearly upsetting the object in the process. She had been so fixed on watching the child, she hadn't heard him coming. This time, though, there was no doubting who he was.

No small figure of a man indeed; he was quite simply the most imposing figure Eleanor had ever faced. Taller even than her brother, broad through the shoulders, just his arrival made the room seem inimitably smaller. Eleanor watched as he headed toward the desk, noting his height, well over six feet, the blackness of his hair that swept just below his coat collar.

He wore a belted plaid in shades of dark red, white, and green, with a length of it draped carelessly over the shoulder of his dark woolen coat. The collar of his shirt was open loosely underneath and his face was darkened by the slight growth of a beard, as if he hadn't shaved in days. His tartan stockings and buckled shoes were mud-spattered and his hair was ruffled about his forehead from the wind. His eyes were so dark, she couldn't tell their color, his mouth held no hint of a smile. With his rough looks and potent presence, Eleanor couldn't help the thought that the title "Devil of Dunevin" suited him most aptly.

Her heart, she noticed then, was pounding.

"I'm Dunevin," he said, "laird of the castle and this isle. I'm the one who posted the notice you saw in Oban. Please, won't you sit?"

He spoke as someone who'd been educated in the south with only the slightest hint of a burr. His voice was low

timbred, deeply and quietly compelling like the distant roll
of thunder one heard before a storm. It was the sort of voice
that brought gooseflesh running up the arms of young maidens.

Eleanor was one such maiden.

Dunevin motioned toward the chair she had previously
occupied and said without preamble, "Fergus didn't tell me
you were so young."

Still struck by the sight of him, the sound of him, the
presence of him, it took Eleanor a moment to respond. "I'm
sorry?"

"What are you, miss, all of eighteen?"

His direct almost blunt manner of speaking broke her
from her bemusement of him and she answered after first
clearing her throat, "I am one-and-twenty, my lord."

He raised a brow. "Indeed? One-and-twenty?"

"Well, nearly." She shifted beneath his unblinking stare.
"In any case, I assure you I am quite able to manage."

The viscount watched her, mentally measuring her, she
knew. He was wondering what a seemingly genteel young
lady was doing in a place like his remote island alone. His
silence was beyond unnerving.

"I'm afraid Fergus didn't tell me your name, Miss . . . ?"

"Harte," she responded without thinking, saying the first
thing that came to mind. "Miss Nell Harte."

It was as good a name as any other, she supposed, for it
wouldn't have done to tell him her real one, not when the
names of Wycliffe and Westover were nearly as renowned as
that of Hanover across the kingdom.

"Well, *Miss Nell Harte*," he said, repeating the fictitious
name in a way that made her wonder if he was mocking her,
"from whence do you hail?"

"Surrey," she lied.

"Surrey?" he repeated.

"Yes."

"The seat of my wife's family is located very near there in a small parish called Abinger. Do you know it?"

Eleanor swallowed, caught with indecision as to whether she should stretch her false tale and tell him she did know it, or admit that she didn't and quite possibly alert him to the fact that she knew nothing really of Surrey other than that it was located in the south of England?

"Abinger . . ." she answered quickly on a nod. "Yes. Yes, I do."

"Indeed, then you must have shared the acquaintance of the curate there, Mr. Pevensley. It was he who married me to my wife."

Eleanor nodded on a cautious smile, saying even as her brain screamed at her to shut up, "Indeed I saw him shortly before I departed. He was doing quite well."

What in heaven's name had just possessed her to say that?

"Indeed . . ."

The viscount fell silent, staring at her again with that same direct look that made her want to pull the edges of her cloak more closely about her. Eleanor prayed he wouldn't question her further about the curate. A moment passed. The wind whistled through the window. Eleanor adjusted the cuff of her sleeve.

"References?"

She had been afraid of this, of course, but hadn't been to-tally caught off guard by it. "I'm afraid I haven't any, my lord."

Dunevin looked at her. "No references?"

She shook her head and smiled, folding her hands neatly

on her lap before her. She offered no further explanation.
She didn't have one.

The viscount leveled her a stare. "Miss Harte, forgive
me for being, well, *blunt,* but from what I can see you are
barely out of the schoolroom, you have appeared from out
of nowhere, from Lord-Knows-Where, certainly not anywhere near Abinger, since the curate Mr. Pevensley has
been dead nearly these five years past—"

An embarrassed flush begin to spread across Eleanor's
cheeks.

"—You are applying for the position of governess to my
only child, yet you have no references to show that you are
at all qualified for the position. Quite obviously, given just
these initial observations, I must assume you have something to hide. Your name probably isn't even Harte. So tell
me what makes you think I would hire somebody under
these circumstances to see to the care and education of my
only daughter?"

Eleanor straightened in her seat, refusing to shrink under
his censure, and said in a voice that was surprisingly clear,
"Because, if you'll pardon *my* frankness, my lord, there is no
one else *willing* to take the position."

Dunevin stared at her, silent, quite obviously displeased.

Eleanor opened her reticule and unfolded the notice she
had taken from the wall of the inn on the desk before him.
"I'm told I am the only one to have shown any interest in the
position in some time."

The viscount didn't even bother to glance at it. Instead he
stared at her, hard, his mouth turned in a decided frown.

Eleanor pressed on. "I know that the last governess you
managed to employ left her position nearly a twelve-month
ago. I also know that you have been unable to secure another

for the position since, despite numerous inquiries made across the land."

She sat forward in her chair. "Lord Dunevin, while I cannot go into the details of my background, I can assure you I was raised among polite society all my life, not in Surrey, no, but elsewhere. You are right in assuming I have never served as a governess before, which is the reason for my lack of references. My upbringing, I believe, more than qualifies me for the job. I can speak both French and Latin. I was instructed at the best of ladies' establishments in England. I have poured literally hundreds of cups of tea, have arranged countless dinner menus, and although it doesn't quite look it now," she went on, looking down at her travel-worn gown, "I do know the proper way to dress. I can dance the allemande, the quadrille, the waltz, and dozens of others. I can sew a variety of stitches neatly and evenly. I can cipher. I am accomplished musically. I can recite poetry and quote philosophers. I daresay you'll not find another more qualified for this position in your lifetime"—she took a breath—"so as I see it, you can allow your daughter to languish without an education for another year, or you can give me a chance. That is all I'm asking for, the opportunity to show you that I can teach your daughter the accomplishments she needs to move in society. I assume that is what you are hoping for?"

The viscount stared at her, his expression frozen.

Eleanor sat, returning his stare, half expecting him to turn her out when next he opened his mouth. She had no idea what she would do if he did, where she would go. One thing was certain, if he did turn her out, she was going to have a long swim back to the mainland. She hadn't two shillings left to rub together to keep her.

But, remarkably, he did not turn her out, at least not

immediately. Instead the viscount stood and crossed the room to the window with his hands clasped loosely behind his back. As he stood there, Eleanor noticed the way his dark hair curled just below the collar of his coat, the pensive set of his shoulders. He remained for several minutes, not speaking, just watching his daughter as Eleanor had from that same vantage moments earlier.

From where she sat, Eleanor could see that the child had not moved despite the fact that a soft rain had begun to fall. A moment passed. Two. The rain fell harder, driven by the rising wind. Still, she sat. Still the viscount stood watching.

Finally, when Eleanor was on the verge of running out to fetch the child herself, she spotted a maidservant making her way from inside the castle toward her. She wrapped a cloak around the child's shoulders and drew her up from her sitting place, walking her back toward the shelter of the castle walls.

Still the viscount did not move.

"What is your daughter's name?" Eleanor asked softly, unable to bear the silence any longer.

"Juliana."

Dunevin turned, his face as clouded as the sky outside. "She does not speak."

Eleanor nodded. "Yes, I know."

He looked at her. And then he shook his head. "The locals have already filled your head with their gruesome tales, I see, no doubt leaving nothing out in their descriptions. They likely tried everything to dissuade you from making the crossing"—he paused—"and yet you came seeking the position of governess despite their warnings. Why?"

"Fantastic tales about the misfortunes of others do not interest me, my lord. I have always found that idle gossip is naught but the work of th—" Eleanor stopped herself, hoping he didn't realize what she had begun to say.

"—of the devil," he finished, "or so they say. But tell me, Miss Harte, does the same hold true if it is gossip *about* the devil?"

His look was suddenly so intense, Eleanor could not think of a single thing to say in response.

The viscount left his place at the window and returned to the desk to open the top drawer. "It seems both of us are in need of each other then. You have made a good argument, Miss Harte. You are hired. Anyone who has sense enough to discount the superstitious stuff and nonsense of the mainlanders most certainly deserves a chance. The salary is one hundred pounds per annum. Are those terms acceptable?"

Not six months earlier, Eleanor had spent a hundred pounds and much more just on the wardrobe for her coming-out into society and without giving it a second thought. That had been Westover money, money that she now knew was intended to hide the truth of the past behind a mask of propriety.

The money she would have now would be earned on her own. The sense of independence that one hundred pounds per annum gave her was worth more than all of the Westover riches.

Eleanor nodded.

The viscount removed some coins from the desk drawer and dropped them into a small drawstring pouch. He then placed the pouch on the desk before her.

"Consider this an advance on your salary. You might do well to use some of it to purchase a pair of sturdy shoes and a more serviceable overcoat. Winter comes fast to the isles, Miss Harte, and you won't find much use for kid slippers here. My gillie, Fergus, can make arrangements for you with the cobbler in Oban."

He crossed to the door and opened it on where the very man stood waiting. "Fergus, please show Miss Harte to the nursery floor." He turned to her. "You will find my daughter there now. Dinner is at six, we keep country hours here. If you have need of anything else, Fergus will see to it for you."

Eleanor stood to leave, wondering at Dunevin's sudden urgency to be rid of her. "Should I not speak with Lady Dunevin first before going to meet your daughter, my lord?"

Dunevin's face lost all expression. He stood, for a short time frozen by her words. "I'm afraid that won't be possible, Miss Harte. Lady Dunevin is dead."

And with that, the Devil of Dunevin Castle swept from the room just as suddenly as he had come.

Chapter Two

The Dunevin nursery was comprised of three rooms perched at the topmost floor of the castle's main donjon, or tower. Accessed by a succession of turn-pike stairs nestled in each of the keep's corner turrets, the task of getting there alone was no easy undertaking.

The first flight of stairs took them to the floor above the main hall, where they then crossed the upper gallery to the adjacent turret. No sooner had they reached the next highest floor than the stairs had come to an end again and they were made to cross to the third turret in order to continue on to the next flight of stairs. It went on this way for five floors in a confused sort of zigzag pattern until, by the time they reached the nursery at the top, Eleanor had very little confidence at all in her ability to find her way back unassisted.

The viscount's manservant, Fergus, whose task it was to direct her through this tangled skein of stairs and towers, explained that the ancient keep had been constructed in that manner specifically as a means of defense. "It would allow the Dunevin laird the opportunity to escape in times of invasion," he'd said, "through a secret passageway that only the laird and his most trusted servant knew about."

Having traversed the complex labyrinth herself, Eleanor could only agree. If she'd had to find her way alone, she'd

not have made it past the third floor. In fact, on more than
one occasion as they'd made the climb, she'd half expected
to turn a corner on the crumbling bones of some long-
departed intruder who'd wasted away centuries earlier, still
clutching his claymore after getting lost while laying siege
to the place.

The governess's bedchamber, to which Eleanor was directed first and which would be her own retreat in the days
to come, was modest in both size and furnishing. It held a
plaided box bed, one side table, a small chest of drawers,
and a simple washstand in the far corner. The walls, a lime-
washed white over bare stone, had no decoration save a
crude hook that Fergus demonstrated would hold the
"cruisie" lamp he'd brought, an iron ladle-shaped fixture
that burned by way of a rush pith stuck in a shallow depth of
fishy smelling oil.

The room was what was called in earlier days "a mural
chamber," built into the very thickness of the keep's walls
and a twin to the one the viscount's daughter occupied one
door further down the passageway. It was the schoolroom
that took up the better part of the tower's top floor, stretching at great length across the hall.

In contrast to the bedchambers, the walls there were finished in plasterwork and there was a hearth framed in carved
stone, indicating to Eleanor that the room had originally
served as a bedchamber with the two smaller chambers used
perhaps as an adjoining garderobe or servants' quarters. For
all its space, though, the schoolroom contained but a single
window, the only window on the entire floor.

Eleanor stood now, unnoticed in the doorway, contemplating the play of the waning daylight through that one
small window against the child's profile as she sat across the
room. They were alone, Fergus had returned belowstairs

shortly after delivering her there, leaving Eleanor to acquaint herself with the silent young girl whose care was now hers.

Juliana MacFeagh was a pretty child, slender, with hair that was the same endless black as her father's. Still damp from the rain, it curled softly below her shoulders, the length of pale ribbon that tied it back from her face hanging limply over one ear. She wore a light blue frock sashed at the waist over white pantaloons that peeked out from under layers of tartan skirts. Her mouth was small, pursed into something resembling a frown but not quite, and her eyes, large on her delicate face, were of a dark, indistinguishable color.

From the outside, she appeared to be a perfectly ordinary-looking nine-year-old girl, the sort who would spend her days dressing up for imaginary tea parties and arranging her hair in elaborate coiffures. It was only when one looked closer that there was something else about her, something deep inside that kept her distant, somehow untouchable, like a bisque Dressel doll Eleanor had once seen in a shop window on Bond Street in London, lovely to look at, but so fragile, it could only be displayed and never played with.

Eleanor entered the room quietly, crossing the lengthening afternoon shadows that spilled through the window as she came to stand beside her young charge. Juliana remained where she was, sitting on one of the recessed seats that had been cut into the stone wall beneath the window. She didn't move. If she at all realized Eleanor was there, she gave her arrival no notice whatsoever.

"Hello, Juliana," Eleanor said, smiling at her in greeting. "I am Miss Harte, your new governess."

She held out a hand, but the child did not move to take it. She did, however, glance at Eleanor briefly, allowing a slight wrinkling of her forehead, indicating that although she might not speak, Juliana could indeed hear.

A moment passed. Juliana went back to staring out the window, shifting slightly away from where Eleanor yet stood. Behind her the rain trickled spiritlessly down the windowpane, the wind soughing through the courtyard below like a distant moan. Time ticked by as Eleanor searched for something, anything, to breach the interminable silence between them.

"We have a little time to us before the dinner hour," she said. "The rain will keep us from going outside, but I thought perhaps we might find something here to occupy us."

There was no response.

Eleanor said to the back of Juliana's head, "Do you read?"

Again, nothing, so she turned to look about the room for a book or a plaything or anything that might engage the little girl's interest.

The place, she decided immediately, was as bleak and as characterless as a book filled with nothing but empty pages. Except for a single faded map of England that looked as if it had been drawn two centuries before, the walls were bare and painted in a pale nothing of a color that wasn't quite green and wasn't quite beige, but something hideously in between. The furnishings, stiff and unappealing, had been covered in the same lackluster color, a finishing touch to the aura of cheerlessness that pervaded the place. Narrow iron bars flanked the outside of the window, and although likely intended as a measure of safety, it only lent to the impression more of a tollbooth than a haven of learning.

The only other ornament, Eleanor found with dismay,

was a slender well-worn birch rod propped menacingly near the door.

It was no wonder the child spent her time looking out the window.

On the shelves, Eleanor noted a few examples of the typical children's literature, Aesop's *Fables* and the tales of the Grimms alongside Wedderburn's more rudimentary *Institutiones Grammaticae*. Sparse toys that looked as if they'd never been touched by a child's hand stood beside others that had endured through generations of play. One in particular, a wooden doll with painted black eyes and curled flaxen hair, caught Eleanor's eye.

She was a fashion doll, one used by dressmakers in France to display their latest designs in miniature to their English patrons. She was fully dressed in quilted petticoats and a linen shift under a gown with hooped skirts such as those popular in the previous century. But it wasn't the elaborate costume that drew Eleanor to it. There was something in the doll's expression, a twin to Juliana's same faraway look, that brought her to reach for the small figure.

Juliana sprang to her feet, moving from her window seat to pull the doll quickly away. She stared at Eleanor with silent, narrow-eyed suspicion.

"Oh, I wouldn't have harmed her," Eleanor said softly. "I was just going to look at her."

Juliana said nothing. Instead she returned to her seat to once again face the horizon through the window bars. She held tightly to the doll, sitting in that same way a rabbit would when cornered, stiff and unmoving, as if hoping to blend into its surroundings.

Eleanor approached Juliana slowly, lowering onto the window seat beside her. She leaned forward, resting her arms on her upraised knees, as she watched, and waited.

"She's a very pretty doll, Juliana."

Juliana kept her eyes fixed staunchly on the window, making no effort to respond. Her only movement was the soft-breathing rise and fall of her chest.

"You know," Eleanor persisted, "when I was a girl, I had a doll quite like her. She was called a 'Queen Anne' doll but I named her 'Frances' for my mother because she looked just like—"

Eleanor forgot her next words. Juliana had abandoned the window and turned suddenly to look at her. Her mouth may have said nothing but her eyes were filled with such stark longing, Eleanor was taken by a chill that had nothing to do with the inclement weather.

Like her own childhood toy, this doll was obviously a connection for Juliana to the mother she had lost; considering its age, perhaps even a remnant from Lady Dunevin's own childhood that had been passed on to her only daughter. As she sat looking on the torment that filled the child's eyes, for a fleeting moment, thoughts of Eleanor's own mother surfaced, thoughts she had spent the past several weeks since leaving Skynegal stubbornly refusing to heed.

How very much she missed her. For as far back as Eleanor could remember, Frances, Lady Knighton, had been more than a mother to her only daughter; she had been her closest friend. From telling her stories at night to teaching her the intricate steps of a dozen different dances, Frances had shared everything with Eleanor. Even now, if she closed her eyes, Eleanor could almost feel the familiar gentle touch of her mother's hand when she brushed out Eleanor's hair after her bath, a task she had continued even after Eleanor had grown into womanhood.

She remembered fondly her mother's love of wildflowers and the hours she had spent with Eleanor walking through countless country fields, relating little anecdotes about each one they encountered. She remembered the conversations they had shared together, talk of grand balls and the magnificent parties Eleanor would attend when it was finally her time to "come out" into society.

They had planned for that first Season for so long, discussing every detail down to the color of each pair of slippers—even, Eleanor remembered wistfully, what it would be like to be kissed that first time by the handsome young swain who would one day make her his wife.

It will feel as if the earth has stopped spinning and everything around you has vanished into a shimmering white cloud, Frances had told her when Eleanor had asked her one long-ago spring day. They had been walking in Hyde Park, a daily outing for mother and daughter. The daffodils and crocuses had been in brilliant bloom, and Frances had turned to face her daughter with a tender knowing smile.

The first time you kiss the man you love, for that one moment in time, somehow you will have even forgotten how to breathe. Imagine standing in the very midst of a rainbow, my darling girl. Your heart will have wings and for the rest of your life, nothing will ever be the same.

Eleanor looked now on the innocent face of this child who could never again see her own mother, talk to her, share with her, and felt the urge to reach out to Juliana, offer her some small comfort against so great a loss. "Juliana, I—"

The moment was shattered nearly before it had begun when Fergus appeared at the door.

" 'Tis time for you to come doun to sup," he said, throwing a sidewise glance at Juliana, who sat before Eleanor, yet gripping the doll in her arms.

Eleanor let go her breath and nodded to him. "Thank you, Fergus."

She waited until he had gone before turning back to the window, but that rare chance, that brief moment had already gone. Juliana had retreated, her dark eyes sadly distant once again.

Not wishing to press her, Eleanor stood.

"It sounds as if we are expected downstairs, Juliana. I'm not quite certain I can find my way down. I wonder if you wouldn't mind perhaps leading the way?"

Juliana simply stared at her. After a moment, however, she stood and started for the door.

Eleanor followed Juliana quietly as they walked the gamut of upper corridors and towers with only the sound of their skirts rustling against the stone floor and the distant patter of the rain yet falling on the courtyard outside. She tried to think of something to say, some magical phrase that would reach behind that wall of silence to the troubled little girl hiding beyond, but decided to leave Juliana to her thoughts. She had only just arrived and Juliana would need to adjust to this new change in her life. They would have days ahead of them to get to know one another.

The rain had brought on the night's darkness early and Eleanor had taken a candle with them to light their way. Its small flame danced and flickered as they walked, throwing silvery shadows against the beautifully woven arras that hung from the stone walls.

When Eleanor and Juliana arrived at the dining hall, Lord Dunevin was already seated down the length of the polished oak table. The room was large and brilliantly decorated but it wasn't the silver that gleamed in the candlelight or even the beautiful carved marble fireplace that caught her attention. What Eleanor noticed first upon entering the room was that the table was only set for one other person.

"Good evening, my lord," Eleanor said cheerfully, pretending not to notice as they came in. She bowed her head in greeting. "My apologies for our tardiness. Juliana and I were just getting acquainted in the nursery and lost track of the time."

The viscount looked up from the burgundy in his wineglass. "My daughter does not take meals in the dining room, Miss Harte."

The cut of his words brought an immediate chill to the place that even the fire blazing in the hearth could not chase away. Eleanor looked from the viscount to where Juliana stood beside her. She had bowed her head and was staring at the toes of her shoes sticking out from under her pantaloons as if she had just been reprimanded for a misdeed. After a moment of absolute silence, she started to turn for the door, but Eleanor set her hand on her shoulder, stopping her.

"Indeed, my lord," she said, keeping her voice pleasant. "If I may ask then, where does Juliana take her meals?"

The viscount frowned at her. "She sups in the nursery."

Eleanor wasn't surprised by the viscount's pronouncement; a good many members of the nobility chose to live wholly separate lives from their children, only seeing them at scheduled intervals each week and on special occasions and leaving their care to others the remainder of the time. But given the isolation of both their home and her muteness, Eleanor would have thought Juliana better served by the company of others.

"My lord, begging your pardon, but beyond the obvious fact that by the time her meal makes it up all those stairs to her it must be quite cold, how ever can you be certain she is getting the proper nourishment?"

"My servants see to it."

Eleanor frowned at his indifference. "With all due respect, sir, I know of households where the servants would just as soon keep the meat and pastry for themselves while serving the children gruel. Do you think that wise?"

The look that came over the viscount's face then told Eleanor that he wasn't a man accustomed to having his word questioned by anyone, and most especially someone who had so recently entered into his employ. His eyes, a cold dull black gray, caught hers and held them.

"My servants, Miss Harte, have all proven themselves loyal to me through years of service. That same loyalty extends to the members of my family. And need I remind you that you can now be counted among the same servants you have just so gratuitously accused?"

Meant to intimidate, his words didn't have their desired effect, for though he tried very hard to cloak it in callousness, Eleanor saw something else entirely.

Behind that gruff exterior, Lord Dunevin was hiding— but hiding from what?

Juliana's muteness? Did that make her somehow flawed in his eyes? Eleanor knew many families in society who would think so. The slightest blemish, the faintest lisp were easily cause for alarm when perfection was the only ideal. Those who were flaunted it, while those who weren't strove to conceal whatever made them unique for fear of society's censure.

"My lord, if Juliana is to make her way among polite society, she will need to learn proper dining decorum. By taking meals at opposite ends of the house, you cannot possibly know if she has learned the correct holding of her fork, let alone the quietest way in which to sip her soup. In a society where one's every move is under constant scrutiny, many a lady's reputation has been damaged by poor table manners. The only way Juliana can learn and accustom herself to the society of others is to practice on a daily basis."

It took Gabriel several moments to realize that he was staring at his new governess without a word to offer in response. This woman, who had appeared virtually from out of nowhere, who stood only to his chin with flashing green eyes and hair the color of the richest sable, had just blithely challenged him as even most men had never done.

Did she truly not realize who he was? That most would quail at the prospect of simply standing before him, the Devil of Dunevin Castle?

He gave her his fiercest scowl, the one that was known to have sent many a fainthearted housemaid fleeing for the mainland, but she merely smiled, yet waiting for his response. He didn't want to relent, to allow Juliana to stay, but at the same time he was unable to argue against what Miss Harte was saying. Juliana did need to learn how to conduct herself in social situations, for there would come a day when she might no longer have the safety of this isle to hide behind.

Wasn't that the very reason he had hired this governess in the first place? To prepare Juliana for the world beyond these shores? Surely he could manage to sit in the same room with his daughter through the course of one meal.

"Very well," was all he said before turning his attention to his soup which Fergus had just begun ladling out. Juliana remained standing, staring from Gabriel to Miss Harte.

"There, Juliana," the governess said, smiling and pointing to the chair at Gabriel's right, where a place had already been set. She then lowered herself into the chair across at his left. Fergus, ever at ready, hastily brought a service to place before her.

From the moment their soup was served, the meal was seized by a silence far more deafening than the tempest that was making its bluster known against the windowpanes across the room. The storm had moved in suddenly off the firth and Gabriel wondered fleetingly if its unexpected appearance could be attributed in any way to the arrival of their new governess. She was certainly proving to be as unpredictable, as enigmatic as the ever-changing Hebridean skies.

Who was this woman? he wondered, stealing a glance at her as he refilled his wineglass. Thick lashes cast demure shadows against her cheeks in the muted candlelight as she looked down at her supper plate. What was she doing there? Why was she hiding on his isle—or, more importantly, from whom?

He watched as she lifted her soup spoon, making sure that Juliana followed her example, and sipped lightly at the steaming broth, a partan bree that was as smooth as it was tasty, a specialty of the Dunevin cook. He watched the tip of her tongue as it ran along the fullness of her bottom lip. The room seemed to grow suddenly warmer.

Gabriel knew the governess's name wasn't any more Miss Nell Harte than his was Napoleon Bonaparte, but he also knew that whoever she was, she was a lady of good breeding, certainly naïve to have come to his isle alone, but refined and educated, and since that was exactly what he needed for Juliana, she was nothing short of a godsend.

He needed her. He needed Juliana to be taught the social accomplishments that would quickly help her to appear as normal as possible. His time, he knew all too well, was running dangerously short.

Gabriel didn't realize he was still staring openly at the mysterious Miss Harte until she asked, "Is there something you wanted, my lord? The salt cellar perhaps?"

Gabriel looked away and focused straight ahead down

the length of the table at the shadows. "No, thank you, Miss Harte."

Silence followed through four courses that felt rather like ten until Miss Harte finally set down her dessert fork and said, "I noticed your stables upon my arrival on the island, my lord. If the weather will permit, I thought perhaps to acquaint myself with the isle's surroundings tomorrow. Does Juliana like to ride?"

Gabriel looked at her as if she'd just spoken to him in a foreign tongue. While it would be a completely reasonable question to anyone else, she could never realize that to him, it was as impossible to answer as if she'd questioned why the March hare was mad. In the past three years, Gabriel could count on his fingers the number of times he had spent in his daughter's company. He no more knew if she could ride than if she could turn a proper curtsey. But the governess was looking at him, awaiting his response, and so, after a moment, Gabriel spoke, directing his words to the wall paneling at the other end of the room.

"I cannot say with any certainty whether she likes to ride or not, Miss Harte."

"I see . . ." She knit her brow over her cup of tea a moment then said, "I was considering Juliana's curriculum earlier in the nursery and thought perhaps to begin our studies with literature. Does Juliana know how to read?"

"I believe she has a rudimentary understanding, but I am not certain."

"Do you know whether she has been introduced to the classics, if she is at all acquainted with Virgil or Homer?"

"No, I do not."

"Can she cipher? Has she had any musical training?"

This time Gabriel didn't even bother to respond, just shook his head at the wainscoting. Couldn't she understand he wasn't purposely being obtuse—he just truly did not know anything about his own child?

"Can you say with any certainty the date of your daughter's birth, my lord?"

The question had been intended give him a turn, he knew, to pull his attention away from where he had fixed it on the opposite wall.

And it had succeeded.

He looked at her. "February the twentieth, Miss Harte."

Having made her point, the governess simply smiled. "Thank you, my lord. I shall make note of its approach."

The tall case clock standing behind them chose that moment to strike seven of the clock. An hour had passed that seemed more like several. Gabriel suddenly wanted to be anywhere but there, in that room, facing the evidence of the daughter he had neglected these three years past.

He stood, wiping his mouth before setting his napkin beside his dessert plate. "It grows late and I've business to attend to. If you'll excuse me."

The viscount turned from the table before Eleanor could frame any response and without, she noted sourly, bidding his daughter a good night.

He was angry, Eleanor knew, angry at the recrimination of her last question to him. She probably shouldn't have asked it, but his detachment from the concerns of his daughter had been beyond frustrating. In any case, she had succeeded in reminding him that he did indeed have a daughter, a daughter who very much needed his attention. Why he refused to give it was something Eleanor determined to discover.

Eleanor looked beside her to where Juliana was staring at her pudding, which had remained untouched. Like most everything else that went on around her, the child gave the leaving of her father no notice, at least not outwardly. But inwardly, who could know?

Eleanor stood from the table. "Come, Juliana, we shall see if we cannot find something of interest to do in the nursery for the remainder of the evening."

She waited while Juliana rose from her seat, pushed in her chair, and headed slowly from the room. As she followed behind the curious silent child, Eleanor thought to herself that before coming to the island, she had believed there could be no one in the world more lost than she.

She saw now that she had been wrong in that assumption. . . .

. . . Twice.

Chapter Three

G ood night, Juliana."
    The small ormolu clock on the table down the hall struck its ninth dulcet chime as Eleanor closed the door to Juliana's bedchamber softly behind her. It had finally come, the close to a most uncertain day, a day fraught with anxiousness, the beginning of a new life in a most unfamiliar place.

Eleanor started down the passageway but paused outside her bedchamber. If she retired just then, she would only lie awake in the darkness. Even now her head was abrim with flurried thoughts and unsettled questions, so rather than retire, she decided she would go down to the kitchen to see about making herself a cup of tea.

Everyone else in the castle, it seemed, had retired for the night, for the halls were dark and vacant and silent—not even the rain made any sound. Eleanor took the candlestick with her that she had used to read Juliana a story and made her way slowly along each successive flight of tower stairs down to the lower castle floors. She lost her way only once, taking the left instead of the right tower at the last floor, and found herself somehow standing outside the closed door to the viscount's study, where she had first anxiously awaited earlier that day. The coppery flickering light of the hearth fire burned underneath.

Not everyone had retired after all.

Eleanor stood for a moment outside the door, contemplating the mysterious Lord Dunevin. She remembered the direful warnings she'd received of him before coming to the island that day. The people on the mainland had called him a demon, painting him as a grim villain who had committed countless atrocities against any number of hapless victims. Thus far, however, Eleanor had seen nothing to lend credence to those plaintive accusations. Instead of frightening her, the viscount intrigued her as a curious contradiction, a man at odds with himself even in appearance. He was certainly rugged and imposing in stature, but he spoke with such a quiet depth, the voice of a man who sought rather to occupy a place on the periphery instead of the glare of society's censure.

Even with the brief amount of time she had spent in his company, Eleanor had already determined that he carried a dreadful burden. It was in his eyes, so dark and remote and shadowed, and it brought Eleanor to wondering how long he had been without his wife. Had the viscountess died giving birth to Juliana? It might explain why Lord Dunevin seemed so uncomfortable in the presence of his daughter, why he avoided taking so much as a meal with her. Or, perhaps, did he blame Juliana somehow for the loss of his wife?

It had been Eleanor's experience that when somebody lost a loved one, the others in their life were drawn yet closer to them. Dunevin hadn't wanted to be anywhere near his daughter that evening, yet during their interview earlier that day, he had been so very concerned about the education and care she should receive.

Why, Eleanor wondered, why hadn't he simply sent Juliana

off to one of the schools for young ladies many members of
the nobility were so fond of, like her own Miss Effington's
Academy? It would have been an easy solution, yet somehow Eleanor knew there was something more to it, some
other reason that would remain a mystery, at least for this
particular night. She turned from the study door and continued on her way.

The kitchen, she'd been told by Fergus earlier that
evening, was situated outside the great hall through a covered arcade and was accessed by a small turning stair in the
corner tower. As she made her way there, Eleanor half expected to find a place cramped and musty and ridden with
smoke. Instead she came into a spacious chamber with several other smaller chambers branching off to serve as pantry,
scullery, wine cellar.

The moment she entered, the warmth of the arched brick
cooking hearth wrapped itself around her, drawing Eleanor
in like a welcoming embrace. The air was touched by the
mingling scents of the peat that fueled the fire and the
bunches of drying herbs that hung from hooks in the low-
beamed ceiling. Iron cooking pots of various sizes and other
assorted utensils lined the pristine lime-washed walls in neat
rows, and a huge oaken trestle table took up the center of the
room on which she found a small kettle.

She took it and filled it from an earthenware pitcher of
fresh water she found standing nearby then stirred the glowing embers in the hearth, dropping on a fresh brick of peat
before she set the kettle on the iron cooking hook that hung
down from the blackened chimney.

While she waited for the water to boil, Eleanor searched
for the tea, which she soon found in a small caddy chest
tucked in an oaken wall hutch where there were also several
porcelain teapots and cups. She set out the things she needed

and then took up the boiling kettle to prepare the tea, measuring in the fragrant leaves before she set the brew aside to steep.

Wondering if there might be something in the kitchen she could nibble on with her tea, Eleanor turned. She nearly let out a gasp when she found a woman standing in the doorway behind her, silently watching her.

"Goodness," Eleanor said. "I didn't hear you come in."

The women simply shrugged. "I thought I heard someone messing aboot in my kitchen."

She was a stocky figure of a woman of middling age dressed in a simple linen nightshift that tied at her chin and fell to her ankles. Her hair was a pale wheaten brown streaked through with gray and it hung down the middle of her back in a single thick plait.

"I'm sorry to have awakened you. I—"

"You must be the new governess," the woman said, crossing the room on bare feet. She took up the water pitcher from where Eleanor had left it and put it back in its original spot, sweeping a hand over the tabletop as if to whisk away a scattering of crumbs. "I'm Màiri Mórag Macaphee—cook, housekeeper, and resident tyrant."

She turned then and looked at Eleanor, who must have appeared panic-stricken at having been caught invading what was so obviously this woman's territory. The woman smiled, revealing a healthy, easy grin. "But if you'll share a wee cuppa with me, you can call me Màiri."

Eleanor instantly eased. "I am El—, Nell, and yes, that would be wonderful."

The woman looked at her. "Nell, it is then."

Màiri took a second cup down from the hutch while Eleanor strained off the tea leaves and poured, taking both cups to a small table with two chairs that stood in a cozy corner. It sat in the glow of the moonlight coming from a window set high on the wall. Màiri followed, stopping first to fetch a small tin of buttery shortbread, setting it on the table between them.

"You're a bit young to be a governess," Màiri announced over a small bite as she studied Eleanor closely in the moonlight. "Have you no care to take you a husband, lass?"

Eleanor stiffened at the sudden reminder of Richard and the betrayal of her family, a thing she just then realized she hadn't thought about all day. It was the first time she hadn't since leaving Skynegal.

She answered with a vague, "I have no wish to marry."

"Hmm." Màiri nodded. "That's quite a decision to be making at your tender age. Did he break your heart then? What was it? Take himself off with another lass, did he?"

"No, nothing like that." Eleanor stared down at the table as she feigned at ministering to her teacup. "We just didn't suit."

"I see." Màiri looked at her skeptically over a bite of shortbread. "Well, then, 'tis a good thing you found out afore the vows were said, else you might have ended up like Alys, my youngest daughter, who wed herself to a right lazy sort because she couldn't see naught beyond the bonny blue o' his eyes."

Màiri took a sip of her steaming tea, closed her eyes, and smiled. "Och, lass, but that is a fine brew you've made. Finer than any I could make. Wherever did you learn to make such a fine cuppa?"

"Miss Eff—" Eleanor stopped herself before finishing.

Màiri's soft eyes twinkled in the firelight. "Well, whoever this Miss F. is, she certainly knows her way around a teapot."

Eleanor couldn't help but smile at the woman's easy

humor; she liked her already. "The secret is to swirl some of the boiling water inside the pot first to heat it before steeping."

Màiri stared at her. "Is that so?"

But it wasn't tea she was interested in discussing, or Miss F. "So, Miss Harte, where is it you're from then? My guess would be somewhere around Londontown?"

"I, uh—" Eleanor was prevented from answering when Màiri suddenly took up both her hands, peering at them in the moonlight.

"Well, wherever it is you're from, it wasna a working life you led there, that much is certain. Not a bit of rough skin on those hands. The only other leddy I ever saw with hands that soft and pure was the laird's sweet wife, Leddy Georgiana. With your polite talk and pretty hands, I'd almost guess you were one o' the quality yourself." She peered at Eleanor closely then. "But what would a leddy o' quality be doing working 'ere in a place like this now?"

The woman's questioning stare searched for more than Eleanor was willing to reveal. She quickly pulled away on the pretense of taking up her teacup. "My mother insisted that I wear gloves when I was young. It was a matter of great import to her."

Màiri gave a slow nod of understanding. She would press Eleanor no more. Instead she said, "Well 'tis a brave lass you are to come all the way to Trelay to run from your ill-suited beau, but I'm verra glad you did. Miss Juliana needs someone now, poor wee lost lassie. 'Tis a good thing, your coming. So alone she is without her dear mither. And what a blessing it would be to hear a child's laughter once again through these lonely halls."

Eleanor was taken aback by Màiri's words. She had

assumed Juliana had been mute since birth. "Do you mean to say that Juliana once spoke?"

"*Och*, aye, lass. She would to come in 'ere to this kitchen ever'aday chattering for hours whilst I baked. Even when she would be helping me t' roll out the oatcakes, she would be asking questions, that one, curious as a dormouse she was. Been only since she lost her mither that she hasna spoken. Not a word." Màiri shook her head regretfully over a sip of tea.

Eleanor looked at her, curious now. "Màiri, when did Lady Dunevin die?"

Màiri gave a rueful sigh before answering. "'Twas three years ago now and afore you ask wha' happened, I'll tell you nae'abody knows. She simply vanished while walking aboot the isle one day and hasna been seen since. Whether it were a terrible accident or whether Lady Dunevin took her own life, no one can say." She paused. "No one except Miss Juliana, who willna talk to us aboot it."

"Juliana knows what happened to Lady Dunevin?"

"We doona know for certain, but she was with her mither when she disappeared."

Eleanor remembered the words of Mrs. MacIver, the innkeeper's wife in Oban. *He stole his sweet daughter's voice to keep her from telling the truth of his dark deeds. . . .*

"Is it possible, perhaps, that Juliana is afraid to talk?"

Màiri knew immediately what Eleanor meant. She shook her head sternly. "*Och,* lass, doona believe those meddlesome mainlanders who will say 'twas his lairdship that killed his leddy. The laird, he was devastated to lose her, he was. Both he and Miss Juliana, they neither of them have been the same since."

Màiri finished the last of her tea and set the cup down with a decided nod. "But now you have come to the isle to set things to rights." She looked at Eleanor directly. "I feel it in my ane bones, I do. 'Tis you who must heal Miss Juliana's heart."

"Me? I am but her governess and likely a temporary one at that. She doesn't even look at me when I speak to her. I wonder that she even hears me."

Màiri smiled. "Och, aye, she hears you, lass. That she does. That child hears ever'athing. It might not seem like it, but Miss Juliana is there, lost somewhere behind her silence. I have seen it, 'tis in her eyes. She tries hard to hide it, but 'tis there. She just needs someone to unlock the words, miss. And tha' is you."

"But you don't even know me."

"I doona have to ken you, lass. 'Twas three nights afore this one that I prayed to St. Columba, patron of this isle, to bring the wee lassie an angel to save her." She finished on a hopeful smile. "And you are here now. It canna be more destined than that. 'Tis a beginning, your coming here. Aye, a new beginning and a new hope for us all."

It was nearly an hour later when Eleanor finally left the comfort of the kitchen fire to make the winding climb to her bedchamber for the night.

Màiri, she had decided very soon after meeting her, was a woman of inherent warmth and earthly wisdom and her generous manner had put at ease many of Eleanor's misgivings of the day. After those first innocently curious questions, Màiri had accepted Eleanor's reluctance to discuss herself and had turned the conversation to more social topics, telling Eleanor about the manner of life at Dunevin, the sheltered isolation of the isle, the unpredictability of the Hebridean weather, and most importantly, where she hid that tin of shortbread should Eleanor find herself plagued by what Màiri called "the nibblies" in the middle of the night.

By the time Eleanor had returned abovestairs, it was nearing midnight. The light that had shone beneath the door of the viscount's study earlier was nearly gone; but a sparse flicker of ebbing firelight remained.

Eleanor headed for her chamber on the nursery floor, but stopped outside of it, eyeing the door to Juliana's bedchamber down the hall. She remembered how as a young girl she had always found a sense of security in waking each morning to see the break of day through an open chamber door, even imagining it the lamplight of her own mythological Argus standing sentinel for her with his hundred eyes. Perhaps that same gesture would offer comfort to Juliana come the dawn. With that thought in mind, Eleanor started down the hall for Juliana's door.

She turned the handle quietly so as not to awaken her. Inside was total darkness, but she had left her candle burning on the table in the hall, so she moved a bit to where its light could fall on Juliana's bed across the room. When the shape of the room finally came clear, Eleanor froze.

The bed was empty.

Eleanor walked across the room, tugging back the vacant covers. "Juliana?"

There came no response.

Eleanor turned for the hall to retrieve the candle and looked all around the room, in the corner chair, inside the wardrobe even, but Juliana was nowhere to be found. She called to her again before realizing the futility of waiting for a response from a mute child. Her heart began to thud in her chest. She had been a governess but a matter of hours and already she had lost her charge.

Eleanor looked under the bed once more on a hapless

whim before retreating to the hall. She stopped herself there
for a moment to take hold of her scattered senses.

Juliana was *not* lost, she told herself. She was in her own
home, a safe place several stories above the ground. No
harm could come to her. These weren't the Dark Ages when
warring clansmen would come in the midst of the night to
raid and pillage and steal. This was the nineteenth century.
Blood feuds and the like were a thing of the past. Juliana
was inside the castle—somewhere. All Eleanor had to do
was find her.

Before heading for the stairs, Eleanor checked in her own
chamber and then the schoolroom, but to no avail. Juliana
was nowhere to be found.

Eleanor retraced her steps and took the first flight down
to the next floor below and the other bedchambers. She
wasn't certain which of them belonged to the viscount, nor
did she relish the idea of waking him to tell him his daughter was missing, but she was unfamiliar with the lay of the
castle and so conceded she would have no choice but to alert
him.

The first two doors she went to were locked, no answer
coming to her soft knocking. At the end of the hall there
were two doors remaining. Eleanor headed for the one on
the left and raised her hand before she noticed that it was
slightly open. Without knocking, Eleanor pushed the door
softly inward.

The bedchamber she found on the other side was decidedly feminine in décor, touched by the pleasant subtle scent
of lavender. A good many of the furnishings were shrouded
by dustcloths and a quick glance at the hearth in the moonlight revealed it hadn't been used at all recently.

The light bed hangings, the finely spindled bed, the lingering soft scents that filled the air—Eleanor need not have

looked any further to know that this had been the viscount-ess's bedchamber. It was a place that spoke of gentleness and sanctuary, and as she made directly for the bed that stood across the room, she wasn't at all surprised to find someone there.

Juliana lay asleep in the middle of the bed, curved into a tight ball of childish innocence beneath the rumpled bed-covers. The doll Eleanor had remarked on earlier that day in the nursery was tucked safely in her arms. In the light from the candle, the child's face was peaceful, angelic, the dull-ness that had marked her eyes in daylight hidden behind the shelter of her slumber.

Juliana had obviously come here to find the peace she was unable to find elsewhere. Looking on her as she slept so serenely, Eleanor didn't have the heart to wake her, much less direct her back abovestairs. Nor could she leave her there alone, so instead, Eleanor put out the candle, set the smoking taper on the bedside table, and slid quietly onto the mattress beside her.

Chapter Four

Bu dual da sin.
That was his birthright.
—Gaelic proverb

Gabriel sat staring silently into the peat fire that burned in the hearth at his feet, watching as it danced molten amber through the brandy in his glass. It was nearing midnight. He was alone in the near darkness of his study, elbows at rest on the carved arms of his chair, his legs stretched at full length before him.

To anyone looking, he would appear the noble lord at ease, his cravat untied and loose around his neck, the sleeves of his cambric rolled over his forearms—except that his mouth wore a frown and his mood a cloak of disquietude heavier than the weight of any boulder.

He'd spent the past hours since supper at his desk going over some of the estate papers, then later, to this chair, listening to the sounds of the castle retiring for the night, the closing of the doors, the banking of the rush lights, the checking of the window latches that could snap open at a sudden gust blowing in off the firth. The rain had slowed some time before, falling softly now, and it had been well over an hour since he had heard the last footstep, no doubt that of his gillie, Fergus, shuffling out of the great hall for his chamber in the castle's opposite tower.

It had been a long and disconcerting day and Gabriel knew he should have already taken himself off to bed. There

was a harvest to prepare for and the winter beyond that.
Plans needed to be made for the stock and the plenishing of
the isle for the bleak months to come. Sleep, however,
would not come easily for the Dark Lord of Dunevin.

All night, even as he'd been going through his paper-
work, Gabriel's thoughts had been occupied by the events of
the day. The unwelcome image of Juliana's dark absent stare
at supper that night, the memory of what had once been
haunted him still.

Could it really be that just three years before laughter had
spilled from that sweet child's lips like the first dappled sunlight breaking through the clouds after a storm?

It seemed almost impossible to believe that his daughter
had once sung with the voice of an enchanting angel. Just to
hear her calling him "Da" had been each day's utmost reward. A light had shone within her more brilliant than the
brightest star. Each day had been a new and glorious adventure . . .

. . . until Fate had come along to remind Gabriel that
there was a terrible consequence to be paid for his foolish
bid for happiness—one that had stolen both his daughter's
sweet voice—and his young wife's life.

Lady Georgiana Alvington had been all of seventeen
years when Gabriel had first seen her, standing like a fragile golden daffodil across a crowded London ballroom. It
had been spring, he remembered, the beginning of another
society-mad London Season and he had just returned from
the Peninsula after having received the news of his brother
Malcolm's untimely death.

Gabriel hadn't planned to attend any festivities that
evening; he was in London only long enough to see to the
legalities of the estate and the transfer of the title of Dunevin
to him. It was his colonel, Barrett, who had requested that he

go to the ball that night; the hostess, after all, was his colonel's wife.

"You'll have time on your hands in town before you can depart for the Highlands," he'd said with a pat to Gabriel's shoulder. "With the boys all gone to the Peninsula, the dancing partners are scarce and my wife despairs of having her soirée dubbed a disaster."

Colonel Bernard Barrett had been the closest thing to a father Gabriel had ever known, despite the fact that his own sire, Alexander MacFeagh, had lived to see Gabriel's twentieth year. It had been Colonel Barrett who had urged Gabriel to secure his commission into the 105th Dragoons, and then again the colonel who had helped him to sell that commission to a fellow officer when he'd received word calling him back to Scotland.

During the years he had served under him, the colonel had taught Gabriel such things as how to defend himself against enemy attack and how best to determine an opponent's weakness. He had taught him courage, prudence, and gallantry, but most vital of them all has been the true definition of honor.

If the colonel had known the dark truth of Gabriel's family history, he had never revealed it. All those many months they had spent traversing Portugal and Spain after Napoleon, Colonel Barrett had always treated Gabriel with the utmost fairness and respect at a time when many English soldiers had shown a good deal of disdain for their Scottish comrades. Even three-quarters of a century couldn't erase the bitterness of the ill-fated '45.

Yet Barrett had given Gabriel the chance to prove himself both as a soldier on the field of battle and as a man in charge of a company of others, and because of that, Gabriel had gone to Mrs. Barrett's ball, vowing, however, to stay no longer than an hour.

It was at that same ball he had first spotted Georgiana.

She had been standing against the far wall, trying very hard to blend in to Mrs. Barrett's woodwork, along with a bevy of other young ladies fresh from the country, all dressed in the latest fashion, smiling and fluttering their decorated fans in order to catch a young buck's eye.

Something about Georgiana had caught Gabriel's attention, not only that she'd looked quite lovely that evening, her blond hair curled high upon her head, showing off the fragile beauty of her neck and shoulders. The eloquence of her fan, even the smartness of her sleeveless silk spencerette, none of it had kept him looking time and again to that same place against the wall. What had drawn his attention in the midst of that crowded ballroom had been nothing else but Georgiana's eyes.

They had been the palest silver gray, like shimmering raindrops on a moonlit night, and they had held more sadness than he had ever thought possible.

Having been born with a family history as dark and as isolating as his own, Gabriel had easily recognized a fellow victim of unhappiness. He had watched Georgiana on and off that night as she had stood rooted to that same spot on the far wall, dance after dance, while the others had hied off and the merriment had gone on around her.

He remembered thinking what a pity that so pretty a lass should be so obviously miserable. What a pity, too, that no one else in that vast place had noticed.

As he was readying to leave, his promised hour ended, Gabriel happened to catch a remark hissed sharply to Georgiana under her mother's breath, chastising her for a lack of effort in attracting male attention. Something in Georgiana's eyes as she stood frozen by her mother's displeasure had told Gabriel that she'd be facing far worse than sharp words after the ball.

He never knew what came over him; he only knew he would have done almost anything at that moment to dispel that petrified look from her eyes—

—even ask Georgiana to dance.

That single impulsive moment had led to a courtship that resulted in their marriage barely three months later. When he returned to his childhood home on Trelay to take up residence as the isle's new laird, it was with Georgiana as his wife.

It was only when they were in Scotland, a safe distance away from London and its haunting memories, that Gabriel learned the true depth of his new wife's melancholy, a melancholy seated in years of mental abuse at the hands of her mother and the worst sort of physical abuse at the hands of her father.

No matter how gentle, how understanding Gabriel tried to be with her, Georgiana could never prevent herself from stiffening whenever he moved to touch her. She would apologize to him over and over and finally ease enough to share his bed, but after weeks of dutiful lovemaking that culminated each time in her tears, Gabriel had given up altogether any attempt at intimacy with his wife.

By then, however, Georgiana had been expecting their child.

Throughout her pregnancy, Georgiana had openly declared that she was carrying Gabriel's son, almost as if by saying it often enough, she could somehow make it true. He would be called Gabriel for his father, she'd said, ignoring the direful warnings of the women of the island who told her it was bad luck to christen a child while it yet lay within the womb.

Even after Juliana had been born a daughter, Georgiana had refused to believe it—not until she had seen the babe for herself. Gabriel had watched as she had looked upon their child that day, not with the wondrous joy of a new mother, but with that same terrible fear that had so caught him the first time he'd seen her in that crowded London ballroom.

Gabriel assured Georgiana over and over that she had nothing to fear any longer, that the life she had led before wedding him was locked away to the past, but Georgiana still made Gabriel promise her that he would never allow her family the opportunity to abuse Juliana as they had her. They would stop at nothing, Georgiana had said, to get what they wanted.

Wishing only to ease those terrible anxieties, Gabriel had given Georgiana his word, never knowing just how significant keeping it would someday become.

Time had passed quickly and Georgiana had eased into her new role of mother. She saw to every aspect of Juliana's care herself, feeding her at her own breast, delighting in the mess of a finicky eater, the thunder of a two-year-old's tantrum. Gabriel had believed Georgiana happy, truly happy for the first time in her life, free from the dark memory of her own wretched childhood.

He couldn't have been more mistaken.

He knew so very little of what had happened that cheerless winter morning three years earlier. It had been a day much like any other with no indication of the events that would take place.

That day had dawned on a frosty morning, but the sun had broken through the clouds, showering the isle with its radiant light. After breakfast, Georgiana had dressed herself and then six-year-old Juliana for a walk along the heights above the isle's westerly shore, a jaunt they had made often together. She had asked Gabriel to go with them, but he had declined, having a pile of papers to go through for his steward, Clyne.

Instead, he had watched the two of them go, waving from his study window in the tower as they made their way across the frost-dusted machair to disappear over the distant hilltop. The wind had been icy and Georgiana had promised Gabriel they wouldn't stay out too long.

Still, somehow, Gabriel had felt a niggling sense of unease.

If only he had heeded it.

When they hadn't returned several hours later, Gabriel had gone out after them, only to find his daughter alone, wet and shivering above the farthest shore, struck suddenly dumb, unable to tell him where her mother had gone.

One of Georgiana's shoes had washed up on the shore a week later; her body, however, was never found, almost as if she had been carried away by the rolling white mist of the morning. It didn't matter whether it had been a dreadful accident or whether Georgiana had for some reason taken her own life. Standing on that beach, clutching her water-soaked slipper in his trembling hand, Gabriel had felt the full weight of the responsibility for her death as keenly as if he had taken her life himself.

He knew he should have seen it coming. It was a terrible history that had been written nearly three hundred years before, revisiting itself time and again through generations of the *cursed* MacFeaghs.

Gabriel downed the last of his brandy and moved from his place by the fire, crossing the darkened room to where a

large trunk that looked every bit as ancient as the castle itself stood in an inconspicuous spot in the far corner. Flip-
ping back the worn and faded tapestry cloth that covered its
lid, he smoothed a hand against the dark oak underneath,
pitted and scarred through many centuries past.

Gabriel slid a length of silver chain that hung around his
neck from inside the cambric covering of his shirt. On its
end, glinting in the muted firelight, hung the tiny, timeless
key that had hung about the necks of every MacFeagh chief
who had come before him.

The crude iron lock upon the trunk was as much a mystery as the origins of the trunk itself. Marked where various
intruders had tried over time to force it open, the lock had
been fashioned in a manner most mysterious, so that only
the single key that fitted it would release it, a sort of Excali-
buresque relic. Even with the key, only the MacFeagh chief
could open the trunk's lock. To anyone else who dared to try,
the key would prove both useless—and fatal—for death
surely followed for those who had tried, as if the very metal
it had been forged from was somehow enchanted.

It was the only lock worthy to protect the Clan MacFeagh's
most prized possession.

Fitting the key into its place, Gabriel released the catch
that allowed him to lift the lid on a trunk that now lay con-
spicuously empty, barren of the relic that had once lain protected inside centuries earlier.

The ancient ensign-staff of the MacFeaghs had been a
symbol of the clan for as long as history had been recorded,
passed down generation after generation since the clan's
very beginnings. Because of the MacFeaghs' connection to
the bishops of the priory at Trelay founded by St. Columba
all those many centuries before, many said the staff had
been fashioned from the wood of the very *curragh* in which

the holy saint had sailed from Ireland and was therefore certainly blessed. Legend described the staff as both long and sturdy, magically indestructible, made of a gleaming white wood of unknown origin. History dictated that for as long as the MacFeagh chief held the ancient relic, the clan would prosper—and prosper they had for several hundred years.

Led by the great Murchardus Maca'phi, the clan had reigned unchallenged over not only Trelay, but several of the neighboring isles during the earlier centuries. Once honored as the hereditary keepers of the records for the ancient Lords of the Isles, the clan's present misfortunes began in the early sixteenth century when, legend says, an ancestor of Murchardus, a Murdoch MacFeagh, the chief at the time, fell under the curse of a witch from the nearby isle of Jura.

History recorded that Murdoch, a great bear of a man with the trademark dark MacFeagh hair and eyes, had been sailing in his *bhirlinn* when a fierce squall had suddenly risen up against him, tossing him and his crew helplessly into the icy waters of the firth. He had fought the treacherous swells valiantly, listening to the dying cries as each of the others had perished, until, exhausted himself, he'd lost consciousness.

When next he awoke, he found himself lying beneath the warmth of a pile of furs in a sea cave by a crackling fire. The haggard old witch who tended the blaze told MacFeagh she had saved him from drowning by means of a magic spell, bringing him to the safety of her cave home on Jura.

MacFeagh had been so grateful to her for saving him, he'd promised to reward her with one of his many prized possessions. He remained with the witch to mend for several days, but when his strength returned and the time came that he thought to go back to his own home, which he could see through the mist on the adjacent isle, the witch stubbornly refused to give him up, drawing his boat back time and again by means of a magical tethering thread.

MacFeagh had no choice but to remain her unwilling guest, tortured by the sight of his beloved home so near yet so far from reach. Until he managed to gain the witch's trust enough to learn of a hatchet she had that could sever the enchanted thread she held him with. Late one moonless night, MacFeagh stole the hatchet and cleaved the thread to escape from her, arriving home to the relief and joy of his worried family while the angry wail of the witch carried behind him on the sea wind.

The following day, the witch presented herself at MacFeagh's door, demanding that he fulfill his promise of the gift of his most prized possession. But when he offered her a marvelous jeweled brooch, she refused, saying she would only accept the ancient and renowned staff of the MacFeaghs in exchange for her having saved his life.

Murdoch refused, offering her goods and riches beyond all imagination, but still she demanded the cherished staff. Unwilling to part with his hereditary relic and unsettled by her dark presence, MacFeagh had the witch carried away and warned her never to return.

By the time the next morning dawned, three of the chief's five children had mysteriously perished, found lying in their beds, their faces peaceful in sleep, as if their very breath had been stolen from them. Grief-stricken, MacFeagh went immediately to the trunk, only to find that the ancient staff was missing, removed somehow through a means by which the lock hadn't been opened.

In its place lay a scrap of crude parchment. Written upon it were with these words in ancient Gaelic:

For nine hundred years, and then one hundred more,
any creature or beast you allow past your heart's
door, will soon slip away and suffer death's most
telling stone, while helpless you watch on, forsaken
and alone. Only here on this misty isle might the
truth be found, St. Colomb's staff will loose the curse
by which you are bound. One of pure heart and
eye will right the wrongs of the past, to bring
about an end to the suffering at last!

From then on, and over the next three centuries, the loved ones of every MacFeagh chief would often perish suddenly and under extreme circumstances—drowning, fire, even accidental falls. It seemed that whenever a MacFeagh made the mistake of allowing someone close to his heart, the curse would return with its fatal Midas touch, just as the witch had prophesized that long-ago day.

Because of this, the enduring MacFeagh chiefs had become a clan of distant, untouchable men, watching helplessly while without warning those around them fell victim to the witch's bitter curse. As a boy, Gabriel had rarely seen his father, the great Alexander MacFeagh. His care and well-being had been seen to by his mother, Lillidh, while his father had spent his time grooming his elder brother, Malcolm, for the reclusive role of MacFeagh chief.

Malcolm had been a diligent student, carrying on the dreaded legacy well, growing into a fierce man as cold and callous as their father. Everyone had predicted that he would serve well as laird, for he allowed nobody close to him, not even their mother.

But no one had foreseen Malcolm's untimely demise, a freakish accident that had occurred after he had mistakenly eaten the poisonous monkshood instead of the horseradish root he'd intended. Thus no one could have predicted the sudden inheritance of Gabriel, the second son.

Gabriel had been ill-prepared to assume the damned role of MacFeagh chief. Unlike Malcolm, he hadn't been raised to bury his emotions behind an impenetrable wall of cool indifference, eschewing all feeling, all compassion. As such, Gabriel made the fatal mistake of caring for Georgiana, of trying to help her—and, ultimately, it had led to her death, perpetuating the common belief that the MacFeaghs murdered their own, and proving to Gabriel that he had to do whatever he could to protect his daughter from a similar fate.

During the course of the three years since Georgiana's death, Gabriel had done everything he could to avoid spending anything more than a few moments in the company of his daughter on any given occasion. He made certain she was cared for, seeing to it that she was properly clothed and fed and that her every physical comfort was looked after by the handful of servants who had proven themselves loyal and trustworthy to him and his family.

But it was as close to her as he could allow himself to get to her.

To talk to her, care for her, know her at all would put Juliana's life too much at risk—and he had already made that mistake once. It wasn't a mistake he had any intention of repeating.

Thus Gabriel would do everything in his power to keep from loving his daughter.

If only so that he could spare her life.

Chapter Five

Eleanor opened her eyes slowly to the blossoming new light of the morning—

—and the unexpected sight of Juliana standing at the side of the bed. Her hair was still tucked neatly beneath her frilled nightcap as she stared at her in stony silence. The window behind her revealed that the hour was yet early, the sun barely starting to climb in the dappled morning sky. For the first few moments, Eleanor wondered what had awakened her. She couldn't recall having felt Juliana rise from the bed or even nudge her to wake. But something had awakened her.

Searching her memory, she remembered a sound, like the dull thumping of a foot—a foot of someone standing very close to the side of the bed.

"What is it, Juliana?" she said, sitting up on the bed. Her neck twinged from the uncomfortable position she'd been in all night, poised at the edge of the mattress beside Juliana. "Is something the matter?"

Juliana didn't respond, not even with a nod or shake of her head. Instead she turned and walked across the room to the door, that same ambiguous expression on her face as she opened it quietly and then stood beside it, waiting.

Waiting for Eleanor to leave the room.

Was she angry, Eleanor wondered, that she had awoken to find someone, a stranger, with her in her mother's bed? Perhaps she considered it an intrusion on a last sacred connection between mother and daughter. Eleanor hadn't considered that the night before when she had decided to remain with Juliana. Her only thought had been to keep watch over her, to make certain she didn't go wandering elsewhere through the castle in the dark of the night.

Deciding that it would be best to go along with the child's wishes, Eleanor got up from the bed and crossed the room to leave. She hadn't dressed in her nightclothes the night before after finding Juliana missing, so she still wore the pale blue muslin gown, now hopelessly wrinkled, that she had worn to supper. Her hair was mussed, half hanging from its pins. A bath and a fresh gown would certainly be in order before breakfast.

Eleanor started for the hall to leave, until she noticed that Juliana hadn't followed her. She turned to see that she was at the bed again, pulling up the rumpled bedclothes. She smoothed out the wrinkles in the coverlet. She set the pillows to rights. In moments, there remained no indication that anyone might have slept there at all.

The ritual ease and practice of her movements told Eleanor that the child had done this many a time before. How long had Juliana been coming there to her mother's bedchamber to sleep? Since Lady Dunevin had died? Did no one else in the castle know of her nightly visits there?

When she was finished making up the bed, Juliana turned, snatched up her doll from where she had set it on the chair beside the bed, and walked quietly from the room, shutting the door behind them. As she fell into place behind her, walking down the shadowed hall, Eleanor decided that

Màiri had been right in what she'd said to her in the kitchen the previous night.

There was something there behind Juliana's silent stare after all.

The rain that had dampened the previous afternoon continued throughout the following morning, waning to a misty drizzle by midday. The temperature in the isles proved a good deal colder than that on the mainland, spurred by a biting sea wind that blew in fiercely off the channel to the west with such constancy that the stark trees along the coast were forever bowed in an easterly direction.

Rather than trouble anyone to haul buckets of water to her chamber in the tower, Eleanor had taken a quick bath in a small antechamber off the kitchen in a wooden tub with water Màiri had heated over the hearth fire. The shock of stepping out of the water's warmth onto the cold stone floor with bare feet had stripped away the last remnants of her fatigue. Eleanor quickly realized that the thin fashionable silks and decorative muslins that made up the whole of her wardrobe would provide very little comfort against the bitter island chill.

Her fingers prickled even now as she worked to fasten the numerous tiny buttons that lined the front of her lilac-colored muslin daygown. Thank goodness she had sleeves, narrow and reaching to her wrists. Still, she would have to see about getting herself some of the warmer woolens that were the staple costume in the isles. Until then, Màiri had loaned her one of her own heavy pairs of woolen stockings and a thick woven tartan shawl with which to keep warm.

After taking a breakfast of tea, bannocks, and Màiri's hot porridge and fresh cream, Eleanor and Juliana retreated abovestairs to the confines of the nursery and the heat of the small hearth, where she kept a kettle of tea simmering throughout the day to warm them. Eleanor had left word with Fergus that his lordship was invited to call on them there to discuss Juliana's curriculum. Hours later, however, Lord Dunevin still had not shown any indication of joining them.

Eleanor spent a good part of the morning sorting through the numerous books and maps and other printed material she'd found in the schoolroom. She scribbled notes to herself about them on a parchment she had found in the drawer of the corner desk while Juliana merely sat at the window as she had the day before, watching as the rain moved off into the sea and the sun pushed its struggling light through the dank autumn clouds.

Other than the thumping of her foot early that morning, Juliana had made no further effort to communicate with Eleanor, taking her breakfast in silence while Màiri had chatted over tea with Eleanor.

Eleanor had set out a children's storybook earlier that morning, hoping she might glean something of Juliana's likes and dislikes from it, but Juliana had barely given it notice and it sat, yet untouched where she had placed it on the schoolroom table.

Setting aside the dwindling pile of books she had left to go through, Eleanor sparked on an idea. She crossed the room and took down a box of small painted alphabet tiles she had found earlier that morning before returning to the table near to where Juliana sat.

Sitting in one of the two small chairs, Eleanor spread the ivory tiles out upon the tabletop with the painted letters facing upward. Some of the tiles had one-letter, others two-letter combinations of consonant and vowel. When she had finished placing them all, nearly filling the tabletop with them, Eleanor turned to regard her silent young charge.

"Juliana, I found these tiles earlier today and I thought perhaps we'd try a little game together . . ."

She might as well have been in another room or even on another planet for all the notice Juliana gave her. Without affording the slightest indication that she had heard her, Juliana remained sitting as she was, curled upon the window seat, the back of her head facing to the room, as she stared out at the dim horizon, oblivious to anything and everything else around her.

What was it, Eleanor wondered, that so drew the child's attention to the sea?

"Please, Juliana. I would very much like to teach you, but I cannot do this alone."

Eleanor knit her brow in frustration, when Juliana continued unresponsive. She would not give up on this child, not like everybody else.

She tried again. "I do not know what your other governesses were like, Juliana, but I promise you I only want to help you. Won't you please help me to help you?"

There passed a silent moment before somehow, blessedly, Eleanor's words seemed to break through to her and Juliana turned slowly from the window to look at her. Her expression spoke more loudly than any words ever could. Her eyes were dark and open and filled with hope.

This little girl wanted to be saved. But from what?

Somehow, Eleanor determined, she would find out.

She motioned toward the opposite chair. "Won't you come and join me for a moment?"

Juliana slid from her window seat and tentatively approached the small table. She lowered herself into the opposite chair, her eyes moving about the scattered letter tiles before she turned her attention to Eleanor, waiting.

Eleanor smiled, the spark of hope seizing her inside. "I want you to know that I will never try to make you speak. If you do not wish to, then you needn't ever utter another word. I understand. But if there is ever anything you wish to communicate to me, if you are cold and would like a shawl, or if you are hungry, there are ways other than speaking to do so."

Juliana stared at her, listening—oh, thank heavens, yes, listening. Eleanor drew a hopeful breath.

"First, I thought perhaps we'd try something with these tiles."

Eleanor reached for the storybook she had given Juliana to read earlier that morning. Picking up several of the tiles, she spelled out *B-O-O-K* with them. Then she looked to Juliana, who read the tiles before looking up at her again.

Eleanor would have sworn she saw a flicker of something there, the smallest indication that she wouldn't shut Eleanor away. Anything was better than the obscure silence.

"Now it is your turn," Eleanor said with a quick nod of encouragement. "Choose anything you wish."

Juliana looked at her a moment, then turned to peer about the room. Her gaze fell immediately upon a small wooden horse painted in red with worn wheels and a frayed string by which it could be pulled. She got up to retrieve it from where it sat on a shelf and set it on the table. Looking through the scattered tiles, she picked up one and then another and another until she had spelled out a single word with them.

H-O-R-S-E.

Eleanor smiled, a warmth moving over her, as if the sunshine had suddenly broken through the lowering clouds.

They were communicating.

She tempered her excitement and said, "Very good," as she looked about the room for another object to spell. "Okay, now it is my turn again."

On they went through several more—

B-A-L-L

M-A-P

S-O-L-D-I-E-R

C-A-N-D-L-E

—labeling various objects about the room until it fell to Eleanor's turn once again. But this time she didn't go searching through the shelves for some other item to place on the table.

Instead she pushed aside some of the tiles that were yet scattered about the tabletop. Then taking her time, she set down her next batch of letters neatly in front of where Juliana was sitting.

F-R-I-E-N-D.

Eleanor watched, breath held in anticipation as Juliana read the word, her head bowed. She could see Juliana begin to chew her lip before she slowly raised her gaze to hers. A moment later, their eyes locked.

Eleanor drew a slow breath, feeling as if she were standing before a long locked doorway, waiting to see if she would be allowed inside. She could see the uncertainty play across Juliana's face, this child who had hidden herself away from the world for so long. Silently, she prayed that Juliana would give her this one small chance.

"I would very much like to be your friend, Juliana," she whispered.

Eleanor didn't press her to respond, but instead waited. They sat there, just the two of them, listening as the hall clock ticked away the minutes. Outside, a dog barked in the courtyard below the window. A few moments later, Juliana reached one hand slowly forward, timidly, forming a word with some of the tiles that yet remained on the table.

Y-E-S.

Juliana looked up from the tiles. Their eyes met again and Eleanor smiled, her throat tightening as she blinked back the emotions that rushed within her.

"Juliana, I—"

The door across the room opened suddenly, without a knock. The wonder of that special moment between them was abruptly shattered.

"His lairdship will see you in his study now." Fergus stood there, staring at them from across the room.

The man certainly had a proclivity for poor timing, Eleanor thought. Just like the night before, he had come at the very moment when Eleanor had finally been making progress with Juliana.

Juliana turned so quickly from the table that she scattered the few remaining tiles to the floor. In a flash, she was back at her place on the window seat, her back to the room once again, staring out at the dusky expanse of sky and stormy sea.

Eleanor frowned as she bent to retrieve the tiles from the floor. "You may tell his lordship I shall be down directly."

Fergus didn't respond, but remained at the door, watching as she deposited the tiles into their box. His unexpected arrival had brought a marked chill to the room. His expression as he looked on the room seemed almost irritated, as if he believed Juliana had swept the tiles purposely off the table.

"Thank you, Fergus," Eleanor said, dismissing him. In a hapless effort to bring back the warmth of the special moment before his arrival, Eleanor took up the hearth tongs and dropped a fresh peat brick onto the fire, stirring it to flame. When Fergus didn't immediately move to leave, she added, "Was there something else?"

The older man stared at her in a manner that almost seemed intended to intimidate her. "No, miss."

He turned then, and vanished down the hall.

Eleanor stood and brushed her hands over her skirts to smooth them, wishing she could brush away the chill of that man's presence with it. Not everyone, it seemed, would be as welcoming to her new place in the household as Màiri had been.

"Well, I shouldn't keep your father waiting," she said. "Will you be comfortable here alone while I am gone, or would you like me to ask Màiri to join you till I return?"

Eleanor's spirits dropped when Juliana didn't respond. Hoping that she hadn't lost what little ground she had gained by the morning's exercise, Eleanor came up behind her and placed a hand gently on her shoulder. "I shall be right back."

Juliana remained fixed on the window.

Disheartened, Eleanor turned and quietly left the room. She would not lose hope. She had reached Juliana once, broken through her silence. And she would do it again.

Minutes later, she was standing at the open doorway to the viscount's study. He was seated inside behind his great desk with a large deerhound—probably the one she'd heard barking—stretched like a sprawling furry carpet before the hearth. The dog picked up its great head at her arrival, watchful as she knocked softly on the doorjamb.

"My lord?"

The viscount looked up at her from the paper he was reading. He wore a pair of spectacles that softened the intensity of his dark gaze, making him appear more a scholar than a fierce Highland chieftain.

"Miss Harte," he said, motioning her forward. "Good day to you. Please come inside."

Eleanor crossed the room to sit on one of the two tartan-covered chairs that sat at cross angles before his desk. The dog, curious about the sudden stranger, rose from the hearth and slunk across the length of the carpet to nose at her feet. Sitting as she was beside the lanky height of him, they were very nearly eye-to-eye.

The viscount scowled at the dog and said in Gaelic, "Cudu, *a-sìos*. Sit down."

"Oh, no, it is all right."

Eleanor held out her fingers to the stately hound, who glanced once at his master before he sniffed at her outstretched hand with his narrow wet nose. After a moment, he lowered his elegant head in hopes of a good scratch behind his grizzled ears. Eleanor willingly obliged and from that moment, her feet had the welcome warmth of a furry companion.

Lord Dunevin folded his hands before him on the desktop and looked at her. "Fergus left word that you wished a moment to discuss Juliana's curriculum with me."

Eleanor cleared her throat on a nod. "Yes, my lord, although in truth I had rather hoped to discuss this with you *in* the schoolroom."

The viscount stared at her incredulously, and Eleanor was reminded once again that she was no longer his social equal, Lady Eleanor Wycliffe, heiress to the Westover fortune, but his employee, Miss Nell Harte. She decided she should soften her tone.

"My apologies, my lord. I didn't mean to speak disrespectfully."

He shook his head. "Not at all. I was a bit occupied this morning," he offered by way of an explanation.

Eleanor caught herself studying the line his beard-shadowed chin and the few strands of dark hair that fell over his forehead. She wondered if the line that creased his brow ever eased. She wondered if he ever smiled. When she realized he was staring at her, she quickly broke away and turned her attention to the notes that she had made earlier that day in the nursery.

"Yes, well, the materials I found in the schoolroom are, on the whole, adequate, but I noted several fields of study that weren't represented that I would recommend be included in Juliana's education."

"Indeed?"

"Yes." She handed him her notes, sitting forward in her chair. "I took the liberty of listing some additional subjects I thought might prove beneficial."

The viscount took up the page. At first it appeared as if he might only give it a cursory glance, but something she had written caught his attention and he gave it a second, more thorough study.

He glanced up at her. "Astronomy? Botany? And this last one, do I read it right? Anatomy?"

Eleanor nodded.

"Miss Harte, I'm not of the mind to turn my daughter into a nine-year-old bluestocking. I had thought more along the lines of teaching her to write a pretty letter or play a pleasant tune upon the pianoforte, or even arrange a proper supper menu. What could anatomy possibly have to do with preparing my daughter to someday manage her husband's household?"

Eleanor felt herself stiffen against that all-too familiar and insular concept that to be a wife, mother, and gracious hostess were the very heights of womanly ambition. That same belief, that naïveté was "charming," and helplessness a longed-for virtue that she had swallowed all her life, like a spot of afternoon tea with her fingers held just so, and which, in the end, had only left her feeling betrayed and utterly vulnerable.

It was a mistake she had no intention of perpetuating through the next generation.

"As a matter of fact, my lord," Eleanor said then, pulling back her shoulders to sit up straighter in her chair, "I do think that a basic education in anatomy is most beneficial to a woman, even, it could be argued, more so than to a man. For who is it, sir, who is physically charged with the task of bringing forth new life? How much less terrifying that would be for a woman who has a basic education in the mechanics of the thing instead of blithely floating along on the belief that babies are delivered by fairies in the middle of the night, left upon the mother's pillow cooing and smiling to be discovered upon awakening the following morning?"

Eleanor's voice had risen to the point that even Cudu had lifted his head to look at her in astonishment. Her bout of indignation had brought a most appealing color to her face, the enthusiasm that she'd spoken with lighting her eyes a deeper green than they already were.

Gabriel wasn't accustomed to anyone, much less a woman, standing up to him so boldly. Most everyone he encountered feared the very sight of him, agreeing with anything he said even if it opposed their own views.

He was, after all, the Devil of Dunevin Castle.

But this woman . . .

He found himself wondering what it would be like to kiss the mouth from which those fiery words had come, and then he wondered where the hell that thought had come from.

He looked away from her, focusing on the letter he had been in the process of responding to at her arrival, a bland

and wordy bit of account from his solicitor, George Pratt, in London, anything to take his thoughts away from the fullness of her bottom lip.

"Actually, Miss Harte, here in Scotland the belief is that the fairies come to steal babies at night, not to deliver them."

The governess mistook his attempt at diverting his thoughts for ridicule at something she so obviously felt strongly about.

Her eyes flashed with an angry green fire. "Scoff at it all you like, sir, but I know of what I speak. Ignorance is never an asset. It is a weakness that victimizes women far more than it ever protects them."

As he looked on her bold eyes and heat-flushed cheeks, Gabriel wondered what had happened in her life to make her feel the burdens of her gender so keenly. There was no doubt she had been raised among elite society. Her manner and speech told adequately of that and she was educated far above even the most privileged members of her sex.

Just who was Miss Nell Harte? Where had she come from? Was she married? He didn't know why, but for the fleeting moment that thought filled his head, his shirt collar grew uncomfortably tight.

What should it matter if she were wed with a flock of offspring waiting for her at home? She obviously didn't wish to be wherever it was she had been, and she was the best candidate to teach Juliana the ways of society.

Even more so, she was the *only* candidate.

If she wanted to instruct his daughter in the patterns of the stars or the Latin name of every weed on the isle, so be it. When she had completed Juliana's education, she would go back to whatever—or whomever—she had left behind, and he could return to the solitude of his life with Juliana's future welfare secure.

"Once again you have proven your point, Miss Harte. I am convinced that Juliana could only benefit from the subjects you have mentioned. You may have full use of my library whenever you wish. You should find the materials more than adequate for your purposes, as over the past centuries my ancestors were great collectors of the written word in a variety of subjects. If there is anything else you find you need, we can see about acquiring it from the mainland."

The governess looked momentarily astonished. She said nothing, simply nodded in response. That one small movement of her head brought a single tendril of chestnut-colored hair to slipping from the stricture of her coif, trailing softly along her cheek, a cheek that looked as if it would be smooth as silk to the touch.

"Is that all?" Gabriel asked, fast growing aware of the increasing intimacy of the two of them alone in that room with only the woolly bulk of his dog stretched between them.

"Yes, my lord. I thank you for your refreshing open-mindedness toward Juliana's education. It is a most admirable manner of thinking for a man of your rank."

Gabriel wasn't sure whether he should take that as a compliment or a personal affront to his gender. He wasn't given the time to decide, for she stood then and turned to leave the room.

As she passed by the front of his desk, Gabriel caught the scent of her, a captivating mixture of flowers and spice. She may as well have struck him cold.

As she walked from the room, Gabriel found himself watching the gentle sway of her hips beneath the delicate pale muslin of her skirts. The room seemed to grow suddenly hotter. His breathing was coming fast. He realized a dangerous and wholly primitive tightening in his groin. It startled him and scared the living hell out of him all at the same time.

What in perdition was he doing? He wasn't some untested school lad dreaming of having a go between the luscious legs of the headmaster's daughter. He was a man, a man who knew better, a man who had learned all too well the perils of giving in to his emotions.

He was a man who hadn't lain with a woman in longer than he could remember.

This woman had been on the isle, in his home, all of one day and he was sitting there contemplating the softness of her skin, losing himself in her fragrance. Had he learned nothing after Georgiana? How many more innocent people had to suffer because of him?

Gabriel knew all too well what he must do. He must become the son of his father, the great Alexander. He must become cold and aloof, utterly unaffected. He would maintain that same hard-edged armor that had served the lairds of Dunevin for generations. And that meant one very clear thing, as well.

He must avoid being in the company of his mysterious governess at all costs.

Chapter Six

Gabriel stepped swiftly from the jetty onto the deck of the weather-worn skiff that bobbed lazily on the rippling waves at the shore.

It had dawned a clear morning, cool and crisp, the sort of day that brought everyone out after too many days of having been tucked away by the warmth of the peat fire.

It wasn't often the western seaboard was treated to such favorable weather so late in the season. The waning autumn months were more often obscured by low-hanging clouds or battered by the constant howl of fierce seaward winds. When they were blessed by unexpected fair weather such as this, it almost seemed like an unplanned-for holiday.

Earlier, Gabriel had decided to spend the day closeted in his study answering correspondence and reconciling the estate ledgers. But upon spotting the boat from his study window, and watching as it was readied for its voyage to the mainland, he had decided that the ledgers could wait for a more inclement day.

The waters of the firth tugged at the small craft as Gabriel shaded his eyes against the brightness of the sky, filling his lungs with the salt and mist and chill of the brisk sea air. A day like this, spent out on the open sea, was just what Gabriel needed to clear his head, banish the images that had plagued him in sleep, images of a particular governess with glinting green eyes and a mouth that begged to be tasted.

"*Là math dhut, Dòmhnall,*" Gabriel called in Gaelic greeting to Donald Duncan MacNeill, one of the island's tenants, who was preparing the boat for departure.

The few crew members were yet on the shore, stocking up on fresh water and bidding farewell to wives and mothers who were pressing them to take extra clothing should the weather take a sudden turn.

Gabriel took a moment to peer out over the easterly horizon, looking toward the distant mainland that rose through the dawn's drifting haze. There, hidden behind the scattering of isles that made up the Inner Hebrides, lay their destination of Oban, the quaint coastal town and hub port of all of Argyllshire.

"This morning's wind should afford us a swift crossing," Gabriel said.

"Aye, my lord," Donald answered, speaking in his native Gaelic, even though, like Gabriel, he had learned English at an early age. "We'll surely make good time this day."

Donald was only a few years younger than Gabriel's two-and-thirty, and had been born on Trelay, as had his father and his father before him. He had only left the isle once in his lifetime, at seventeen when he had gone to serve in one of the mighty Argyllshire Highland regiments against Napoleon on the Peninsula.

Donald had returned within a year of leaving after he'd taken a stray shot through his calf, from which he'd eventually recovered, but which had left him with a pronounced limp that had since christened him with the nickname of "Lame Donald" to those on the isle. He captained his crude craft twice weekly to the Scottish mainland, taking passengers to Oban, picking up the post, and retrieving supplies for the other crofters that couldn't be grown or manufactured on the isle. In appreciation for his performing this charitable duty, the other folk of the island saw to his small stock of cattle and sheep, and the potato and barley crops that would feed Donald and his young family through the coming winter months.

As he stood on the deck of the small sailing skiff, Gabriel was anxious to be away, unwilling to waste another moment of the day's glory. The small crew of four others had already boarded and were ready at their various stations. In minutes, the final details for their departure were completed.

"Shall I help you to push off?" Gabriel asked even as he reached for the twisted root rope that tethered the skiff to the rocky pier.

"Aye, my lord, that would be—"

MacNeill hesitated, looking out past Gabriel toward the distant castle hill. "A moment, my lord."

Gabriel turned from the hawser to see two figures making their way quickly down the pathway toward the jetty. They were too far away to see clearly, but both were dressed in skirts and cloaks with one quite a bit smaller than the other.

The taller figure's arms were waving in an obvious effort to draw their attention. This, Gabriel thought, was precisely *not* what he needed this day.

"Yoo hoo!" called out a reedy voice as the two approached. "Good morning, Lord Dunevin."

She was breathless from hurrying down the hillside and her hair had come loose from its pins. It was burnished a rich auburn brown from the sun and framed her cheeks and nose, pink from the chill air, most appealingly.

"I understand from Màiri that you are going to the mainland today," she said, stating the obvious, he gathered, in hopes of an invitation to join them.

Gabriel looked at her. "Yes, Miss Harte, we are."

If he at all thought his prosaic response would have deterred her, he was quickly proven wrong.

"Well then, I'm so glad we caught you before you departed."

Without waiting for an assisting hand, she stepped quickly onto the deck, turning with a swish of her skirts to take Juliana's hand and help her onto the boat behind her. She then went for Donald, putting out her hand in greeting.

"How do you do? I am Miss Harte, Miss Juliana's new governess. I wonder if we might tag along to town with you today? It is such a lovely day for a sail."

MacNeill doffed his ragged fisherman's cap, revealing the crop of bright red hair that sprouted underneath. He grinned broadly. "Donald MacNeill at your service, Miss Harte."

The governess returned the smile, charming the Scottish sailor and his entire crew to their teeth. "Please, call me Nell. Everyone does."

Everyone but me, Gabriel thought.

He looked at her. "What are you doing, Miss Harte?"

Her easy smile vanished and she turned to regard him with eyes of curious unease—*green* eyes of curious unease.

"Why, I am taking your own advice, my lord."

"My advice?"

"Indeed. According to your cook, Màiri, I can purchase a pair of sturdy shoes in Oban quite cheaply."

"And I believe I told you that Fergus would see to it for you."

"Yes, but I saw no reason to take him away from his other duties when I could see to the errand just as easily myself. I am also in need of some more suitable clothing and, well, Fergus couldn't very well have seen to the purchase of my underthings, now could he?"

An image of her clad in her chemise flashed before his mind's eye. Gabriel scowled, although he certainly couldn't disagree that she needed clothing more befitting the isles.

Even now, she was dressed in a high-waisted gown of checked light cloth and dainty heelless slippers, as if she were going off on a round of social calls instead of sailing up a windy sea lane. If she continued dressing like that, she would catch pneumonia in a month's time.

"Besides," she went on, "this way I can be sure of the fit, and with the weather so fine, I thought it a perfect first outing for Juliana and me."

Beside her, Juliana was looking at her father as if she expected him to refuse their passage.

Though his first sense told him that he should, he also knew that Juliana had been shut away inside the castle for too many weeks without venturing out-of-doors. Even yesterday, a quiet moment by the sea had been spoiled by rain. Thus he couldn't argue against a healthy dose of sunshine and fresh sea air.

He also knew he couldn't very well just suddenly cry off from going himself without causing question, so instead he muttered, "Very well," and reached once again for the mooring ropes.

Once they were free, the sloop slid easily away from the pier, pulled by the swelling waves as her stout woolen sail filled with the bracing wind. The crew took their places at the thwarts, readying themselves at the narrow oars, and at Donald's command in Gaelic of *"Tiugainn!"* they all pulled back in unison.

The boat heaved forward. They were headed out to sea.

As they sailed, the air was filled with the rhythmic sound of the oarsmen's chant, an ancient song that aided them in keeping their movements in sync. It was a practice long seated among the isles and various verses had been handed down through generations of seafaring men.

In between each stride, Gabriel was treated to an earful of Miss Harte's nonstop chatter as she told Juliana about things she knew, and alternately asked Donald about things she did not.

"You see this here, Juliana? This is the front of the boat, called the 'prow,' and the rear is called the 'stern,' is that not correct, Mr. MacNeill?"

Even before he could answer, she turned and asked, "Oh, and what is that little island there called, Mr. MacNeill?"

"Oh, that be Eilean Olmsa, miss. There is a legend that says when the Bonnie Prince came to Scotland back in '45, 'twas there he first landed afore moving on northward to Barra."

"Indeed?" The governess's eyes lit with curious excitement as she scanned the rugged shoreline of the tiny islet as if searching for the lost Stuart among the rocks and overgrowth. "Do tell the tale, Mr. MacNeill . . ."

While Donald began recounting the same stories of the Jacobites they'd been told since childhood, Gabriel busied himself with checking and rechecking the halyard on the opposite side of the craft, thankful for the brisk chill of the wind against his face and neck, anything to draw his attention away from those damnable green eyes.

This woman had a light about her, an indescribable radiance that shone in her tireless inquisitiveness and passionate nature. She had a face that displayed every emotion she felt like an open book.

She was *intoxicating*.

The journey up the firth was not by any means a brief one; it would take them till nearly midday to reach Oban Bay. At no time during their journey did Miss Harte ever seem at a loss for words.

Juliana, in contrast, never uttered a sound. She sat as she always had every day for the past three years, staring at the far-off horizon, oblivious to all the activity going on around her.

Still, Gabriel couldn't help but be astounded by his new governess. She never gave up. Unlike any previous governess who had quickly detached herself from any social interaction with Juliana when the child wouldn't respond, Miss Harte continued to talk to Juliana as if they were carrying on a nonstop conversation. She included her in everything that was going on around them, even asking her questions as if she had no notion that only one of them was talking.

The next hours passed quickly. Just over halfway to the mainland, the skiff cut to where the firth began to narrow between the larger isles of Mull and Jura. The winds here began to pull the small craft more strongly as they swirled and whistled through the moody sea corridor, sending a salt-sea spray shooting upward from the beaked prow with each wave they crested.

At the customary spot, the oarsmen suddenly stopped, stilling their movements and lifting their oars high in the air, allowing Donald to steer by way of the rudder expertly over the choppy waves.

It grew quiet. Even Miss Harte seemed to sense the change as they sculled further inward toward Oban. Soon, a distant and familiar roar began to rise from the east, growing louder, it seemed, with each swell they rode.

"*Och,*" said Donald as he kept a firm hand on the ship's

rudder, "sounds as if the *cailleach* is in a fine temper this morn, it does."

"*Cailleach?*" the governess asked.

"Aye. Do you hear that, Miss Eleanor? That roar? 'Tis the Hag of the Isles, the roar of Corryvrecken. 'Tis a most fearsome tidal whirlpool that lies off the northern coast of Jura there." He pointed toward the nearest coastline, where three distinct peaks rose through the hovering mist. "You and the little lassie there had best find a firm handhold. Sailing will likely get rough 'ere for a spell."

"Is it dangerous?" Miss Harte asked, eyeing the eastern horizon with some consternation. Her bubbling enthusiasm for their leisurely sail had suddenly waned.

"Aye, it can be, for those who doona ken the ways of the waters of Lorne," Donald said. " 'Tis called Coire Bhreacain by the Gaels, 'Prince Breacain's Cauldron,' and it comes from a legend almost as auld as these same isles. They say that hundreds of years ago, back when it were the Picts and the Gaels who dwelled on these ancient lands, there came a Prince Breacain one day from far-off Norway, seeking the hand in marriage of the beautiful daughter of the Lord of the Isles.

"But the lord, he intended to truly test this young prince afore he'd give up the precious prize o' his beloved daughter. So he told the prince he must anchor his galley for the length of three days and three nights in the churning flood tide that roars a'tween Jura and Scarba. If he made it through the third night to morning, he would win the hand of the lord's lassie.

"Many a sailing ship had gone to her grave in those treacherous waters, so to better prepare himself, the prince hied his way back to Norway to consult with the mystic sages. These wise men studied their ancient scrolls and prayed for direction to the Norse deities. Finally they returned to the prince with their advice."

"What did they tell him?" Her eyes were wide with wonder.

"They bid him to take three ropes with him to the Kingdom of the Isles, one spun of wool, another of hemp, and the third made of the hair of pure and true maidens. Well, needless to say, many a Norse lassie gave over her silken tresses to the handsome prince for his rope, but wha he didna know was that one lass"—Donald shook his head dolefully—"*och,* she wasna so pure. Unknowing of this, Prince Breacain sailed swiftly back for the isles, ready with his three ropes and confident to face the challenge that the Lord of the Isles had put to him."

Gabriel found himself staring in fascination at the expression on the face of Donald's one-woman audience. Forgotten was her unease at the roar that now surrounded them; she was utterly captivated by the old tale.

Gabriel, in turn, was utterly captivated by her.

"What happened when the prince went back?" she asked.

"On the first night," Donald explained, his voice growing hushed over the sound of the sea, "the rope made of wool broke, but the prince managed to weather the pull of the tide and see his way through to morn. On the second night, the hemp rope fared no better. Still Breacain prevailed. The third rope did hold fast through the third night just as the sages had promised, until a terrible storm arose from the west and the one strand that contained the hair of the impure maiden broke, weakening the rest of the rope. Just afore the dawn, Breacain and his ship were carried away by the raging flood tide, doomed never to win the hand of his princess. But his faithful dog snatched the poor prince's lifeless body from the churning waters and dragged him to the shores of Jura, where he was then buried in the cave that bears his name to this day."

By now, the governess was staring at Donald with an expression of pure and utter veneration. Even Juliana had become entranced by the story, pulling her gaze away from the distance to give her attention to MacNeill.

Gabriel stood silently applauding the sailor's effort, for in the time it had taken Donald to relate that old and colorful tale, he had managed to sail them clear of any danger from the roaring flood tide. Even now, its howl was slowly fading into the mists behind them.

Only a short time later, they drifted to a halt at the busy pier in Oban.

Gabriel jumped off the skiff first to see to securing the mooring ropes, then immediately went back to assist the others onto the pier. The past hours had been a trial for him, being in such close company with Juliana after having spent the past months doing everything to avoid her. He had to continually remind himself of the dangers of so much as enjoying her company.

Thus when he felt the touch of Juliana's fingers in his, he stopped himself from a greeting smile, tempering it with a curt nod as she stepped onto the pier.

He reached lastly for Miss Harte, who stood waiting at the skiff's prow. In the moment that she stretched her leg over the hull to the pier, the boat took a sudden lurch, pitching her forward into his arms. She looked up at him in stark surprise, so close to him that he could feel the warmth of the sharp exhale of her breath against his chin, that same alluring scent of her overrunning his senses.

His body virtually leapt in response. The warmth of her against him, the smell of her, the *womanliness* of her press-

ing so intimately against him brought his groin to tightening
and his pulse to pounding.

It was a feeling he hadn't felt in some time.

It was a feeling that felt good against him.

She was staring at him, her eyes wide, dark hazel green,
her mouth slightly parted. He could kiss her so easily, and
somehow he knew she would let him, even as he knew he
had to get away from her.

Immediately.

Gabriel set her to rights and stepped awkwardly away.

"We must leave no later than two of the clock if we're to
make it back to the isle by nightfall," he said more abruptly
than he had intended.

Without waiting for her response, he turned away from
her on the pretense of rechecking the tightness of the mooring hawsers, leaving Eleanor to stare in befuddlement at the
unyielding wall of his back.

Chapter Seven

There was a steep flight of stone steps, slick from the sea mist, that led up from the crowded pier to George Street, the main thoroughfare of the tiny hamlet of Oban.

The small Highland fishing village had sprouted up within only the past thirty years or more, around the eastern curve of a picturesque sea-swept bay. It was scarcely more than a string of thatched cottages and lime-washed houses with high-pitched roofs, and though there was no church, there were two small inns, a Customs House, a distillery, and a scattering of other trades all centered largely on the fisheries that made up the bulk of the village's sparse economy.

Set at the foot of a towering, tree-lined mountain, Oban was sheltered from the keen Hebridean winds by the verdant isle of Kerrera across the bay, and dominated on its northern end by the fortress of Dunollie.

This ancient castle was the seat of the Clan MacDougall, now a crumbling ruin, although it had once been the stronghold of the kings of Dalraida. The present MacDougall chief still occupied the land, living in a house built of the castle's own stone right after the defeat of the '45. All that remained of the original stronghold was the ancient keep, standing like a sentinel above the sheltered cove at the precise spot where lofty mountaintop met endless sky.

Eleanor decided that it would be wiser to begin their outing with some place familiar, and so she headed off first down George Street, walking the short distance to the inn where she had stayed earlier that week. She thought to ask the innkeeper's wife, Mrs. MacIver, where she might find her much-needed shoes.

They had to step quickly to skirt an oncoming pony cart and Eleanor took hold of Juliana's hand to pull her along safely. She did not, however, let go after the cart had gone, and was delighted to see that Juliana did not pull away.

When they entered the dimly lit front parlor of the inn, there was no one immediately about, although Eleanor could hear muffled voices coming from the rear of the place. She looked down at Juliana and smiled, directing her to a small rustic-looking bench set beneath the small front window.

Eleanor turned just as the innkeeper's wife came into the room, wiping her hands on her apron.

"*Och,* lass, but you gave me a fright just now. I dinna hear you come in, but I canna say I am surprised to see you either. I expected you'd be back. As I said to you afore, few have ever lasted more than a night's time on that accursed isle. But not to worry, we still have your room ready for you. Will you be wanting to stay for just one night, then, or longer this time?"

Eleanor shook her head. "Oh, no, I'm sorry, Mrs. MacIver, but you are mistaken. I do not mean to take a room. I have decided to stay and serve as governess on the isle. I only just—"

"Governess?" Mrs. MacIver's eyes had gone wide as the harvest moon with disbelief. And then she spotted Juliana sitting behind Eleanor. Her mouth fell open in astonishment and it took her a full minute to find her tongue. "You are going to stay there on that wicked isle and tend to that demon's child?"

Eleanor scowled unhappily at the woman. "I'll thank you not to speak in such an impolite manner in front of Miss MacFeagh."

"She *is* the demon's child, she is, sure as her da has stolen away her voice."

"That is enough, Mrs. MacIver."

"Then why doesna she speak?"

"Perhaps because she has nothing to say. I would also remind you that the fact that she doesn't speak does not prevent her from *hearing,* so I would ask you to hold your tongue against any further commentary. Now if you would be so kind as to direct us to the village shoemaker, we will take ourselves off from your parlor and be on our way."

Mrs. MacIver shook her head dolefully. "*Och,* lass, but 'tis a grievous mistake you're makin', A most grievous mistake."

"Then it is my mistake to make. The shoemaker, Mrs. MacIver, if you please."

The woman frowned at her, obviously displeased that she had failed to convince her to her nonsensical allegations. "He's doon the road a bit on the bay side near to the end of town. Has a big black bear of a dog that lays by his door a'day, lazy as a lump in a pudding. Just look you for that beast and you canna miss findin' the place."

Eleanor thanked the woman and held out her hand to Juliana, who took it quickly, no doubt as eager as Eleanor to be out the door.

It was as she was reaching for the handle to leave that she first spotted the notice tacked next to the door in the precise place where she had days before discovered the advertisement that had taken her to Trelay.

This time, however, it wasn't an offer of employment.

NOTICE

A monetary reward of substantial sum is offered for
the safe return of one Lady Eleanor Wycliffe
of the esteemed Westover Dukedom.
The lady is of fair complexion with brown hair
and green eyes and was last known to be traveling
alone through the northern Highlands. Please contact
His Grace, the Duke of Westover, or his heir,
Marquess Knighton, with any information.
No expense will be spared in the search for her.

Eleanor felt all color drain quickly away from her face.
Oh, good God, she thought, they were hunting for her.

The notice had to have been posted within the past two
days, since she had stayed at the inn so recently and had not
noticed it before. She wanted to question Mrs. MacIver
about it, to ask who had brought it and when, but worried
any interest she showed might draw the woman's attention
to the fact that the subject of the notice was quite obviously
herself.

She was surprised, in fact, she hadn't realized it already.

Eleanor glanced over at the woman who was busying
herself with some flowers she was arranging in a small vase.
Pretending to search through her reticule, Eleanor waited
until the woman had turned for a moment, and then quickly
snatched the notice from the wall, shoving it carelessly inside her bag.

Once outside, Eleanor paused to take a deep breath. Her
first thought was to return to MacNeill's skiff and simply
wait there until it was time to leave, and she would have, except that she really needed to purchase her shoes. Perhaps it
was the only notice posted, she thought hopefully. And if it
wasn't, she would just have to make sure that she found and

removed any others, starting, she decided, with the shoemaker's cottage.

As they started down the roadway in the direction Mrs. MacIver had suggested, Eleanor looked upward toward the mountains and noticed that the skies were beginning to cast over. She hoped that it wouldn't rain again.

They hadn't walked very far before they came upon a small, vine-clad cottage that had what looked like an open-ended barrel sticking out the top as a chimney. Lying in front was indeed a most prodigious black dog sprawled before the door. His eyes were closed and his breathing was slow and heavy and he seemed to pay them no mind as they quietly approached. He didn't move, didn't so much as lift his head—

—until they were within a few feet of him.

He jerked upright, placing himself between them and the door in one swift movement. In the next moment, he started barking like a hellhound.

Juliana froze at her side. Eleanor quickly put herself between the girl and the barking dog. Holding the child's hand tightly in hers, Eleanor took one cautious step closer toward the door. The dog bared his teeth and glared at her.

"Is anyone there?" she called feebly to the house, hoping to somehow alert the dog's owner inside, as if her quivering voice would do that more than this creature's unholy din.

There came no response, so she released Juliana's hand to step slightly to the side and closer to the single window. She tried to peek inside its filmy pane. "Excuse me, is anyone there?"

As she moved a bit to better see between the ragged curtains, she heard the dog give a low growl. She turned to look, drawing in a sharp breath.

"Juliana, no!"

Juliana had stepped forward and had extended her hand to within a few inches of the dog's grizzled snout. Eleanor's first instinct was to pull her from harm's way, but she feared that if she moved too quickly, the dog would become startled and lash out.

It was then she noticed that the dog was no longer growling. Instead he had lifted his great snout upward, sniffing curiously at Juliana's outstretched fingers. Eleanor caught her breath, silently praying. The dog gave a soft whine and then licked Juliana's hand, pushing his head under her fingers for a scratch.

Juliana smiled and stooped down before the beast, gently petting him.

"Aye, I thought I heard someone calling. Good day to you, miss."

A brawny man, perhaps in his later twenties, with muddy blond hair and amber-colored eyes, came around from the back of the ramshackle cottage. He wiped his fingers on a cloth before holding out his hand to her in greeting. "Seamus Maclean at your service."

Eleanor smiled and shook his hand. "Good day to you, Mr. Maclean. I am Miss Nell Harte, and this is Miss Juliana MacFeagh. We've come looking for some shoes."

"MacFeagh?" He eyed Juliana with much the same look as the annoying Mrs. MacIver. "Would that be the MacFeagh from Trelay?"

After the earlier conversation at the inn, Eleanor's defenses prickled immediately. "Yes, sir, that is right. We have come from Trelay. I am the governess on the isle now."

"Governess, aye?" His smile no longer gave the impression of friendliness. Instead it seemed almost to mock her words.

Eleanor frowned at him.

"So this is her, the wee quiet one. Aye, though she carries the unfortunate mark of her da's coloring, she still has the light o' her mither's gentle beauty, she does."

Had this man known Juliana's mother? Perhaps the viscountess had come to town for shoes herself. His words, however, and the distinct emotion he spoke them with, gave an indication of a far more familiar relationship.

Maclean must have remembered then that they had come to give him business, for his tone changed almost in an instant. "You've come looking for shoes, you say?"

"Yes. A pair of half boots should suffice quite well, if you please, Mr. Maclean."

The shoemaker grinned broadly. "You're no' from the Highlands, are you, Miss Harte?"

She would have thought that her obvious lack of a Scottish accent would have given that bit of information away, but she simply shook her head and said, "I come from England, sir."

"A Sassenach, you say? Well, I canna say I've ever seen or even heard of something called a ha'boot. Most Highland lassies doona wear any shoes a'tall."

Eleanor frowned. "I see. Well, apparently I've come to the wrong establishment then. I'm sorry to have troubled you, Mr. Maclean." She turned to leave. "Come, Juliana."

"Aye, you must be from the Lowlands indeed, ready as you are to rush off e'en afore I've finished what I'm saying."

Eleanor stopped and looked at him, waiting.

"I cannot make you this ha'boot you speak of, but I can make you a bonny pair of Scottish brogues that'll serve you much better than those wee fancy slippers you're wearing now. I'll need to measure your feet first, though, to get the fit right."

He walked over to the door of the cottage, opened it, and

stepped back, motioning for Eleanor to proceed ahead. Eleanor hesitated a moment, hoping she wouldn't regret having come, wondering if she dare trust him long enough to stay. She decided her need for the shoes outweighed her misgivings. She nodded for Juliana to come and started for the door.

Eleanor ducked inside the low doorway and found herself standing in a single cluttered room that took up the entirety of the cottage's interior. A crudely built hearth was set against the far wall, looking more like a haphazard stack of flat stones, the smoke from which filled the room more than it escaped through what was indeed an open-ended barrel chimney. A blackened kettle simmered there and variously shaped tools and utensils hung in a scattered mixture from every spare bit of wall space.

Thankfully, there was no sign of another notice like the one she had removed from the inn. She rather doubted he could find room for it on the wall anyway.

Maclean crossed the room to quickly dust off a small wooden bench by the hearth and then motioned for her to sit while he retreated to the far corner for some tools.

Eleanor removed her slipper and made to hand it to him when he returned.

"Wha's that for?"

"For you to measure my foot with, sir."

Maclean grinned again, shaking his head as if she had just said something amusing. "I canna form a brogue from that bonny bit o' nonsense."

He sat down on a small stool before her and held out his hand, quite obviously expecting her to deliver her foot into it.

Maidenly modesty apparently had no place in the Highlands.

Eleanor slowly lifted her foot to his waiting palm while making certain that the hem of her skirts went no higher than her ankle.

Maclean moved his hands deftly over her stockinged foot, testing several leathern shoe forms against the length of it. There was no attempt at delicacy in his touch. Rather the manner in which he worked was filled with a casual familiarity that made Eleanor increasingly uncomfortable.

When she felt his hands move upward under her skirts past her ankle to her calf, Eleanor stiffened. "I beg your pardon, sir, but . . ."

"That's enough, Maclean."

Eleanor drew a startled breath at the sudden and unexpected gruff voice coming from behind them.

She turned to see Lord Dunevin standing just inside the cottage doorway, filling it with his imposing stature, his face crossed by a stern frown.

The dog, she realized, had never made a sound to forewarn of his arrival.

"I believe you have sufficient measurement to make the lady a competent pair of brogues. Now get on with it."

Maclean grinned, his eyes fixed coldly on the viscount. "Ah, well, when I awoke this fine morn I'd never 'ave believed I'd find the Devil of Dunevin Castle standing in my parlor door. How does the mighty Lord 'Done-Her-In' fare these days?"

Dunevin's eyes narrowed perilously as he advanced into the room. His dark head nearly glanced the smoke-blackened rafters above them. "We've a boat to catch in order to return to the isle by nightfall, Maclean. Just get the lady her brogues and be quick about it."

The men faced each other through several tense moments.

Still grinning that cold smirk, Maclean then turned to Eleanor. "I'll take but a moment, lass."

He stood and departed through a door at the rear of the cottage.

Alone now with only the heavy silence between them, the viscount looked at Eleanor, his expression chillingly grim.

"You would be wise, Miss Harte, not to allow a Scotsman such liberties, and especially in front of my daughter."

Eleanor stared at him, dumbfounded. "Liberties? I beg your pardon, my lord, but Mr. Maclean was fitting me for a pair of shoes. Yes, he did become a bit too familiar and at the moment you interrupted, I was on the very verge of rebuking him."

"A man like Maclean would care very little for your polite rebuke." He glanced quickly at Juliana before saying, "I will await you outside."

Eleanor didn't know who she wanted to cosh on the head more, Maclean for his crudeness, or Lord Dunevin for his unfounded accusation. He made it sound almost as if she had been flirting with the Scots cobbler. Even worse, he had inferred that she could not handle herself, that all would have been lost had he not happened upon the scene when he had to save her.

She fought against the urge to inform him in no uncertain terms she was quite capable of taking care of herself, that she had had the situation well in hand. Instead she could but set her feelings aside and smile when she noticed that Juliana was watching her. She waited silently for Maclean to return.

He did, after nearly a quarter hour, carrying with him a pair of the leather-laced shoes the Highlanders called brogues.

Eleanor slipped one of the thin-soled coverings easily over her foot and then pulled tightly on the leather thongs that crisscrossed the top of her foot to tie it. The shoe fit with the snugness of a glove, the softly treated leather molding itself delicately to the contours of her foot. Despite his impolite behavior, Maclean certainly knew his trade.

As she took a few steps to test the fit, Eleanor noticed that the sides of the shoes had been left unstitched in places. Maclean must have noticed her uncertainty in looking at them and explained.

"The sides are left open like that to allow water to escape, else you'd be sloshing about like an otter whenever it rains."

They were certainly like no other shoes she had ever worn before, but as she became accustomed to the flexible fit of them, Eleanor found she quite liked them.

"Thank you, Mr. Maclean. They are very nice. I especially thank you for making them so quickly. What do I owe you, sir?"

He was putting away his tools, his back to her. "Three shillings. They wear out quite easily, so for that price I'll make you up another pair and send it over the next time MacNeill makes the crossing."

As Eleanor reached to place her coins on his work table, Maclean turned to look at her. Gone was the smirking grin and mocking amber eyes. Instead his expression had turned suddenly grave.

"Be careful on that isle, lass. It is a mournful, forsaken place. If you should ever find yourself in danger, always remember Uamh nan Fhalachasan, 'the Cave of the Hidden.' Ask Màiri where it is. There is a secret chamber at the back of it that even he doesna know of. Keep it to yourself, lass, and tell no one of it. Doona make the same mistake that Lady Georgiana did."

His stare was so fierce that Eleanor could only manage a short nod, averting her eyes nervously as she turned and called for Juliana.

As she made for the door, she wondered if the confrontation earlier between Maclean and Lord Dunevin had had less to do with her than it had to do with whatever history there was between the two of them, a history that she suspected had something to do with the former viscountess.

As they emerged from inside the cottage, she was more than a little surprised to see Lord Dunevin still been waiting for them outside.

"The brogues fit well?"

He seemed to have forgotten the unpleasantness from inside the cottage.

"Yes, indeed, my lord. They are most comfortable."

"Good. I'll escort you to the pier then," and he started down the dirt path leading away from the cottage.

"Oh, thank you, my lord, but Juliana and I are not yet finished with our sightseeing. We've yet another hour or more and I thought to explore the ruins of Dunollie before finishing my shopping in town. I do appreciate your kind offer, but I believe I can take it from here."

He mumbled something she didn't quite hear.

"I beg your pardon, my lord?"

"I said I will accompany you to wherever else you need to go."

Eleanor thought for a moment, then nodded, thinking this a good opportunity for him to spend some time in Juliana's company. Perhaps if he saw the progress she was already making with his daughter, he wouldn't be so reluctant to spend time with her himself. In fact, Eleanor thought further, she would do whatever she could to prolong the outing for just that purpose.

"Shall we go, then?"

They spent the next half hour climbing the steep, over-grown path that led up the thickly treed hillside to the castle ruins. The view over the secluded bay and distant isles there was breathtaking, a rich palette of colors, greens, purples, and reds, that stretched for as far as the eye could see and beyond. The isles of Mull and Lismore and the Morvern Peninsula were clearly seen from this lofty vantage, making it easy to see why this particular site had been chosen for the fortress.

Built at a time when most all travel was done on water, anyone approaching within the distance of ten miles would be easily spotted.

While they were there, climbing about what had once been the seat of ancient kings, they encountered the present MacDougall chief, Patrick "Peter" MacDougall, who had watched their approach from the house he occupied a short distance away from the ancient keep. Despite his advanced age of nearly eighty years, he had made the walk up the hill to greet them and had spent nearly an hour telling them wondrous tales of the MacDougalls through history. Eleanor thought him a warm and genial host.

Leaving Dunollie, they made their way back down the hillside path to town. As they strolled quietly along George Street, each lost in their own thoughts, Eleanor couldn't set aside the nagging sensation that they were being watched.

And they were.

One place in particular drew the curtains closed when they passed and children who were playing at Tom Tiddles scattered and squealed as their mothers called them in. Every quaint cottage and house they passed along the way was like so many of the lines of decorated ladies at a London ball, whispering to each other from behind their lace-edged fans.

It was utterly ridiculous, Eleanor thought, this unfounded fear the entire town had of Lord Dunevin. He was a man, not a monster, merely out taking a pleasant stroll in fine weather with his daughter. Dunevin pretended not to notice the villagers' actions, still the frown he wore deepened the further along they walked.

Eleanor stopped at a couple of the waterfront shops to purchase lengths of sturdy woolen for skirts, a few pair of thickly knit stockings, and chemises made of the white twilled cloth called "cuirtan" that Màiri had advised her to get. She ordered several more and tried to ignore the shopkeeper's expression when she learned they were for delivery to Trelay. She was relieved, however, to note that no other place in the village had another notice posted about her missing.

By the time she was finished, Eleanor had spent nearly all of the coin Lord Dunevin had given her as an advance on her salary, but there was still enough left for one more item, one she had purposely saved enough to buy.

They came to a small shop nestled near the pier, a haberdashery of sorts whose front window was filled with everything from wooden spindles to timepieces. Eleanor had remembered the place from her previous visit to the village, had remembered something in particular she'd seen.

"Excuse me, my lord, but there is one last place I wish to stop."

Lord Dunevin glanced quickly at his timepiece. "The hour grows late, Miss Harte."

"I'll only be just a moment, my lord. I promise."

He nodded curtly and Eleanor turned for the shop, which by now Juliana instinctively followed her into. While Juliana was gazing at some small painted pictures of sailing ships set up near the back counter, Eleanor quickly made her purchase, thanking the shopkeeper with a smile as she turned to leave.

With this last purchase tucked under one arm, Eleanor returned with Juliana to where Lord Dunevin awaited and they walked in relative silence to the pier.

Donald MacNeill was standing ready at the skiff, chatting amiably with a fellow boatman, when they approached. MacNeill smiled at Juliana in greeting and spoke quietly to her as he helped her on board, in sharp contrast to the many villagers they had encountered that day who had looked on the child quite as if she carried the plague.

Once Juliana was settled safely upon one of the thwarts, Donald then reached to assist Eleanor aboard. "Tha's a fine pair o' brogues you've gotten there, Miss Harte."

"Thank you, Mr. MacNeill. Mr. Maclean tells me he will have a second pair ready by the time you come to the mainland again."

"Then I'll be certain to fetch them for you."

Eleanor nodded her thanks and joined Juliana.

It had been a pleasant day despite the boorishness of Maclean, Mrs. MacIver, and the other villagers. There had been several occasions during the course of the day when Eleanor had noticed Juliana actually listening to her and not lost to her own silent world. Eleanor had delighted in her progress to reach the child, a sign, she believed, of even better things to come.

"Juliana," she said as she sat beside her on the skiff's small bench seat, "I have something I want to show you."

Eleanor removed the cloth covering from the small extending spyglass she had just purchased at the haberdashery.

"Do you know what this is?"

Juliana took up the brass piece in her hand and studied it closely, turning it over several times in her hand. She looked at Eleanor.

"It is called a spyglass." Eleanor took it and extended it to its full length, about a foot and a half of interconnecting pieces. The light of responding curiosity that sparked in Juliana's eyes was priceless.

"You look through it on the small end here and it makes things that are far away look closer." She pointed it out toward the isle of Kerrera as they sailed down the sound for the firth beyond. "Here, why don't you try it?"

Eleanor sat back and watched as, Juliana placed the glass near her eye and looked out at the horizon. Her brow knit in concentration as she looked, drew back, and looked again, taking the glass away time and again to compare the true distance with the one she saw through the glass.

"Amazing, isn't it? Do you like it?"

Juliana simply stared at her, but her eyes spoke her agreement clearly.

"Then it is yours."

Juliana remained still through a long moment. Then she did the most extraordinary thing.

She smiled.

It wasn't a wide, ear-reaching grin, but instead the shy tentative smile of one who had gone too long without doing so. Eleanor thought to herself that she would have paid the cost of one hundred spyglasses if it would have taken that to see just this one moment of Juliana's happiness.

"Look there." She pointed outward, watching as Juliana went back to peering through the glass. She sat back on the seat, relishing the sea air against her face, the freedom of soaring over the waves. It was then Eleanor noticed Lord Dunevin sitting across from them.

He was watching Juliana and her smile, unaware of Eleanor's silent scrutiny. His gaze as he stared at his daughter was filled with such softness, such unconscious longing that Eleanor could feel his emotions almost as clearly as if they were a tangible thing.

This was not the face of a man who didn't care for his child. Lord Dunevin loved Juliana with the tender adoration of a true father, but for some imperceptible reason, he just didn't want anyone else to know it.

And that left Eleanor with one lingering thought.

Why? What was it that made him hide his affection, as if he was somehow afraid to let anyone else know how he truly felt?

Chapter Eight

The journey back from Oban was uneventful, a quiet voyage touched by a vibrant sunset of mixed pinks, purples, and oranges shimmering over sleepy gray waters that glistened like glass in its ebbing light.

The image of Trelay as they approached, limned by mists and colorful light was the most beautiful, breath-stealing sight Eleanor could ever imagine, and she stood on the ship's deck, awed by it as they slipped across the dark waters to dock at the jetty.

The coming back seemed to take twice as long as getting there, and they arrived back at Dunevin shortly after dark.

They were greeted with a simple supper of barley bannocks, cheese, and sliced roast pullet which Màiri had kindly thought to have ready for them when they returned. Màiri asked about their outing, thrilling over Juliana's spyglass, and then quickly reported to Gabriel on the doings at the castle in his absence.

Soon after their meal, the day's activities began to make their effects known, bringing on quiet thought, wide yawns, and fast-drooping eyes.

They all retired early, shortly before nine, and once again, Eleanor had gone down to the kitchen after seeing Juliana to bed for a cup of tea with Màiri. Once again she returned abovestairs to find Juliana missing from her bed, curled asleep in her mother's bed, and joined her there.

Early the following morning, they shared a simple breakfast of oatcakes and tea, sitting at the small table by the warmth of the kitchen hearth while Màiri flitted about the place in preparation for the baking she would do for the upcoming Michaelmas holiday.

The festival of St. Michael, patron saint of the sea, brought an end to the month of September, the traditional end of the harvest, when rents were paid and thanks were given for a bountiful crop.

Màiri's two married daughters, Alys and Sorcha, had come that morning from the mainland to help their mother to prepare. While they checked that there would be enough meal and other food stuffs for the traditional Struan Micheil cake that would be the highlight of the celebration, Màiri sat with Eleanor and Juliana, telling them of the sacred holiday.

"Ev'ryone on the isle takes part in the celebration," she explained, "beginning on the Sunday afore St. Michael's Day, a day we call Dòmhnach Curran, when all the women and young lasses of the isle of every age gather the carrots from the fields. 'Tis a tradition that is long seated in the isles. You and the wee one must take part with us, too."

Eleanor was delighted to accept.

The weather had continued fair and after finishing their breakfast, Eleanor saw that Juliana was dressed warmly in a woolen frock and stockings against the chill outdoors. Eleanor tied the thonged laces of her new brogues snugly and the two of them set off for the craggy hills beyond the castle to spend the day exploring the isle through Juliana's new spyglass.

As they crested the first hilltop, Eleanor turned back once and thought she spied a figure standing at one of the castle

windows. At their distance apart, she could not see that the
figure was Lord Dunevin, nor could she see his troubled
frown as he watched their departure from his study, his
thoughts haunted by another such outing three years before,
one from which only one had come back.

The sun seemed content to hide its morning warmth behind a mottled covering of autumn clouds, the wind blowing
in off the firth brisk and chill, tugging at the ends of their
overcoats as they walked. Eleanor wore the warmest gown
she had, an ashen gray velvet with sleeves that reached to
her wrists off a closely fitted bodice buttoning along the
front. Her new woolen stockings provided ample warmth
against the cold, but she had brought along a spare pair for
them each just in case they might need them.

Within a half an hour, the carefully wound chignon into
which Eleanor had fashioned her hair that morning had
grown slack, drooping further and further down the nape of
her neck. A quarter hour more and Eleanor gave up the effort of keeping it confined altogether, pulling the pins that
secured it from her hair and letting it fall in a loose tangle
about her shoulders.

As they walked along, they stopped now and again to in-
vestigate some curious speck on the far horizon, numerous
herring boats, an occasional shearwater soaring close to the
water's surface in search of a fishy snack, and the bobbing
rounded head of a curious gray seal who seemed somehow
to be following them.

Juliana constantly stopped to peer at the creature while
Eleanor chatted pleasantly to her about the island landscape,
remarking on the abundance of wildflowers they encountered this late in the season. They gathered woodruff and
other herbs for Màiri to freshen the linen presses, tucking

them in a small willow basket she had given them before
they'd left.

As they made their way over brae and glen, they met with
several of the tenants of Trelay. The whole of the island was
governed by Lord Dunevin, and those who lived outside the
castle proper occupied land that was divided into separate
crofts or small holdings, which they farmed both to feed
their families and to earn their living.

Most often, the crofters would not earn enough from the
land to sustain themselves, so they would supplement their
incomes with secondary trades such as fishing, kelping,
weaving, or in providing other services, as Donald MacNeill
did in delivering the island post and ferrying goods and people between Trelay and the mainland.

The crofts they passed stood alone, not in clusters as was
common in the villages of England, and they usually con-
sisted of a thatched-roof cottage built alongside a "drystane"
enclosure used for keeping sheep and goats. The materials
used for constructing the cottages came from the land itself,
stones of every size and shape heaped one upon another to
form patchwork walls around an earthen floor beneath a
thickly thatched roof.

Some had a crude chimney, or *lum,* through which the
smoke from the perpetually burning peat fire escaped. Others simply allowed the smoke to hover above their heads,
making its way out slowly through the small crevices and
openings in the thatch and turning the rafters inside a glis-
tening black.

While some might look on such seemingly impoverished
conditions of living as miserable, the crofters, Eleanor found
were a happy, congenial folk. All greeted them with friendly
smiles and welcoming warmth, stopping in their work in the
fields to wave and call out in Gaelic greeting.

Whenever they happened close upon a cottage, they were immediately invited inside to partake of whatever refreshment was at hand, milk, tea, whiskey even, despite the fact that for some, it was all they had. Everyone treated Juliana with the respect due the daughter of their laird, calling her the "Wee MacFeagh." If they felt any awkwardness about the fact that she didn't speak, they did not show it. Even Lord Dunevin was only spoken of as a good laird, a chief who saw after the well-being of his people, a reaction so very different from that of the mainlanders they had encountered the day before.

It was while they were visiting with the family of Donald MacNeill, the boatman who had taken them across to Oban, that Eleanor began to hear more of the history of the island and its reclusive, mysterious laird.

She was sitting at the sturdy oaken table, enjoying the warmth of a fresh cup of tea in her chilled hands while Donald's eldest son introduced to them as "Donald the Younger," took Juliana out with him to watch as he brought in the sheep from where they grazed.

Donald's wife, Seòna, was stirring a savory-smelling stew that simmered in an iron kettle over the hearth fire while their toddler son, whom they called "Wee Donald," played happily with a ball of yarn at his father's feet. It was tradition in the isles, they had explained, to name sons for father and grandfather to ensure that an honored name carried on.

Seòna was a young woman, very close to Eleanor's own age, with soft brown hair that she wore pulled back from her cheerful face beneath the netting of a snood. Her feet were bare beneath the colorful plaid of her skirts and she wore a saffron-colored chemise beneath a dark-colored bodice that laced loosely at the waist, for she was with child, one which she hoped would be born a lass, she said, for she could come up with no other fitting nicknames for another Donald.

"'Tis a good thing, your coming to the island to look after the wee MacFeagh," said Donald then, nodding over his cup of tea, and echoing the words of Màiri that first night Eleanor had been on the isle.

"Aye, a verra good thing," Seòna added as she tossed bits of the potato she'd been chopping into the stew. "'Tis been too long since we've seen a new face on the isle, it has."

"Were there many governesses at Dunevin before me?" Eleanor asked. She noticed that Donald cast a momentary glance at his wife before responding.

"Not many, one or two"—he paused—"three or more, but then Lady Dunevin has been gone to us these three years past. Afore she died, she cared for the child herself with the help of a maid."

"Who has cared for Juliana since then when she has been without a governess?"

"Màiri mostly. Sometimes his lairdship's gillie, Fergus. He's a mon who has served the lairds of Dunevin for generations. 'Twas an honor for him to see to the wee one, it was."

Eleanor nodded, watching Juliana outside the small window as she knelt to pet the sniffing nose of one of the fleecy lambs who had just come in. She wondered that perhaps Fergus's outwardly gruff manner toward her was due more to having her, a stranger, suddenly assuming responsibilities he'd formerly held.

"Has Lord Dunevin been laird of the isle for very long?"

"Only the past ten years or more," Donald answered on a nod. He offered her an oatcake fresh and hot from the fire. "He was on the Peninsula and at university afore that."

"Lord Dunevin fought against Napoleon?"

Eleanor knew a number of her family's acquaintances

who had gone abroad to serve, Robert Edenhall, now Duke of Devonbrook, Bartholomew Tolley, all friends of her brother, Christian, whom she had known since childhood. She wondered whether any of them might be acquainted with Lord Dunevin.

"Aye, the laird was the fiercest soldier I've ever seen," Donald continued. "We were together at Corunna. The man lost three horses beneath him but he ne'er faltered. 'Twas as if the enemy shot somehow couldna touch him. A loss to the regiment, it was, when he left us."

"He was injured?"

"*Och*, no, lass. He was called back to Trelay when his brother Malcolm died suddenly and left him as the new laird. The MacFeagh are one of the oldest of all the clans. The last living direct descendent of the MacFeagh couldna risk his life 'gainst the French. Lord Dunevin had his duty to the clan and the people of this isle and so came home to wed Lady Dunevin and settle in. Then the wee one came and all was well, until . . ."

Just then, Donald the Younger and Juliana came into the cottage from outside. Eleanor wondered what Donald had been about to say, but decided it was a conversation that would be better kept for another time.

She turned a warm smile on Juliana, whose face had touches of color at her cheeks from the brisk wind. Her eyes, framed by the wisps of her dark hair that had blown loose from its ribbon, were vibrant and animated.

She didn't need to say a word for Eleanor to know she had enjoyed her outing with the young Donald; it showed clearly in her expression.

"Well, we have taken up enough of your time," Eleanor said, rising from her chair. "It is past time we were heading back to Dunevin now. Thank you so much for your hospitality."

"Would you be needin' Young Donald to walk you the way back?" MacNeill asked. "It grows late."

Eleanor shook her head, pulling on her overcoat. "I believe we can find our way, but thank you for the kind offer."

Linked arm in arm, Donald and Seòna bid them farewell, inviting them back for another visit whenever they wished, which Eleanor could already guess would be often. She had enjoyed herself at the simple croft very much. They were warm, friendly people and one of the few families on the isle who spoke English as well as the native Gaelic.

Outside, the sky had already begun to darken to night even though it was only late afternoon. Eleanor and Juliana had not made it any further than the crest of the first hilltop before Donald the Younger came following from behind with a wooden pail swinging in his hand.

"Ma sent me to fetch some milk for our supper. If you doona mind it, I thought I'd walk with you since we seem to be headin' the same way."

Eleanor smiled and nodded, turning to wave her thanks to Donald, who stood watching from the cottage doorway behind them.

Donald the Younger was fifteen and already stood taller than his da, whose red hair had been passed on to his son. His lanky arms were well-muscled beneath the linen of his sark from his constant work on the croft. A bright lad, he knew every landmark they passed and pointed out a good many of them, recounting the legendary tales surrounding each seemingly insignificant rock or tree that dotted the endless landscape.

"That there," he said, pointing out a large rounded stone that rested alone, looking quite out of place, on the machair.

"That is 'The Lifting Stone.' 'Tis said that the stone was thrown 'ere all the way from Eire by the great Fingal himsel'. It was used as a test of a man's strength, though only few could move it and none certainly in this lifetime. And that," he said, pointing outward toward what appeared to be a small recess on the side of a far hill, "that is one o' the MacFeagh's Hiding Places."

"One of them?" Eleanor asked.

"Aye. Legend has it that the last great MacFeagh, Malcolm MacFeagh—not the laird's brother, but another—was hunted down by enemy Macleans there. They chased him from spot to spot and finally caught him hiding in a cave with his great black hound. There were two entrances to the cave, as there are to this day, and he stood guard at one entrance with his mighty claymore while the hound kept watch at the other, but they shot him through with an arrow by way of an opening in the cave roof. It's been since then that the MacFeaghs lost their ruling place over the three isles and were exiled here to Trelay."

"But why did the Macleans wish the MacFeaghs harm?"

Young Donald simply shrugged. *"Och,* 'twas a long-standing feud, as most feuds are, the reasons for it lost over time."

Eleanor was suddenly reminded of the shoemaker in Oban, Seamus Maclean, and the obvious hostility between him and Lord Dunevin the day before. She wondered if their enmity was a last, enduring remnant of this same, age-long feud.

While Donald had been telling his tales to Eleanor and Juliana, he had nearly filled his wooden pail from the black cow who stood sedately grazing on the hillside. His chore completed, they started for the shore, chatting as they went about ancient clans and bitter feuds and the like. The sun was nearly gone over the western hills, and the mist that seemed ever to cling to the isle had begun to roll in slowly off the sea, dappling the landscape around them.

As they approached the shore, right at the point where the grassland gave over to sandy dune, there stood a curious, conical-shaped hillock, nearly as tall as Eleanor, surely man made, as perfectly shaped as it was.

"What is that?" Eleanor asked, standing by as Donald proceeded closer toward it.

"Oh, 'tis just a *sithan*," he answered as if it were as common as an English hedgerow.

Eleanor waited quietly for the explanation she knew had to be coming, her mouth falling open in astonishment when, as without so much as a "Watch me now," Young Donald proceeded to pour a goodly portion of the milk from his bucket into the top of the hill where a small opening had been formed.

He poured until the milk nearly overflowed it, then stood and waited several moments while it slowly receded into the ground. He then turned to Eleanor and as matter-of-factly as one could possibly speak, said, " 'Tis for the *sith*."

She looked at him, incredulous. *"Sith?"* was all she could manage in response.

"Aye, 'the Still Folk.' They live in those small hills. We of the isle call them 'Fairy Knowes.' 'Tis a long known fact that if you offer the wee folk some o' your ane milk, they will ne'er bring their mischief to your house. 'Tis they who make the green fields grow so rich for the cows to live on so that we will have their milk to sustain us. 'Tis only fittin' then that we should then give some of our bounty back from whence it came."

Had she been talking to him thus in one of the numerous London ballrooms that had been the setting for her life before coming to Trelay, Eleanor would have believed the boy a likely candidate for Bedlam. Still Folk? Fairy Knowes? But somehow, standing on the shore of this rocky, mist-swept isle, where the unknown was as much a part of life as the known, she couldn't entirely dismiss his superstitious logic.

Even as they turned to walk away, bidding Young Donald and his half-filled milk bucket farewell, Eleanor found herself looking back to the peculiar grassy mound just once, to see if maybe something strange and unexpected had suddenly emerged.

Like a wee person.

As they continued on their way back to the castle, the skies seemed to be growing darker by the minute, the mist settling in thickly, making it difficult to see if they were still heading in the right direction. Juliana began to walk closely by Eleanor's side, her small hand soon finding its way into hers as they picked their way over a rocky, desolate mull that was slick from the incoming tide.

Eleanor tried to ease Juliana's growing apprehension by chatting to her about Young Donald's unusual stories, all the while secretly hoping that the next hill they climbed would be the one she had turned back from hours earlier to look at the castle.

She wasn't too terribly worried, though, for she knew that eventually, even if they were walking in the wrong direction, they would arrive at one of the crofters' cottages and she knew the crofters would be more than happy to offer them shelter until the morn.

They had to climb a cragged outcropping in order to continue on their course and Eleanor stopped to help Juliana up before her. Then, grabbing a handhold on the rough granite while tucking her toe onto a footstep, she pulled herself up behind.

Through the swirling mist, she could see Juliana standing several feet in front of her, looking out toward the distant sea that crashed on the rocks below them. As Eleanor came up beside her, she could see that the child's eyes were fixed widely, her face suddenly an ashen white.

"Juliana, what is it?"

Juliana did not move, not even to look at her, in response.

Eleanor looked out across the water to see if she could find what had so caught the child's attention, but saw nothing through the dense swirling mist. She reached for Juliana's hand and tried to lead her away, frightened by the strange look in her eyes.

"Come, Juliana. Let us get back before it grows much darker . . ."

It was almost as if the child's feet had taken root to the ground, so fixed was she on that distant shore.

Eleanor murmured to her, soothing her, trying everything she could think of to draw her away, but to no avail.

Then, in the very next moment, Juliana began to tremble.

Eleanor knelt down beside her, patting her hand. "What is it, Juliana? What is wrong? Please, tell me . . ."

Juliana wouldn't respond. Eleanor was fast growing panicked now, too panicked to realize the uselessness of her words. Her heart was beating anxiously as she looked all around, trying to find something, anything, to pull Juliana's attention back to the present. It was as if she were fixed in some terrible trance, unreachable even though she stood right beside her. Eleanor stood helplessly, desperate as she searched the thickening darkness around them.

Blessedly, after several moments, she spied a flickering lamplight glowing off in the distance, but she couldn't leave

Juliana standing there alone, trembling so fiercely. She cried out for help, praying that whoever it was would understand her enough to come to their aid.

Seconds later, the lamplight began to move in their direction. Eleanor blinked back frightened tears as a figure of a man of middling age whom she immediately recognized as one of the crofters they had seen earlier that day, emerged from the darkness and mist.

He spoke to her in Gaelic, but she had no way of responding. All she could manage was to wave her hands about.

"Please, go find Lord Dunevin . . . the laird . . . Mac-Feagh . . ."

Finally the man nodded to her. He pressed his flickering *cruisie* lamp into her hands and turned, jogging off into the thickening darkness. Eleanor simply stayed at Juliana's side, trying once again to calm her, talking softly to her, begging her to come away and return home to the warmth of the kitchen fire, where Màiri would be waiting.

She had no notion of how much time had passed. It could have been moments. It could have been hours. The next thing she realized was the thundering sound of approaching hoofbeats and Cudu's bellowing yowl.

"It is all right now, Juliana. Do you hear that? Your father is coming."

Eleanor turned just as Lord Dunevin crested the hilltop, pulling his mount to a halt close by. Cudu trotted forward from the mists, sniffing at Juliana's hand.

Still she did not move.

"What are you doing here?" Dunevin barked at Eleanor as he leapt down from the saddle. "You should have been back hours ago."

The tears that Eleanor had managed to keep at bay all that

time suddenly gave way as she sobbed out her response. "We were walking back—and we had to climb up from the shore, here—but Juliana, she just stopped and wouldn't move—and then she began shaking like that. I couldn't quiet her no matter what I tried to do . . ."

"Just get her out of here!"

Lord Dunevin's face was darker than the skies around them. Eleanor was frozen with fear. When she didn't immediately move, without a word of warning, he stalked forward and seized her roughly about the waist, lifting her carelessly onto the back of his horse. He then took up Juliana who still stared frozen and trembling out to sea, and lifted her to sit before Eleanor.

"Take her back to the castle."

"But I don't know the way—"

"Now!"

The viscount slapped his horse hard on the flank and the beast leapt to action, nearly dragging Eleanor and Juliana both to the ground. Eleanor grabbed for the reins and a handful of the horse's mane while clutching Juliana against her, praying that the horse knew its own way back to the castle in this darkness.

Tears stung at her eyes as its flying hooves ate up the distance. The wind was bitterly cold against her face and hands but she barely noticed. She was fast growing senseless.

It seemed as if in moments they had arrived at the castle courtyard.

As the horse trotted to a stop, Eleanor called out for help and slid from the saddle, gently guiding Juliana down before her. Màiri came running from inside, pulling off her tartan wrap to place it gently around Juliana's still shivering shoulders.

Without a word, Màiri led Juliana inside. Eleanor followed

behind to the nursery, where the two women quickly removed Juliana's shoes and coat and eased her back onto the pillows on her bed.

They tucked a woolen blanket up around her but she was still trembling, though not as violently as before. Her eyes, however, were yet fixed in that same frightening, frozen stare.

"What in heaven's name happened to the lass?" Màiri asked on a whisper.

Eleanor shook her head, utterly at sea. "I do not know. We had gone to visit the MacNeills and were just walking back to the castle. All was well. I was chatting to her about something, I don't even remember what, and we had to climb some rocks. I helped her up first and when I came up behind her, she was just standing there as if she had turned to stone. She wouldn't move no matter what I tried to do. She just kept staring like that. When she began to shake I grew so frightened. Has she ever done anything like this before?"

Màiri's eyes were suddenly grave with a most haunted darkness. She nodded slowly. "She has. Only once. The day her mither disappeared."

Eleanor felt as if all the strength suddenly left her body. She had to grab onto the bedpost so that she wouldn't crumple to the floor.

The housekeeper shook her head. "I'll fetch some tea with a bit o' the valerian in it. 'Twill help to calm her. I've a notion it would do you some good, too."

Eleanor could barely manage a nod as Màiri turned to leave the room.

Alone with Juliana again, she'd never felt more helpless than she did at that very moment. She wanted to know what had brought on this sudden change in the child's behavior.

Had she said something, done something, wrong? Even more, she wanted to know what she could do to bring Juliana out of it. Eleanor felt so helpless, so alone, so *lost*. She would do anything to take that hopeless look of shock from that child's sweet face. Anything . . .

On instinct, Eleanor sat down on the bed beside Juliana and drew her up gently into her arms, rocking her as her own mother had her as a child when she'd awoken in the night from a terrible nightmare. Softly she hummed to her while smoothing a hand over her damp hair, closing her eyes and praying to the heavens that Juliana would come around.

After a few minutes, the trembling quieted, but Eleanor stayed as she was, rocking and humming, quietly soothing this child who had so easily and so quickly stolen her way into her heart.

Gabriel took the steps to the nursery two at a time, his jaw set, his hands clenched tight into fists. He had spent nearly all day standing at his study window, watching the hills and waiting for them to return. The longer they remained gone, the darker his mood had become until, when night had begun to fall and the mists had drifted in off the sea, he'd convinced himself that history had once again visited its damnable curse upon him.

He'd already had his horse saddled and was readying to go out in search of them when Angus MacNeill, a crofter on the isle and cousin to Donald, had come running breathless into the courtyard, telling him where they were.

As he spurred his horse around, racing off in the direction Angus told him, Gabriel couldn't help but blame himself. It was he who had brought this on, he'd told himself. If he hadn't begun the day before to loosen his reserve, allowing himself to enjoy the sight of Juliana's delight in the spyglass Miss Harte had given her, none of this would have happened.

The progress the governess had made with Juliana so quickly after her arrival had truly astounded him, certainly, for none other had been able to breech the protective wall that Juliana had surrounded herself with after Georgiana's death. Even worse, though, Juliana's progress had begun to give him hope, hope that their lives might be better, no longer cast in the shadow of fear.

Why could he never learn?

Now, less than a couple of days after hiring her, he was on his way to dismiss the very person who had finally managed to reach his daughter. He had been so angry at himself for relaxing his guard the day before. Coming back to the castle, he had turned that anger on the governess, thinking to dismiss her for his own failing.

But as he stepped into the nursery doorway and opened his mouth to speak the words that would send that remarkable woman out of their lives forever, his voice died in his throat, and the helpless fury that had built with every step back to Dunevin vanished.

Standing there watching her as she held his daughter, giving Juliana all the love and compassion she had been denied for so long, he knew he could no more dismiss her than he could keep himself from loving his own child.

For the smallest of moments, he would have sworn that he was watching Georgiana again sitting on that bed, rocking their daughter to sleep as she had so many times. A tightness overtook Gabriel inside as he fought to control his warring emotions. He had thought that by keeping himself away from Juliana as he had since Georgiana's death, he had been protecting her from ever being touched by the curse that seemed ever to plague his family. But trying not to love someone, a child of one's own flesh, was like a living hell.

Standing in the doorway, Gabriel looked on the two of them for one moment more, then without a word, without a sound, he turned and walked away. Followed by the soft tune the governess had been humming, touched by the way she had gently stroked Juliana's forehead as she drifted off to sleep, Gabriel knew that he'd only been fooling himself.

Chapter Nine

Eleanor stood framed in the doorway of Lord Dunevin's study, watching him quietly from across the room.

The viscount had sent word through Fergus early that morning requesting her attendance *as soon as was convenient*. That had been several hours ago. She had delayed purposely in coming, taking time with their breakfast and then afterward sitting with Juliana in the nursery for a time, reading a bit of poetry aloud.

After the events of the previous day, there could be no favorable reason for his wanting to see her. Dunevin would dismiss her, Eleanor knew, because of what had happened the day before. She could not, however, put it off indefinitely.

Though Juliana had calmed down overnight, she seemed to have withdrawn even further into herself, no longer interested in her spyglass even; content to sit at her window seat alone.

It was now late morning, just after eleven, and the viscount was sitting at his desk, scribbling something. A pot of tea stood beside the desk on a standing tray. He had removed his coat, wearing his everyday attire of kilt and simple cambric sark, the full sleeves of which were rolled back loosely over his forearms. A single streak of sunlight beamed in through the open drapery beside him, precisely lighting the desktop where he wrote. She wondered fleetingly if he had chosen that particular placement for the desk because of it.

As Eleanor watched him, he swept a hand carelessly through his dark hair, pushing it back as he rubbed his eyes beneath his spectacles. He was a man so very different from any other she had known. All her life, she had been surrounded by men of polished gentility, a good many of them fops who pinched snuff till they sneezed, wore high starched collars that made them look like ostriches, and who fretted for days over which leg they should put forth in a bow to make themselves look most fashionable.

But this man, this dauntless and inscrutable Scot, was as far from that image as was possible.

No mincing buck he, he was a mixture of the unconventional and the noble with an infinite strength of mind as well as of body, primitive in a way that only added to his mystery. He was rugged, yes, even imposing, but with a quiet strength that need never be demonstrated, who didn't need to bluster and pose in order to go noticed in a crowd. His commanding height and presence alone did that.

But it was his eyes, she decided then, that were most remarkable. Dark, compelling, intelligent, they had the striking ability of being able to convey with but a simple glance exactly what he was thinking without his needing to utter a word. Those same eyes could, however, in the very next moment, become as unreadable, as inscrutable as a moonless night.

As she stood there studying him, Eleanor wondered suddenly if he had ever smiled. Lightness somehow seemed to elude him. She wondered what caused him to guard his heart so closely. She wondered what the touch of his hands would be like.

Where in heaven had that thought come from . . . ?

Eleanor shook her head, returning her attention to the present situation, that of his summons for her there that morning.

She knocked softly on the doorjamb. "You wished to see me, my lord?"

The viscount looked up from his paper, his stare immediately seizing her. He removed his spectacles and set down his pen. "Miss Harte, please come in."

His voice was stiff, matter-of-fact, chillingly unemotional. She walked into the room slowly, trying to ignore the lurking feeling of dread that weighted her footsteps as she crossed to sit in the chair before him.

Smoothing her skirts over her knees, Eleanor lifted her eyes to look at him. He watched her for several moments, silent, his hands clasped before him on the desk, his mouth set in a stark line.

Dear God in heaven, he was going to dismiss her.

"Miss Harte, as you might have already guessed, I have called you here to discuss yesterday's incident with Juliana."

"My lord, I—"

He held up a hand. "Miss Harte, please, allow me to finish."

"*No,* my lord. I have something to say first."

Eleanor sat forward in her seat, looking away from his stunned expression. She focused instead on a small porcelain curio of a dolphin that stood at the corner of his desk. If this was to be it, she had every intention of speaking her piece before he sent her packing.

"There is no need for you to finish, sir. Indeed, I already know what you are going to say."

The viscount sat back in his chair, folding his arms before him, one brow incredulously raised. "Do you now?"

"Yes. You think to dismiss me from service as Juliana's governess because of what happened yesterday, but I'll have you know I have no intention of abandoning that child."

She was letting her emotions get the better of her, she knew. Eleanor looked at him directly, softening her next words.

"I know you believe you made an error of judgment in hiring me, but you are wrong. I can help Juliana. You saw her when she was looking through that spyglass, how she had begun to respond. I don't know what happened yesterday, what I did to cause Juliana to react the way she did, but please do not allow my carelessness to put an end to her progress. You need not pay me, my lord. I will stay on without wages and continue to work with Juliana regardless."

The viscount sat quietly considering her words as the clock behind him ticked off several long moments. His face gave no hint of his thoughts, no indication of whether she had succeeded in persuading him. Finally he answered her.

"Very well, Miss Harte. You have convinced me to your opinion. You will stay on."

"Oh."

Gabriel watched as an uncertain moment of confusion played across the window of her face. She was like an open book, her thoughts so easily readable. She had expected more of a disagreement from him, obviously. No doubt she had spent the morning preparing, mentally rehearsing all sorts of arguments to combat his reasons for firing her. She was puzzled at his ready agreement, perhaps even wondering if she had heard him right. And then she looked at him.

It hadn't taken her long at all.

"You weren't planning to dismiss me, were you?"

He shook his head, hiding his mirth behind a disguise of nonchalance.

"But why did you let me go on like that, saying all those things to you, knowing in the end it wouldn't matter . . . ?"

Because I wanted to watch the fire light up your green eyes. . . .

Gabriel cleared his throat against that sudden vagrant thought. "If you will recall, Miss Harte, I attempted to explain, but you would hear none of it."

That drew her more upright in her chair, her head cocking slightly to the side. Gabriel tried to ignore the single twisting curl of sable brown that fell against her shoulder.

"Oh. You are right. I apologize, my lord."

"No apology is necessary. However, I do need to give explanation for Juliana's behavior yesterday. In truth, it was through no fault of yours, Miss Harte. Has anyone yet told you of Lady Dunevin's death?"

She looked at him. "Only that she was out walking with Juliana one day and vanished without any apparent explanation."

Gabriel nodded solemnly. "I had gone out to find them when they hadn't returned and it was on that particular precipice you had climbed yesterday where I found Juliana without her mother, standing trembling in much the same manner. I can only presume that Lady Dunevin slipped from there and Juliana could do nothing to help her. It was a terrible, unavoidable accident. Juliana had never gone back to that place since."

"Until yesterday."

Eleanor's voice was filled with remorse. The light in her eyes grew dim and she shook her head regretfully. "I am so very sorry."

"Please do not blame yourself, Miss Harte. You couldn't have known. I hold myself wholly responsible. I should have told you of it before you went out."

Eleanor sat for several moments, her brow slightly furrowed as she reflected on all he had just told her. Gabriel allowed himself the silent pleasure of her presence.

Somehow, if it were possible, she looked more lovely this morning than ever. She had pulled her dark hair back, pinned it high upon her head in a topknot of loose brown curls that framed her face elegantly. It was a style that revealed the slender grace of her neck, the arch of her brow, the soft curve of her cheek.

Gabriel wondered what she could be thinking. Did she doubt his explanation of Georgiana's death? Did she, like so many others, believe he had somehow done away with his own wife?

But when she looked at him again, he did not find the icy suspicion, the condemnation he had seen so often in the eyes of others. What he saw behind those green depths was profound compassion and something else, something tender and honest and impossible to describe.

It was something he had never before seen.

The impact of just that look startled him, and his reaction must have shown on his face, for she suddenly stood from her chair.

"Well, you no doubt have much to do," she said. "I won't keep you any longer."

Thinking it was probably better that she go, he agreed. "Yes, thank you, Miss Harte."

She nodded and turned and Gabriel returned to his letter writing, scribbling in response to his steward in London.

And in regard to . . .

"My lord, if I may trouble for you just another moment."

Gabriel lowered his pen, glancing back at the door, where she was standing with her back to him now as she faced his bookshelves.

"Yes, Miss Harte?"

She said to the shelves, "I wonder, does your library contain any Gaelic literature?"

It was probably the last question he would have expected to hear. "Yes, of course. Poetry mostly, though." He was intrigued. "Do you read Gaelic, Miss Harte?" He didn't recall her having mentioned it during their interview.

She shook her head, letting go a resigned breath. "No, I'm afraid I do not."

She did not move to leave. Gabriel continued to watch her as she surveyed the many titles in the towering cases.

"Is there a particular shelf on which I might find them?" she asked. "The Gaelic books, I mean."

Gabriel stood and crossed the room to join her. "Something in particular you are looking for?"

"A grammar would be ideal, but I'd probably be expecting too much . . ."

Curious now, Gabriel surveyed the shelves for her. "There, on the topmost shelf."

She smiled at him. "Oh, thank you, my lord. Please don't allow me to keep you from your business. I can reach them with the steps."

Gabriel pulled the rolling library steps from the corner, setting them beneath the shelf she sought, then returned to his desk and his letter while she picked through the books on the shelf. He had only written a sentence or two before he found himself glancing back to where she was sitting now on the topmost step, her feet tucked neatly beneath her, skimming one of the books she had lying open across the tops of her knees. A bit of her hair had fallen into her eyes and her mouth was moving in silent recitation of what was written there, her brow knit in intent study.

"Miss Harte?"

She lifted her head, looking at him from behind the stair railing, "Yes, my lord?"

"May I ask what you are doing?"

"Certainly. I realized yesterday when Juliana and I were walking about the isle that very few of the people here are familiar with the English language. It was most distressing when I was attempting to communicate with Mr. MacNeill when I needed help with Juliana. Since I am in essence the stranger here, I thought perhaps in my spare time I might endeavor to learn more of the native tongue."

Gabriel was stunned by her uncommon sagacity. Most people not of the Isles thought the natives backward for their inability to speak the King's tongue. She, however, understood their pride for the language of their ancestors, and even sought to teach it to herself. "And you mean to do this simply through reading?"

"Indeed. It worked quite well with Latin."

"Do you mean to say you taught yourself the Latin language?"

"Well, mostly, although I did have the benefit of my bro—" She stopped herself. "Few ladies are permitted instruction in such a masculine tongue, my lord. English and French have for some reason been deemed the only languages fit for the female mouth. But I love to study history and so much of it is recorded in Latin, I determined that I would learn it."

She was truly the most remarkable creature had ever met. "But I'm afraid you won't find the Gaelic as amenable to your efforts, Miss Harte. It is an auditory language; it must be learned with the ear, not solely with the eyes."

"Oh, I see." She thought for a moment. "Perhaps . . . ?" She shook her head. "No, that wouldn't likely be appropriate."

"What were you going to say, Miss Harte?"

She hesitated, reluctant, then answered, "I was going to ask if perhaps you would be willing to introduce me to the language, at least some of its pronunciations and conjugations, then perhaps I would be able to continue from there on my own. At least to get a rudimentary understanding of the language. But you are a very busy man with many more significant obligations than to remedy my ignorance."

Her suggestion intrigued him, partly because of her lively enthusiasm for learning, a thing most ladies did not have, but mostly because of his own love for the natural language of his heritage—and a bitter regret that since the failed '45 and the proscription that had followed, Gaelic was slowly fading into obscurity all across his homeland.

Gabriel left his desk, crossing the room as he motioned for her to come down from the steps. He took the book she had been reading, a collection of ancient and modern Gaelic poems and songs, and glanced quickly through the pages.

"Come, sit for a moment. I'm not that busy that I can't take a moment to enjoy a bit of poetry."

She smiled brightly as he motioned for her to take one of the two chairs nearest the window.

"The primary difference between English and Gaelic," he explained, "is that some of the consonants do not always carry the same sound, depending on where they are in a word. So in order to learn Gaelic, you must forget a good deal of everything you were ever taught about English."

He stole a glance at her. Her eyes were absolutely alight with enthusiasm, giving her entire face a sparkling vivacity. He was immediately struck by it.

"For example," he continued, "let us first discuss the letter *B*. When it is found at the beginning of a word, it carries the same sound as the English *B*." He glanced at her again. "As in the word 'beautiful.'"

Their eyes locked for a single brief moment that was so poignant, it felt quite as if time had stopped. Neither spoke or made a movement. The room grew measurably warmer and it had nothing to do with the fire rolling in the hearth. Finally reluctantly, Gabriel pulled his attention away from the emerald sea of her eyes.

"When the letter *B* is found elsewhere in a word, it carries the sound more of an English *P*. To make matters even more confusing, often you will see the letters *BH* together in Gaelic. They can make the sound of an English *V* or *W* as in this word here: *leabhar.*"

"*Ly-orr,*" she repeated easily. "That's a pretty word. What does it mean?"

Gabriel held out his hand to her, handing her the—

"Book."

She nodded, smiling. "Cudu," she said, glancing at the carpet, where the hound napped. "Is that Gaelic, as well?"

Gabriel nodded. "It is from the Gaelic *Cù-dubh.*"

"No doubt the name of some great ancient hero like Fingal or cuChulainn?"

"I'm afraid it isn't anything quite as romantic as that," he replied. "Quite simply, it means 'black dog.'"

She laughed at that, a rich, delightful sound that hadn't echoed past these ancient walls in a long, long time. The music of it was more seductive than anything he could remember.

"You are jesting, my lord. Teasing me, surely."

He looked at her.

"Oh, goodness, you are *not* jesting, are you?"

Gabriel shook his head, looking down at the hound who, as if listening to their conversation, rolled onto his back with all fours in the air. He couldn't resist a small scratch to the beast's belly, smiling as one leg twitched reflexively against his fingers. "It was the only name he would ever respond to, after trying a score of others that were much more illustrious."

He glanced up at her and froze. Her eyes were sparked in the sunlight. His pulse leapt.

"Would you perhaps read a page to me, and then translate it into English so I might get a sense for the flow and intonation of the words?"

Gabriel nodded. "Very well. Choose one."

She flipped through several pages in the book, browsing pages before settling on one. She laid the book upon the table between them so that they could both read together, he aloud, and she following along on the page.

Their heads were bent closely as Gabriel began to recite the poem she'd chosen, an ancient Erse verse titled "Aisling air Dhreach Mna"—"Vision of a Fair Woman."

As he spoke the words in his native, lyrical tongue, she bent her head closer to the page as if to somehow absorb the words written there. As she did, he was caught by the scent of her, that exotic perfume that had struck him before. Gabriel soon found himself reciting the poem from memory instead of reading off the page as he studied her face, her inquisitive eyes, the lushness of her lips, the gentle curl of her hair. When he finished, he repeated the verse for her in English:

> *Tell us some of the charms of the stars . . .*
> *Soft and fair as the mountain snow;*
> *Her two breasts were heaving full;*
> *To them did the hearts of heroes flow.*
> *Her lips were ruddier than the rose;*
> *Tender and tunefully sweet her tongue;*
> *White as the foam adown her side*
> *Her delicate fingers extended hung . . .*
> *Unfolding their beauty in early spring . . .*
> *And her eyes like the radiance the sunbeams bring.*

When he finished, he watched in absolute silence as she lifted her eyes slowly to meet his.

The air around them became charged with the spark of intimacy. They were so near to one another, eye to eye, face-to-face, their breaths mingled between them. In that same moment, he knew what she would do. And he knew that he would let her.

Gabriel sat perfectly still as Eleanor leaned toward him, closing the space between them to touch her lips softly to his.

He closed his eyes. Her mouth was still beneath his, the stillness of a maid who had never before kissed or been kissed. Gabriel tipped her chin softly upward with his fingertips and deepened the kiss, drinking in her warmth and light and gentleness.

She responded to his touch as a woman, instinctively opening to him, giving him the gift of her intrinsic innocence.

Too many years of living in emotional exile, of being feared and reviled and haunted by the very world around him, came together in one blinding moment of priceless freedom. This woman, this one incredible creature, did not, had never seen him as the monster everyone else did. With her, for the first time in his life, Gabriel could truly forget the darkness of the past, the legacy of his family history, and simply live.

But the forgetting could only last as long as their kiss went on. It was knowing this and hating it both at the same time that brought Gabriel to reluctantly pull away from her.

He felt the warmth vanish almost immediately. He watched her face as she hovered between dream and reality, her eyes yet closed, her lips wet from his mouth. Slowly her eyes drifted open and she stared at him wordlessly, unwilling to shatter the moment they had shared together.

He spoke softly, saying her name for the first time. "Eleanor . . ."

It struck her like the shock of a chill wind, drawing her up and away from him as she blinked in alarm. She was so stunned, so dismayed, she never realized he had not called her "Nell," but had used her true Christian name.

"My lord, I am so sorry." She put a hand against her mouth. "I . . . I don't know what caused me to do that." She pushed abruptly away from the table, nearly tipping her chair back in her haste to be away. "Please forgive me."

Gabriel shook his head, to tell her she had nothing to apologize for, that she had done nothing wrong but something so right, but she had already turned and was rushing from the room.

He wanted to call her back, even as he realized he could not. He'd stolen a moment, a brief breath-stealing instant in time where the darkness that followed him had ceased to exist behind the warmth and sunlight of this woman's kiss. It had been joy and light and freedom all at once. Yet, as always, the clouds of reality had returned.

No matter how much he wanted, he could not outrun it.

He was the Devil of Dunevin Castle, the Dark Lord of Trelay.

She was a creature of gentleness and beauty and light.

What had he to offer her other then the darkness, the anguish and misery that were his inherited cross to bear?

Chapter Ten

Nearly every spare moment over the following fortnight was taken up with the preparations for the St. Michael's Day, or Michaelmas, celebrations. The castle kitchen was hectic with activity from early morning till late into the night and Eleanor and Juliana took part as often as they could when they weren't involved with their lessons or other activities.

As governess, Eleanor wouldn't as a rule have been involved in the work of preparing, but she defied convention, throwing herself into whatever task was at hand to occupy herself, making certain she always had *something* to do, if only to keep her from remembering what a fool she'd made of herself with Lord Dunevin.

Even now, she couldn't quite understand what had happened that ineffable day, what had caused her to do something so bold, so *brazen,* as to kiss Lord Dunevin outright like she had.

At first, she had told herself that she had simply, inexplicably gotten caught up in the rich lyricism of his voice, the beautiful words of the poem he'd read to her that day. Even now she could see it so vividly, the way he'd been looking at her so intently, his eyes captivating and dark, his voice warm and beautiful, she'd forgotten that he'd been reading from a book and not speaking those fluid words to her directly.

It was only later, as she had lain awake in the middle of the night, reliving those few magical moments, that she realized she had wanted him to speak those words to her, wanted it so badly, she'd somehow convinced herself he truly had.

As if a man like him, handsome, noble, incredibly mysterious, would ever recite those words to someone like her. To the viscount, she was little more than a member of staff—an utterly foolish member of staff—even though, in truth, she was more.

How had she ever gotten into such a complicated situation? To the rest of the world outside this far-off isle, she was Lady Eleanor Wycliffe, missing heiress to the Westover fortune. Had they met one another in a London ballroom instead of on this distant isle, would things have been any different? She wondered what he'd think, what he'd say, if he knew the truth.

Even if he could overlook the fact that he was her employer, eventually she would have to tell him the circumstances of her birth. How could a man with a proud lineage such as his ever consider an involvement with some nobleman's bastard daughter?

Shaking away that most troublesome thought, Eleanor turned her attention to where it was needed more, to Juliana, who sat on a high stool at the central kitchen table, helping Màiri to roll out a fresh batch of bannocks for supper.

Blessedly, Juliana had overcome the frightening episode on that dreadful precipice, and within days had begun taking part in the Michaelmas activities. To avoid any further upset, Eleanor made certain they did not return to that part of the isle on any of their excursions. Instead, they kept close to the castle proper and immersed themselves in reading, music, sewing, and various other exercises, many of which Eleanor employed to show Juliana how she might express herself differently than through speech.

With the help of Màiri and Donald MacNeill, Eleanor's first venture was to undertake the repainting of the school-room walls, forever banishing the drab beige-green behind a pristine coat of fresh whitewash.

The difference of doing just that had been astounding, but Eleanor had had other thoughts, as well. With some of the natural dyes used for coloring the local wool, they created other paints with which to further adorn the walls. By mixing and trying different colors, a diverse palette was created, and once ready, Eleanor then set the task to Juliana of what should decorate the walls.

"The schoolroom is *your* place," Eleanor had told her, handing Juliana several small brushes made from birch branches and bent grass, as well as a collection of different pointed leaves and feathered quills to paint with. "Cover it with whatever you feel inside."

After a few tentative efforts depicting a flying gull and a shy flower, Juliana finally set to the project, deepening her focus to create a scene Eleanor later recognized as Trelay, the heathery hills, the rugged sea, and atop it all, the tower of Dunevin looking out like a faithful sentinel. She spent hours at it, showing true interest for the first time in something other than the view outside that window. While she painted and colored, Eleanor would read to her aloud from Shakespeare or Virgil, or spend some quiet time herself practicing the Gaelic pronunciations Màiri had been teaching her.

Since that day in Dunevin's study, Eleanor had only seen the viscount a handful of times. She and Juliana no longer took their meals in the dining parlor with him, but instead spent more and more time with Màiri in the kitchen. If it seemed odd to Màiri, their sudden company there, she said nothing. She accepted Eleanor's explanation that she simply sought to balance Juliana's education of the running of a household by showing her firsthand the inner workings of the kitchen, the true heart of any house.

If Eleanor did see the viscount, it was only in passing, with a pleasant "Good day to you, my lord," as she and Juliana went about their daily routine. He, too, seemed content to avoid their company. If she needed something from his library, Eleanor waited until she was certain he was away from the castle before going to his study. It wasn't a difficult thing to do, for the estate was involved in the business of the harvest and preparing for the coming winter, so he was rarely at home during the day.

Time passed quickly. While occupied with her activities, Eleanor could successfully hold her thoughts about that day and their kiss at bay—at night, however, when she would lie in the darkness with a sleeping Juliana beside her, she would find herself thinking back on that morning, the curious siren's song of his voice as he had read her those ardent words written centuries before, the glory of that fleeting kiss that had so stolen her breath.

She knew now that her mother had been right. That first kiss had been wonder-working, mystifying, utterly enchanting. She truly had forgotten for that moment how to draw a breath. It had been nothing at all like Lord Monning's son, young James Crockett, whose sloppy fumblings the night of her first London ball had only brought her to giggling when he'd struck his forehead on a low-hanging tree branch after he'd backed her against the outside balcony banister. Nor was it anything like the polite parting peck on the back of

her gloved hand that had been the all of what Richard Hartley had ever given her.

Whatever it was that had possessed her to kiss Lord
Dunevin as she had, it had been more magical, more incredible than she could have ever possibly imagined. It defied
definition, filling her with warmth and softness and aware-
ness and hope all at once. Everything about that day, the two
of them, had felt so right, so real, so . . . as it should be. It
was as if the world had for that moment stopped its spinning, suspended among the stars if only so that the thrill of
it all could go on just a tiny bit longer.

But then, all at once, their kiss had ended, pushing the
world back into place with a jarring nudge, and leaving her
awash with the horror at what she'd done, the humiliation,
haunted each night by the memory of it.

Eleanor wondered if the emptiness of it would ever go
away, the feeling of having lost something that in truth she'd
never possessed, but had for one moment stolen.

Would the memory of the touch of him, the salty scent of
his hair, the warmth of his breath, ever go away?

She resolved that she would simply have to keep herself
constantly busy until it did. Thankfully, there was much to
do for the approaching holiday.

The Sunday before St. Michael's Day, Eleanor and Juliana joined a gathering of the other women and girls from
the island who had assembled on the castle courtyard.
Armed each with a special three-pronged mattock, dressed
in colorful skirts and bodices, their hair bound beneath
bright kerchiefs, The entire assembly of them made their
way to the thriving fields outside the castle proper.

There, Màiri and Seòna MacNeill instructed Eleanor and
Juliana in the ancient method of cutting the special *torcan*,
an equal-sided triangle around each carrot, before pulling it

from the earth and dropping it into the bag that hung from their waists. Lilting songs were sung as the women worked, and there was much gaiety, and a touch of rivalry as to who would get the most and finest of the carrots.

Once, Eleanor pulled out a forked carrot and within seconds she was surrounded by the others, all smiling and congratulating her in bubbly Gaelic, for such a find was a sign of great luck, she was told.

Afterward, when they had returned to the castle, the carrots were washed and tied in bunches with a scarlet-colored three-ply thread, most of them then stored away until the feast day later that week.

But at Dunevin, Màiri explained, it was tradition for one carrot to be chosen from each bundle and included with that evening's meal.

Eleanor and Juliana helped Màiri in the kitchen all through that late afternoon, preparing a special supper that would be attended by all the people of the castle, the viscount, Màiri, Fergus, Eleanor and Juliana, the groomsman, Angus, from the stables, as well as Donald MacNeill and his family. It was a private custom practiced by the laird's family and repeated through each successive generation. The more formal celebration on St. Michael's Day would come later that week on Friday when all of the island families would take part.

As a young girl growing up in the sterile and socially proper Wycliffe home, Eleanor had never felt a true part of the inner workings of the household. The separation between servant and lord had always been a most definitive thing, and she had rarely seen what went on beyond the green baize door.

Here, on Trelay, that division was less distinct. Because of it, there was more a feeling of all hands doing their part.

For Eleanor, the notion of something as simple as baking before coming to Trelay had meant nothing more than simply writing out the instructions for the cook on what to prepare for that evening's meal. But here at Dunevin, baking meant putting your hands into a soft oatcake dough, kneading it with her own hands, and rolling it out for cutting. She baked it herself, turning it—only once—on the iron *greideal,* savoring its pleasing scent as it mixed with the smoky heat of the peat fire crackling beneath it.

This community, this belonging, was a feeling that affected not only Eleanor, but Juliana as well. Even now, as they stood together in the kitchen, two of Màiri's aprons doubled about their waists, their faces dusted with oat flour, a light of elfin delight shone in Juliana's dark eyes that was truly extraordinary.

Looking on her as she carefully cut out the rounded cakes, Eleanor came to realize that in the short time she'd been there, this enchanted place and its wistful native daughter had stolen completely into her heart.

It was as if her life before had been merely a stopping-off point, a brief respite on a journey to a place where she would find . . . she would find . . .

"Well, it looks as if we're aboot ready t' serve," Màiri said, interrupting Eleanor's thoughts before she'd had the chance to decide the answer.

Eleanor and Juliana quickly removed their aprons, splashing away the flour dust from their faces at the small wash tub in the corner. Màiri handed Juliana a willow basket that had a fresh batch of warm bannocks tucked beneath a linen inside.

"You can carry this, lassie. Miss Harte, Mrs. MacNeill, and I will see to the rest."

Together, the four of them made their way from the kitchen across the vine-draped arcade to the castle's donjon.

In the dining parlor, Lord Dunevin and the others had already gathered around the crimson light of the fire that blazed in the great stone hearth. The table had been freshly polished and set with plateware of delicate china and glimmering silver candleholders the likes of which a number of the guests had never seen.

Night had already come and the moon hung high and bright in an uncommonly cloudless sky. The wind blew in softly off the firth. It was a fine ending to a most pleasant day.

"'Tis time to sup," Màiri said cheerfully to the others as she and Seòna began to set out the fare, each dish a singular representation of food grown or raised on the isle.

There was kail brose, a sort of thin porridge, with tatties and herring, roast grouse, stewed turnips, and the traditional haggis, which Màiri had promised Eleanor tasted much better than it looked. An assortment of warm bannocks and scones, a fresh cranberry tart, and a flummery had been prepared for dessert.

The meal, however, would start with that day's harvest of the carrots picked that morning and stewed in a tasty broth.

Fergus served while Màiri and Seòna finished arranging the various dishes about the dinner table. Donald MacNeill the Younger took the seat beside Juliana while Eleanor took the chair across, nearest the head of the table where the viscount sat. Eleanor smiled when she noticed Young Donald's eyes nearly as wide as the dish before him as he looked uncertainly at the assortment of flatware before him. Eleanor took up her napkin, unfolding it in her lap before subtly pointing out the proper utensil to him.

He grinned his thanks, his face coloring nearly as red as

his hair. The viscount took his seat beside her. Eleanor looked at him briefly.

He was dressed more formally than was his custom, wearing a rich coat of dark green velvet over a white linen shirt with knotted cravat and the kilt. As he lowered himself into his chair, their eyes caught. Her heartbeat jumped, and she smiled nervously.

Was he, like she, remembering the kiss they'd shared?

"Miss Harte, good evening," he said, nodding to her.

"Good evening to you, my lord."

When everyone was finally seated, Lord Dunevin stood, raising his glass of claret in a toast.

"Today we celebrate another successful harvest at Dunevin. We thank the Lord for keeping us safe and in good health and for feeding our families well with this good food."

The others around the table all raised their glasses, saying "Aye," before they drank in unison.

Eleanor chatted amiably with Seòna. Talk was of the coming festivities for St. Michael's Day, at which, Seòna told her, there would be horseracing, much dancing, and music.

As she was speaking, Eleanor took up her fork; since she had found the lone forked carrot that morning, she was given the honor of leading the meal. She tried not to notice the eyes of everyone looking on around her as she went to take the first bite.

"Stop!"

Eleanor froze, the fork poised just outside her mouth. She turned in surprise to Lord Dunevin, who had just spoken so sharply.

"Is something wrong, my lord?"

Without a word, he plucked the fork from her hand. "Do not eat it."

He stood, crossed the room, and tossed the carrot, fork and all, into the fire. "None of you eat any of it."

Màiri looked at him in alarm. "My lord, is something the matter?"

Gabriel had gone from his seat and was circling the table, taking each person's plate from the table. "That was not a carrot Miss Harte was about to eat. It was *iteotha*."

A gasp rose from around the table.

Iteotha. Eleanor silently repeated the word he'd said to herself.

It wasn't one she was yet familiar with.

"I do not understand," she said. "What is it? What is wrong?"

But no one would answer her.

Instead they all stared at each other as if they'd just heard of the coming of the apocalypse.

When all the plates had been cleared away, Lord Dunevin returned to his place at the head of the table. He clasped his hands before him and looked at her gravely. "It was hemlock, Miss Harte."

Eleanor's mouth dropped. "Hemlock?"

He nodded. "It is very similar to the wild carrot of the isle in appearance and only someone familiar with both can tell the difference between them. Had you or anyone else here eaten it, the results would have certainly been fatal."

Eleanor was taken by a sudden chill and instinctively wrapped her arms around herself. It wasn't until two moments later that she realized Lord Dunevin had just saved her life.

"But, my lord," Màiri explained, her voice trembling with upset, "I checked them, each and every one."

"Màiri, I'm sure it was only an accident," Eleanor said in effort to calm her. "I probably picked it myself. I wouldn't have known the difference whereas you and the others would have recognized the plant in the field."

Màiri shook her head. "But we havena seen any of the *iteotha* here on the isle in years." She began to lose the battle to her tears. "Sweet Mary in heaven, 'tis just like when we lost the laird's own brother, Malcolm . . ."

The viscount looked at Donald MacNeill. "Is he on the isle?"

MacNeill hesitated before he slowly nodded. "Aye, my lord. I brought him over just this morning."

"Who, my lord?" Eleanor asked.

Dunevin's fingers were gripping the stem of his wineglass so tightly, Eleanor thought sure it would snap.

"Seamus Maclean," he said as if the very words brought a bitterness to his mouth. "His family lives here on the isle and he comes each year to celebrate Michaelmas with them."

"But we did not see him at all today."

His dark eyes shifted suddenly to her. "I would not be so eager, Miss Harte, to jump to the man's defense."

"I am not, sir," she said. "I just cannot think of a reason why Mr. Maclean would wish to poison me."

"You cannot know if it was you he'd intended the hemlock for. Any one of us could have taken that first bite. You, me, Màiri, even Juliana . . ." His voice dropped off suddenly.

Eleanor knew exactly what he was feeling, how the mere suggestion of such a terrible harm coming to Juliana filled him with a sense of helpless terror. She felt it, too.

"But why would Mr. Maclean want to poison anyone at this table?"

Eleanor looked at the myriad of faces around her. Oddly, none of them seemed to be as confused as she. They all looked as if they weren't too terribly shocked and she realized then that she was still the outsider here. She also realized that there was something more to this that no one else was saying.

And then she remembered the story Young Donald had told her.

"You cannot truly believe that he would do something like this because of that senseless feud?"

Lord Dunevin's eyes narrowed. "Who told you about . . . ?"

Eleanor noticed that Donald MacNeill shot Young Donald a stern look, easily figuring out where she had heard the tale.

She quickly sought to divert the man's attention.

"But you can't very well accuse the man without some sort of proof."

"I've proof," Fergus suddenly said from his place at the other end of the table. The grizzled man stood from his chair. "I saw that Seamus Maclean flirting with young Catriona after the carrots were gathered this morn."

"My sister's Catriona?" Màiri asked, obviously horrified.

"Aye."

But it all made no sense to Eleanor. It had to have been a ghastly accident, nothing more. A stray root of the hemlock must have somehow gotten tossed in with the other carrots without anybody noticing. There had been so much singing and merriment that morning in the fields, so many hands picking through the garden, surely that had to be it.

Wasn't it?

The others sitting around the table were now eyeing the other dishes, wondering, no doubt, if anything else had been tampered with.

Finally the viscount spoke.

"Màiri, I˙know you worked very hard on this fine meal for us all, but I'm afraid I cannot risk anyone's well-being on the chance that something else might also have been tainted. We'll have to dispose of everything. I am truly sorry."

Màiri's eyes were weeping as she nodded quietly. "I've some cheese and a mutton ham in the larder we can partake of instead, my lord. I know it hasna been touched by anyone."

The viscount nodded, and Màiri, Seòna, and Fergus began the task of clearing away the waste of their unfortunate feast. The mood in the room had quickly turned grim with foreboding.

Eleanor looked to where Lord Dunevin yet sat at his place heading the table. His eyes were focused blankly on the glass of claret before him, his expression profoundly troubled.

"What will you do?" she asked, trying to push aside a vagrant image of warring clansmen heaving mighty claymores in bloody battle to exact revenge.

"What choice have I?" he answered in quiet torment. "I can simply watch and wait to see if he will try again now that this effort has failed."

Chapter Eleven

In the last days before Michaelmas, Juliana spent more and more time working on her wall painting until it seemed she wanted to do nothing else. Even the promise of Màiri's sweet treacle bread and a cup of warm milk early that chilly morning couldn't entice her away.

She would spend hours at it at a time, silently drawing, never tiring, adding freely to the mural as she enhanced the image first with tangled, windswept trees and distant shadows of the various standing stones that peppered the rolling landscape. Later, figures of some of the more familiar inhabitants of the isle began to take shape, scattered here and there about the idyllic setting.

The painting itself was really quite good. Even at her young age, Juliana showed the keen eye for detail and use of color that was the mark of many a talented artist. Even more remarkable was that somehow, without any instruction, she seemed able to capture the very personality of each figure she drew simply by the manner in which she illustrated them.

There was the family of MacNeill all standing outside their small thatched croft, fleecy sheep teeming around them like landlocked clouds while Donald sailed by on the murky waters of the firth in his small skiff.

At the opposite corner, Juliana had brushed in the imposing structure of Dunevin, with its the shadowed figure of the viscount standing high on the castle tower, Cudu flanking his side, a misty pair of silhouettes against the sullen clouds that stretched across the sky overhead.

Below them, the tender figure of Màiri stood out on the castle yard, her trademark apron tied around her waist as she tossed bits of feed to the scattered chickens while Angus, the Dunevin groomsman, watched on from the open stable door.

Each day, some new image would appear on the mural. When Eleanor thought Juliana had finished, she would add something more to it.

Just the day before, she had spent a great deal of time drawing in the small, round-headed figure of the little seal who often followed them when they walked along the shore, peeking from behind the water's surface. And that morning, she had begun sketching in yet another set of figures, this time a pair of them standing closely together at the water's edge while a third waved to them from a rocky mull overhead.

At first, Eleanor had thought the two figures nearest the water were meant to depict her and Juliana with their skirts hitched up to their knees as they had waded out several mornings ago to gather periwinkles for Màiri's stew. The water had been so cold their toes had tingled for a full hour afterward.

But when Juliana had enhanced the figure that was waving to the two from afar with dark hair and eyes, dressing it in a pale green frock very similar to one of her own, Eleanor realized that the one waving was meant to be Juliana. The other two, she surmised, were likely meant to be herself and Young Donald, who had joined them in the winkle pool that day.

It was that part of the painting Juliana was now perfecting, her dark head bent closely to the wall as she traced in some careful detail with the tip of a feather dipped in black. Guessing that she would be involved in the project for some time, Eleanor had just decided to spend some quiet time on her Gaelic studies when Fergus suddenly appeared at the nursery door, his weather-worn face nearly eclipsed by the tilt of his ragged blue bonnet.

"Màiri says 'tis time to come down to bake the *struan* cake now."

Eleanor nodded to him. She had forgotten that she had asked Màiri if she and Juliana could help with the baking of the traditional cake for the St. Michael's Day feast the following day.

"Thank you, Fergus. We shall be right down."

As she set aside her book, Eleanor noticed the Scotsman staring with keen interest at Juliana's mural.

"It is very good, isn't it?"

"Aye," he answered, looking intently at Juliana, who had turned to face him. "A good likeness, indeed."

Juliana turned away then, stowing away her paints and brushes.

"Has the laird seen this?" Fergus asked.

"No, not yet. I thought to wait until Juliana was finished before showing it to him."

The quizzical look in his eye brought her to wondering. "Do you suppose Lord Dunevin could be angry that we painted over the walls without first checking with him?"

Fergus shrugged. "I canna say what the laird would or wouldna like. The laird is the only one t' tell you that."

And with that, the man turned and shuffled out of the room.

The man always spoke so matter-of-factly, never stating

anything beyond what was necessary to get his message across. At first, Eleanor had thought the man hadn't liked her, his manner so brusque and at times even callous. She had since decided that he simply spoke with everyone that way.

Eleanor looked over to where Juliana was now standing by the window. The expression on her face looked suddenly uneasy. "Oh, do not worry, Juliana. I'm sure your father won't mind that we painted over the walls. In fact, once he sees the wonderful work you've done, he'll surely thank us for the improvement we've made."

She seemed to ease, and Eleanor smiled. "Are you finished cleaning up?"

Juliana nodded. Together, the two of them made off for the stairs.

The kitchen was ablaze with light from a scattering of candles, *cruisie* lamps and tin lanterns, and the glowing hearth fire whose welcoming warmth could be felt all the way to the outer corridor. The pleasing smells of baking and fresh herbs filled the air, mingling with the earthy wooded scent of the fire. Màiri's two daughters, Alys and Sorcha, both robust and of the same easy manner as their mother, were there, helping to get things prepared.

Though they each had taken husbands from the mainland, the two young women visited their mother often, coming over at least weekly on Donald MacNeill's skiff since the death of their father five years before, when Màiri had given up the family croft for a pair of rooms off the kitchen at Dunevin.

Sorcha, with what must have been her father's dark hair and high forehead, was the elder of the two and currently in the later stages of pregnancy with Màiri's first grandchild. She was the picture of maternal contentment, with soft eyes, her hand frequently at rest on her swollen belly. The family had been doubly blessed for Alys, who more resembled their mother and was perhaps a few years younger than her sister, had brought the news just that week that she, too, was expecting to deliver her first child late the following spring.

Eleanor often found herself looking on the two, Alys even younger than she was herself, both married and now establishing their own families. She wondered wistfully if the time would ever come when she would know what it was to be a wife, a mother. . . .

"I think we're a'ready now," Màiri said, handing Eleanor and Juliana each one of her voluminous aprons.

The process of baking the traditional Michaelmas *struan* was as celebrated an event as the time-honored cake itself, created through a series of steps and ingredients that was followed stringently each year.

Oats, barley, and rye were ground together into meal in equal parts in the circular stone quern that stood in the kitchen corner. It was the custom for the eldest daughter to bake the cake; this year, Màiri passed that honor on to Juliana, teaching her the proper way to moisten the meal with some milk, tossing in a handful of bogberry and caraway, adding a dollop of honey as they shaped it into its traditional three corners on the heated flagstone where it would bake.

The fire itself was fueled not by the usual peat, but by symbolic branches that had been gathered earlier that day, oak, rowan, and bramble, woods that were considered sacred among the isles. While the cake gained in consistency, Màiri and Juliana took three basting feathers they'd plucked from one of the Dunevin cockerels, and applied a smooth batter of eggs, cream, and butter to form a custardlike covering that glistened in the firelight.

After being blessed, this sizeable *struan* would be shared

by everyone at the feast the following day. Any leftover meal was then made into smaller individual cakes for those family members who were absent or had died.

While Màiri set out each tiny cake, quietly mentioning the name of each departed member of their families, Eleanor felt a touch of sadness, reminded of the bitter separation from her own family so far away.

So many times over the past weeks Eleanor had wanted to write to her mother. She'd begun countless letters, thinking to assure Lady Frances not to worry, that all was well, but just couldn't seem to find the words any further than the salutation.

What could she say? If she revealed to her where she was, Eleanor knew Lady Frances and Christian would both come immediately to Trelay to fetch her back, back to a life that no longer felt anything but false. The truth was Eleanor wasn't ready to go back, not now, not yet. Juliana had made such progress, especially recently. She needed Eleanor, but even more than that, Eleanor needed her.

In Juliana, Eleanor saw so much of herself. Though she hadn't lost the will to speak, from the time she'd been a girl, Eleanor had somehow stopped being heard. She had seen only what others had wanted her to see, had done what had been expected of her without really wondering, without questioning. Only now did she understand why they had never visited the duke, her grandfather, even though he'd lived less than a mile from their London house. Only now did she recognize the veiled hostility, the bitter resentment, that had always simmered beneath the surface.

It was this realization that had helped Eleanor to come to terms with the truth of her birth, that had allowed her to forgive her mother and Christian for the decisions they'd made in keeping it from her. Had it been Christian who had been born in her place, Eleanor couldn't honestly say that she wouldn't have made the same sacrifices he had to protect her. Society was cruel to anything less than ideal; in the same way that Juliana was shunned for her silence, Eleanor would have been shunned for her bastardy. And how easily she herself could have faced the same circumstances as her mother, wed to a man she did not love, living day in and day out with unhappiness and resentment. How many of her friends from Miss Effington's had done just that? Countless many—even Amelia B. hadn't been able to avoid it.

After Michaelmas, Eleanor told herself. After Michaelmas when the harvest was complete and life on the isle settled in for the winter, she would write to her mother and assure her all was well. She would not tell her where she was, but would promise to explain when the time was right. Lady Frances would understand, for she of all people realized that there were times when things were better left unsaid. . . .

It was with that thought that Eleanor shaped her own batch of the tiny cakes, silently designating each, *Mother . . . Christian . . . Grace . . .*

By the time they had finished with the baking that night, the moon was high in the star-dusted sky and several dozen little cakes were set out in neat rows to cool on the trestle table. Before leaving the kitchen for the night, Màiri broke off a tiny bit of the Michaelmas cake, tossing it to the fire, as was custom, "as an offering" she said, "to safeguard the house against the evil deeds of the underworld for the coming year."

The festivities were to begin early the following morning with the circuiting of the isle's ancestral graveyard in a gesture to honor those who'd departed.

Shortly after dawn, Eleanor and Juliana came quickly

down the tower stairs, munching their morning bannocks as they tied on their bonnets and headed off to join the others already gathering on the green outside. Màiri and her daughters were already waiting for them when they came into the great hall below.

"Have they already begun?" Eleanor asked, hoping they hadn't slept too late.

"Nae, not as of yet, lass. But we'd best hurry else we'll miss the morning blessing."

They headed off quickly across the hall to leave, but Eleanor hesitated when she happened to spy Lord Dunevin through the open door of his study, standing at the window.

"What is it, lass?" Màiri asked when she noticed Eleanor had not joined them at the door.

Eleanor walked Juliana over to her. "Is Lord Dunevin not planning to join in the festivities?"

"*Och*, no. The laird doesna ever come doon for the revels."

"Whyever not?"

Màiri's expression grew clouded, her voice dropping to a quiet murmur. "Come, lass, you remember the terrible things Seamus Maclean said to you? About the laird? The mainlanders talk to the island folk, too, stories get passed around, and well, the laird just believes 'tis better for everyone if he stays 'ere at the castle."

"Oh."

But Eleanor was still staring at the study door, mulling Màiri's words over in her thoughts. Gossip or no, it wasn't right that he should stay locked away from one of the most important events taking place on his own isle with his own people.

He was the laird, *their laird*. For too long, the islanders had been listening to the false words of others, superstitious nonsense that had been added to and embellished for so long now, there was no longer any fragment of truth to the stories.

Lord Dunevin was not some black magic wizard who had cast a terrible spell on his own daughter to steal her voice. He had never been responsible for crop failures, foul weather, or the fact that one of the mainlanders' cows had a white marking shaped like a lightning bolt on its neck. The people of the isle had spent too much time now believing Lord Dunevin to be something he'd never been. It was past time they were acquainted with their true laird.

Màiri bent down to help Juliana tie her bonnet in place. "Shall we go, then?"

But Eleanor wasn't moving. "Màiri, why don't you take Juliana and go on ahead. I'll catch up with you shortly."

Màiri looked at her, knowing immediately what Eleanor planned to do. "Very well, lass. We'll see you on the hill. But doona be disappointed if you fail to sway him. We've tried in years past to no success."

Eleanor nodded to them, watching as they all departed, baskets in hand. Only when they had gone, closing the door behind them, did Eleanor turn for the viscount's study.

Dunevin was still standing at the window when she walked quietly into the room. Even at a distance from him, she could see his stance was tense, like a collie watching over his flock, sensing a predator but unable to see it. His arms were folded before him and he looked as if his thoughts were deeply troubled. He had said nothing more about the near-accident at dinner earlier that week, but Eleanor knew the incident preyed heavily on his mind. It had preyed heavily on the minds of them all.

Cudu lifted his head from where he lay on the carpet as Eleanor came fully into the room, rising up on all fours to greet her. Lord Dunevin noticed the dog's movement and turned. He glanced at her only briefly, and he said nothing before returning his attention to the scene outside the window.

She said to his back, "I thought certain you'd be outside on the green, my lord, readying to ride that great beast of a horse of yours to victory in the race this morning."

The viscount shook his head. "No, my place is here where I can watch over it all. Didn't you know? That is what lairds do."

His tone tried at levity, but he wasn't fooling anyone. Most especially not her.

"Hiding yourself away only gives them that much more to talk about, you know."

He turned to her as if trying to feign that he didn't know what she was talking about when, in truth, he knew very well. "I beg your pardon?"

Eleanor moved to join him at the window. "I was just thinking that if you took part in the festivities of the day, assumed your true and rightful place as laird of these people, they would all see that there is nothing to those ridiculous stories the mainlanders keep bandying about. Keeping yourself locked away like this, a silhouette in a tower window, only implies that you have something to hide." She stared directly at him. "Which you do not."

Gabriel turned then to fully face her. Vibrant green eyes that somehow saw straight to his soul blinked back at him. His insides tightened just to look at her. He thought again of how closely she had come to eating that hemlock, how the curse that plagued his family had nearly worked its wrath on another, this time an innocent bystander. She believed it was merely a terrible accident. Did she yet realize that her life was at risk solely because of him?

Or was that her purpose in coming there? Had she come

there that morning, suggesting he do something he had longed to for years but had never dared even consider to test him somehow? Did she think to see if he would admit that there was indeed something for him to hide?

But as he looked into those eyes, losing himself in their luminous emerald depths, Gabriel knew that her intentions were only true, because reflected in her eyes he saw something he had never seen in the eyes of any other.

This woman believed in him.

He told himself she was simply naïve, too unaware of the danger she was in. It was that same naïveté that had allowed her to kiss him that day, in this very room, having no earthly idea that as she had been falling dreamily under the spell of that sentimental old poem, she had at the same time been kissing a demon.

"Tell me, my lord," she said then, breaking him from his thoughts, "what would it take to get you to leave that window and walk with me to the hill to stand with the others?"

A blessed miracle, he thought to himself. He said instead, "I beg your pardon?"

"A round of piquet, perhaps?"

She crossed the room to the gaming table without even waiting for him to respond and opened the drawer, removing a deck of cards from inside. She arched a brow above a most cunning smile.

"I propose these stakes," she said. "If you should best me, you can stay there at that window all day and watch the day pass from afar. You can allow the people of your isle to continue to believe false tales and implausible conjecture about you. But," she went on, "if I win, then you must accompany me to the hill and take part in the festivities today. Including," she concluded, "racing your horse on the course later today."

At first, Gabriel thought she was jesting, until she cut the deck and began to shuffle the cards. She had no idea of what exactly she was proposing. He, the Dark Lord of Dunevin, take part in the Michaelmas celebrations?

His next thought was to decline her proposition, tell her to leave him to watch as he always had before, alone and haunted by memories, even as he turned from the window and headed for the gaming table.

Perhaps he would just accept her wager and best her at the hand. It would serve her right. He was, after all, an excellent piquet player.

But so, apparently, was she.

Six deals later, she had thoroughly trounced him.

Gabriel sat back in his chair and stared at the cards fanned out on the table before him in stunned disbelief. "Wherever did you learn to play like that? You play with a ruthlessness worthy of White's!"

Eleanor took up the cards proudly, shuffling them with the ease of a practiced gamester. "I learned from the aunt of a very close family friend. Instead of spending our afternoon visits pouring tea, she and I played at cards. She is quite a sharp." She stood then, setting aside the deck and pulling on her gloves in an obvious prelude to leaving. "Are we ready then, my lord?"

"Ready?"

"Yes. To leave. We wouldn't want to be late."

She didn't even consider the possibility of his refusing. Gabriel looked at her, contemplating his decision. He had never been one to walk away from a debt. She had beaten him fairly. And he reasoned that if he were down in the thick of things, he could keep closer watch on Seamus Maclean.

He would go.

"On one condition," he added.

She turned to him, her eyes alight beneath the brim of her bonnet. "Yes, my lord?"

"That you cease with the 'my lords' and 'sirs.' Anyone who was able to best me so thoroughly at cards should certainly call me by my given name."

"But, my lord, is that at all proper? For someone who is in your employ?"

"It is proper if I say it is proper."

"Oh."

When next she spoke, her voice was noticeably softer. "But I'm embarrassed to say I don't even know what your name is."

His eyes held hers. "It is Gabriel."

She smiled softly as if the name pleased her. "Very well, *Gabriel*."

It was the first time in his life that the sound of his own name brought his pulse to racing.

"Well, then, shall we go?"

He turned from her then, lest she notice that he was flushed despite the chill in the air, and took up his coat.

As he pulled it on, she said from behind him, "If I am to call you by your given name, then I must insist that you do the same."

He turned to face her. "Very well, Eleanor."

Eleanor. For the briefest of moments, Eleanor feared the end of her charade as Miss Nell Harte. She searched his eyes. Had he somehow learned the truth of her identity? Had he seen a notice like the one she'd taken from the inn wall, one she'd somehow missed?

But she saw nothing to indicate that he had chosen that name for any reason other than it was the more formal version of "Nell." If he had known the truth, if he had seen a notice and somehow figured out it was her, he surely would have revealed it to her long before now.

They left the study then and walked quietly together down the graveled pathway leading to the hill where the others had already gathered for the blessing of the *struan* cake. The day had dawned clear and bright for this wondrous time of celebration; the sun midway to rising, struggling through the mist in the distance all pink, lilac, and pale green while reflecting in the waters and burnishing the entire hillside in a mixture of rich colors.

As they took their place among the small congregation of others, Eleanor noticed looks of surprise and wonder at Gabriel's unexpected attendance. She could feel the stiffness of his reaction even as he stood beside her among these people whom he governed, but whom he had avoided for so long. After a short while, when he saw that there were no protests, no bitter remarks whispered amongst the gathering, he began to ease.

Those who knew him, like Donald MacNeill or Màiri, simply looked astonished, pleasantly so, that he had decided to come. Others, those who had rarely if ever seen him in person, looked on him as if they weren't quite sure how they should feel. It had to be difficult, she assumed, to think on the man suddenly standing amidst you as the devil incarnate.

Only one person, Seamus Maclean, showed any hint of contempt as he glared at Gabriel from where he stood beside what appeared to be the members of his family.

Gabriel and Eleanor stood quietly with Màiri and Juliana as the priest began to speak in Gaelic, blessing the day and the fruits of the harvest, the prosperity of the isle, the health of the people and their laird. As if the very heavens realized the specialness of the day, a salt-scented gust of sea wind blew suddenly over the hilltop, dispersing the mist that hovered around them to reveal the rugged, austere beauty of the ancient landscape while the priest's lyric voice carried like a mystic song on the lifting breeze.

When the service was finished, not a single person moved from where they stood. Everyone turned as if waiting, and Eleanor realized that it was Gabriel's place as laird to lead the circuit around the final resting places of those no longer a part of the isle. It was a tradition he had avoided for too long.

He looked at Eleanor, sensing the same, but reluctant to take such a forefront so soon after emerging from the shadows of his long-held obscurity.

She smiled at him and watched as he finally walked to where the priest stood waiting.

But even after he had gone forward, the others waited, watching her now.

"You must go with Miss Juliana and follow the laird," Màiri whispered quietly to her. "The laird and his family all walk together. 'Tis tradition."

She nodded and took Juliana's hand, walking slowly after him. The others fell into place behind her.

They walked in a quiet procession once around the graveyard filled with ancient carved crosses and stones from centuries past before they dispersed to allow each family to make their own private offering to their departed loved ones. St. Michael's morn was a time for remembering, for reaffirming one's roots, for knowing from where one had come. It was a security, a pride, Eleanor would never truly know.

Some offered prayers, others bits of cake and bread. Eleanor found herself kneeling beside the stones of the graves of those families who were no longer a part of the isle, pulling stray weeds and smoothing away scattered bits of leaves and twigs.

It was just as she was readying to make her way back down the hillside when she felt Juliana loosen her hand from hers and begin to walk away on her own.

"Juliana?"

But the little girl just kept walking, crossing the green to where the laird's ancestors were interred in a separate parcel of the cemetery, higher up on the hill.

Eleanor didn't try to stop her, but followed quietly behind, watching as Juliana paused before the beautifully carved stone cross that symbolically marked the final resting place of her mother. With all the innocence and tenderness of the child she was, Juliana reached down and placed a single daisy flower she'd picked, laying it gently at the base of the cross. Eleanor was so moved by the gesture, her eyes clouded with heartfelt tears. She never heard him approaching.

" 'Tis a man with little conscience who can stand before the graves of those he put there."

It was Seamus Maclean's bitter voice that hissed closely to Eleanor's ear, like a menacing cloud come to cover the sun's light. Angrily, Eleanor wiped a hand across her teary eyes and turned to face him.

"Even less of a conscience is shown by the man who would disrespect the significance of such a day in order to satisfy his own resentment."

The two stared at one another through a long moment before Seamus's father came up alongside, taking his son by the arm to pull him along. "Away, lad. 'Tis no good will come of this."

Seamus yanked away from him. "No, Da, she needs to know." He turned to Eleanor, his eyes glinting with emotion. "Listen to me, lass. He's the devil tha' one. I tried to save the other lady, but I was too late. He will lure you into his trap sure as he did her. It's in 'is eyes, lass. Look at them. Dark as the depths of hell they are. No life behind them. Get out now, afore it is too late."

Eleanor stared at the man in stony silence.

Maclean gave a bitter smile, shaking his head. "Look you up there at all the crosses and headstones of those who have perished at the hands of the MacFeaghs. The evidence speaks for itself, lass. See how many have gone to their graves because of that godforsaken clan. Doona be another to join them, lass. Hie yersel' away afore it is too late for ye."

Loath to listen to his spiteful insinuations any longer, Eleanor turned away from him and headed off up the hill to join Juliana. But as she wove her way slowly through the carved stone crosses and wind-battered headstones that peppered the hillside, she found herself glancing unwittingly at the names and the dates that had been inscribed upon them.

There was *Liùsaidh MacFeagh, died aged seven and ten months,* in the sixteenth century, *Iseabail, infant daughter of Alexander MacFeagh, Murchadh Macfeagh, born 1710, died without issue 1733,* and the least weathered of the markers which read *Georgiana MacFeagh, Lady Dunevin, taken from this lonely isle in 1817.*

There were so many, one could see why it would be difficult to put it off to unfortunate coincidence. Still as she gazed across the hillside to where Gabriel stood conversing with the priest, she could not bring herself to give credence to Seamus Maclean's terrible accusations.

There had to be some other explanation for the incidents that had darkened this place and these people. But what?

Eleanor felt a tugging on her arm and turned to see Juliana's sweet dark eyes looking up at her. The answer to it all lay with this one child, hidden behind a wall of frightened silence. Only Juliana knew the truth of what had happened to her mother. Only she had been with her last before she'd disappeared. Somehow, someway there had to be a key to unlocking it.

And Eleanor determined that she would find it.

Chapter Twelve

After the morning's more spiritual observances, the mood of the day shifted, like the moon giving way to the sun, from a feeling of serene commemoration to another of lively merriment and high celebratory spirit.

Winter was coming to the islands and Trelay had been blessed by a bounteous harvest that would see them all through the meager months ahead. St. Michael's Day was a day of rich reward after weeks and months of toilsome work. This was a day of giving thanks for a season of abundance and prosperity at a time when other districts of the Highlands and western seaboard were struggling against land clearances, steadily increasing rents, and economic failure.

Out on the green that stretched in a lush fusion of soft meadow grass, white clover, and dandelion from the castle proper to the lower shoreline, games and amusements had been set out for the children to amuse themselves while the adults took part in the day's traditional horse race.

Gabriel had taken himself off shortly after the ceremony of the morning and hadn't returned since. Eleanor hoped that he hadn't decided against taking part in the rest of the day's activities, retreating back to his study window to watch from afar. She couldn't, she knew, press him to stay, but inwardly she hoped that he had been encouraged by the reactions of the islanders, many of whom had even approached him that morning on the hillside to wish him well.

For the *oda* race, the horses would run on the sandy stretch of rugged shoreline that extended from below the castle's venerable walls to the rock and stone jetty that served as the island's pier. It was a length of about a quarter mile of uneven terrain that was peppered with an assortment of natural obstacles, everything from timeworn standing stones to dense clumps of sea moss and scattered pieces of driftwood that had washed up with the tide.

As the others made their way down the hillside to where the racers were at that moment assembling on the strand, Eleanor looked through the crowd, shading her eyes as she studied the faces of the others.

She did not see Gabriel among them.

Màiri noticed her searching and came up beside her, tucking her arm loosely around her waist.

"If you ask me," she said with her usual infinite wisdom, "'twas a miracle you convinced him to come out e'en this morn, lass. Be happy you managed to accomplish that. He's been apart from this all so long, it may take him some time to feel comfortable 'ere."

Eleanor simply nodded, trying to stave off her disappointment, and turned to help with the other activities.

For the children, Màiri and Seòna had furnished tubs filled with a sudsy mixture made from crushed soapwort stems and various other herbs that they could pour into carved wooden "pipes" to blow clumps of bubbles all about the place.

Later that evening, there would be games of Hoodman Blind and Tigh, while the adults danced at the *cuideachd*.

While the older children pranced around, trying to see who could blow the biggest bubble, Wee Donald and some of the younger ones sucked on spoonfuls of sugar that had been twisted into bits of paper for a special sweet treat. Eleanor was heartened to see that the other children easily took Juliana into their collective fold, accepting her muteness without any outspoken remarks and with only a little curiosity.

When a boy of about six asked Juliana her name, to which she responded with a silent stare, another little girl named Brìghde, very near Juliana's age with curly blond locks and bare feet beneath the ragged hem of her woolen skirts, took it upon herself to act as Juliana's attendant, introducing her to the others as "My friend, Jwee-lhànna." Even now, they lay on their bellies, ankles crossed behind them and noses nearly to the ground, one dark head bent closely to one light, searching through a thick patch of clover for the one bearing the charmed four leaves.

Would that the mainlanders they had encountered that day in Oban could take a lesson from the innocent and unprejudiced perspective of a child, Eleanor thought, watching them with a soft smile.

When it came time for the race to begin, Eleanor walked with Màiri and Seòna to the edge of the course to stand with the others already assembled. It looked as if most every family on the isle had come out for the festivities that day, for easily over two hundred or more of all ages stood along the periphery of the race's course.

A line of nearly a dozen riders had congregated at the starting point, a motley assortment that included most every sort of beast from riding horse to pony, plow horse to nag.

There was even a mule that looked quite as if it might doze off at any moment, its head hanging low to the ground, its eyes blinking to a snooze. They were all without both saddle and bridle, the riders by tradition made to direct their mounts by means of their skill alone and a simple leading rope.

"I wagered old Angus MacNeill a batch of blaeberry scones that your Donald would win this year, Seòna," Màiri said as they waited for the race to begin. "I even gave Donald a special bit of sugar for his mare with the promise of another if she can beat that Seamus Maclean's nasty old hack to the finish line."

"And what is your prize from Angus if Donald should win?" Seòna asked with a tilt of her brow and a mischievous grin.

It was a subject of frequent mirth among the women that Màiri's interest in the widowed crofter was a little more than friendly acquaintanceship. She often asked after him to Seòna and Donald, and Old Angus could almost always be found sitting in the Dunevin kitchen, sharing a wee cuppa with Màiri while she worked.

"If I win, Angus has to turn a reel wit' me at the *cuideachd* later tonight."

At Seòna's sidelong glance, she added, "I ken what ye're thinkin' by the look on your face, Seòna MacNeill. Doona be getting' any matchmakin' thoughts into that pretty head o' yours. 'Tis simply because I miss dancin' so much without my Torquil 'ere these past five years."

Seòna glanced knowingly at Eleanor. "And I suppose all those cakes and fresh bannocks and blaeberry scones you keep takin' over to Angus's croft are because you worry the man canna feed himsel'?"

Màiri lifted her chin stubbornly, but her plump cheeks

pinked modestly and she gave a slight smile while Seòna and Eleanor chuckled behind her. "*Whish,* you brazen lasses, the race is nearly ready to start."

The riders were poised to set off when Young Donald, who was readying to strike the signal to start using a tin pan and a stick, suddenly lowered his arms, looking up toward the castle heights. Everyone turned at once to look at what had caught his attention, just as a lone rider, silhouetted by the high sun, started coming down the hill toward them.

A murmur of excitement bubbled through the crowd.

"Well, you'd better get to baking those scones, Màiri Macaphee," Seòna said. "I think your chances for winning that wager just went astray."

Eleanor's heart bounded when she caught sight of Gabriel making his way down the hillside toward them. With the wind tugging at his hair and the late morning mist curling around the legs of his prancing black horse, he looked like an ancient Highland warrior readying to do battle. She felt the urge to rush over to meet him, but held it in check as he quickly closed the distance to the shore.

"Sweet Mary in heaven," Màiri said, shading her eyes along with all the others against the light of the sun. "'Tis the laird. He's goin' to race this year."

Word spread quickly throughout the assembly, sending a headlong rush of excitement rolling across the brae like the swift autumn wind. Even the children stopped in their play to watch as Gabriel cantered his great hunter past the astonished faces of islanders to the starting point.

Young Donald was staring with his mouth agape as Gabriel took his place in line.

"I hope you don't mind an additional rider," Gabriel said, urging his horse forward alongside Donald MacNeill's mare, who looked suddenly like a pony beside the viscount's pretty black hunter.

Like the other riders, Gabriel had changed from his fine coat and dress kilt into a pair of the traditional riding trews that hugged his legs almost like a second skin beneath the fullness of his linen sark.

Eleanor suddenly understood why Gabriel had vanished earlier.

Gone was the genteel austere lord to be revered and watched from afar. In his place was a man who fit in easily with the others, every bit a Scot.

He looked splendid. His dark hair ruffled in the wind blowing in off the firth, tousling about the sharp angles of his face, the roughened line of his chin, the hooded darkness of his eyes. Eleanor could but stare at this man who looked so noble, so powerful, so incredibly handsome.

He looked at her and she smiled, appalled to feel herself blushing like a giddy schoolgirl, and shyly looked away. That smile vanished when she happened to notice the look of unconcealed hatred that had crossed Seamus Maclean's features as he glared at Gabriel from the other side of the line of riders.

Noticing her watching him, Seamus suddenly backed his horse from the ranks.

"Maclean," Donald MacNeill called to him, "what're you about? Are you for quittin' the race e'en afore it's begun, mon?"

A chorus of Gaelic whispers soughed through the gathering.

Seamus spat into the ground at his horse's feet before responding. "Nae, Donald MacNeill. I jus' see nae good reason to waste my time t'day. 'Tis obvious to all 'ere who'll win the race now. 'Tis the mon with all the money who can afford to buy himsel' the best piece of horseflesh."

An astonished silence followed, sparked by several audible gasps from the crowd. People shook their heads in disbelief that Seamus would dare direct such open hostility toward the laird. Others simply stared.

A threatening wind blew in off the shore, whistling through the stark coastal trees. No one moved or made a sound, so quickly did the festive mood of the gathering change.

Though Seamus Maclean didn't himself live on the isle, his parents had all their lives, leasing land directly from Lord Dunevin. As such they were at his mercy. Few lairds if any would tolerate such an open show of disrespect. Most would make an example of this blatant insolence to serve as a reminder to the others of the true order of things.

Eleanor stole a quick glance at Seamus's father and mother, who stood across from her. They were of an older age, no longer able to toil away on the land, and the looks on their faces were stricken with panic by the gravity of the situation.

It was only through Gabriel's grace and goodness that they had a home to rent and plot of land to sow; it could just as easily be taken away without cause, without warning, without recourse. At a time when Highland lairds were swiftly clearing their lands of the people who had farmed it for generations for the more profitable venture of sheep farming, words like those of Seamus were both imprudent and perilous.

Everyone watched Gabriel for his response, waiting in tense silence for his final judgment. When it came, even the gulls flying overhead fell silent.

"If it was my horse you coveted, Maclean, you should have taken advantage of the opportunity to steal him last night for today's race."

He looked at Eleanor then, explaining, "There is an ancient custom that on the eve of St. Michaelmas, any horse may be appropriated for the race the following day without fear of punishment, provided the horse is returned afterward to its rightful owner unharmed. Most of the men here spent the night watching over their own horses and ponies in the fields."

He glanced a moment at the mule beast, who had, in fact, by now dozed off. "Well, except perhaps for Olghar there. No doubt he left the byre unattended all night in hopes some unlikely fool would take that lazy beast off his hands."

Several of the islanders laughed at that, while the mule's owner, Olghar Macphee, grinned at Gabriel's jest. The crowd began to ease, sensing their laird's benevolent leniency.

"I posted no guard on my hunter," Gabriel went on. "I even left the stable unlocked because I hadn't planned to race today and thought perhaps someone else might like to borrow him, but no one bothered to take him. It doesn't seem fair now not to let him stretch his legs today with all the other horses. I had no choice but to come and ride him myself in the race."

Murmurs of agreement arose from the assembly gathered. Others turned angry glances and whispered muttered curses at Seamus Maclean for his failed attempt at ruining the happy gathering.

"But," Gabriel went on, "I will make a concession to you, Seamus Maclean, so that it cannot be said that the race was run unfairly in my favor. My horse will bear the weight of two riders through the course while everyone else rides alone. That should sufficiently even the stakes."

Those islanders who understood English seemed to agree, translating Gabriel's offer to Gaelic for the others. All around the assembly, people began to nod and comment on their laird's integrity and goodwill. One man even suggested that Olghar's mule beast, as dispirited as it looked, race riderless to even the odds the other way, eliciting a chorus of good-natured laughter.

Eleanor was so busy looking around at all the others, reading their reactions, that she never noticed Gabriel had walked his horse over to where she and Juliana stood with Màiri and Seòna. Only when he was standing right beside her and she felt the nudge of his horse's muzzle against her arm did she turn about.

"Eleanor?" he said, looking down at her from the back of his great beast.

"Yes?"

It wasn't until she noticed that the eyes of everyone around her were focused solely on the two of them that she realized what he was doing.

"You wish me? To ride with you, my lord?"

Gabriel never had the chance to answer her, for cheers of encouragement immediately erupted from all sides, urging her to "Do it, lass," and "Ride with the laird."

Before she could comprehend what was happening, Eleanor felt herself being hoisted somehow onto the horse's back, turning to sit before Gabriel with her legs dangling over one side. She stared at him in breathless astonishment.

"Hold tight, lass," Gabriel whispered to her on a half grin. "This will likely prove a bumpy ride."

He turned his horse without using his hands, guiding it back into its place in the line of other racers solely with pressure from his knees. Eleanor threaded her fingers into the wiry hair of the horse's mane, her heart racing, her hands trembling, hoping to the heavens that she wasn't unseated the moment they started off.

"Riders at ready!" Young Donald called out then, raising his tin pan gong again as he readied to strike the starting signal.

Eleanor felt Gabriel tighten his arms around her, took a deep breath of the mingling scents of formidable horse and even more formidable man that surrounded her and held it, closing her eyes as Donald lowered his hand to strike the gong.

She felt the horse's muscles bunch in expectation beneath her.

The signal sounded.

They leapt forward in response.

That same breath she'd been holding left her in a rush of pure exhilaration as she was jerked back, falling against the solid wall of Dunevin's chest. She fought desperately to stay seated, her hands soon letting go of the horse's mane and working their way slowly around Gabriel's arms as he urged them on even faster.

The wind bit at her cheeks and nose, stinging her eyes to tears as her hair tumbled helplessly from its pins, but she barely noticed. All she could see, all she could think about, all she could feel was the man whose arms were around her.

They were racing at breakneck speed across rough and treacherous terrain, but Eleanor had never felt safer in her life. She could let go, she knew, and still he wouldn't let her fall. He would never let her fall. But none of that mattered. She didn't want to let go of him. She wanted to feel the tautness of his arms beneath her hands, the warmth of his body so close to hers, the salt-spiced scent of his neck as she allowed the motion of the horse beneath them to push her further back until she was leaning fully against him.

With the spray of the incoming tide beneath thundering hooves dampening their faces, they bounded over a fallen stone, crashing through shore brush and marram as they began to close in on the jetty that stretched its way outward from the shore in front of them. At the jetty, they would have to make a sharp turnabout before heading back, retracing the course to where they'd begun and where the burgeoning crowd of islanders awaited, cheering on the racers even now behind them.

As they came to the jetty, there were three of them running closely together, Donald MacNeill, Seamus Maclean, and Dunevin's steed carrying them both. It would make the sharp turn on this narrow strip of shoreline even more difficult to execute, but Gabriel showed no signs of slowing.

Neither did Seamus or Donald.

If anything, they all urged their horses on faster, hooves cutting deeply into the wet sand and graveled shell beneath them as they raced closer and closer to the rock pier.

Once at the point where they had to make the turn, Seamus cut left inland toward the green of the machair, while Donald cut right, galloping out in a wide arc to where the waves lapped hungrily at the shore. Gabriel would have to make an even tighter turn, a difficult maneuver without the use of a bit to direct the horse, and as he went into it, leaning and tightening his knees around the beast's girth, Seamus cut him off suddenly from the side, making it that much more difficult to shift.

The hunter faltered, uncertain, nearly unseating them

both, and Gabriel had to pull on the leading rope to bring
them to a sudden stop or else risk sending one or both of them
plummeting downward against the tumbled rocks of the jetty.
As he managed to set them each to rights and turn the horse's
head back in the other direction, Seamus set his whip hand to
slapping against his steed's flank, shouting out an unearthly
curse and frightening the poor beast into a panicked gallop as
he headed for the finish line.

Gabriel snaked an arm around Eleanor's waist, pulling
her even more tightly against him so that she was sitting
atop his thigh and quite nearly across his lap. His chin
brushed her temple, the roughness of it rasping against her
forehead as he looked down at her.

"Hold tight to me, lass. We're about to sprout wings and
fly."

Eleanor barely managed to get one hand around his arm
before he set his heels hard against the horse's sides and they
were off, hooves flying, wind screaming in her ears as they
crashed through the foam and raced down the pebbled
shoreline in relentless pursuit of the other two riders.

They first overtook Donald MacNeill, whose mare was
tiring visibly, her smaller legs no match for those of the two
larger horses. Gabriel's hunter ate up the distance between
them easily, galloping past in a flurry of sand and sea spray
to the encouraging shouts of Donald himself as he cheered
them on.

They pounded over the shoreline, drawing slowly closer
to Seamus and his steed a distance ahead. A screen of peb-
bles and sand from the horse's flying hooves began to pep-
per them. Eleanor turned her face into Gabriel's neck to
avoid the debris, the scent and the heat of him filling her
senses.

She scarcely noticed when they hurtled past Seamus's

horse in a quicksilver flash as they closed in on the finish line. Not until she heard the uproar of cheers from the crowd around them did she realize they had just won the race.

Gabriel slowed his horse first to a canter and then to a trot, taking them along the stretch of brae to the heathery hillside beneath the castle. Even after they had stopped, Eleanor hadn't let loose of Gabriel, not until they were surrounded by a crowd of the islanders all cheering and congratulating them for the exciting victory.

Gabriel let go of the leading rope, loosening his embrace, and swung his leg around, dropping to the ground. As the others crowded thickly around him, he took Eleanor by the waist and eased her gently to the ground, tightening his hold around her again when her legs threatened to buckle suddenly beneath her.

"Steady now, lass," he said softly to her. "You seem to have lost your land legs. I thought that sort of thing only happened at sea."

At sea . . .

They were the perfect words to describe the unusual way she felt at that very moment. Her senses were giddy, her thoughts so much in chaos she could only manage a weakened smile.

"A kiss for the lady from the winner," called out a sudden voice that sounded curiously similar to Màiri's.

As if in a dream, Eleanor could but watch, wide-eyed, mystified and totally bewildered, as Gabriel lowered his mouth to hers and kissed her there before all.

A chorus of cheers resounded around them but Eleanor barely heard them. Somehow, in the space of a few moments, they had gone from governess and lord now simply to woman and man, all propriety, all stricture between them departed in the very blink of an eye.

The sounds of the rest of the world around them, the crowd, the wind, the crash of the surf on the shore, all of it faded into an oblivious haze. The only sound she could hear was the rapid pulse of her own heart beating a rhythm all its own as she gave herself over completely to the kiss and the man whose lips touched hers.

It was over far, far too soon.

As Gabriel pulled his mouth away, his dark eyes capturing hers and holding her suspended, Eleanor knew in the very next moment what it was that had caused this to happen.

She had fallen in love with Gabriel.

She loved this man with every hope, with every dream she had ever held close to her heart. It was nothing like the cordial affection that she had felt for Richard Hartley, what she had thought in all her maidenly ignorance had been the beginnings of love.

What she felt for Gabriel was something else, something infinitely more, undeniably stronger. It was fire, it was gale, it was a bottomless sea all at once. Even now, she wanted him to kiss her again no matter who stood around them, and never ever stop, not even when the moon had risen high in the sky and the magic of the night surrounded them. She wanted to feel his hands against her skin, the heat of him touching her in places she had never been touched. She wanted to lose herself in the dark endless depths of his eyes every day for the rest of her life.

It was utterly all-consuming and breath-stealing, this sudden realization she faced about herself. She wanted to love this man who the world had forsaken and heal his tortured heart. She wanted to spend her days living on this island, watching Juliana grow and helping her to find her way in the world. She wanted to breech the distance between father and daughter and show them the way back to each other again.

She wanted all this and more, so much more, but first Gabriel would have to know the truth of her, of her ancestry, of her reasons for running away from the life she'd lived before. She would have to tell him she was not really Miss Nell Harte. She would have to reveal that she was Lady Eleanor Wycliffe, the illegitimate Westover heiress—even if doing so might very well destroy whatever future they might have had.

These troubled thoughts must have shown clearly on her face for Gabriel stood before her then, looking down at her with those dark eyes soft with concern.

"Is something wrong, lass? You look as if you're not happy we won the race."

She looked up at him, uncertain, frightened at what she knew she must do. What would he do if she were to tell him right there, that moment that she loved him? Would he think her fanciful? Would he think her a fool? Even worse, would he turn away?

Would he be angry she had lied to him, leading him to believe she was someone she was not?

It was a risk she had no choice but to face. What she felt for Gabriel was too real, too special to surround with a lie. She would have to lay her heart, her life, her future on the line to him, but not here, not now.

This wasn't the time or the place to tell him. This was a day of celebration for so many reasons, not the least of which was his own "coming out," his emergence into his rightful place in the world. To undermine it now would be nothing short of a calamity.

So, instead, Eleanor simply smiled, looking into the eyes of the man she loved, and shook her head, saying quietly, "I always knew you would win."

For he had won more than just the race that day.

He had won her heart as well.

Chapter Thirteen

The weather held fair all through the day, kissed every now and then with brief washes of sunlight that stretched gently from behind the scattered clouds like ribbons of fanfare on May Day.

Many agreed there hadn't been such a fine Michaelmas on the isle in more years than most could remember. Others attributed the curiously clement skies to the unexpected but wholly celebrated appearance this year of the isle's reclusive laird.

After the excitement of the race that morning, the islanders had retreated inland from the shore to the verdant machair beneath the castle heights where the men and boys of the isle then squared off into teams for the traditional games of "shinty."

It was a competition steeped in tradition. The men were armed with the slender curved *caman* stick and a small wooden ball made from an elder gnarl the size of an apple, and the play of the game was both hard and fierce as each team labored to drive the ball successfully into the opposing team's hail marked clearly by two makeshift stacks of stones on either end of the playing field.

There were scraped knees, bruised heads, and for one, a broken front tooth. Rules were unwritten, although ancient custom prevailed. Tempers would flare, and disagreements often erupted, sometimes coming to blows, but always it was the play of the game that decided the true victor.

When the sun had declined and the skies had darkened too much for further play, the assembly retired back to Dunevin Castle for the feast, the Michaelmas lamb, and the *struan* cakes that had been baked by the women the night before.

Each of the island families brought food from their own crofts to contribute, and the tables were filled with numerous cheeses and partan pie, cakes and scones, howtowdie, puddings, and biscuitlike treats called whim-whams. Heather ale and birk wine flowed freely, loosening tongues and freeing gay spirits. All around there was a feeling of good cheer. By the time night had fallen on St. Michael's Day, the dancing was well under way.

On the moon-kissed courtyard outside the castle donjon, burnished in muted torchlight and whispering shadows, circles of dancers moved in whirlwind harmony, hands clasped, arms linked, weaving in and out of one another in time to the lively tune of the piper and fiddles. Brightly colored skirts swished and swayed around bare feet and slender legs. Hands clapped. Feet stomped. Laughter and gaiety filled the air, while in the far-off corner, sitting alone at the end of one of the many trestle tables that had been brought out from the great hall for the feast, the laird of Dunevin watched over it all with thoughtful dark eyes.

It had been a day of celebration for many reasons. As laird, Gabriel was protector and ultimate caretaker for every person, from eldest graybeard to newborn nursling, on the isle. He was lord, master, benefactor, their trials were his trials, their preservation his bounden duty. Being an island community only made them that much more vulnerable.

Today, however, was a day when he could find peace in knowing that the people of his island, the island that his ancestors had safeguarded for centuries, would have sufficient food and shelter to last them through the harsh months ahead.

It wasn't always so across the Highlands. All around the western seaboard and further out even to the more remote isles of Lewis and Harris, places once inhabited by great Gaelic kings were being wholly abandoned out of necessity, the land no longer affording the barest sustenance for the people who had lived there through generations. The industry of kelping, which so many had grown to depend upon to make their living, was steadily declining since the defeat of the Napoleon, leaving them with only the unpredictability of farming or herring fishing on which to survive.

Even worse, the people on some of the other nearby isles were at the very mercy of a system that offered them little in the way of protection against greedy tacksmen and absentee landlords who valued pounds far above the livelihoods of their minions. Gabriel refused to adhere to this new system of estate management. Despite the darkness of their past, the MacFeaghs, lairds of Dunevin since time immemorial, had always been as one with the needs of their people—patriarchs of clan and kin—and he meant to see that tradition preserved.

All through the day and evening, Gabriel had been approached by the people of his isle, people who had avoided him just as much as he had them for the past three years since Georgiana's unexplained death. It was almost as if he had been away on a journey to far-off lands, returning to their gracious welcome.

Across the courtyard, Gabriel watched his daughter, Juliana, who would one day take his place as benefactor on this lonely isle. The change she had undergone in the past weeks was beyond astounding. Not a month before, he had thought her lost forever, an empty shell of a child who shunned human contact. To look at her now as she sat playing with another little girl, Brighde Macphee, whose parents had changed the spelling of their own last name years earlier in order to differentiate their family from his, could only be called a miracle.

The two of them together were the picture of innocence, skipping together in a circle beneath the flickering light of the rush torch beside them, their faces kissed with smiles, their eyes alight with excitement. It was just one of so many revelations that had touched this special Michaelmas.

What was it, he wondered, that was so very different? Was it simply the festive mood of the day? The thankfulness for the abundant harvest? But even as he wondered this, Gabriel knew the reason for this sudden rebirth stood now among the line of dancers, clapping her hands in time to the music, the torchlight reflected in those incredible green eyes.

She called herself Miss Nell Harte; but he called her the answer to a prayer. He had hired her in hopes that she would prove a suitable governess for Juliana, someone who would teach her the social accomplishments she would need to one day be wife and mother.

Instead, the woman had proven herself a virtual angel in disguise.

Gabriel watched Eleanor quietly now as she linked hands with Young Donald MacNeill amid the burgeoning circle of the other dancers, trying to mimic the steps of a lively reel she had only just learned, laughing at herself when she misstepped and trod upon his toes. Her thistledown laughter was like music to his ears, a madrigal that had been unspoken at this castle too long. Her smile shone brighter than the harvest moon overhead . . .

"I ken what ye're thinkin', laird."

Gabriel broke from his musings, looking beside himself to where Donald MacNeill had suddenly appeared. He arched a bland brow. "You can read thoughts now, can you, MacNeill?"

The man simply stared at him, seeing right through his weak attempt at detachment. "Have I no' known ye since we were lads, laird?"

"Aye, you have."

"Did I no' fight with ye at Corunna 'gainst that demon Napoleon?"

"Aye, you did."

"Then I think I can say that I ken wha' ye're thinkin' "

There were few on the island who would dare speak so openly to Gabriel, just as there were few who knew Gabriel, really knew the true MacFeagh, and not the legendary Dark Lord of Dunevin that the people on the mainland filled their children's nightmares with.

MacNeill fell quiet for a moment, then added, "If my Donald was ten years older, you'd have you a sure fight on yer hands. I think the lad's smitten wit' her."

Gabriel turned to look at MacNeill, his expression suddenly grave. "And a better man for her he'd be."

Donald shook his head, scratching his rusty hair beneath his natty blue bonnet. "How is it a mon as rich as you can be so bloody stupid?"

"I ask myself that same question all the time. You would think I'd have learned well enough. I thought I had learned, with Georgiana. I let her get too close and she suffered because of it. I cannot allow myself to repeat that mistake again with this lass."

No matter how deeply she might touch my soul . . .

"Tha's not what I mean and you know it." MacNeill was getting angry now, his words sparked with feeling. "Tha' old witch's curse only has its power because you give it that power." He tapped a finger to his forehead. "You give it the power to rule you in 'ere. You fight it e'ery day in yer mind. Ye're consumed wit' it." Then he flattened his hand against the front of his woolen shirt. "But it's 'ere, in yer heart that you must finally put that curse to its rightful rest, laird. Banish it and be on wit' yer life afore you end up old and bitter, dying alone just like . . ."

"Just like my father."

MacNeill stared at him, fearing he'd gone too far, touching on a subject of great anguish for Gabriel.

The great Alexander MacFeagh had been what some would call a medical miracle, walking, talking, breathing, while devoid of any hint of a heart. Remarkably, he had lived to the ripe old age of seventy-nine that way.

Gabriel had been four the first time he remembered seeing the man, his dark hair and fierce stolid eyes sending the lad backing away to the safer haven of his mother's skirts.

"Ye've coddled the lad, woman. Look at 'im! I ne'er should 'ave given over his care to ye like I did. Should 'ave raised 'im like I did young Malcolm here, to be a mon worthy of the name MacFeagh. Ye might as well start dressing 'im in skirts and tying ribbons in 'is hair!"

With twin looks of disgust, his father and his brother had turned away from Gabriel then, their laughter echoing across the courtyard, ridiculing him as they went.

It was another three years before he saw his father again. Never again did he back away from him, but Malcolm had grown into manhood, as fierce and heartless a man as their father, and so Alexander had had no need for another son.

Gabriel looked out at the swirling sea of dancers on the courtyard while silently considering Donald's words. Most of his life, he had been surrounded by people who had either feared, ridiculed, or reviled him. His mother had died shortly after he'd turned seven and from then, he was sent away to a series of boarding schools. No one had ever dared believe in him.

Until he met Eleanor.

Since she had come into his life, he found himself wondering what it would be like to have someone to share this island with, someone who held his same affinity for its people and their ways. He imagined being with a woman who wouldn't flinch when he touched her, who set his pulse to racing just with a simple look from her bottomless green eyes. How easy it could be, he thought, watching as Eleanor linked arms now with old Angus, taking a twirl with the ruddy-cheeked Scotsman while Màiri and the others around her cheered. How easy it would be for him to fall in love with her . . .

But he could not erase the history no matter how much he wished it, the dark history that yet plagued him and that put her at such great risk.

Gabriel noticed that the dancing had stopped and everyone was moving off from the center of the courtyard to sit at the tables or stand off in the evening shadows. He saw Eleanor making her way to the small dais where the piper and the fiddlers had assembled, carrying something tucked under her arm.

Màiri came forward from the crowd then to stand and face the others.

"Aye, but ye're all in fer a treat now, you are. It took

some doing"—she glanced at Eleanor beside her, smiling—
"but I've managed to convince this sweet lass to share the
talent she has that she's been hiding from us all."

Talent? Gabriel found himself sitting more forward on
his seat. He watched as Eleanor came to stand at the front of
the musician's platform. In her hands she held something
slender and dark. When she lifted it up to her mouth, he realized it was a flute she meant to play. The entire courtyard
hushed as she took her first soft note.

The dulcet tones of an old Scottish air familiar to
everyone seated there drifted sweetly from her fingertips,
whispering across the courtyard, filling the air with ancient magic, and entrancing everyone seated before her.
Like the famed piper of Hamlin, her sweet music drew
each listener in, each note of her plaintive tune rushing
across the assembly like a siren's song carried by the drifting wind.

Gabriel stood, completely forgetting Donald MacNeill
behind him as he walked slowly from the shadows, spellbound as she played on, her eyes closed, lashes resting
lightly on her cheeks, more evidence indeed that she was an
earthly angel, for only in heaven could such sweet music be
heard.

Not typically a ladies' instrument, Eleanor played the
flute as though she'd been born to it, her fingers moving easily over the keys. Many around the courtyard had closed
their eyes, swaying softly to the rhythm of the breathy
melody. Others simply stared as if afraid to so much as blink
lest the vision before them suddenly vanish.

When she finished, ending the lilting tune on one gentle,
sweet note, there was silence for a long moment afterward.
Nobody moved or uttered a sound. It was as if she had lulled
them into a dream. Then, as if those assembled were sud-

denly shaken from that dream, they applauded, cheering out, standing and surrounding her with their praise.

Eleanor smiled shyly, bowing her head before she turned to back off the dais.

"Nae, doona go just yet," called the piper, who struck up a lively tune, accompanied by the fiddler. "Play wit' us, lassie!"

Eleanor stood as they began to play and listened for a few moments, following the tune, memorizing its notes. After the first chorus, she joined in and everyone got up at once to dance. Just as quickly as the mood had shifted to one of softness and whispers, it had turned back to the liveliness and vigor of before.

Gabriel saw Màiri standing off to the side of the dancing with Seòna beside her, watching the dancers as they whirled and skipped. Quietly, he walked over to them.

"Good e'ening, laird," Màiri said warmly. "A fine *cuideachd* we're havin'. Is no' Miss Harte a bonny fine musician?"

Gabriel couldn't seem to take his eyes off Eleanor as she played, her expression alight as she tossed her head with the trill of her tune. "Yes, she is quite an accomplished flutist. I had no idea."

Màiri grinned. "Nae a'one of us did. I only happened to be walkin' out one night late and heard the loveliest of strains coming from out on the hillside. I thought to me'self that it must be the faeries for who else could there be making such magical music on a moonlit night? I stole closer to catch a wee look at them and was astounded when I found not any o' the wee folk, but our own young miss sitting atop a big stone, playing a lovely song all alone. She said she'd played her fife since she were a wee lassie, that it often gave her ease, but that she mostly played for hersel'. It took a lot o' convincin' to get her to play for us all t'night."

"Well, I'm pleased you did."

Gabriel watched then as Eleanor, who had finished playing with the others, crossed the courtyard, heading for the door that led inside the castle. He waited through the next dance, and when she didn't immediately return, he decided to follow after her.

Excusing himself from Màiri and Seòna, he headed for the castle door.

Màiri glanced sidelong at Seòna, her mouth touched with a small grin. "Keep the gillie occupied for a while, won't you, Seòna dear? His master will no' be needin' him tagging along behind 'im this night."

Seòna nodded knowingly, and headed across the yard to where Fergus was sitting with some of the other islanders, chatting over a mug of ale. Always a most resourceful lass, she soon had the man engaged in a conversation that he had no hope of extricating himself from.

Her work done, Màiri glanced up at the top window in the castle tower, whispering to herself, "St. Michael, if ye're a'listenin', 'tis time fer you to work your magic."

Eleanor placed the separate pieces of her flute inside its velvet-lined case, smoothing a fond hand against the polished rosewood and silver keys that still shined as if new, before tucking it back inside the chest of drawers in her small chamber. Despite her initial reluctance, it had felt good to play, to lose herself in the music, to be a part of the celebration of this very special day.

She stopped for a moment, smiling as she thought back on the happy scene yet engaged outside, the ending of a time of coming together for all, and the hope for a new beginning, too.

She turned for the door and started down the hall to leave, but hesitated outside the open door of the schoolroom. Across the room at the window, she could see the glow from the torchlight in the courtyard, could hear the laughter of the revelers and the plucky tune of the fiddle, echoing into the night.

She crossed the floor to the window seat Juliana was so fond of and looked out onto the scene below. She soon spotted Juliana sitting with Màiri and Brìghde, and smiled to herself. Of all the wonderful things of that day, theirs had to be the most special. Somehow, through the grace of God, or St. Michael, or all the angels in the heavens, Juliana had found a friend.

It was inexplicable. All day, the two girls had interacted with one another as easily as if they were carrying on a conversation, but Juliana never had to speak a word or even make a gesture. Brìghde, whom Eleanor found to be a most precocious child, spoke to Juliana, answered her, questioned her, and somehow knew exactly what she would have said had she said it herself. It was as if Juliana had spent all those years of silent anguish in isolation waiting for this one girl, and from the moment they'd met, it had all magically melted away as the two of them played and danced the night away together.

It was just one of the mysterious things that happened on this distant island for which there was no reason, no logical explanation. Wee folk, faeries, kelpies, even ghosts that wandered aimlessly in the mists at night, there was something about this place that seemed somehow supernatural, an ancient spirituality, an enchantment that made the impossible seem possible and had one believing in things they'd never believed in before.

It was that same Gaelic mysticism that had given Eleanor's heart over to Gabriel.

All through the day, her thoughts had been only of him, wondering what he would do, what he would say if he knew her true feelings. She wished she could look in a pool of water, or a cup of tea like one of those fortune tellers who set up tents at the country fairs, and see what the future held for her, for them.

As she sat looking out on the castle courtyard, she remembered something Màiri had told her earlier that day, that if a maid said the name of the man she loved to the St. Michael's moon, he would come to her in a dream.

Silently, Eleanor stood before the window, staring up at the moon and the stars and endless heavens stretching out over the turbulent sea, and whispered softly to herself.

"*. . . Gabriel.*"

Almost in the same moment, she heard a soft sound behind her. She turned and her breath left her in a rush of wistful disbelief when she saw Gabriel suddenly standing there before her.

The dream had come true.

She didn't speak. Nor did he. Cloaked in the near darkness, they simply stared at one another in silence.

He looked like a spectral vision, all cloaked in shadows and silvery light. Was he real? Or was he some flight of her imagination? At that very moment, Eleanor didn't even care. Just looking at him, having him near, made her heart race and her breath come in quick gasps.

Gabriel crossed the room slowly, coming to stand before her at the window. His eyes watched her closely, his features etched in the muted moonlight, bold, bewitching, clearly chiseled. He looked as if he wanted to say something, but knew not what.

It was precisely the way she felt, too.

To convince herself that he wasn't a wildering dream, Eleanor reached up and touched Gabriel tenderly on the side of his face, tracing her fingertips along the scuff of his jaw, delighting in the texture, the roughness, the *maleness* of him. His eyes held hers captive, his skin was warm to the touch, and she could see the beat of his heart pulsing steadily against his throat.

She wondered what it would be like to put her mouth against it. She wondered if it were possible for her to take flame just standing before him. Until he stepped even closer, to where his legs, bare beneath the kilt, brushed her skirts, taking her face on either side with his great hands and tipping her mouth upward for his kiss.

And then she wondered no more.

Eleanor closed her eyes and utterly melted against him, flattening her hands against the cambric that covered the heat and hardness of his chest as he kissed her more deeply than she could have possibly imagined.

He smelled of the open air, salty and new, and of the smoke from the rush fires that burned even now on the courtyard beneath them. She felt his hands curve around to the back of her neck, raking upward through her hair to dislodge its pins, caressing her until his fingers were overflowing with a riot of loosened curls.

Eleanor dropped her head back into the cradle of his hands, arching her neck, drawing in a breath deeply as he moved his lips downward, over the line of her chin, her neck, to bury his face in the curve of her shoulder. Her skin tingled with life, her limbs had turned to limpid honey, and she felt herself falling with him as he lowered them both onto the scattered cushions of the window seat behind him.

"Oh, lass, we shouldna be doing this."

His burr was more pronounced now, mesmerizing her as it rolled so easily off his tongue.

Eleanor rose up before him, sitting on her knees, and reached for him, sliding her hands around his waist. She rested the side of her face against the solid warmth of his chest and whispered to the night.

"I wished for you to come to me in a dream, and now you are here. Do not wake us from it so soon, Gabriel. Forget about the rest of the world outside this room for now. Forget who I am. Forget who you are. Let us just have this one night to keep us for the rest of our lives."

They were all the words he needed to hear.

Gabriel took Eleanor up in a move of pure desperation and dragged his mouth across the tender flesh of her shoulder, tasting her, caressing her with his tongue as his hands trailed down from her hair to work the small buttons that lined the back of her gown. She felt the bodice loosen around her, felt it fall beneath the pressure of his mouth, and arched her back, wanting it gone, wanting nothing between them but his mouth and his hands on her breasts.

The moment he touched her, closing his hand over her fullness, Eleanor was seized by a riot of breathtaking sensations. They whirled throughout her body, causing her to draw him as closely to her as possible. She wanted to touch him everywhere, to know his body like her own. She wanted him to touch her, wanted him to keep touching her and never, ever stop.

She threaded her fingers through the silky darkness of his hair and gasped out loud when she felt his mouth on her breasts, nuzzling her, tasting her, suckling her until she thought she would cry out from the intense pleasure of it. She pressed her hips closer against him, desperate for fulfillment, and moved with him as he shifted them on the window bench, easing her back onto the cushioned seat as he came to stand before her cast in muted moonlit shadow, all heat and magic and utterly man.

He looked anxious. He looked uncertain. He looked as disconcerted by the fire between them as she was.

"I love you, Gabriel."

The words were spoken even before she realized she had said them. Her heart stilled for the briefest of moments as she watched his face timidly for his response.

Perhaps it was the darkness, the shadows, the play of the light, but it looked almost as if his expression had suddenly shifted from one of intensity and desperate desire to stunned denial. A chill fell over the room, dousing the flame that had burned between them with one swift sweep.

"Gabriel . . . ?"

He shook his head. "You don't know what it is you're saying."

"But I do know. I've never known anything more."

He broke away, closing his eyes. His fists were clenched tightly at his sides, and Eleanor felt the pall of his rejection all the way to her soul.

She wrapped her arms around herself, covering her nakedness, suddenly shamed in the face of his unyielding response.

He didn't return her love.

Gabriel looked at Eleanor and cursed out loud in Gaelic at the darkness, striking his hand against the hard surface of the wall where Juliana had painted her mural. "Damnation, lass, it cannot be. It can never be. Don't you see? I cannot

forget who we are, no matter how much I might want to. It
can never be."

Tears welled thickly in Eleanor's eyes, swelling, burning,
spilling down her face, and inside, deep inside, something
twisted painfully.

She just stared at him, silent, awash with humiliation and
heartbreak, her throat so tight she couldn't utter a word as he
turned, vanishing from the room just as quickly as he had
come, as if waking from a dream, leaving her sitting alone
and forsaken at the window.

Chapter Fourteen

Gabriel looked with bleary eyes on the despairing darkness of his study.

He blinked to clear away his fatigue, and glanced quickly at the small clock on the table beside him, reading its face in the muted moonlight.

It was early morning, closing in on dawn. The hearth at his feet no longer so much as flickered, unattended the past hours that he'd spent slumped in his chair, locked behind the isolation of his closed door, trying to banish the image of Eleanor's vulnerable and stricken eyes from his memory.

The copious quantity of brandy he'd drunk earlier had not numbed his senses as he had hoped it would. Instead it had given him a splitting headache behind thoughts that remained too damnably clear for his liking. He had wanted to lose himself, lose his thoughts and regrets in a dim drunken haze. He had wanted to surround himself with obscurity and darkness, anything to put what had happened, what he'd done—what he'd *not* done—forever out of his mind.

But nothing he'd tried, not the brandy, nor the darkness, nor the sullen isolation, had succeeded, and he knew no amount of denial would ever take away that last moment between them, the hopeful sound of her voice when she'd spoken those three telling words.

I love you . . .

It was the first time in his life, that he could remember hearing those words from someone other than his mother. They were words that offered everything of another person, their heart, their body, even their soul, words that made up poetry, filled pages in books, became plays acted upon the world's stage.

They were words that asked and hoped, begged and waited—waited for an expression of the same feeling in return, words that were a most precious gift, but that because of the past, he could never allow himself to accept.

As he sat in that chair, glaring at the carpet beneath his feet, Gabriel cursed the bloody ancestor who had brought this darkness down on all of them centuries before. It was fortunate the man was already dead, for at that moment, Gabriel felt certain he could kill him.

But he couldn't, he knew, do anything more about it, except . . .

Incensed, Gabriel got up from his chair and crossed the room to the corner trunk, bent on taking the damnable scroll of parchment that had haunted him and his ancestors so unbearably long and consign it to the place it truly belonged— the crimson fires of hell.

Gabriel yanked at the key, breaking the silver chain from around his neck, and unlocked the trunk to open it. Taking up the scroll from inside, he read the ancient witch's words one final woeful time.

*For nine hundred years, and then one hundred more,
any creature or beast you allow past your heart's
door, will soon slip away and suffer death's most
telling stone, while helpless you watch on, forsaken
and alone. Only here on this misty isle might the*

*truth be found, St. Colomb's staff will loose the curse
by which you are bound. One of pure heart and
eye will right the wrongs of the past, to bring
about an end to the suffering at last!*

Nine hundred years be damned, witch!

With a sour sneer, Gabriel dropped the lid down on the trunk with a hollow thud and turned for the hearth behind him. But he stopped in midstride when he noticed Cudu getting suddenly to his feet and trotting over to the door. He sniffed at the space underneath, whining softly, and turned to look at Gabriel in the moonlight. He pressed his nose to the door again and sniffed some more. After several more whimpers, and an insistent scratch, the dog gave out a mournful, unearthly moan.

"Dè tha ceárr, Cudu?"

Gabriel walked over to him to see what was the matter.

The dog scratched at the door again, groaning at Gabriel to open it. As soon as he turned the handle, Cudu darted through, moving swifter than Gabriel had ever seen him go, heading at once to the tower stairs across the hall.

As a rule, the dog was historically indifferent—very little if anything ever disturbed him, thus Gabriel decided he would follow to see what had caused the beast to become so uneasy.

He never even realized when he dropped the tattered scroll to the carpet.

They clambered up the first flight of tower stairs and the moment Gabriel opened the door at the top, Cudu sprinted off down the hall, heading in a straight line for the next set of stairs as if he were somehow mysteriously being summoned there.

He did the same when they reached the third level, and it

was as they were coming to the door at the top of the stairs that opened onto the fourth level that Gabriel first noticed the acrid smell of smoke.

He pulled the door open and Cudu scrambled through, rushing to the last set of stairs—the stairs that led to the nursery level.

Gabriel felt a moment of true panic.

The circular stairwell that led to the nursery was filled with white smoke that billowed and grew the nearer he came to the top of the stairs. At the last step, in the moonlight from a window set high in the wall, he could see that more smoke was seeping from underneath the small door.

Cudu was panting more from upset than exhaustion, scratching at the stone beneath the door as if to dig his way through.

"Gabh nam," Gabriel said, shooing the dog away.

He reached for the door handle, noticing it was warm to the touch. When he tried to turn it, he found the door staunchly locked.

Gabriel stared at the door, baffled for the moment. Something wasn't right. How? How had the door gotten locked? He hadn't even known there was a key.

He jiggled the handle again, pummeling the door in a moment of frustration when it refused to yield. He let go a breath and told himself to remain calm.

Perhaps Eleanor had found a key somewhere, in her chamber or in the nursery room, and had locked the door as a measure of safety.

Safety from what?

Gabriel pounded on the door.

"Eleanor! Juliana! Can you hear me?"

There came no response, but he could hear a faint crackling sound coming from the other side of the door—like fire feeding on wood.

Bracing himself against the solid wall of the tower behind him, Gabriel lifted his foot and kicked at the door hard, once, twice, before it finally gave, slamming open on the other side. He felt a wave of raw heat roll against him from the other side, his panic running over when he saw the flames licking at the walls of the schoolroom, reaching out for the hallway in front of him.

Gabriel shouted out again, calling for Eleanor and Juliana both, but there came no reply. He ran for the first door, Eleanor's chamber, and slammed himself against it, shouting out her name again.

The room was dark inside, no window to light it, and filled with so much smoke he could barely see.

"Eleanor!"

There came no answer and he crossed the room, kicking at the furnishings, tossing anything he encountered out of his way, only to find an empty bed.

"Damnation!"

Gabriel turned and rushed for Juliana's door further down the hall. Again he found the bed empty. Where in God's name were they? He looked down the hall to where the flames burned steadily in the schoolroom.

Oh God, no . . .

He tried to go in, shouting out to them again, but the fire was too great, the smoke too thick, the heat from it all too intense. What if they were inside, somehow unable to answer him? With the door to the stairs locked as it was, their only other way out would have been the window. But it was barred. They wouldn't have been able to escape. Could they be lying there among the smoke and flames unconscious? They had to be. Where else could they have gone?

Gabriel snatched the coverlet from Eleanor's bed and began to beat at the flames, trying futilely to fight his way inside the room. He needed someone else to help but daren't leave them. As he attacked the flames again, he heard a voice coming suddenly distant to him.

"Gabriel?"

He stilled, listening in the darkness. "Eleanor? Where are you?"

"I am at the stairs."

The stairs? His confusion was immediately superceded by his profound relief that she was safe. "Juliana?"

"She is with me. What is happening?"

"Run down to the courtyard and find Fergus and anyone else who is still there. Tell them there is a fire in the schoolroom."

Blessedly, a good many of the islanders had decided to spend the night in the courtyard or in the stables rather than make the long trek home in the darkness to the opposite sides of the isle. Soon they had a team of them running buckets of water up each flight of stairs while others still dropped ropes from the windows on the middle castle floors.

Fergus soon joined Gabriel and together they alternated running buckets up to the nursery floor to try to douse the fire. When he managed to advance far enough into the room to see, Gabriel threw a chair across the room, breaking out the window to allow the smoke to escape.

Outside on the courtyard, Eleanor gasped, watching the glass from the window fall and the smoke billow against the castle tower overhead. The orange light from the fire glowed menacingly against the dark, early-morning sky. She tried to think of what could have possibly caused the fire to start, especially so late in the night. She and Juliana had been out of the nursery all day, involved with the Michaelmas festivi-

ties, so the hearth had never even been lit. When they had
left the nursery that night, she had taken the candle with
them to light their way down the stairs.

Some time later, the smoke coming from behind the bars
of the window had slowed to a scuddlng drift. Inside, the
flames had mercifully been extinguished.

It had taken hours to put out the fire; dawn was now
breaking on the eastern horizon, shining its colorful mixture
of morning light through the drifting haze of dulling smoke.
Out in the courtyard, Màiri flitted about like a nervous
mother hen, bringing damp cloths from the kitchen to wipe
soot from faces and fresh water to ease the smoke-stung
throats of those who were seated about.

As she stood there, looking around at all the faces,
Eleanor said a silent prayer of thanks. If not for the help of
the other islanders, the fire would surely yet burn, and the
ancient stronghold of Dunevin would have been destroyed.

Eleanor didn't see Gabriel when he first came out into the
courtyard, but when she noticed him talking with Fergus by
the stables, she nearly started to cry. His clothing was
scorched, his face indelibly blackened from the fire and he
looked ready to drop from exhaustion. Still, he stayed out in
the courtyard for some time, thanking each one of the islanders who had taken part in the salvage, informing them
all that because of their efforts, the fire had been successfully confined to the uppermost tower floor.

They were all very fortunate. With the exception of a few
minor burns and some stinging eyes, there had been no in-
juries. Though the damage in the schoolroom was extensive,
the rest of the castle remained intact. It would take quite a
bit of effort, but the nursery could be rebuilt.

Later that day, Eleanor sat quietly in the study, absently

browsing through the titles in the library while Juliana napped, when Gabriel finally approached her.

"I had hoped to find you here," he said, coming into the room behind her.

Nearly all evidence of the events of that morning were now gone. Gabriel had bathed and changed his clothing, although his face still bore a certain redness from the intense heat of the fire. His expression, however, looked as if he carried the very weight of the world upon his shoulders.

Eleanor set aside the book she'd been reading, and came down from the library steps. "I had thought to do some reading while Juliana napped. I had hoped to talk to you as well."

"And I you." He looked at her. "But, please, you first."

Eleanor took the seat before his desk, folding her hands gently into her lap. The gesture suddenly brought to mind the first day she had come to the isle, the apprehension she had felt at meeting him, the anxiousness of starting a new life in an unknown place. How long ago that seemed now. How different things were, so very different.

She looked up at Gabriel and was seized by the memory of the night before, his arms around her, his mouth to hers, not a handful of hours earlier. She tried to forget the humiliation of having blurted out her inmost emotions so stupidly, tried to forget the sorrow of watching him turn away from her in disgust. How utterly ridiculous she must have seemed to him, professing her love when what had happened between them was probably no more to him than a dalliance between master and servant.

Eleanor drew herself up to face him, keeping her voice clear, calm, and matter of fact. "I wanted to talk to you because I'm sure you are wondering why Juliana and I were sleeping in the viscountess's chamber last night and not in the nursery."

"The reasons why matter very little now against my utter relief that you were."

"Still, I think you need to hear my explanation, if only for Juliana's sake."

Eleanor paused, searching for the right words. "The first night I came to Dunevin, I discovered Juliana missing from her bed in the middle of the night. I eventually found her in her mother's chamber, and instead of forcing her to return upstairs to the nursery, I decided it would be better to allow her to remain. It was obvious she had been going there for some time. I gathered that sleeping in the bed of her mother offered her some sort of comfort. So, instead, I stayed with her."

"Right down the hall from me every night." Gabriel shook his head sadly, "I had no idea she was going there."

"I don't think anybody did. But how fortunate it is that she had after the accident of the fire last night."

"Yes. The fire." Gabriel sat in the chair beside her. "That is what I wanted to talk to you about. That fire was no accident, Eleanor. It was set—deliberately."

Eleanor took a moment to fully grasp what he was implying. "How can you be so sure?"

"The door leading to the nursery off the stairs was locked—from the outside. I'm assuming you didn't lock it when you came down to Georgiana's chamber."

Eleanor shook her head.

"So that would indicate someone else had locked it—with the intent to keep you and Juliana inside. Had you both been there, with the window barred as it was, you would have been unable to escape."

He paused a moment before going on, "There is more. I

also found a candlestick turned onto its side on the floor in the nursery room where the fire was started."

"A candle? But who would—?" Eleanor looked at him then, knowing his thoughts immediately. "You suspect Seamus Maclean is responsible for the fire?"

"He was very cross after losing the race yesterday morning. In fact he left without returning. He did not participate in the games, nor did he come later for the feast and the dancing. No one has seen him since he ran in the race yesterday morning."

"Perhaps he returned to the mainland."

Gabriel shook his head. "Unless he swam there, we would have seen him sailing out of the bay. Because of the range of the currents off the channel, the jetty is the only safe place to disembark from the whole of the isle."

"But his parents. Surely they can tell you if he was with them last night at their croft after the *cuideachd*."

"I have already sent Fergus off to bring them here to Dunevin so I can question them, with Seamus if he is with them. We should know very soon just where Maclean was when the fire broke out."

Gabriel stood then, circling to his desk. "In the meantime, however, I have come to a decision." He looked at her. "A decision that effects both you and Juliana. I have decided to send you both to London to stay until the repairs on the castle are made and I have determined who it was who set that fire and can handle the matter accordingly."

"London?" Eleanor didn't bother to hide her dismay at his unexpected announcement. "But why so far away?"

"Because it is far enough that Seamus Maclean cannot harm you there. It isn't just the fire, Eleanor, but the incident with the hemlock, too. I cannot take a chance a third time. It is better this way. There will be no possibility of him reaching you there."

"You believe it is me he seeks to harm?"

Gabriel looked at her. "Both incidents have directly involved you. I cannot pretend to deny it is a possibility. Nor can I fail to do whatever I can to protect Juliana either. So to London you will go. With the ready resources in the city, you can continue Juliana's education there more adequately than you can here. I own a house there, part of the Dunevin viscountcy. It is usually let to others for the Season, but at this time of year, it is always vacant. I will draft a letter for you to take to my solicitor, Mr. George Pratt on Buckingham Street. He will assist you with hiring the necessary staff and will secure you whatever funds you might need."

"It sounds as if you mean us to stay there for some time."

"It could take some time to repair the damage from the fire."

Eleanor frowned. "Somehow I believe that is an excuse."

Gabriel shook his head. "Call it whatever you prefer, Eleanor, but I've made my decision."

Eleanor's emotions started to get the better of her, her eyes stinging with the threat of tears. She blinked them back. Annoyed at herself for giving in to such an utterly female response, she got up from her chair and crossed the room to stand at the window.

She stood for several minutes, arms crossed before her, watching as Angus, the groomsman, took the ponies out from the stables to graze on the machair while he mucked out their stalls. She thought to herself that she had planned to teach Juliana to ride the little gray one, a sweet little mare Angus called "buckie-faalie," the local name for the primroses she was so fond of eating.

There were so many things she had planned for them to

do. She had hoped to pass some of the coming winter months teaching Juliana how to stitch her first sampler. And they were supposed to help Màiri make conserve from the cloudberry and bramble they had gathered.

Now they would be a world away from this place.

Eleanor spotted Màiri below the window then, hanging out the laundry to dry on the branches of the elder trees that grew around her herb garden. Eleanor and Juliana's clothing had smelled so strongly of the smoke from the fire that Màiri had had to use poppy root and bracken ash to dispel its pithy trace. Eleanor mused bitterly that she had promised Màiri she would help her with the chore.

Instead, she was going to be packing it all away to go to London—the very place she had run from.

Eleanor turned from the window, angry at the way things were turning out, angry at Gabriel, too. "You are doing this because of me."

Gabriel knit his brow. "You?"

"Yes, because of what I said to you last night." She started back for her chair, lowering into it. She tempered her cross tone. "I'm sorry. I should never have said that to you."

"That has nothing to do with it, Eleanor."

"It has everything to do with it. I acted improperly. But please don't punish Juliana by sending her away from the only home she has ever known because of my indiscretion."

Gabriel's eyes darkened, his expression turning suddenly vague. He stared at her for some time, not moving, not saying a word, as if he were at war with his own private thoughts.

Finally he spoke. "There is something you need to know," he said quietly then. "The hemlock, the fire; these are not simply coincidental accidents, Eleanor."

Eleanor's pulse thudded at his suddenly ominous, seemingly remorseful tone. What was Gabriel saying? She sat at the edge of her seat, waiting for him to continue, trying to ignore the cold shiver that was making itself felt along her arms and neck.

Gabriel got up from his chair and walked to the far corner of the room, where he stood before a large, very old-looking wooden trunk covered by a faded tapestry table cloak. She wondered how she had never noticed the trunk before as she watched him take a key from a chain around his neck and open its lid. He removed something from inside then and turned to face her.

Gabriel said nothing, simply handed her a small, worn, very old-looking scroll of parchment.

Eleanor took it, carefully unrolling it. The words written upon it were in Gaelic and she could only make out some of what it said, words like "nine hundred years" and "death" and "curse" and something about St. Columba's staff.

Eleanor looked up at Gabriel, confused. "I do not understand. What is this?"

Gabriel shook his head. "I forgot you cannot read Gaelic."

"I understood some of it. Something about a curse and St. Columba's staff. This looks very old, as if it were written centuries ago."

"It was."

Gabriel reached for the scroll to take it, as if just by holding it, it could somehow harm Eleanor.

He sat in the chair beside her. "Do you remember yesterday morning, when we made the circuit to the Dunevin graveyard?"

She nodded.

"I'm sure it couldn't have escaped your notice that the MacFeagh ancestry have some of them met with early and untimely deaths. It certainly escapes nobody else's notice, least of all mine."

Again, she simply nodded.

"No doubt you have been told that a good many people believe we, the MacFeaghs, somehow sinisterly do away with our own."

Gabriel glanced at her briefly before continuing. "It is an observable fact that the people of my family die, often and quite young. It is a sequence that has been repeated time and again. It will seem to stop for a while, but inevitably, it begins anew. And in a manner of speaking, it was the MacFeaghs who brought it on."

Gabriel then related for Eleanor the story of his unfortunate ancestor and the Jura witch who had saved him and then set down the curse that would punish him and his kind forever, finishing with the legend of the St. Columba staff that had vanished so many years before. "And since that time, whenever a MacFeagh laird has allowed himself to care for someone close to him, they have died through mysterious circumstances.

"And she left behind this?" Eleanor asked, motioning toward the scroll.

Gabriel nodded. "Since this has been going on for some time now, you can surely understand why people believe I, and my ancestors, are, well, *demons*."

Eleanor fell silent, thoughtful for the moment, ruminating on the incredible story she'd just been told. Of anyone else, at any other place in the world, she would immediately have thought the tale a made-up deception, a farcical effort to explain away something much more nefarious.

But not on this isle—and not with this man.

"I was just about to burn that damned thing last night before I discovered the fire in the nursery."

Eleanor looked in his eyes and saw fear there. "Is there a part of you that believes the fire happened because you had decided to destroy the scroll?"

Gabriel didn't answer. He didn't need to.

Eleanor sat face-to-face with the torture, the anguish he had lived with throughout his entire life, and could only think of one thing to say in response.

"Then do it, Gabriel. Do just that. Burn this horrible piece of history so you never have to read its vengeful litany again."

She swept up the scroll from his desk and held it out to him. "I will do it with you."

Gabriel looked at Eleanor as if she'd just run mad. But then, after only the barest moment of uncertainty, he took the scroll and walked with her to the hearth.

They stood facing the slumbering fire that burned in the iron grate. Eleanor watched Gabriel, watched the play of emotions across his face, fear, acceptance, resolution. And then slowly, Gabriel extended his hand and dropped the scroll onto the fire.

After a moment, they saw it catch, waited while it took flame, and continued to stand and watch until there was nothing left but smoke and ash.

A calm came over the room, like the most peaceful spring morning. Nothing terrible had happened to them because of what they'd done, there was no supernatural retribution. Instead, there was quiet, and warmth, and a feeling of absolute righteousness.

"I could tolerate it," Gabriel said softly to the fire, "if it were only myself who had been touched by it. But that damnable curse stole my daughter's mother from her when she needed her most, it stole her voice, and now it threatens to steal my daughter as well."

Gabriel looked back at Eleanor, his eyes filled with stark grief. Eleanor thought she would weep from it.

"Georgiana's family has written," he said, his voice rough with emotion, "threatening to petition the Crown for custody of Juliana if I do not relinquish her to their care. It is not out of any concern for her that they do this. Georgiana left a sizeable inheritance to Juliana that she will be due upon reaching her majority. I promised Georgiana long before she died that if anything ever happened to her, I would never allow her family to take our daughter. Georgiana's upbringing was one of nothing but abuse and she feared every day that Juliana would somehow face the same, almost as if she knew what would someday happen."

"Can they possibly take her?" Eleanor asked.

"I've corresponded with my solicitor who tells me that he doesn't believe the Crown would forsake the rights of a father to his child, but there is the chance that Georgiana's family will accuse me of her murder. With my family's less than sterling reputation, and with the fact that Juliana will no longer speak, my solicitor cannot guarantee what the outcome would be. They will say I have abused her in some way to keep her from speaking. They will say anything in pursuit of their greed. They could make rigorous attempts to force her to speak out against me. At the very least, a scandal would most certainly come about the likes of which has never been seen against a peer, and it would ruin Juliana's chances for a happy, secure future."

Eleanor shook her head. "Scandal. Damnable scandal."

"It was for that reason I hired you to be her governess," he went on, "in hopes that if she could be taught the best social skills, I could somehow stave off Georgiana's family long enough to see Juliana safely married." He scoffed then.

"As if the fact that she doesn't ever speak wouldn't be enough to keep any man worthy of her away."

As he'd spoken, pouring out the anguish he'd kept locked away for so many years—too, too many years—Eleanor dawned on something so elementary, so patently obvious, but something Gabriel somehow refused to acknowledge.

No matter how much he tried to tell himself he didn't, he *did* love his daughter with every shred of his entire being. No man who cared nothing for another would trouble so very much, would carry the staggering burden he had for so long.

She realized, too, that it was for this very reason he had reacted the way he had the night before when she had revealed that she loved him. It was the words he feared, those three simple little words. Somehow, it was as if he believed that by speaking those words, admitting to them, it would call the wrath of the demons of the past upon him.

Realizing this, Eleanor was suddenly filled with a sense of new, dauntless hope—and a perfect and logical solution to it all.

She looked at Gabriel, sitting up straight in her chair. Facing him openly, she spoke the words that suddenly filled her heart to bursting.

"Then as I see it, you have only one choice in the matter. You must marry me, Gabriel."

Chapter Fifteen

Gabriel looked at Eleanor as if he now did truly believe she'd just run stark-raving mad.

"What did you just say?"

Eleanor stared at him. "I believe I just proposed marriage to you."

She fell silent a moment as if to come to terms with what she had just done. "But if you think about it, really, it is the best solution to your predicament. With a wife, and a mother for Juliana, Georgiana's family wouldn't stand any chance of succeeding with a petition to the Crown. You said yourself she needs a mother's influence. You must know how much I care for her; she means everything to me, and you must have seen how she responds to me."

Gabriel shook his head. "Of course I have, but did you hear nothing of what I just told you? About my family history? About the fact that my family members have been mysteriously dying for centuries?"

Eleanor refused to back down. "Yes, Gabriel, I heard every word of what you said, but I am choosing not to be dictated by it. You burnt that terrible scroll in the hearth. I watched you do it. As far as I'm concerned, it no longer even exists. Curse or no curse, you"—she corrected herself—"*we* must do whatever is necessary to make certain

Juliana doesn't come to harm at the hands of those despicable people."

Gabriel fell silent. His expression was troubled as he became lost to his thoughts. It was only then Eleanor realized there was something more, something else she had forgotten in all her enthusiasm, that could very well prevent them from marrying.

She had to tell him the truth of her illegitimacy.

"Gabriel, you just told me something terrible about yourself, about your past, but something over which you had no control, despite the fact that it affected your life very much. Before you make any decision about what I have proposed, there is something you first need to know about me."

Eleanor reached for the folded scrap of paper she had tucked inside her pocket. It was the notice she had taken from the inn wall in Oban, the one offering the reward for her return. She had found it earlier that day when she and Màiri had been gathering up the clothing that had gotten damaged by the smoke from the fire. She had hidden it away, determined to dispose of it. She decided now it would best explain what she had to say.

Gabriel took up the notice, barely giving it a moment's glance.

"Yes?"

Did he not realize what it said?

"Did you read it? The woman described in that notice . . . it is me, Gabriel."

He stared at her. Finally, he said, calm as day, "Are you saying I should claim the reward?"

Eleanor didn't know whether he was jesting or not. Instead she looked down at her hands, suddenly regretting she had ever lied to him, leading him to think she was someone she was not. "I just thought you should know that I am not

Miss Nell Harte." She looked back into the darkness of his eyes. "I apologize for the deception, but I . . ."

Eleanor forgot the rest of her words when she noticed Gabriel suddenly opening his desk drawer and removing something from inside. It was a scrap of paper which he then placed on the desk before her.

She looked up at him, stunned. It was a twin to the notice from Oban she had just given him.

"How long have you known?"

"Since the day we went to Oban."

Weeks had passed since then. "Yet you said nothing in all this time. Why?"

"Because I knew you must have had your reasons for wanting to keep your true identity anonymous."

"I do—or rather I did. Anymore, I just do not know." Eleanor suddenly wanted very much to unburden herself, to let go of the anger, the pain, the humiliation she had kept locked away inside herself for so long now. More than that, she wanted to tell Gabriel the truth.

"Gabriel, I left my family because I had learned that the man who I believed was my father was not, in truth, my father. I had always been told that my father had died shortly before I was born, the victim of a sudden nameless illness. I discovered in the worst of all ways that this was not true. The man the world knew to be my father, Christopher Wycliffe, had died fighting in a duel against the man who my mother had been unfaithful to him with, a man named William Hartley, Earl of Herrick."

"And?" Gabriel asked, sensing there was more.

Indeed there was.

"When these men met on the dueling field, my father—Christopher Wycliffe," she clarified, "was killed. But Lord Herrick, who had shot him, didn't leave the field that day either. He was also killed—by my brother, Lord Knighton, who had picked up my father's pistol and shot him as he was leaving. The only reason I was told any of this was because I was being courted by the heir to Lord Herrick, a man named Richard Hartley."

"A half brother you didn't know you had."

She nodded, stunned at how calm and matter-of-fact he was being. "Richard had asked me to marry him, and knowing that I could not, my brother had no other choice but to tell me the truth. If I had never met Richard, I still would not know that I am quite possibly illegitimate."

"Possibly, but not certainly."

Gabriel's eyes held hers with nothing other than clear, profound compassion. "As far as I'm concerned, you are the same person you have always believed yourself to be, Eleanor. No one can take that away from you."

His words touched her so deeply that Eleanor felt as if she might begin to cry at any moment, and so said nothing.

"That must have been very difficult for you all. Eleanor, I have heard tell of your brother, Christian, even in my limited social sphere. He is, from all accounts, a man of great honor and integrity. Since he would have been quite young at the time, I would assume, whatever the circumstances with Lord Herrick were on that dueling field, he reacted out of emotion and not with any malicious aforethought."

Eleanor nodded. "I know that now. At the time Christian told this to me, I was so hurt and felt so utterly betrayed by him and my mother, I couldn't see what this had been doing to them, the burden they had carried for over twenty years. They lived in fear each day that the truth would somehow be exposed. As you are all too aware, society can be most cruel in matters of scandal. They feared for my future. So that is why I wanted to tell you this before you made any decision about your future and Juliana's. This could all still come to light. It would be"—she searched for the right word—"difficult for any man to consider marriage to a lady everyone suspected had been born on the wrong side of the blanket."

Gabriel simply looked at her and said, "Actually, it isn't difficult at all. In fact, it's probably the easiest decision this man has ever made.

"Eleanor, I have decided to accept your proposal."

They were married along the way to London at the very place Eleanor had threatened to run away to with Richard Hartley, Gretna Green—actually a tiny hamlet of a place outside of Gretna called Springfield, just the Scottish side of the River Sark.

After inquiring locally, they were directed to The Queen's Head Inn, a tiny tumbledown "clay daubin biggin" nestled at the bottom of Springfield Hill on one side of the turnpike road to Longtown. Across the road, another public house, the Maxwell Arms, had recently set up as competition in this most lucrative venture—what was known to most as the "Clandestine Marriage" trade.

Gabriel spoke with the innkeeper, Mrs. Johnstone, a cheery woman who spoke with a hinterland dialect and who had greeted them at the door. She referred them to Mr. Robert Elliott, the local "parson," who apparently spent his days sitting in the public room of the inn, nursing a mug of ale while waiting for just such an occasion.

Mr. Elliott performed the short ceremony right in the public room of the inn with Mrs. Johnstone and her servant, Sawney, standing by as witnesses. Juliana and Brìghde attended the bride, traveling companions after Màiri had privately revealed to Eleanor that Brìghde's mother, Eibhlin, had been despairing the night of the *cuideachd* that her mother, who lived in London and who was slowly dying from an illness, had never seen the granddaughter who was named for her.

Eibhlin was in her eighth month of pregnancy and could not safely make the trip, so Eleanor had offered to take the little girl along with them so that Brìghde could meet her namesake before it was too late, much to Eibhlin's obvious gratitude.

When Mr. Elliott suddenly called for a ring to secure the legalities of the ceremony, Eleanor was startled to see Gabriel produce one from his coat pocket.

"Màiri gave this to us," he said quietly only to her. "She said it had blessed her marriage to Torquil for thirty-five years before he passed away, and so it would thus bless ours for at least twice that long."

Eleanor blinked back tears as he slid the plain gold band onto her finger. It was the most touching gift she had ever received, more precious than any jewel or diamond.

After a quick mug of ale, requisite, Mrs. Johnstone said, to toast in the new union, they were off across the border and into Cumbria by dusk.

They finally broke their journey at a benighted little village called Kirkby Lonsdale just off the main London road between the lakes and the dales of Yorkshire.

In the darkness, they couldn't see much more than the sparse candles lighting the small windows of the stone cottages that lined the winding road to the village's center. It was there they stopped to look for the closest inn.

It was market time, which unfortunately meant that all of the inns in the village were full—except one. A local farmer directed them to a small graystone building on the outskirts of town called quite simply "The Graystone," where they came upon the proprietor of the place, named fittingly enough Mr. Gray. He was a man whose appearance very much suited his name.

He had one room left to let, he told them, and the tariff included clean linen, coals for the fire, and ample servings of Mrs. Gray's own hearty breakfast for them all the next morning. The room was the best of the house, he assured them—complete with a bed that even royalty had once slept in.

"'Twas my own uncle Ethelred Gray that served Queen Elizabeth back when she were a young miss, e'en before she became our greatest queen. 'Twas she that gave him that bed from her own chamber at Hatfield, and it's been in the family ever since. I myself were born in that bed after my mother had labored for forty-two hours." He glanced at Gabriel then, adding on a wink, "We've polished it up a bit since then."

In the face of such an auspicious history and with no other choice left to them, Gabriel promptly rented the room, and without a moment to spare, for as Mrs. Gray was off preparing the room and stoking the fire, another traveler came in asking for accommodation.

They repaired abovestairs, filing down the narrow hall toward the room to which Mr. Gray had directed them. Gabriel opened the door on what would have probably been a quite comfortable chamber—had it not been utterly bulging inside with what was undoubtedly the largest bed Eleanor had ever seen.

It was a dark black walnut monstrosity of a thing, carved on every possible space, a big four-poster that would have had to have been disassembled to get it through the door and then reassembled piece by piece inside the small room. Even then, it would have been quite a chore. The finial tops of the posters grazed the low-beamed ceiling and were thicker than most tree trunks. There was scarcely enough room left in the small chamber to walk around it.

Eleanor took one look at the place and immediately began to laugh.

Gabriel, however, failed to share her amusement at the ridiculous situation.

"I'll bed down in the stables with Fergus and the driver."

"You'll do no such thing," Eleanor said, stepping in the middle of what narrow path there was between the door and the bed, preventing him from leaving. "This bed is big enough for all of us. Faith, I think it is big enough for the entire village as well." And then she looked at him and said quite seriously, "I'll not sleep alone on my wedding night, my lord."

Even if it was a wedding night that they would spend with two nine-year-olds tucked on the bed between them.

"We will be leaving early in the morning," Gabriel finally muttered, as if to say he would deign to tolerate the situation for the night only for that reason.

Eleanor laid Juliana, who had fallen asleep in the coach an hour or more before, on the middle of the downy mattress, then helped Gabriel to divest himself of a clinging Brìghde. She edged around the room and began getting herself ready for bed while leaving Gabriel to stand by, still as one of the carved posters on the bed.

Gabriel watched as Eleanor pulled the pins deftly from her hair and let it fall down her back in a free cascade, removing her pelisse and draping it neatly at the end of the bed before she kicked off her slippers and set them on the floor beneath.

Then she turned to face her new husband.

"I wonder if you would help me with the buttons on the

back of this gown," she asked casually. "I fear I might do myself an injury in these close quarters if I try to unfasten them myself."

Gabriel nodded silently as she came before him, turning her back to him. He had to push her hair away from her neck to see, sweeping it gently over one shoulder and exposing the slender line of her nape to his eyes.

His pulse bounded at the scent of her hair, floral and fresh and soft as thistledown.

Gabriel set to working the buttons, his fingers fumbling nervously as his thoughts ran wild with images of Eleanor stepping out of the gown, naked and beautiful, turning to face him with open arms. It took him some time to get the buttons unfastened and by the time he'd finished, his breathing was coming fast, his hands were warm and damp, and his breeches, his lowland attire, were fitting him much more tightly than they had just moments before. There were certainly a good many advantages to the kilt, comfort in situations like the one he now found himself being one.

Eleanor pulled her arms slowly from the narrow sleeves of her traveling gown and lowered the garment so that she could step out of it. As she moved to lay it on the bed with her pelisse, the light from the candle set on the small side table behind her shone through the thin gauzy fabric of her shift, outlining the curves of her figure to his waiting eyes.

Gabriel sucked in his breath, trying to ignore the rounded curve of her breast pressing against the delicate fabric. He wanted to pull her against him and cup its softness in his hand, tasting her with his mouth. He wanted to have her beneath him on that ridiculously large bed and make love to her through the night.

Then she turned to face him, a small grin touching her mouth as she said, "Now it is your turn to get undressed, my lord."

Gabriel nearly buckled at the knees.

Without waiting for his invitation, Eleanor stepped closely to face him. Her hair was burnished by the candlelight, all rich auburn and brown, and Gabriel had to tighten his hands into fists against the sudden urge to twine its silk around his fingers.

Eleanor seized him utterly without a touch, using only her eyes of kindled green fire while she slowly tugged at the ends of his cravat to loosen it. When she slid the length of its fabric from around his neck, he thought surely he would drop to the floor. All the while, she just watched him, her eyes seductively alight.

If she knew what she was doing to him, how she was bringing his blood to the boiling point and his control over himself to the brink, she did not show it. One by one she unfastened the buttons on the front of his shirt, her fingertips grazing the taut skin of his chest time and time again, eliciting incredible sensations that ran throughout his body and straight to his aroused groin.

Standing so closely, Gabriel was overpowered by her distinctive fragrance, the one he'd come to know so well the past weeks since she'd come into their lives. It was a scent that awakened him in the middle of the night and filled his head whenever she passed through a room.

His head was abuzz, his body on fire, and he stood unmoving as she slid her hands slowly beneath the fabric of his shirt, splaying her fingers flat against his chest as she pushed the covering back over his shoulders. The muscles in his belly rippled and tightened in eager response to her soft touch.

"There. Now we are both ready for bed," she said. "Good night, my lord. Sleep well."

At that moment, sleeping was the last thing Gabriel was ready for.

When Eleanor lifted up on her toes to kiss him lightly on the mouth, Gabriel seized her by the arms and pulled her against him, kissing her hungrily, deeply with his mouth and his tongue and his lips. He took in every essence of her, reveling in the heaviness of her breasts pressed tightly against his chest as she leaned into him.

He could have drawn her to the bed and made love to her right there, except that in the next moment, Juliana stirred on the bed, her movement rustling the bedclothes.

As if he was suddenly sixteen again, and had been caught kissing the headmaster's daughter at Eton, Gabriel abruptly pulled away.

Juliana did not wake, and was soon sleeping heavily again, her breathing humming lightly in the silence. Gabriel and Eleanor stood face-to-face for several moments, each caught in the lingering exhilaration of the utterly sense-stealing kiss they had shared.

Neither dared end the moment.

Eleanor was the first to speak, breaking the snowy silence between them. "Please douse the light when you get into bed," she said with a soft smile.

She turned, climbing onto the great bed, sliding across the mattress to the far side of the two slumbering girls, leaving Gabriel no choice but to take the nearer side.

As he snuffed the candle and lay down on the mattress, trying not to disturb the sleeping girls, Gabriel was taken by an image of fiery green eyes, moistened lips, and breasts white and filling his hands.

He then spent the next hour counting the oaken beams of

the ceiling above them in the moonlight, trying to dispel that same image.

Eleanor was the first to awake the following morning, opening her eyes to soft morning sunlight pouring in through the small window set in the wall above the bed. The delicious aroma of Mrs. Gray's eggs and bacon breakfast cooking in the kitchen below tempted from the other side of the door.

Lazily, she extended her arms, above her, feeling refreshed, invigorated, utterly alive. She hadn't slept so well in as long as she could remember and she decided it must have been solely because of Mr. Gray's incredible bed.

Surely a bed so extraordinary would give one an extraordinary night in it. She decided then that if they ever made the trip to London again, they would have to make certain to stop in Kirkby Lonsdale and ask for this same room.

Eleanor sat up on the mattress, ready to face the day, and promptly stilled at the scene that met her eyes.

Stretched beside her across the mattress, Gabriel lay with his face peaceful in sleep. His hair was mussed around his forehead, softening the chiseled lines of his face. Juliana's dark head lay tucked up against his shoulder, while one of Brìghde's small arms had flung outward in sleep to curve around his neck.

Somehow, in the middle of the night, the girls had squirmed their way around him until now he was totally and utterly surrounded by them. And when Eleanor looked closer, she saw that he was actually smiling in his sleep.

Lying back on the bed, Eleanor curled against the slumbering trio and closed her eyes, deciding she would just drift back to sleep for a little bit longer on Mr. Gray's Incredible, Extraordinary Bed.

                              *   *   *

The perpetual haze of London's bleak coal smoke awaited like a murky shroud long before they ever reached the city's sprawling outskirts. Even as far out as Chiswick, the stench of gutter waste and the smell of rotting market produce and fish made itself known while autumn leaves that had left the trees stark for the coming winter littered the roadway in front of them, swirling around the coach wheels as they drove by.

Eleanor could remember how as a child she had always been seized by a juvenile thrill of excitement when approaching the metropolis from the country, leaning out the coach window all along the road from Ealing, waiting to catch that first glimpse of Kensington and Hyde Park Corner, after which she knew they would almost be there.

The feverish bustle, the mingled crowd—the grating, chirping, humming, clopping, whirring, swishing noise of it—all had simply enchanted her beyond imagination. She had pictured dashing highwaymen hiding out behind the trees of Knightsbridge, waiting to call out "Stand and deliver" and divest them of their riches. She'd imagined the ghost of old Queen Anne herself watching from the top floor window of Kensington Palace, which she was purported to haunt.

But as they drove now along the populous Strand and under Wren's Portland stone Temple Bar, where the heads of traitors had been piked not a century earlier and where the figures of Charles I and II watched them pass underneath, Eleanor felt none of the charm, none of the pent-up excitement of her youth.

Instead, she found herself looking around at all the muck and mess and mire, at the people and the carriages and the houses that blocked out any hint of sunlight, longing for a

glimpse of a mist-ringed standing stone with a pair of ful-
mars souring overhead and Cudu stretched out like a Turk-
ish carpet across the stone floor of the great hall.

Their coach stopped first off Chancery Lane at the offices
of Gabriel's solicitor, Mr. George Pratt, a stout-looking man
with quite the bushiest eyebrows Eleanor had ever seen—
more one brow than two—set beneath a thinning pate of
grizzled hair. Upon being introduced to them, the native
Scot had greeted Eleanor and the two girls warmly.

"A pleasure it is, Lady Dunevin, Miss Juliana, and Miss
Brìghde. Welcome to London Town."

He was the first to have referred to Eleanor by her married name and she found she liked the sound of it.

She was Lady Eleanor Wycliffe no more.

Mr. Pratt took a moment to discuss a bit of business with
Gabriel before he furnished the keys to the Dunevin town
house on Upper Brook Street, a place Eleanor knew very
well. Just off Grosvenor Square, it was a quiet residential
street lined with neat fashionable homes only a few blocks
away from her brother's London residence, Knighton
House, at Berkeley Square.

As they made their way to Upper Brook after leaving Mr.
Pratt, they passed through Berkeley Square, and Eleanor noticed the polished brass door knocker in the shape of a
pineapple hanging outside the front door at Knighton House,
indicating to all that the family was in residence. A shiver
ran through her as she knew a sudden urge to open the carriage door and climb those small stone steps to the door.

Gabriel must have noticed Eleanor staring at the red brick
façade, the place she had called home almost all her life,
when the coach was suddenly stopped by an influx of traf-
fic. The look on her face must have been something akin to

miserable indecision because he leaned toward her and asked, "What is it, Eleanor?"

She looked at him and smiled, pushing away her clouded thoughts. "That is my family's house," she said. "The window there at the top behind the tree is my bedchamber. The flowers in the boxes beneath the lower windows were planted by my mother and me just this spring."

The front door opened then and Eleanor gave a little gasp at the sight of the Knighton butler, Forbes, brushing a bit of dust from a small rug over the front railing.

Gabriel sensed her torment at feeling almost as a stranger before something that once offered utter security. "Do you wish to stop in?"

Eleanor thought a moment but then shook her head. "No. Not now. Not just yet. I would like to get us settled and come up with some idea of what I shall say first. There is so much for me to talk about with them, I don't really know where to begin."

Gabriel smiled at her and said in a voice that sounded much like Màiri's, "The beginning is usually the best place to start anything, lass."

As the coach began to pull away, Eleanor thought she caught a glimpse of a figure, a silhouette, passing by one of the lower floor windows.

Her breath caught and she watched until she couldn't watch anymore, saying silently to herself, *I have come home, Mother.*

Chapter Sixteen

After removing their baggage to the house, Eleanor set the girls to washing their faces while she carried out her first formal duty as lady of her own household.

She met with Mrs. Wickett, the housekeeper Mr. Pratt had hired, who was Màiri's opposite in almost every way imaginable.

From her tall lanky figure to her quiet disposition and her very, very polite manner of speaking in a way that while perfectly affable, didn't convey an ounce of warmth or feeling beyond its delivery, she only left Eleanor longing more for their home on Trelay.

Eleanor set Mrs. Wickett and the two maids who'd been hired with her to the task of preparing the chambers for that night. While they aired the linen and shook out the dust from the carpets, Gabriel, Eleanor, and the girls took a carriage drive down Piccadilly before finally leaving the carriage to walk along St. James Street and the surrounding area for some shopping and impromptu sightseeing.

They walked along Pall Mall, showing the girls the gardens of St. James and the spectacle of Carlton House, the London palace of the former Prince Regent, deserted now since his ascension to the throne earlier that year, after he'd spent nearly three decades on its total reconstruction.

All red brick with an impressive Corinthian portico, inside it was said to rival Versailles in grandeur. A graceful double staircase that curved to meet on the first floor, and then divided again to meet on the floor above was the showpiece of the great hall, along with Ionic columns of brown marble and exotic decoration brought all the way from China.

After looking with a child's awe all the way up to the top of its roof, Brìghde declared that she should marry this prince and live in his pretty former house with Juliana and her pet lamb, whom she affectionately called "Woolly."

Eleanor and Gabriel then had to let the news fall that the prince was already married, in fact was no longer a prince, but the king, and had refused to allow his wife to be crowned queen because he didn't like her.

To which Brìghde immediately amended her declaration, deciding instead that she would find another, different prince with an even prettier house than this Carlton, who wouldn't refuse to let her be queen.

As they circuited to Piccadilly again, Eleanor watched Gabriel take Juliana's hand to cross the bustling street in front of them. Her heart filled with love for this man, who had avoided his daughter out of fear for so long, now seeming to try to make up for all that lost time in one day.

The change in him was astounding. As they walked along the row of shops, Gabriel talked to Juliana, showing her the sights, and accepting her silence as a thing he should not try to force her to change. Perhaps it had been Brìghde's ready acceptance of Juliana's muteness as simply a part of her, but once Gabriel arrived at that same acceptance, the rest had simply fallen into its proper order all on its own.

They stopped for a while at Hatchard's and purchased several books both to augment Juliana's studies as well as begin Brìghde's, for she would be joining Juliana and some of the other island children at a school Eleanor had proposed to Gabriel during their journey to London. She would teach the children to speak English, writing, reading, and simple ciphering, and they, in turn, would continue her education in Gaelic.

After Hatchard's, they had tea and buns at Mrs. Collins' Tea Shoppe, where Eleanor had to stop herself from laughing out loud when she spotted a young lady, very like herself not too long before, sitting with her mother in her "coming-out" wardrobe, being reminded of the proper angle of her fingers as she took her tea.

Those rules, those strictures, that whole existence suddenly seemed as if it had been a lifetime ago.

They paid a visit to a tailor on Jermyn Street to purchase some new cravats for Gabriel and bought Màiri an assortment of pretty silk ribbons in every color imaginable from the milliner. While Gabriel went off with Juliana to the stationer's shop to purchase some new writing quills and sealing wax, Eleanor and Brìghde browsed the shop windows on Old Bond Street, commenting on a display of bonnets that were decorated with bunches of fruits.

"I wouldna know whither t' wear it or eat it," Brìghde said with the wisdom and common sense of a child.

It was as they were turning the corner where they had planned to meet back with Gabriel that Eleanor suddenly heard a voice calling out to her from behind.

"Eleanor! I can't believe it is really you!"

Eleanor turned. She froze when she spotted Richard Hartley jogging up the pedestrian walk to meet her.

He was dressed elegantly in a suit of buff and navy blue, his dark hair brushed stylishly beneath the brim of his tall beaver hat, his boots polished to a marvelous sheen, every inch the fashionable buck.

"Richard," was all she managed to say before he seized her gloved hand, kissing it warmly.

"I have been going absolutely mad over worry for you," he said. "After I had discovered you'd left Town, I wrote to you in Scotland, but then thought perhaps my letter did not arrive safely when I didn't receive your reply. Then I wasn't certain if you were still in Scotland, so I wrote to your brother, but he did not reply either. So I decided you must be on your way back to England and that I would just come back to town to await you. I wanted to apologize for leaving you as I had in the middle of the Season without much in the way of an explanation. I called at Knighton House and left my card two days ago, but again, no reply. Till now." He beamed. "It is good to see you again. When did you get back to town? Had enough of wild Highlanders in kilts, did you?"

Eleanor glanced around, searching for Gabriel on the crowded walkway. "We only just arrived back in the city this morning."

"This morning?" He laughed. "And already you're out shopping. You must have gone mad up north without Bond Street." He seemed suddenly to notice Brìghde standing at Eleanor's side, holding her hand and staring at him with her usual open curiosity.

"Hello," Richard said. "I am Lord Herrick."

"I am Brìghde. Your hat is very tall." She looked up at Eleanor. "I can see myself in his boots they are so shiny."

"Richard," Eleanor interrupted then, "have you not spoken with my family?"

"No. I was detained longer than I had expected in Yorkshire. You probably thought I'd forgotten about you." He paused long enough to realize her tense expression. "Is something the matter?"

Before Eleanor could frame a response, Gabriel and Juliana came around the corner to join them on the footpath. Juliana, uneasy at the sudden stranger and as if sensing the awkwardness of the situation, came to Eleanor's side and tucked her hand in hers. Gabriel stood close beside her, closing the protective ranks around Eleanor, and though he spoke not a word, it was obvious their relationship was more than passing acquaintanceship.

A good deal more.

Eleanor watched as in the space of a moment, the expression on Richard's face turned from one of elation at having run across her, to one of confusion, to one of speechless, overwhelming dread.

"Richard," she said quietly in effort to break the terrible silence that had somehow descended upon that busy city corner, "allow me to introduce you to my husband, Lord Dunevin, and our daughter, Miss Juliana MacFeagh. You have already met her friend, Brìghde. Gabriel, girls, this is a friend of mine." She looked at Richard. "A good friend, Richard Hartley, the Earl of Herrick."

Richard was staring at Gabriel, who stood several inches taller and even now drew stares from the other pedestrians passing by. After a moment, he looked at Eleanor again, his eyes suddenly dull and vacant with realized catastrophe.

"You are married?" he asked, as if he didn't quite grasp the concept of what he'd been told.

Then, suddenly, as if shaken by unseen hands, every modicum of gentility and politeness he'd ever been taught came to surround him like a protective cloak. Richard stood straighter, putting on a face of polite indifference, and extended his hand toward Gabriel. "Dunevin, an honor to make your acquaintance."

Gabriel shook his hand. "Herrick."

Richard glanced at the girls and nodded.

"Yes, well," he said, obviously struggling to come to terms with what stood before him in the face of such a public arena, "I wish you all the best on your marriage." He bowed his head to Gabriel. "Lord Dunevin."

He then looked at Eleanor, his face rigid against the high points of his fashionable collar. "Lady Dunevin. I can only say I'm sorry my letter didn't make it to you successfully while you were in Scotland. My loss is obviously Lord Dunevin's gain."

With that, he bowed his head and turned, walking away from them down the pedestrian path, his back as straight and stiff as the lamp post.

He never once looked back.

Eleanor hadn't realized she was still standing there, staring at his retreating back while people strolled around her until Gabriel finally spoke.

"Are you all right, lass?"

She looked at him, filled with such sudden terrible remorse that her eyes were blurred with tears. "I never expected to see him here. I didn't know what to say to him. Oh, God, Gabriel, he should never have had to find out that way."

"There was nothing else you could do."

She gave over to her tears. "But what if he had been my mother? Or Christian? I cannot imagine seeing them for the first time outside a . . . a hat shop!"

Brìghde tugged on Eleanor's sleeve, asking her why that man with the shiny boots had made her so sad. Juliana just took a step closer to her side. Suddenly Eleanor wanted to get off that crowded street corner and back to the house as quickly as they could.

Gabriel must have sensed her thoughts, for he hastily hailed them a hackney that was parked around the corner. Within minutes they were rolling toward Upper Brook Street this time avoiding a pass through Berkeley Square.

That night, they stayed in for supper, eating a quiet meal which they had had to send Fergus out to fetch from a nearby pub since Mrs. Wickett had spent most of the day provisioning the kitchen.

After supper, Eleanor saw that Juliana and Brìghde were quickly bathed and dressed in their nightclothes, then tucked them both into bed in a chamber just across the hall from her own.

As she closed the door behind her, Eleanor could hear Brìghde whispering to Juliana in the darkness and knew the two would probably spend half the night standing at the window, watching the carriages roll by under the light of the gas lantern at the far street corner. It was much the same sort of thing she had done as a child.

An hour later, Eleanor sat alone in her chamber, brushing out her hair at the dressing table with long, contemplative strokes.

She had taken a bath to wash away the travel dust and to try to ease the lingering troubled thoughts of the day. She wondered how Richard was doing, if he would ever forgive her, and if he did, what she would say to him when next they met. She thought about her own family and found herself longing to see them. She felt so suddenly isolated, and so utterly unsettled.

Several times that day, Eleanor had wanted to do nothing more than climb in that coach and drive straight over to Berkeley Square to see her family, but she hesitated each time, her mind at a loss for what she would say, how they would react to her new situation. Would they like Gabriel? Would they welcome Juliana and her muteness into the exalted Westover family?

Eleanor was still sitting at her dressing table, staring blankly at her reflection in the looking glass when Gabriel knocked softly at her door.

"A footman just brought this to the door for you," he said, handing her a folded and sealed letter.

It was addressed to her as "Lady Dunevin" and it bore the Herrick seal.

She looked up at him. "It is from Richard," she said as she broke the seal to open it.

It was not, however, from Richard, but instead from his mother, the dowager Countess Herrick, inviting her to tea the next morning.

"Matters needing to be discussed" was written at the bottom of the page. Eleanor knew immediately what that "matter" would be.

Eleanor handed the letter to Gabriel so he could read it.

"Will you go?"

"I do not know. I don't want to hurt anyone else. This has already brought on so much unhappiness for so many people."

Gabriel nodded. "If you would like, I will go with you. Give it some thought first, lass. You needn't decide right now. Sleep on it for the night and you can make your decision in the morning."

She looked at him and smiled, bolstered by his supportive words. "Thank you, Gabriel."

"Good night then, lass." He nodded and turned to leave. "Sleep well."

He was almost to the door when she called to him.

"Gabriel?"

Gabriel turned but remained at the door as Eleanor stood to face him across the room. For several moments, they stared at one another in spellbound silence. Neither one of them had to speak to know what the other was thinking for the past weeks, every moment of that time had been leading to this one special night.

The waiting was over.

At the silent invitation in her green eyes, Gabriel kicked the door closed behind him, never taking his eyes from hers. He stood across the room, tall and powerful, and Eleanor felt herself blush at the light of something strange and wild in his eyes.

But one of them was going to have to move.

It was Gabriel and he strode across the carpet, sweeping Eleanor up and into his arms with one swift movement without saying a word. Eleanor gasped, realizing a thrill of excitement, and locked her hands around his neck as he carried her to the bed.

"Shall I snuff the candles?" she asked.

"Does it need to be dark, lass?"

"Well, I thought . . . I mean, that is what I heard . . ."

Gabriel chuckled deep in his chest. "Is that what your schoolgirl friends told you?"

Eleanor thought of her dear friend Amelia B. and the nights they had spent whispering beneath the bedcovers. She wondered if her father's whist partner, now husband had carried her to bed, too.

"It isn't fair, you know," she said to him, frowning. "Men are practically born knowing these things. You talk about it as if it were nothing more than . . . a horse race. Girls are only left to their imaginations and the small *on-dits* whispered by older sisters and cousins." She pulled a face. "Such as snuffing candles."

Gabriel stretched upon the bed beside her. "I imagine you've been told that some lasses prefer the dark so they won't have to look at their husband's faces. They can shut out the miseries of their unhappy lives, doing their wifely duty, and pretending that it is a secret lover in their bed instead of an insensitive husband."

Gabriel made to reach for the candlestick. "So which is it you prefer, lass, your husband, or a secret lover?"

Eleanor looked at him and smiled, hooking her hand around his neck and pulling his mouth down to meet hers. She said on a breath before their lips met, "I don't have to choose, husband, because I have them both in the same package."

Their bodies met in a twisting of arms and legs and mouths as Gabriel kissed Eleanor deeply and completely, stealing her breath and sending her senses soaring to the heavens. He pulled away from her, and she watched him in the candlelight as he stripped away his shirt, tossing it to the floor behind him.

"Hmm, husband, looking at you I think maybe candles are a good thing."

He nearly laughed. "Will you think so when I'm standing without a stitch to cover me? Some ladies shudder at the sight of the privy parts on a man's body."

Eleanor sat up before him and trailed a finger along his arm to his chest. "You do remember that I was a student of anatomy, my lord."

Now he did laugh, deep and smooth and utterly sexual. "Ah, lass, you do me in."

Their eyes caught and in a sudden instant, all mirth was gone. In its place was pure, living desire.

Gabriel kissed her again, long and slow, brushing his fingers back over her ear and twisting a strand of her hair in his fingers. Gently he tugged on that strand of hair, pulling back her head as he moved his mouth over her chin to taste her neck.

She moaned softly in response.

Three tiny ribbons tied in perfect bows fixed the top of her nightrail closed. Three tiny tugs and they were bows no more, and Gabriel was pushing the fabric over her shoulder with his mouth, kissing her along her collarbone and sending delightful chills running down her back and over her breasts, where she craved to feel his touch.

Somehow, Eleanor didn't know how, Gabriel had gotten her night rail down around her waist. He lay her back upon the bed, softly in the pillows, and she watched him in the candlelight, watched his eyes ignite with black fire as he took in the sight of her nakedness.

"Oh, lass, if I had had a governess who looked like you when I was a lad, I'd have been much more assiduous in my studies."

"It is a good thing you did not," she whispered to him as he ran his fingers slowly over her breasts, trailing a finger downward between them to the flatness of her belly. "Else it might be her here with you now instead of me."

Gabriel pressed his mouth to the taut peak of her, saying against her breast, "Oh, no, lass, having you in my bed is the only way it should ever have been—and the only way it shall ever after be."

He closed his mouth over her nipple and Eleanor arched her back, realizing a heated pulling deep inside of her, a yearning, a desperation that begged to be fulfilled.

As he suckled her breasts, sending magnificent sensations running through her body each time he drew on her with his mouth, Gabriel eased her night rail down over her belly, sliding it whisper soft over her hips. He dropped his hand against her bare hip and stroked her there, moving his fingers in gentle circles as he lifted one leg, bending it at the knee, caressing her softly on its underside.

Eleanor felt a heated rush between her legs and dropped her head back against the downy pillow, closing her eyes and waiting, waiting, waiting for his touch against her there.

She drew in a deep slow breath when she felt his hand running along her thigh, felt his fingers touching her, parting her, stroking her. He kissed her across her belly and down to her hip, then sat up on the bed to look down at her in the candlelight.

"You're more beautiful than I ever imagined. All those nights I lay awake in my bed thinking about you. How'd I ever get blessed with such a fine bonny lass?"

She whispered to the night, "It was fated."

He moved his fingers against her again and Eleanor sucked in her breath as she was overwhelmed by a thousand different shimmering sensations. When he slid his finger inside of her, she lost all sense, all reason, all reality.

How could he, with just one tiny touch, make her feel the way she was? It seemed almost impossible, but the more he touched her there, the more he moved his fingers against her, the stronger that feeling became.

She felt if he should suddenly stop she would lose something very precious, and so she moaned out to him, begging him never to stop, lifting her hips from the bed as the sensations pulsed and grew, pulling, reaching, desperately reaching for whatever it was that awaited her, until suddenly she was there, lost in a shower of gasps and swells and shivers so fierce she thought she would take flight. Her body throbbed deep within.

Slowly his fingers left her. Slowly Eleanor eased against the bed. Slowly she opened her eyes to see him watching her intently.

She knew that what they'd just shared wasn't all that lovers shared, that there was more, much more, but she couldn't possibly imagine anything going beyond the fantastic gift he'd just given her.

Eleanor watched in silence as Gabriel stood from the bed and shed his breeches, never taking his eyes from hers until he was naked and standing before her. His body was magnificent, all bronze skin and dark hair and hard heated muscle. She fixed her gaze briefly on his sex, standing erect from his groin, then looked into his eyes.

Without a word, he slid beside her on the bed and pulled her against him until she could feel the velvet hardness of him stroking her thigh. She shifted her leg to press against him there and he moaned into her mouth as he kissed her.

"It will hurt, yes?"

Gabriel looked at her, seemingly startled by her question. "Yes, but only for a moment. After that, you shall forget it ever pained you."

"That is what I thought."

"And how d'ya know this, lass?"

"Once, when I was thirteen, I overheard two older boys bragging to one another about what they had done with the daughter of the local grocer."

"And what had they done?"

"Things. Things that had to do with numbers and how far under her skirts they had gotten, things that sounded more like sport than anything intimate. Nothing at all like this."

"Aye, well there's a big difference between men and boys."

Eleanor grinned at him, pressing her hips forward against the heat of his hardness. "Yes, I am aware of that."

Gabriel buried his face against her neck as he shifted them, opening her legs and lifting her knees around his hips. He came up on his hands above her, watching her eyes as he slowly pressed against her.

"If I hurt you too much, just say so and I will stop."

"I don't care about the pain, Gabriel. It hurts me not to have you inside of me. Please just make me your wife—utterly and completely."

His eyes changed then, bright with desire, and Eleanor held her breath, waiting for what seemed like an eternity until with one unyielding thrust, he joined them forever.

The pain was instant and sharp and gone almost as quickly as it had come, consigned to fleeting memory for the rest of her life. In its place was a warm delicious throbbing, a craving and a desperation that cried out for the fulfillment of him deep inside of her. She could hear his breathing ragged against her ear and kissed him gently on the side of his face, whispering his name as he struggled to compose himself.

"It has been a long time, lass, so long I no longer remember anyone else. I fear I may come undone if I hold back from you much longer."

"Then don't," she whispered to him. "Don't hold back. Take me, my love. Take me. Now."

Gabriel drew a breath sharply and moved his hips, drawing back from her with desperate slowness. Eleanor watched his face, fixing her eyes on his as he began to move within her, gently at first, then coming faster, sinking into her with longer thrusts, over and over until he was desperate against her.

Sweat beaded at his brow as he struggled and fought, racing toward that place, that special place he had taken her only moments before and was taking her again. Each thrust touched her deeper than the last, each movement filled her with exquisite pleasure, until, with one deliberate thrust, Gabriel broke free, groaning out her name and pulsing deep inside of her once, twice, thrice, again and again, until he was utterly and completely spent.

Gabriel's arms were trembling as he tried to maintain his rigid posture above her. Eleanor reached up to him in the softness of the candlelight. Laying her hands gently against his chest, she drew him down to where he was resting his weight fully against her, his head against her shoulder, his arms around her neck.

Moments later, he lifted his head, kissing her, and looked deeply into the depths of her eyes.

"I love you, lass, more than I ever imagined a man could love. I'll not fight it any longer."

And then he kissed her, not deeply, not passionately, but tenderly, with the sacred promise of the future.

It was beyond anything Eleanor could have ever imagined.

Chapter Seventeen

Eleanor stepped down from the hackney coach onto the curved drive of Grafton Street to stand before the imposing façade of number five, the London home of the Dowager Countess of Herrick.

She thanked the driver, removing two coins from her reticule, and then watched as he clicked to his horses and moved slowly down the lane, vanishing around the next corner. She remained standing on the footpath for several moments, just staring at the pristine Georgian town house tucked in the corner of the lane, whose front windows gleamed like ice in the morning sunlight.

Her hands lay tucked away inside her ermine muff, a new purchase from the shopping excursion the day before, protected from the biting autumnal wind that blew its way over the housetops, stirring the fallen leaves across the cobbles at her feet. Other pedestrians walked casually past and the clip-clop of horses pulling carriages sounded distantly behind her. Still she stood there, wondering just what this visit would bring.

It was evident Richard had told the dowager about seeing her the day before. Did the countess know the truth about the past, about Eleanor's parentage? Or was she simply

seeking to call Eleanor to task for rejecting her son's proposal of marriage so abominably?

Finally realizing, of course, that she couldn't just continue to stand outside in the freezing wind all day, Eleanor
climbed the three short steps to the front door, rapped upon
it, and waited.

"Yes?"

The Herrick butler stood stalwart as a flagpole before her.

"Good afternoon. I should like to see Lady Herrick, if
you please."

"And whom shall I say is calling?"

"Eleanor, Lady Dunevin. I believe she is expecting me."

He nodded and opened the door for her to enter. He motioned toward a small carved bench set just inside the door.
"You may wait here while I see if her ladyship is receiving."

The house was warm inside, elegantly furnished, and
smelled of fresh flowers and early morning baking. Eleanor
took her hands from inside her muff, removed her bonnet
and gloves, and sat to wait.

She could hear the faint murmur of conversation coming
from down the center hall, too muffled, though, to discern
any of the words. A clock hanging on the wall beside her
chimed the half hour. A chambermaid came down the narrow flight of stairs, bobbing a curtsy with a quick "milady"
as she passed on her way to the back of the house. Outside,
a bread seller called out "Hot loaves!"

The butler returned moments later.

"Lady Herrick will receive you in the parlor now. May I
take your coat?"

Eleanor handed him her muff and bonnet while she unfastened the buttons at the front of her pelisse, turning when
he moved to assist her with it. "Thank you."

"This way, my lady."

He led her down the hallway past several doors and a tall case clock to a room set at the back of the house, away from the noise and diversion of the street.

It faced out onto a walled private garden through a large window that afforded a pleasant glimpse of the morning sunlight. The butler stopped at the door to allow her to proceed before announcing her.

"Lady Dunevin, my lady."

The dowager countess sat on a settee facing the door as Eleanor came into the room. Her head was covered by a frilled muslin cap and in her lap she had an embroidery frame on which she'd been stitching a small bird.

Her expression wasn't one that was easily discernible, her mouth set in a line that was neither frown nor smile, her eyes clear and watchful, the same pale gray as her son's.

She nodded wordlessly at the chair nearest by, indicating Eleanor should sit.

"Lady Herrick, it is an honor to make your acquaintance," Eleanor said as she sat and folded her hands on her lap. "Thank you for inviting me today."

"I wasn't so certain you'd come."

Eleanor looked at her, immediately sensing a deeply seated bitterness. "Lady Herrick, please know that I—"

The dowager held up her hand, silencing Eleanor's next words.

"When Richard first came to tell me he had begun courting someone at the beginning of the Season, I was, of course, thrilled as any mother with a son of marriageable age would be. The name of Wycliffe, however, was the very last one I would have ever expected to hear."

Eleanor looked down at her hands, humbled by words this woman had obviously been waiting quite some time to say.

"It was as if the past twenty years had simply melted away," she went on. "I should have told him the truth right then, but I must admit to a certain curiosity about you. I decided to wait until Richard asked to bring you to meet me, thinking that the moment I saw you, faced you, I would surely know . . . I would surely be able to tell . . ."

". . . if I had been fathered by your husband," Eleanor finished for her.

The dowager looked at her, searching her face, no doubt for some sort of resemblance to the former earl. "I didn't know if you had ever been told the truth. A part of me thought that you had and that you were trifling with Richard in a game meant to reopen old wounds."

"Lady Herrick, I would never—"

"Another part of me wondered if you were as much a victim in the events of the past as Richard."

Her voice softened then. "I decided I would wait because I knew if you were truly a product of what took place all those years ago, then Frances would never allow you to go through with a marriage to Richard."

Eleanor shook her head. "I do not know who my father was. I don't suppose I ever will truly know."

Lady Herrick stood suddenly and walked to the window to stare out at the garden beyond. She was quiet for a time, leaving Eleanor to simply sit and wait till she was ready to continue.

"Frances and I were as close as sisters in our youth. We went to school together. We even came out together. We always said we would one day get married to our husbands on the same day at the same church. I always knew that she loved Richard, just as I knew he loved her. But her family had had other thoughts in mind, particularly when the heir to the Duke of Westover came calling."

She turned to face Eleanor again. "She did try, your mother, in the beginning, to make a life with your father, but when the heart is given elsewhere, marriage can be more confining than the loneliest, most forsaken prison." She shook her head. "I know it all too well.

"I knew that William was going to meet your fath—" she stopped and corrected herself. "I knew that William was going to meet Christopher at dawn that morn. I knew Frances well enough to know that she could never deceive Christopher into believing someone else's child was his. I stood at the window that faced out toward the Westover estate all morning, watching for his return. When he didn't appear by the afternoon, I knew what had happened. I didn't find out that Christopher had died, too, until weeks later. I don't know whatever became of my husband."

"Lady Herrick, that morning—"

She shook her head. "No explanations, please. I do not wish to know what happened that morning, Lady Dunevin. It was an inevitability long in the making, a tragic end to a tragic beginning for us all. I left that part of my life behind when I left the country to move permanently to London. I have never gone back and I have no intention of ever revisiting it."

She crossed to a small writing table in the corner and opened a drawer, removing something from inside. She walked over to where Eleanor sat and handed her a small hinged box about the size of a deck of cards. Eleanor opened it to reveal a painted miniature tucked away inside. Its subject was a handsome man of about thirty years in a powdered wig and frock.

She looked to Lady Herrick, who yet stood before her. "This is—?"

The dowager simply nodded.

Eleanor searched the likeness for some connection, some similarity to her own features, the tilt of his brow, the set of his mouth, but found nothing, only unanswered questions.

He had been a handsome man, and it was easy to see why her mother had fallen in love with him. Gently Eleanor replaced the image in its box and returned it to the countess.

"I am so sorry."

"My only regret is that my son had to be hurt by all of this. Even now he doesn't understand your reasons for crying off any more than he understands why you married another so quickly. He simply believes you grew tired of waiting for him to return from Yorkshire, that his letters never reached you, and that he waited too long. And I have done everything I can to prolong that belief."

The dowager paused. "I have not told him the truth about his father and I do not intend to. At least not now. Like your brother, Richard was made to grow up far too quickly after his father's death, assuming the responsibilities of the earldom at too early an age. He idolized his father—he still does to this day—and he has worked very hard to be a son William would have been proud of. I think he has succeeded and I will not take that away from him right now.

"I know I have no right to ask this of you, but I would be most grateful if you would keep our visit today and the things we have discussed between us. The past is the past, Lady Dunevin. There is nothing we can do to change it now. The day may come when Richard should know the truth, but to tell him now would only be cruel. He has already been brought low. Please do not deliver him another terrible blow so soon."

She looked at Eleanor vacantly. "In the best interests of both yourself and my son, I believe things are better left unsaid. You are newly married and have no need of any scandal."

Eleanor lifted her chin at the dowager's thinly veiled insinuation that she had perhaps married Gabriel quickly and deceptively in an effort to protect herself from scandal.

"My husband was told the truth about my parentage, my lady. *Before* we were married."

Lady Herrick looked somewhat surprised by her statement. "My apologies, Lady Dunevin. I made an assumption about you based solely upon the suddenness of your marriage. That was unfair. Indeed Lord Dunevin must be a very exceptional man."

"He is. He is unlike any man I have ever met before."

Lady Herrick smiled. "Then allow me to congratulate you, Lady Dunevin, on avoiding the confinement of a loveless marriage. Your affection for your husband is clear to anyone who looks at you."

Eleanor stood, sensing that the time for her to leave had arrived. "Thank you, Lady Herrick, for taking the time to speak with me so honestly." She extended her hand. "I am in your debt."

"And I am in yours."

They started toward the door.

"I wonder, Lady Dunevin, if I might offer you a word of advice?"

Eleanor nodded.

"Do not judge the actions of your mother or your brother too harshly. They only did what they thought best for you under the most difficult of circumstances. Frances has already been punished enough by all of this to last the length of three lifetimes. Despite what has happened between us, I should hate to see her punished again."

Eleanor looked at her. "Thank you, my lady. If she could

know of your concern, I am certain my mother would appreciate it."

The countess simply nodded, a wistful light crossing her eyes. "But as we both know, that can never be. Some wounds are better left to heal."

After bidding the dowager good day, Eleanor retrieved her things from the butler, who saw to the task of asking the Herrick footman to summon her a hackney home.

As she stood waiting on the footpath, Eleanor's first thought was to return to the town house and sit with Gabriel and the girls for a quiet afternoon. She longed for the security, the happiness they offered. But as she climbed into the carriage and settled upon the squabs, she realized there was another place that she needed to go to first.

"To where, my lady?" asked the driver.

"To Hyde Park, if you please."

Frances, Lady Knighton, was a woman of most scrupulous habit, performing her same rituals each day with but very little variance.

She awoke at five of the clock each morning to wash her face with lavender soap and cold water before taking a breakfast of toasted bread and tea precisely at six.

She took milk in her tea, not cream, and no sugar, and she preferred strawberry jam on her toast, although she had been known to stray to gooseberry every so often as well.

She spent an hour each morning reading quietly in the parlor and, weather permitting, every Thursday morning at ten, before most of London society had even begun to stir, she strolled the three short blocks to the Stanhope Gate leading into Hyde Park.

She sat in the same place each time, taking the third bench to the right of the entrance just off the Lover's Walk pathway that was partially hidden behind a rather large oak that had sprung from two trunks. There she passed the next hour tossing bread crusts to the birds and squirrels while the city awoke around her and the sun climbed to the highest part of the sky.

Today the weather was colder than in recent days, the wind carrying with it a brisk bite, so Frances had brought along a lap blanket to cover her legs while she sat. It was a thick woolen covering woven for her by some of the tenants' wives at Skynegal, the Highland estate of her son, Christian, and his wife, Grace. The crisscrossed tartan design was done in muted shades of dark red, green, black, and white, and it was fringed along the edges. It was a pretty piece.

Frances had come to this place whenever she was in London for nearly the past twenty years. It was a quiet corner of the park, away from the most traveled promenades, and she always found a sense of peace here, a solace that a person could only find when truly at one with nature. The wind soughed softly, the waxwings trilled from the treetops above, but today she found no peace in this place, no solace, only troubling thoughts of her missing daughter, Eleanor.

As she watched a small squirrel collecting acorns at her feet, Frances wished she could somehow, someway go back in time to right the wrongs she had committed so many years ago. At the time, she had been so very young and so very, very foolish, filled with ideas of conquering the world.

The feelings she'd had for William had seemed so eminent, so vital to her existence. She realized now they could never have had a future together; and their love affair had only added fuel to the fire of youthful defiance.

Frances's parents wouldn't have dared to reject the heir to the Duke of Westover no matter how much she might have pleaded with them otherwise. Christopher had known that her heart was given elsewhere, yet he'd truly believed he could make her happy, that someday, after he had showered her with gifts and riches and a suffocation of affection, she would somehow inexplicably change her feelings for him from friendship to the desperate, obsessive love he felt for her.

In the end, however, even that friendship had gone, leaving Frances with nothing but the bitter shadow of resentment—for Christopher, for her parents, and for a society that had left her its powerless victim.

It was the children, Christian and Eleanor, who had suffered the effects of her mistakes the most, and no mother with an ounce of compassion in her heart for those whom she had borne would wish any such pain upon their innocence. At the age of nine, Christian had gone from good-natured boy to the role of nobleman, a man who'd shouldered a burden from then on that would have toppled most.

In order to secure Eleanor the protection of the Westover name, Christian had given over his life into the hands of his grandfather, the old duke, allowing that embittered man to dictate his life's path in exchange for his silence about the question of Eleanor's paternity.

He'd done it to protect Frances, she knew, to keep her from being ostracized as an adulteress, and Frances had only agreed to his understanding with the duke out of fear for the life of her unborn child.

Oh, would that she could erase the memory of that horrible night so long ago, the night she had told her husband she quite possibly was carrying another man's child.

Christopher had sat so silent that night, staring at her with an expression unlike any she had ever seen. His eyes had been frighteningly vacant, glazed, somehow unreal. His skin had been ashen white.

Only later had Frances realized that he had known the truth all along, even before she had told him.

"Who is the father?" Christopher had asked, his voice filled with a fearsome calm.

"I do not know," had been her reply, not because she had sought to deceive him, but because, in truth, she had continued to do her duty as Christopher's wife whenever he had visited her bedchamber.

"Then I will raise it as my own. This is nothing new. Devonshire houses countless brats whose origin is questionable. Brookridge even paid his wife to take a lover so that he could get himself an heir despite his well-known impotence. I shall just be like one of them, pretending not to know the truth.

"You will not see him again," he'd said then, rising from his chair and crossing the room to his desk. "I'll not tolerate being made a cuckold before all the world."

"Christopher, I promise you it will never happen again . . ."

His face twisted in anger. "Spare me from any more of your hollow promises, madam. You made another promise not so long ago when you married me before God, vowing to *'honor and keep thee only unto me.'*"

Moments later, Frances had watched him take out his pistol case. "Christopher, what do you mean to do?"

"I mean to ensure that I am never again made to wonder whether my child is my own."

"But I swear to you—"

"You swear? You swear!"

He grabbed her roughly by the arm, yanking her up from her chair hard against him, his face snarling, inches from her own. "What you say no longer matters to me, wife. I am finished with your lies and deception."

It was in that moment Frances knew that the obsessive passion of love Christopher had felt for her before had suddenly and irrevocably changed to the far worse passions of hatred and jealousy.

Christopher took up his quill and scribbled something upon a parchment, taking his time in dusting it to dry, folding it, sealing it with a dollop of wax into which he pressed his signet ring. He called out the door to the Westover footman, who appeared in seconds.

"What are you doing?" Frances asked.

He ignored her and spoke to the footman. "Deliver this posthaste to the estate of Lord Herrick. Make sure to give it to no one but the earl."

The Herrick estate, Hartley Manor, was but two miles to the west of the Westover estate.

Christopher turned to her. "Did you think I planned to do away with you when I took out my pistol case, Frances? Sorry to disappoint you, but it's your lover I intend to kill this night."

Frances had grown desperately frightened. "Christopher, please, don't do this."

He opened the case and removed one of the carved dueling pistols from inside. "Spare me your tender concern for your lover, madam."

"It is not him I am concerned about, Christopher. It is you. You are not thinking logically."

"Neither were you when you opened your legs to another man."

Frances had flinched as if his sharp words had actually struck her. The memory of them stung even now. "Be reasonable. Please. William is a known excellent shot."

"As should be any man who would sleep with another

man's wife while at the same time betraying one he had called friend."

Frances attempted one final appeal. "Christopher, if you care not for me, please don't do this to Louise. She has a young son to raise."

He merely scoffed, beyond any reason by then. "If you had had such a care for the feelings of the woman, you wouldn't have bedded with her husband. I wonder, does the good Lady Herrick know that the woman she considers her closest friend in life might very well be carrying her husband's child? Tell me, is Herrick at Hartley Manor right now, on his knees before her, salving his conscience?"

Frances simply stared at him.

"As I thought. The man is too much of a coward to face up to his transgressions. Herrick's wife should thank me. I am doing her the favor of never having to know the torture of having her heart rent in two as I have."

In the end, Frances had been unable to do anything more than hopelessly watch from the isolation of her bedchamber window as Christopher, his father the duke, and then nine-year-old Christian, whom they had roused from sleep to view this spectacle, to know what his mother had done, disappeared into the darkness of the Wiltshire moors in the early morning hours.

She hadn't moved from the spot by midmorning, when only two of the three who had gone had returned alive, the third draped lifelessly over the back of his horse.

Still, despite the bitter tragedy of that terrible dark time, Frances couldn't truly regret it all, because out of it, out of the anguish and heartache and loss, had come her most precious daughter.

From the night she was brought into the world and delivered into Frances's arms, Eleanor had been nothing short of a blessing from the angels. It had been six months since Christopher's death, and the pregnancy had been the only thing that had kept Frances from giving up on life completely, the pregnancy and the faith of her son. Enlightened beyond his ten years, Christian had become Frances's immediate champion, doing whatever he could to shield his newborn baby sister from harm.

He had willingly filled the role of brother, friend, and father figure, and had never once censured Frances for the choices she had made in events of the past. Eleanor had grown into a bright, affectionate young woman, filled with promise for the future—a bright shining light in their lives—until all of it came crashing down upon them those few months ago when the truth could no longer remain hidden.

After Christian had revealed the terrible details of the past to her, Eleanor had fled, vanishing into the night. She hadn't written, hadn't been seen since, despite the reward that had been offered for her safe return and inquiries made across the land by both Christian and the old duke, whose guilt over what had happened had brought on a total turn.

Elias Wycliffe, the fourth Duke of Westover, had spent a good part of his three-and-seventy years abusing the power his wealth and illustrious title had afforded him. To those outside the family, he was a man of shrewd intelligence, whose knack for investment and frugality had amassed him a fortune not even the Crown knew the true extent of. To those inside the family, however, he was both tyrant and dictator, Napoleon at his worst, directing the lives of those dependent upon him like pieces on his own personal chessboard.

The day Frances had been presented before him as the

prospective bride for his only son, Christopher, the duke had made his feelings about her abundantly clear.

"You should congratulate yourself, my dear. You have single-handedly elevated your family to a status they couldn't have dared dream about otherwise."

But being a part of the Wycliffe clan came with its price, a price that in the end was far too dear. The resentment, the bitterness could only go on so long, before it would overflow. Sometimes it took a tragedy to get others to truly realize the depth of their deeds. That tragedy was Eleanor.

When Eleanor had vanished after learning the truth of the past, Christian and the old duke had engaged in the bitterest war of words. Two lifetimes of resentment and pain erupted and for the first time in his life, Christian had taken the opportunity to unburden himself of all those many years that he had stood by, silently suffering for the protection of his mother and Eleanor. In turn, the duke shed his impenetrable armor and the truth behind his heartlessness came to light— a lifetime of shame and regret at not having fought for the woman he had loved.

In the end, faced firsthand with the terrible damage his pride had wrought, the duke had broken down, blaming himself for Eleanor's leaving. Miraculously, the two men, grandfather and heir, pulled together and expended every effort, sparing no expense in finding her. The duke had vowed once she was found, he would spend whatever time he had left trying to make amends for the deeds of the past. But it had been so long without any word, any hope, Frances despaired of ever seeing her daughter again, of ever holding her in her arms, if only so that she, too, might beg her forgiveness for having hurt her the way she had.

The sun that morning in Hyde Park had climbed above the treetops and a carriage or two had recently passed by, indicating that the hour grew late, so Frances decided to return to Knighton House. Christian and Grace were to arrive from Skynegal that afternoon, and their friends, the Duke and Duchess of Devonbrook, who had also just returned to town, would be coming for supper that evening. There was much to do.

Frances stood and folded the blanket she'd brought, tossing the last few crusts of bread she'd brought to the squirrels at the foot of the oak beside her. As she turned for the gate that would take her from the park, she caught sight of a figure making its way slowly along the pathway.

It was a woman, she could see, but her distance was too great for Frances to discern her identity. Still there was something about her, something very familiar in the way in which she walked, something that reminded her suddenly of . . .

Frances stood for several moments, just watching her, hope leaping in her breast with each step the woman took closer.

Oh, St. Christopher in heaven, could it truly be . . . ?

Frances wondered if she were dreaming. In the very same moment, she hoped against hope that she was not.

"Hello, Mother."

At the first familiar sound of her daughter's voice, Frances lost the struggle against her tears. She dropped the blanket heedlessly to her feet and sobbed softly as her daughter came home into the circle of her open arms.

"Oh, my dearest, my dearest daughter," she said, stroking Eleanor's arms as she held her tightly to her. "I have missed you so very much."

"And I have missed you."

Frances pulled back only for a moment to look on the face she had nearly given up hope of ever seeing again.

Eleanor looked different somehow, older, wiser. Her eyes no longer held that youthful bounding spirit.

Frances shook her head sadly. "Eleanor, I am so, so sorry for hurting you."

"I know, Mother." Eleanor brushed a tear from her mother's cheek with a gloved finger. "And I am sorry for leaving as I did without telling anyone where I was going. I just needed to get away, to sort through everything."

"Of course you did, dear."

She looked deeply into Frances's eyes. "Mother, there is much we need to talk about. Things have changed in my life, things you need to know."

Frances's motherly intuition immediately sharpened. "What is it, dear? Is something the matter? Whatever it is, we will sort it out. All that matters is that you are safe and you have come back home to stay."

"But, that is what I needed to tell you. I haven't come back—to stay, that is."

Frances stared at her, stunned. "Eleanor, please. I know you are hurt by what you learned, but if we could just talk, if I could just explain—"

"Mother, I am married."

"To—to Richard?"

Eleanor shook her head. "To someone else."

Frances's face froze in a mask of shocked disbelief. "No, dear. It cannot be. You did this because you were distraught over what you had learned. You weren't thinking sensibly. You were just reacting to your emotions, as anyone would under such circumstances. We will have the marriage annulled. Yes, that is what we will do."

"Mother, no." Eleanor looked at her deeply. "I do not want my marriage annulled. I love him."

Frances fell speechless.

Eleanor went on to explain. "Yes, I was upset after what Christian had told me, but that is not the reason why I married Gabriel. I married him because he needs me, and because I need him, too. He knows everything about me, about my past, and he loves me. I truly believe that all of what happened, with you, with Christian, at Skynegal, it happened for a reason. It led me to him."

She motioned toward the bench where Frances had been sitting. "Come, Mother, let us sit for a spell like we used to and I will tell you everything that has happened to me."

Frances sat listening attentively as Eleanor related everything to her, how she had made her way through the Highlands to Trelay, her role as governess to Juliana, the tender feelings that grew into love for Gabriel. She even told her about the events of his past and Gabriel's current trouble with his former in-laws.

"Eleanor, dear, forgive me for asking this, but you say no one knows what became of his first wife. You said twice there were incidents, a fire and some sort of poisonous carrot in your dinner? These are not simple coincidences, dear. What if"—Frances chose her words carefully—"what if your life is at risk, too?"

"Mother, Gabriel did not have anything to do with Georgiana's death or anyone else's for that matter. He was at the castle when she disappeared. Only Juliana was with her and she cannot tell us what happened. When his brother died, Gabriel was abroad on the Continent and when the fire broke out in the nursery, he nearly killed himself because he thought Juliana and I were there. Do not forget that it was he who stopped me from eating that hemlock." Eleanor softened her tone. "There *is* a logical explanation for what has gone on. I know there is, and I just need to find it."

Frances quickly realized she could not persist with her

misgivings. Whatever she may think or suspect, Eleanor was no longer the impressionable young girl of her youth. She was a woman grown with a mind all her own, something Frances and the rest of the family were going to have to learn to trust in.

"How long will you be in London then?"

"I'm afraid not long at all. Only to see to whatever legalities must be put into place to protect Juliana."

"But dear, you were married at Gretna Green among strangers. At least allow your mother to give her only daughter a proper wedding surrounded by our friends and family."

Eleanor smiled. "We shall have a wedding, Mother, at Dunevin. Everyone will come."

Frances nodded. "May I at least meet this man who has stolen my daughter's heart? And your new daughter." Frances gasped then, covering her mouth with her hand. "I am a grandmother. Oh, good heavens!"

She hugged Eleanor tightly to her.

"Tonight," she said then. "You must come to dinner tonight, all of you. Christian and Grace will be arriving later today and will only be in town briefly. We are having the Devonbrooks over for supper tonight and would love very much to meet your new family. At eight?"

Eleanor smiled at her, nodding her head.

"At eight."

Chapter Eighteen

The coach carrying Eleanor, Gabriel, and the girls arrived on Berkeley Square at precisely five minutes before eight, beneath the light of a full autumn moon that hovered low against the London church spires in the distance.

On the southwest corner of the square, shaded by a pair of twin great elms stood the imposing façade of Knighton House, London home to the Marquesses of Knighton for nearly a century past.

The tall bow windows facing the street were ablaze with light from inside. From behind the coach window, Eleanor looked up past the parlor two floors to the window that looked out from her former bedroom. She searched the darkness through the trees, looking . . . she smiled to herself when she spotted a single candle lit upon the sill; it was a long-standing tradition among the Wycliffes that anytime a family member returned from a visit elsewhere, they would find that candle burning in their window, like a beacon to light their way home.

Gabriel stepped down from the coach first, turning to assist Eleanor and the girls behind her. The girls looked especially pretty this evening, each in new frocks—Juliana in pink, Brighde in blue—with lacy pantalettes peeking out from underneath.

Brìghde, who was more accustomed to woolen, tartan skirts and bare feet, was especially proud of her new kid slippers and pristine white silk stockings. She showed them to everyone they met, even the hackney coachman who'd driven them there.

Earlier that day, Frances had sent over Thérèse, who had been Eleanor's ladies' maid since the beginning of that Season. The sprightly maid had cried for nearly fifteen minutes when first reunited with her mistress, and afterward promptly set to arranging Eleanor's hair in a lovely curled coiffure that swept high upon her head with small ringlets dangling down the back of it to her nape.

Afterward, Thérèse had ministered to the girls, curling their hair with fire-heated tongs in tight corkscrew curls and tying them up high upon their heads with soft satin ribbons.

They looked like angels.

Upon seeing them coming down the stairs to leave, Gabriel had declared them his princesses for the night, a comment which had elicited a squeal from Brìghde and a bright smile from Juliana.

Gabriel, too, had taken special care with his appearance for the evening and Eleanor was touched by his efforts to make a good impression on her family. His face was cleanly shaven and his hair had been neatly trimmed, curling darkly just below his collar. His coat was a dark, rich bottle green atop slender black breeches and polished boots that reached to his knees.

They would love him immediately, she thought, still amazed every time she saw him since coming to London, how very different he looked from the rugged kilted Scottish laird she had fallen in love with.

Thérèse had brought several of Eleanor's gowns with her from Knighton House and Eleanor had chosen to wear the pale blue-green silk, a favorite and one that held happy memories for her for it was the same one she had worn the day Christian and Grace had married.

Charlie, the Knighton footman, was standing ready at his post, grinning widely as they approached.

"Good evening to you, Lady Eleanor. 'Tis good to have you home again." He tipped his hat to Gabriel and the girls. "My lord and misses."

He opened the door for them to where the Knighton butler, Forbes, already awaited. "Lady Eleanor, welcome home."

"Forbes, 'tis good to see you. Allow me to introduce my husband, Lord Dunevin, our daughter, Miss Juliana MacFeagh, and her friend, Miss Brìghde Macphee."

Forbes bowed his head respectfully to Gabriel and nodded to the girls as he secured their cloaks.

"They await you en masse in the parlor, my lady," he said as he headed for the back of the house to stow their cloaks.

The parlor was situated down the center hall and as they approached, Eleanor could hear the murmur of conversation coming from within. She set her hand on Gabriel's arm and took Juliana's hand with the other while Brìghde took her place at Gabriel's other side.

Together, they headed for the parlor.

Conversation quickly dropped off to silence after they stepped into the doorway. Everyone was there, Frances, Grace, the Devonbrooks, even the old duke, whom Eleanor was more than a little surprised to see.

Everyone was there, except Christian. He was not anywhere to be seen.

For the smallest of moments, no one spoke, they just looked at one another in awkward silence, as if no one quite knew what to say first. Fittingly, it was Grace, standing close by, who, as hostess now at Knighton House, welcomed them in.

"Eleanor, welcome home. We are all so happy to see you."

She crossed the room and embraced Eleanor warmly, whispering, "I have missed you terribly. Christian is so dreadfully grumpy when you aren't around."

The Grace Eleanor faced was a stunningly different woman from the meek maid who had married her brother six months earlier. This Grace exuded a confidence and a radiance that glowed all the way from her elegant blond coiffure to her perfectly matched slippers and silk gown.

Eleanor smiled at her efforts to ease the tension of the situation. "I missed you as well."

"You must be Lord Dunevin," Grace said then, extending her hand in greeting to Gabriel. "I am Grace, Eleanor's sister-in-law. Until you happened along, I was the newest member of this clan. Welcome to the family."

Eleanor had briefed Gabriel beforehand on the formalities of each person's noble title, and so Gabriel took Grace's hand, bowing over it politely. "Lady Knighton."

"Won't you please come in and meet the rest of the family?"

From that moment, chaos descended. Everyone started talking all at once, pressing forward to welcome Eleanor home and to meet Gabriel and the two girls.

So many questions. So many hugs.

How had they met?

Where had they married?

Were they planning to stay in the city long?

Eleanor got lost in a sea of welcoming faces and embraces, until suddenly she sensed someone standing beside her.

She turned to find Christian waiting. She smiled.

"Christian."

"Oh, Nell."

Her brother barely managed to utter his favorite pet name for her before he crushed her against him, stealing her breath and holding her tightly.

He whispered into her ear, "I'm so sorry," and didn't release her for several moments.

Eleanor could feel him struggling to hold his emotions in check, and she regretted all the worry she had caused him. It was a struggle she lost herself and her own tears fell freely against the shoulder of his jacket as she wept at seeing him again.

Finally, she eased away. "Come, brother, there is someone I wish for you to meet."

Eleanor took Christian's hand and led him across the room to where Gabriel stood with Juliana. "Christian, I would like to introduce you to my husband, Lord Dunevin. Gabriel, this is my brother, Lord Knighton."

The two men shook hands. As they exchanged polite greetings, Eleanor took a moment to watch her brother.

Like Grace, Christian had changed in the time she'd been away. He no longer shouldered the burden of the dreadful secret that had done so much to alter the course of his life. His smile was freer, his manner easier. He had come to terms with himself and the past, and doing so had obviously allowed him to finally see the beauty of his wife, a wife that had been chosen for him, untainted by resentment. She was so happy for them both.

Christian hunkered down to kneel before Juliana, who immediately moved a step closer to Eleanor's skirts.

"It is a pleasure to meet you, Miss MacFeagh," Christian said to Juliana. "That is a very pretty dress you have." He extended his hand to her in greeting. "My name is Knighton and I would like it very much if I could be your uncle."

Juliana looked at Eleanor, who smiled and nodded her encouragement. After a moment, Juliana lifted her hand slowly from behind the fullness of Eleanor's skirts and placed it tentatively into Christian's.

Christian stood, smiling, still holding her hand, and led Juliana over to the small aviary where Frances's pet canary bird was chirping on his perch from all the excitement.

He was wonderful with Juliana. Everyone was. Eleanor beamed.

"Well, now that we've all dispensed with the introductions," Grace said from the parlor doorway, "Forbes tells me that our supper is ready to be served."

The group made their way collectively across the hall to the spacious dining parlor where a formal supper had been laid out upon the long mahogany table. The best Knighton silver had been brought out, polished until it gleamed beneath the light of the chandeliers above them, and the cut crystal goblets had been taken from storage in the pantry, only the finest for this most special occasion.

Eleanor took her usual seat at Christian's left, seating Gabriel on her other side with Juliana between them. The Duchess of Devonbrook, Catriona, had disappeared upstairs only to return moments later with her three-year-old son, James, a perfect miniature model of her husband the duke, Robert, dressed in ankle-length trousers, short coat and shirt ruffles.

Catriona sat James in a Chippendale high stool at the far corner of the table between her chair and her husband's directly across from Brìghde, who soon had the boy involved in a serious discussion about the curliness of her hair.

The meal progressed quickly, through five separate

courses, with delicious food, a warm fire, and pleasant conversation. The others all asked about Trelay, where it was located, what it was like to live there so far from what was
considered modern society, how long their journey from
Scotland to the city had been. Eleanor told them all about
their hasty wedding at Gretna and their stopover in Kirkby
Lonsdale with Mr. Gray's Incredible Bed. Gabriel and
Robert discovered they had both served on some of the same
battlefields on the Peninsula.

After the meal, everyone withdrew to the parlor for tea,
port, or whatever other refreshment was at hand. Brìghde
and Juliana took turns playing with young James on the carpet before the fire, making card houses out of Christian's
best whist deck.

"Nell," Christian said as he settled onto the settee beside
Grace, port in hand, "how about some music? It's been too
long since we've heard you play. And perhaps my lovely
wife would accompany you on the pianoforte?"

He took up Grace's hand and kissed it, staring deeply into
her eyes.

Eleanor couldn't help but smile, watching the two of
them so happy now that Christian had banished his own personal demons from the past.

When he had married Grace earlier that year, they had
been virtual strangers at the altar. It was a marriage that had
been arranged by their grandfather, the duke, and Grace's
uncle, a beginning based on resentment and financial advantage. Their rocky beginning had had to weather some
stormy waters. It had taken some time, and a chase that had
led all the way to the Scottish Highlands, but now it was
plain to see that Christian had won his wife's heart, and she
had won his as well.

Somehow, too, in all the upheaval and heartache of the

past Season, the duke and Christian had come to some sort of accord with one another. It had been so bitter between them for so long. The time had been when the two men would hardly bear to sit in the same room with one another. But now they spoke cordially, discussing politics and other news of the day, and seemed well on the road to mending their lifelong rift.

It had been a year of new beginnings for them all.

Grace stood from the settee, but instead of heading directly for the pianoforte, she stopped a moment in front of where Juliana was sitting, speaking to her in a quiet whisper that only Eleanor and Juliana could hear.

"Juliana, usually when I play, my maid, Liza, sits beside me at the pianoforte and turns the pages for me. But Liza is not here with us in London because she is in Scotland getting ready to marry a most handsome man named Andrew MacAlister. So I wonder if I might entreat you to take Liza's place beside me tonight?"

Juliana looked at Brìghde and then to Eleanor. Eleanor stood and held out her hand.

Together the three walked to the corner of the room.

Gabriel sat in the far corner filled with a sense of true completion as he watched his daughter walk hand-in-hand with his wife across the room. He remembered a time when he had thought having Juliana speak again was the most important thing to him. But in the time since she had been with them, Eleanor had shown him that Juliana need not be considered odd or even cursed for her silence, that she was just as beautiful a girl as she had always been. Because of it, because of Eleanor's unique perspective, he had come to accept the possibility that he might never hear his daughter's laughter or sweet singing again. He would always have the memory of it and the days ahead of them. And nothing could replace that.

As Grace set her fingers to the keys and Eleanor took up a flute, a twin to the one she had at Dunevin, Gabriel glanced around the room, watching the faces of these people he now called family. All of them, had gone out of their way to make them feel welcome and secure, accepting them into their fold without question, without judgment.

Realizing this, it was easy to see now why Eleanor was such an extraordinary woman.

Gabriel watched Eleanor from across the room as she lost herself in the music she played, closing her eyes and moving her head to the gentle air of the stirring melody. She was a woman who gave everything of herself without a thought of receiving in return, a woman who had the uncanny ability of seeing beyond a person's outer veneer to the true spirit that lays sometimes hidden deep within.

His feelings for Georgiana had been based on concern, pity for the deplorable situation in which she had lived. He'd loved her, yes, but in a way that was so very different from the way he loved Eleanor. So, so very different.

With Eleanor, Gabriel had shed the fear that had haunted his days for so long. When he looked into her eyes, the man he saw reflected there was a man without the terrible shadows that had plagued him all his life. Eleanor believed in him, and she had made him believe in himself again, too. If it took the rest of his days, he was going to show her just how deeply, how completely she'd touched his life.

Eleanor finished her piece and everyone applauded, calling out for more. She looked briefly at Gabriel before she bent down and whispered something into Juliana's ear. Juliana looked at Eleanor, her face filled with hesitation, before finally she nodded and slid from the bench to stand beside Eleanor.

Eleanor handed Juliana her flute.

Not a person in that room made a sound as Juliana took a tentative breath and set the flute to her lips to play. Not a complicated tune, still the music of it drifted from Juliana's fingers like the trilling of a bird. Gabriel was spellbound.

He remembered the sound of her sweet child's voice singing that same song once from the castle courtyard years ago. He had believed it was a joy he might never again know.

Until now.

Somehow, without words, without uttering a sound, Juliana had found a way to sing again. Her singsong melody filled his soul and Gabriel felt the long hidden emotions inside of him swell and grow. His throat constricted and he took a deep breath.

She finished the piece and even the duke stood from his chair, calling out *"Brava!"* along with the others. Juliana lowered her eyes and stared shyly at the floor. She didn't see Gabriel crossing the room toward her until he had lowered onto one knee in front of her. Very slowly she lifted her head to meet his eyes.

"That was the most beautiful song I've ever heard, Juliana."

And then, for the first time in what seemed like forever, father and daughter embraced.

Eleanor lay awake on the bed, staring out through the sheer curtains on the window at the white light of the moon above the trees. She had tried to fall asleep, turning this way and that on the feather-stuffed mattress, but could never quite find a place that offered her comfort.

It wasn't the bed, she knew, or the moon shining through her window that was making her feel so restless. It was the thought of that same moon shining down on a magical castle set on a misty island surrounded by bottomless blue sea.

If she closed her eyes and focused very hard, she could almost see it, the endless sky, the hills that stretched out to the shore, carpeted in every possible shade of blue and purple and green all mixed together. She closed her thoughts to the sound of the carriages driving by outside and searched for Màiri's soft voice humming some old Gaelic ditty. She longed for the scent of fresh bannocks off the fire, of evenings sipping tea by the peat fire, of the gentle distant *baa*ing of the sheep on the machair. She yearned for the sight of her rugged Scotsman standing in kilt and sark.

Much as she had wanted, needed, to come back to London, much as she loved seeing her mother and Christian and the others again, Eleanor simply wanted to go home.

As if sensing her troubled thoughts, Gabriel turned quietly in the bed and took her gently against him, wrapping his arms around her from behind.

"You're not easy, lass," he whispered against her hair. "What is troubling you?"

Eleanor let go a discontented breath. "I don't belong to this place any longer, Gabriel. It is another place that calls to me now."

He kissed her ear, nuzzling her neck. "I feel it, too, love. It is like the sky before the storm, refusing to allow any moment of still. I've been thinking of Dunevin, too, longing for it for the first time in my life, but I just did not want to take you from your family so soon after you had been away from them so long."

Eleanor turned onto her side to look at Gabriel in the near-darkness. His face was etched in moonlight, his eyes soft and sleepy and just the sight of him filled her heart to bursting.

"They are my family and I love them all, but you and Juliana are my home. You are my life. Please take me home, Gabriel. I do not want to look out on row after row of buildings and smoke. I don't care to hear the brick dust man cursing the butcher at the street corner. I certainly don't want to see another young girl being scolded for holding her teacup the wrong way. I want to look out and see nothing, nothing at all but the blue"—she looked into his eyes—"and you . . . and our children running down the castle hillside."

"Children?" He blinked at her in the darkness.

It was a subject they had never discussed. Before now.

"Yes, Gabriel. I want to give you a son. Our son."

"Oh, lass . . ."

Gabriel wreathed his fingers into her hair and took Eleanor's mouth in a soft, tender kiss that lasted as long as either of them dared not breathe. Beneath the bedclothes, Eleanor hitched her leg gently over his, hooking them limb-to-limb, body-to-body. She could lie like that forever, she thought to herself, warmed by the touch of his skin, the gentleness of his hands, and never ever feel alone again.

"I have decided something else," she said to him when the kiss had ended, but their mouths were still touching softly and their breaths mingled between them.

"What is that, lass?"

"I've decided I do not much care for you in breeches."

Gabriel smiled, then chuckled softly against her lips, touching his tongue lightly to hers as he slid his hand against her bottom under the bedcoverings.

"Well, that is a good thing to know, lass . . ."

He pulled her hips forward slowly against him and she could feel the hardness of him swelling against her.

". . . especially since I'm not wearing any now."

Eleanor fell silent, their eyes locked, but only for a moment before she said, "I don't know if I can believe you, sir. I'm afraid I'll have to ask you to prove it."

And prove it he did.

Twice.

Chapter Nineteen

Eleanor sat reading quietly by the fire in the front parlor while Juliana and Brìghde lay stretched out upon the carpet at her feet, painting across big sheets of paper with watercolors.

To look at them, flat on their bellies, feet crossed behind them, one would question why they had any paper at all. There was more paint splashed across their noses, cheeks, and fingers than anywhere else.

As Gabriel had promised, they were to leave the city to return to Trelay first thing the following morning. It had been a week since their arrival in London and so much had happened in that short time, it seemed as if a full month at least must have passed.

Mr. Pratt had met with the solicitor for Georgiana's family earlier that week, and after apprising them of the change in Gabriel's circumstances, they had wisely decided to abandon their pursuit of a petition to the Crown. Their marriage, coupled with the Westover reputation, had been adequate persuasion for them to temper their greed. Furthermore, Juliana's legacy from her mother would thereafter be put into a trust so that it could not legally be squandered before she reached her majority.

Afterward, they had visited with Brìghde's grandmother,

who lived alone in a small tumbledown place in Cheapside. Gabriel had hired a physician, who upon thorough examination of her, diagnosed that the cause of her illness was due only to the acrid air of London and was not, as they had first thought, life-threatening. If she moved from the city, he predicted, she would certainly make a full recovery. Thus, when they departed for Scotland in the morning, Brighde's grandmother would be traveling with them as well.

Christian and Grace had departed the day before to return to Skynegal with the promise to ferry down to Dunevin sometime the following month. Robert and Catriona, the Duke and Duchess of Devonbrook, meanwhile, would be stopping in when they returned to their estate, Rosmorigh, in the Highlands for the winter.

Eleanor had invited everyone to travel to Trelay for Hogmanay, when she and Gabriel would be married again, this time among the mist and the green and an altar of ancient standing stones along the castle hillside. They would be surrounded by their families and friends and all the islanders, with the stirring song of Dunevin's resident piper carried on the sea wind.

For now, it was just Eleanor and the girls at the town house that afternoon. Gabriel had gone off earlier to retrieve the last of Eleanor's belongings from Knighton House, numerous trunks and boxes and crates that he was sending on ahead by separate coach and that would be waiting for them when they arrived back on Trelay.

Eleanor had spent that morning penning several pages of chatty correspondence to Amelia B., apprising her of all that had taken place while Mrs. Wickett was busy bustling about—as much as the staid Mrs. Wickett could endeavor to "bustle"—seeing to the details of closing up the house till next Season.

Eleanor had just finished reading a chapter in her book, leaving Mr. Darcy regretting his behavior toward Elizabeth Bennett, and thought to ask Mrs. Wickett for a cup of tea, when she happened to catch a glimpse of Brìghde's painting spread out at her feet.

It wasn't so much the colors, but the image that caught her eye, for it was nearly an exact copy of the mural Juliana had been painting upon the walls in the Dunevin nursery. This time, though, Brìghde was lending a hand to it, and Eleanor watched with curious interest as she would draw a bit, then glance at Juliana as if to ask if it was right.

This went on for several minutes, concentrating on the figures of the two in the water and the one on the hilltop, the bit that Juliana had never been able to finish in the nursery because of the fire. It was almost as if, somehow, mysteriously, Juliana had told Brìghde exactly what to draw—but of course that wasn't possible. She hadn't spoken a single word.

Finally, after another few minutes of this peculiar silent interaction, Eleanor leaned closer to them.

"Brìghde, what are you doing?"

The child swept a stray blond curl from her eyes, leaving a smear of blue paint across her forehead. "I'm drawin' in Jwee-lhanna on top o' this hill. She doesna want to do it hersel'."

Eleanor sat more forward, bending to look at the drawing closely. "How do you know that she doesn't want to do it?"

"Because she told it to me, my lady. That's why."

Eleanor was puzzled. "She told it to you? What do you mean? How did she do that?"

Brìghde giggled. "She told it to me in her thoughts, my

lady. Can you no' hear them? 'Tis clear as the birds singin' outside in the trees, it is."

Eleanor stilled, listening closely, but heard nothing, nothing but the silence.

"Are you saying you can hear what Juliana is thinking?"

Brìghde splashed a bit of paint on the drawing. "Aye."

"Right now? Right this moment?"

"Aye."

"How, Brìghde? How can you hear her thoughts?"

She shrugged. "I doona know. It just happens, is all. It's been that way since St. Michael's Day."

Eleanor's heart began to beat faster. "So are you saying Juliana is talking to you? Even now?"

Brìghde looked at Juliana, scrunching her forehead as if she didn't understand something, then smiled softly and nodded. "Aye, but I doona ken her meaning, my lady. She said she misses her doll. That is why she had me draw it for her here."

Brìghde pointed to one of the two figures in the water.

Eleanor drew in a startled breath. For Juliana, that doll was Georgiana. She looked at the painting again. Why did it suddenly look as if the figures in the drawing were struggling?

"Brìghde, is that Juliana's mother there?"

Brìghde shook her head. "Oh, no, my lady. The lady Georgiana is here."

She pointed to the rounded head of the seal peeking our from the waters. "You see, when the sea came to take her, she didn't really leave like the man said she would. She became a *selkie* so she could watch over Jwee-lhanna."

Eleanor remembered the day they had taken that first excursion on the isle, how that small seal had seemed to follow them. Surely not . . .

Eleanor pointed to the other two figures. "Brìghde, why is Juliana's doll in the water?"

Brìghde glanced at Juliana, then answered simply, "She says because the man took her there and gave her to the sea, but he told Juliana she must never speak of it, not a word to anyone, or else the sea would take her da away, too."

A chill seized Eleanor, prickling along her neck. Through her drawing Juliana was revealing to them what had happened that day to her mother, using the doll to keep from going against the warning of whoever it was who had killed Georgiana.

Eleanor's hands were trembling as she reached slowly forward and pointed to the third figure, the one in the water with Georgiana, the one Brìghde had called "the man."

"Who is this, Brìghde? Who is 'the man' who took away Juliana's doll and gave her to the sea?"

Brìghde looked up at Eleanor and said, "Why, he's the gillie, my lady. The laird's gillie. He's the one that gave Juliana's doll to the sea."

Oh dear God. It was Fergus.

Eleanor felt as if someone had just reached inside of her and stolen her very breath. Her eyes fixed upon the painting, taking in the scene. Suddenly it all made perfect sense.

It had been Fergus all along.

It had been Fergus who had set the fire in the nursery when he saw that Juliana was drawing what he had forbid her to say.

It had been Fergus who had put the hemlock on her dish on St. Michaelmas eve.

And it had been Fergus who had killed Georgiana, drowning her in the sea while Juliana watched on from the shore and then menacing her never to speak of it to another.

It had been Fergus who had stolen Juliana's voice.

Eleanor got up from the settee and looked to the hall outside the door. "Girls, I want you to stay here. I am going to take your picture and put it someplace safe so that we can show it to Lord Dunevin when he returns. I know he will want to see it."

Eleanor took the drawing, its paint still damp, dripping on the carpet, and headed from the room, closing the door softly behind her. She glanced about the hallway but saw no one else nearby. She hadn't seen Fergus all morning and she realized he had likely gone with Gabriel in the carriage to help with the trunks. Eleanor retreated to the kitchen.

"Mrs. Wickett, have you seen Fergus this morning?"

The housekeeper shook her head over a dish of fresh biscuits. "No, my lady, not since supper last night."

Eleanor nodded and thanked her, turning to leave. Her heart was beating so fast in her chest, she had to take several deep breaths to calm it. Her hands were shaking. All she could think about at the moment was finding Gabriel.

She heard a door close at the front of the house then.

Gabriel!

Clutching the girls' drawing, Eleanor rushed from the kitchen for the hall.

But it was empty when she got there and she noticed that the door to the parlor where she'd left the girls was suddenly ajar. He must have gone inside looking for her.

She headed for the door. "Gabriel, I—"

But he wasn't there. Instead, Juliana and Brìghde stood in the middle of the room looking at her in confusion.

Eleanor walked into the room. "Girls, did Lord Dunevin just come home? I thought I heard a door."

"Aye, you did, leddie," came a voice from behind her. "But it weren't the laird. It were myself."

Eleanor turned around to watch in horror as Fergus stepped from behind the cover of the door. A frightful shiver ran along her arms and she realized she still held the drawing.

Fergus realized it, too.

Eleanor moved between him and the girls.

"I can see from tha' picture and the look in yer eye that you know the truth." He glared at Juliana. "I tol' her she must keep her trap shut else her da would be taken to the sea with her ma."

"And she did, so frightened, she couldn't speak at all." Eleanor stepped a bit more between them. "How dare you?" she said, her voice quaking with emotion. "How dare you lie to her like that and terrorize her all this time, filling her with such a horrible fear?"

The man smirked unpleasantly beneath his grizzled beard. "It were a fine clever plan, too, and it was workin' until you came along, askin' all those questions, tryin' so hard to refute my family's curse to anyone who mentioned it."

"*Your* family?"

"Aye. Did ya no' know I were a Maclean on my mither's side?" His narrow eyes glinted at her. "'Twas my grandey who told me all about our witch's ancient curse against the MacFeaghs."

Eleanor felt her stomach roil. The man was actually bragging about being a murderer.

"Why, Fergus? Why would you do such terrible things? Gabriel has always treated you kindly, like a member of his own family."

"Family? Pah!" Fergus curled his lip in disdain. "I was ne'er more than the gillie sent off to do this and do tha'. We Macleans were ne'er good enough for the MacFeaghs, e'en way back to the one MacFeagh what got this all started. A Maclean saved his life, she did, and how did he repay her? By refusing her at e'ry turn. But in the end, we were the stronger for we've had St. Columb's staff all these years, hidden in a place on that isle that even he doesna know of.

. . . that even he doesna know of.

The were the very words Seamus Maclean had spoken to Eleanor the day she had gone to his cottage in Oban.

"The staff is in Uamh nan Fhalachasan," she said. "The Cave of the Hidden."

Fergus's eyes grew wide beneath the ragged band of his bonnet. "How did you . . . ?"

And then he realized. "Seamus Maclean, that bloody fool."

He spat in disgust. "It willna matter, because you will soon join the first Lady Dunevin. Two dead wives and two dead lassies. 'Tis going to be terrible hard for MacFeagh to explain that."

Eleanor caught a movement then out in the hall, spotted Gabriel lingering outside the door, and tried to keep Fergus talking so that Gabriel would realize they were in trouble.

"Why, Fergus? What did the MacFeaghs ever do to you?"

"When the laird's da, Alexander, died, his brother, Malcolm, thought to replace me. Said I was too old to be a laird's gillie anymore. That I no longer fit with the new laird of Dunevin. I couldna let him do that. It would have been a disgrace to me and my family. The MacFeaghs had disgraced us enough already."

"And so you killed him?"

"Aye. 'Twas simple. They all thought it were the salad that did him in." He scoffed then. "They forgot about the secret passageway to the laird's chamber. All it took were one large pillow."

Eleanor could see Gabriel listening at the door. She feared Fergus would notice her looking and so held out the painting with a flourish. "But why, then, Georgiana? What did she do to you?"

"She figured out that it was me who'd done in the laird's brother when she stumbled upon me going into that passageway. She was going to tell the laird. I couldna let her do that. I—"

Fergus noticed Juliana then, peering anxiously toward the door. He turned just as Gabriel rushed through, tackling the older man and tumbling with him against the settee.

The two men struggled against each other and Brìghde screamed, eyes wide as they grappled on the carpet, scattering paints and papers and furniture everywhere. Eleanor quickly drew the girls away, shooing them out to the hallway, and called for Mrs. Wickett to summon help.

By the time Eleanor turned back to the door, Gabriel had a panting Fergus by the throat up against the wall.

"I should kill you now for what you've done to my family." He glanced to the door then and noticed Eleanor and the girls watching him in frozen horror. The look in Juliana's eyes stopped him. She had already been witness to enough in her short life. No more

Gabriel glared at the gillie. "I will not subject my daughter to any more of your madness. I will just rest assured with the knowledge that you will very soon hang for your deeds."

Gabriel held the man tight against the wall until Mrs. Wickett, no longer staid but hysterical with alarm, returned with the magistrate.

After they had led Fergus away, driving him off in chains, it took some time to explain everything to the authorities. Charges would be pressed, an indictment would surely follow, and the magistrate assured Gabriel that a trial could take some time, as long as a year or more. Gabriel referred the matter to his solicitor, Mr. Pratt. He was of no mind to remain in London that long.

They would leave in the morning, as planned, and not a moment too soon.

Epilogue

He's a fule that weds at Yule;
When the corn's to shear, the bairns' to bear.
—Scottish Proverb

Isle of Trelay, December 1820

The seven days that fall between the Yule and the New Year are known throughout the Scottish isles as Nollaig, a time when no work should be done, when there is much eating and gift-giving, a time that is abundant with festivity and cheer.

There was a race on Yule morn to be the first to open the door, for he who "let in the Yule" would be assured of prosperity for the coming year. Each child waited patiently, sure to receive a Yule penny, or bawbee, from their elders. Holly and mistletoe hung from every doorway, for it was renowned throughout the isles that the faeries took cover under their leaves and would protect all who sheltered the sacred plant.

A company of young men would go from cottage to cottage each night, chanting Christmas and Yuletide songs. The people of each house would reward them with bread, butter, crowdie, and other treats for the chanters to feast on later.

Leading this motley group of carolers was Young Donald MacNeill himself, dressed in a bright coat made up of various tartans and topped off by a silly floppy hat. To encourage his audience so that they might reward his company of singers well, he sang quite loud and quite off-key, causing much laughter and bringing the householder to give him a whole basketful of bannocks just so he'd stop.

On the eve of the New Year, a tall candle scented with various herbs and spices was lit in the great hall. It had to be large enough to burn throughout the night to ensure good luck and prosperity in the New Year. Bonfires and torches burned, children recited Hogmanay rhymes. Clouds were studied in the early evening sky and if the largest and fleeciest lay to the north, it would be a year of plenty for man and beast.

It was a time of true rejoicing and there were so many reasons for them to celebrate. Thus it was the perfect time to hold an Hebridean wedding.

Not long after their return from London, Juliana had staggered them all when she came down to breakfast early one morning, took her seat at the table, and as if it were any other day, calmly asked for a bit of salt for her porridge.

Gabriel had dropped his coffee cup.

Màiri had said a prayer of thanks to the saints.

Eleanor had simply smiled, for she had always believed that the day would come when Juliana would finally have something to say.

It had come the very day after Seamus Maclean had shown Gabriel and Eleanor where to find the Cave of the Hidden, where indeed they had uncovered the long-lost ancient Maca'phi staff, and returned it to its rightful place in the old trunk.

From that moment on, it was as if the sun had suddenly dawned on a new and glorious day. And indeed it had.

Juliana laughed, she sang, she remarked on most everything she saw and no one ever complained; there were often times when Eleanor would catch Gabriel just staring at his daughter, listening to her with a smile of utter joy and tenderness.

Frances and the old duke arrived from London shortly before the Yule, bringing with them a surprise that had Eleanor fairly blubbering with delight. Amelia B. had come for the wedding, her entire family in tow, husband and two children, and the old friends had sat up all through that first night, tucked away by the fire in Gabriel's study, drinking numerous pots of tea and chattering like they had when they were school chums.

Christian and Grace arrived from Skynegal on Yule eve with the most blessed news of their expected child sometime the following summer. The Devonbrooks, Catriona and Robert, sailed in from Rosmorigh with young James, bringing with them Robert's brother, Noah, and his wife, Augusta, with their infant daughter, "Gussie," who had her mother's black hair and keen eyes, and her father's easy temperament.

Hogmanay morn dawned to a dusting of new snow across the heathery hillside where, despite the weather, Eleanor still insisted they be wed. As she was readying to make the short walk with Christian to where the guests were already assembled between a scattering of ancient standing stones that overlooked the bay, she heard a knocking on her chamber door and opened it to the unexpected sight of the old duke waiting there.

"Good morning, child. I wanted you to have this."

In his hands, he held a small box wrapped in colorful paper and tied off with a silk ribbon.

"They say it is never too late to make amends. I treated you and your brother ill for far too long. I hope you will accept this as a first token of my regret, and of my hope for your happy future."

Eleanor opened the box to reveal an elegant necklace with a long chain made of finely woven strands of gold. Hanging from it was a rounded pendant carved in gold and colorfully enameled with the Westover crest.

"There is a tiny button," the duke said, pointing to the pendant's side.

Eleanor found it and pushed it, causing the pendant to spring open, revealing an elegant filigree *oignon* watch inside. A moment later, the tiny chinging of chime song began to play from the piece to the tune of one of her favorite Mozart pieces.

Eleanor had never seen anything like it before. She looked at the duke and smiled.

"Thank you. It is so very lovely." She held it out to him. "Will you help me to put it on?"

"It was your father's," he said as he hitched the clasp behind her. She turned and the duke looked at her with nothing but sincerity in his eyes. "Yes, *your* father, Eleanor. He was a great lover of music and would be thrilled at your talent for the flute. I had it made so you would always have a remembrance of him near, even though you never knew him. He was a good man."

"Of course he was," Eleanor said, blinking away tears as she embraced the duke, her grandfather, for the first time in her life. "I shall cherish it always."

That day, the sun broke through the scattered winter clouds overhead, showering the gathering with brilliant heavenly light as Eleanor and Gabriel vowed their lives to one another this second time on that ancient hillside among the snow and the mist and their family and friends.

As they looked out across the bay afterward, Eleanor swore she saw that same small seal that had followed her and Juliana along the shore. She smiled.

That night, as the revelry in the great hall stretched on well into the morning hours, no one noticed when the groom quietly spirited his bride away from the others, stealing up a secluded side staircase that only they knew about.

Gabriel had had craftsmen from as far away as Edinburgh working on the restoration of the castle's top floor for months after the fire; they had finished the new laird's suite just in time for the wedding night.

Gabriel drew Eleanor close as they stood outside the door, kissing her tenderly, this woman who had so changed his whole world. He gazed at her, losing himself in the warmth of love he saw reflected in her green eyes. It was then he suddenly remembered the words that had been written by the Maclean Jura witch all those years before.

One of pure heart and eye will right the wrongs of the past . . .

And that Eleanor certain was. He silently thanked whatever magic it had been that had brought this woman into his life.

"Grace tells me I must carry you over the threshold or risk dire consequences."

Eleanor was nibbling at his ear, anxious to be alone with him. "Then by all means, my lord, you must."

Gabriel swept Eleanor up and into his arms, taking her mouth in a deep and passionate kiss that sent tingles to her toes and made her head giddy with delight. He kept on kissing her as he nudged the door open and crossed the room. He didn't take his mouth from hers until he had laid her on the bed, their new bed in their new suite.

It took Eleanor a moment before she realized precisely where she was. But when she did, her eyes lit with instant delight.

"Mr. Gray's Incredible Bed!" She looked at Gabriel, clearly astonished. "However did you—?"

"It took some doing and a great deal of persuasion, but I managed to convince our friendly innkeeper that we simply could not have our children born in any bed but this one."

"Oh, Gabriel!" Eleanor threw her arms around him and kissed him all over his face. "Thank you! Thank you! It is the finest wedding present a bride could ever receive."

"I had to promise him and Mrs. Gray they could visit in the summer." Gabriel grinned. "Ah, but there is something we must see to before we can ever think of having our children in this monstrosity of a thing." He gave her a look that absolutely curled her toes.

Eleanor beamed, already knowing his thoughts. "Oh, and what would that be, husband?"

Gabriel didn't even bother to answer her. Instead he loosened his cravat, tossing it to the floor, and joined her on the bed, drawing her close, touching his lips to hers so that he could spend the next few hours showing her instead.

Author's Note

Dear Reader:

I hope you have enjoyed your visit with Gabriel and Eleanor, and friends from the other books in this series as we traveled to the misty western isles of Scotland.

Though the isle of Trelay doesn't truly exist, I did base it largely on the two small islands of Colonsay and Oronsay, which lie off the Argyllshire coast of Scotland, near the seaside town of Oban, where Gabriel and Eleanor sailed in the earlier chapters of the story.

The castle of Dunevin is also fictional, although I modeled it on various Highland fortresses, including Duart on the isle of Mull, and Castle Stalker in Argyllshire, both tower houses and both very near to where the story of *White Mist* is set.

Clan MacFie is the most common spelling for one of the oldest of the Scottish clans, so ancient, in fact, that its early history is unwritten. It is claimed by some that the clan did spring from either a fairy woman or a seal woman, but it is generally believed that the earliest members of this tribe of dark haired ancient Scots were the original inhabitants of Colonsay, which they held until they were dispossessed of it in the seventeenth century.

After that time, the MacFies fell the way of other broken

and dispossessed clans, following some of the other, larger clans to the nearby coast and isles.

The magic colour staff of the clan that is mentioned in the story is a true legend of the MacFie clan, and was believed to have protected them for hundreds of years before it mysteriously disappeared around the same time the MacFies lost their ruling place over this windswept corner of Scotland. It has never been seen since, but its image is engraved on several of the carved Celtic tombstones of long-ago MacFie chiefs that can be seen to this day at the sanctuary on the isle of Oronsay, founded, they say, by St. Columba.

If you have ever visited the Isles and Highlands of Scotland, you must know it is truly a place of mist and magic. The ancient Gaelic language blessedly still lingers throughout the isles, and in more recent date, it has even enjoyed a resurgence. History itself whispers across the heathery hillsides like the legendary skirl of the bagpipe, and in some places you can almost begin to believe time has stood still for hundreds of years.

A special note of thanks to my readers who have written to me about the other books in this series. I thank you for your kind words and your requests for me to continue it. I get a thrill each time I read how much you've enjoyed sharing a bit of your time with my characters. I sincerely thank you for that. But what began with *White Heather,* and carried on with *White Magic* and *White Knight,* has concluded with *White Mist.*

At least for now.

Does that mean I will never revisit the friends from this series of stories? I'm a firm believer in never saying never. Perhaps I'll allow Juliana and Brìghde a little while to enjoy their childhood years and then stop back to Trelay in another time, in another story. But for now, at least, it is the isle of

Skye that is calling to me for my next story, the largest of the Hebrides and one touched by every aspect of history. You can read more about this, and any other upcoming stories, on my web site at *http://www.jaclynreding.com* or write to me directly c/o P.O. Box 1771, Chandler, AZ 85244-1771. I'd love to hear from you. Until then . . .

J. R.

**Continue Reading for Jaclyn Reding's
Next Romantic Interlude . . .**

Coming Soon from Signet

Drayton Hall, Northumberland, 1746

"Preposterous!"

Alaric Sinclair Fortunatus Drayton, the fourth Duke of Sudeleigh, bellowed from the far end of the breakfast table.

"What is it this time, dearest?" asked her grace, Duchess Margaret, a striking woman with chestnut hair now streaked with gray. She calmly poured a splash of pekoe into his teacup before refilling her own. She had grown accustomed to her husband's quick temper these five and twenty years past. Though he roared loudly, he rarely did any real damage.

"'The Female Spectator.'" He waved a small printed booklet through the air. "A waste of the paper on which it is printed. This issue deserves the prize for true idiocy. Look here on the first page. 'A Letter in Favor of Woman's Equality to Man.' Equality! Have you ever heard of such a thing?"

"No, dear. I have not."

"Who on earth writes this drivel?"

"I couldn't say, dear."

"'A Lady of Quality' is what it says here. No doubt the offspring of some Whig bast—"

"Alaric—the girls!"

The duke frowned deeply, causing his jowls to droop over the tight knot of his laced cravat as he dropped the pamphlet onto the table in front of him, took up his cup, and swallowed a large gulp of tea. He stared sullenly at the buckle on his shoes. His silence on the matter didn't last for long.

"I say if she dares to write such a thing, this 'Lady of Quality,' she ought to have the backbone to attach her name to it. Let everyone in the kingdom know exactly who she is so they can shame her husband or her father or whoever it is who is responsible for her into bringing the unruly chit in line."

"Yes, dear."

"Discipline, that's what it is. There needs to be discipline in every household. You scold me for keeping such a tight rein on our girls, Margaret, but you could wager your monthly pin money that *our* daughters would never be found authoring such trash." Along the table, five pairs of eyes in varying shades from brown to green peered innocently back. "*Our* girls know the proper order of things, a woman's place and what not. Is that not true, girls?"

"Yes, Papa," came a chorus of feminine voices in response.

The duke smiled beneath his powdered periwig,

utterly pleased with himself as he looked from one to the next down the length of the mahogany dining table, ranging in age from twenty-four to eight. Elizabeth, Isabella, Catherine, Matilda, and Caroline—he'd named them for some of the greatest queens of England. They were all beautiful, intelligent, and refined, even the little one, Caro, who drank her tea as elegantly as if she were dining in state. Through them, the Drayton dynasty would grow and flourish. He would see them all allied with fine husbands of good English stock, earls, marquesses, perhaps even a royal prince. They, in turn would surround him with countless grandchildren to bounce on his knee and tickle relentlessly under their chins.

Looking on them all, the very picture of loveliness, the duke gave in to a familiar sigh of longing. Much as he loved his daughters, beamed with pride whenever they were nearby, there was one thing yet missing from it all. Oh, how he longed for a son.

He stole a glance at his wife. At three and forty, Margaret was still of an age to bear a child successfully. It had been five years since they'd lost their last, too early to know what it might have been. Perhaps they just might yet have time to give it one last try. . . .

The duke was so caught up in his thoughts, he scarcely noticed the dangerous look in the eye of the young woman sitting at the opposite end of the table.

She had been christened Elizabeth Gloriana Regina Drayton after the great Virgin Queen of England to whom her family owed their good fortune these two centuries past. It had been her great-great grandfather, Fortunatus Drayton, who had been awarded the Sudeleigh dukedom for his loyalty and service to the queen during the darker days of her early confinement by her half-sister Mary Tudor.

It was a name the eldest child of the Duke of Sudeleigh had seemed fated from birth to bear. She shared the same straight auburn-blonde hair as her namesake, white skin, slender fingers, and changeable hazel-colored eyes. Over the past four and twenty years, Lady Elizabeth Drayton had grown into a young woman of beauty, pride and dignity. She was taller than most women, with a striking, upright manner of carrying herself that drew stares whenever she walked through a room with her usual brisk and determined pace. Educated above and beyond her gender, she could converse in several languages, was fond of dancing and the theatre, and was as proficient with the needle as she was at both the virginal and lute.

And there was one other way in which Elizabeth resembled the glorious former queen. She rejected any suggestion that a woman couldn't do any job as well, or even better, than a man.

Elizabeth waited until her father was thoroughly engrossed in his newspaper before speaking up.

"Papa? I was just thinking about what you'd said, of that pamphlet you read."

"Yes?" The duke didn't move from behind his newspaper.

"You stated that the pamphlet was 'drivel' and 'a waste of the paper on which it was printed . . .' "

"Yes?"

"Well, I wondered, mustn't there be some public interest in such writings if the publishers of these pamphlets are printing them?"

The room fell instantly silent. Every pair of eyes in the room turned to stare at Elizabeth. Even the footman, Harry.

And the dog.

The duke lowered his newspaper to stare at her. "What did you say?"

Elizabeth sat up straighter in her chair and spoke to be heard down the length of the table. "I simply wondered why anyone would go to the expense and trouble of publishing works such as the one you mentioned if they truly were unworthy of print."

The duke's expression clouded—Elizabeth thought he might surely bellow anew—until she added rather demurely, "I am, after all, merely a woman and so do not have your grasp on such matters."

"Ah, my pet." The duke lightened, utterly unaware of her veiled sarcasm. "You are too young and innocent to grasp the concept of scandal and controversy, so you must allow me to enlighten you.

It is an unfortunate fact of our time that these two things—scandal and controversy—alone sell more papers and books than the greatest examples of literature and learning combined. The more shocking the subject matter, the more copies go into circulation. It doesn't even matter if any of it is true! What it comes down to is the fact that as long as the public continues to devour this rubbish, the publishers will continue to print it and fill their coffers."

Elizabeth wisely waited several moments before adding, "But did *you* not buy one of these pamphlets yourself, sir?"

The duke looked at his wife beside him. "What are you teaching these girls, Margaret?"

"Alaric, the child makes a valid point."

The duke exhaled loudly, turning again to his daughter. "Yes, my dear child, I did purchase the pamphlet," he began, searching for and then finding a suitable explanation, "but only so that I might educate you girls on what is proper and improper reading material." He snatched a book of poetry from the hands of Elizabeth's younger sister Matilda, who was reading over her breakfast, waving it in the air like a war banner. "*This* is proper reading material for young ladies. Graceful words to create graceful thoughts. *This*," he went on, flinging the hand that clutched the pamphlet outward, "is improper reading material, filled with nonsensical words that breed nonsensical thoughts. Remember that, all of you."

"Yes, Papa." Elizabeth stared at her father through a long moment before joining the chorus of her sisters.

The clock in the hall outside struck nine, echoing to the lingering silence of the breakfast room.

"May I be excused from the table, please?" Elizabeth asked, setting her napkin on the table before her.

The duke looked at her. "What are your plans for the day, daughter?"

Elizabeth did not hesitate in her answer. "I thought to give some time this morning to my sampler and my letter writing before mother and I are to go off to the modiste for our fittings."

The duke beamed approval. "Splendid. You've been working so very hard on that sampler, Elizabeth. It must be quite splendid. Will we ever see it?"

Elizabeth eyed Isabella, the sister closest to her in age before responding. "When it is finished, Papa. Not before."

The duke grinned to his wife. "She is a perfectionist, that one, just like her father." He waved a hand. "Off with you then, child. Make good use of the morning's light."

"I intend to, Papa."

Upstairs in her bedchamber, Elizabeth turned the key in the door to ensure that she wouldn't be disturbed. Bright morning sunlight spilled past damask draperies to play across the patterned Savonnerie carpet that stretched across the floor.

She crossed the room to a small willow basket tucked away on the cushioned window seat, removing the scrap of linen she had stretched across a wooden tambour frame. She plicked the needle from where it was tucked at the side and carefully studied the canvas before poking the needle through, drawing the colored thread its length and repeating it for a single perfect stitch. She held it out and admired the result in the light, her work for that day complete. After all, what was it they said? *A stitch in time. . . .*

Having satisfied her word to her father, Elizabeth set the sampler aside. She lowered into the carved chair behind the writing desk that faced out the windows onto the kitchen garden where in the next months brilliant pink cherry blossoms would explode into color. A chorus of sparrowsong light and sweet whistled on the morning breeze, but Elizabeth scarcely noticed. Instead, as she removed the small key she kept tucked in the hidden pocket of her bodice, her father's indignation from that morning echced through her thoughts.

Preposterous. . . .

Idiocy. . . .

Equality! Have you ever heard of such a thing?

Setting the key in a side lock, Elizabeth sprung open the false bottom hidden underneath the top center desk drawer. She removed the small stack of paper sheets from inside, skimming through several of the ones she'd already written until she came upon the one she sought, reading its title to herself.

"A Letter in Favor of Woman's Equality to Man . . . by a Lady of Quality."

She smiled. It was one of her better pieces. Her dear friend and editor had suspected it from the moment she'd submitted it for print. Her father's reaction that morning had only confirmed it.

It had begun with a meeting of pure chance at King's Circulating Library one rainy day in London six years earlier, the very year of Elizabeth's calamity of a season. She had been returning some books just a few short days before they were scheduled to leave the city and return north to Drayton Hall. As she'd stood at the counter, an older woman with a generous mouth and wise eyes had approached to stand beside her.

"Is that Defoe's *Duncan Campbell*?" she'd asked, glancing through the titles Elizabeth was returning while the clerk saw to his business.

"Yes, it is. I've just finished reading it."

The woman nodded. "How did you find it?"

Something about the woman felt familiar somehow, kindred. Elizabeth smiled. "I enjoyed it very much. I would have to say it is my favorite of Defoe's work—even if it isn't truly his own."

"You are saying Mr. Defoe didn't write this?"

"Not on his own, no." Elizabeth went on, "The book obviously credits him with being the author, and perhaps he did write parts of it, but there is a definite presence of another's hand in it, most especially in the way the story illustrates man's dominance over woman, how any freedom is denied them merely for the sake of their sex. Only another woman could have told woman's story so candidly."

The stranger simply smiled as Elizabeth fished in her reticule for the coin to pay the clerk behind the desk. "I wonder who could have assisted Mr. Defoe in his work."

Elizabeth gathered up the other books she was taking home with her. "If I were to hazard a guess, it would be Eliza Haywood. The text echoes with her unique voice. Whoever it is, it is a shame she will never receive the proper credit for it."

"Oh, I think she just has." The woman put out her hand in greeting. "I am Eliza Haywood."

A friendship had been forged that afternoon between two like-minded women who had come from utterly different walks of life. Over the years, they had corresponded through a steady stream of letters. Thus, when Eliza had written to Elizabeth to reveal her plans to publish a periodical called *The Female Spectator*, written strictly by women for women, Elizabeth had been all too happy to contribute.

Taking out a fresh sheet of foolscap, Elizabeth thought for a moment, dipped her quill in the inkwell, and began in her careful, elegant hand:

A Letter from A Lady of Quality Opposed to the Keeping of Young Women at Their Needles . . .

A fortnight later, Elizabeth sat in the Sudeleigh coach, hopelessly watching the passing landscape through the window. Accompanied by her sister, Isabella, and two of her father's men-at-arms, they were headed close to the Northern Border.

"You must have known he'd discover the truth about those letters sometime, Elizabeth."

Elizabeth turned her attention from the window to her sister sitting across from her. With hair the color of black silk that fell in loose curls to her waist and eyes like faceted emeralds, Isabella had none of Elizabeth's own 'shortcomings,' as their father had so furiously pointed out several days earlier when he'd called Elizabeth to his office to reveal that he'd somehow discovered her long-hidden secret.

Isabella was the image of everything that was soft and tranquil in the world. She had the soul of an artist, the elegance of a swan, so different from her elder sister, so accepting of the ways of the world. At times, Elizabeth envied that quality in her almost as much as she found fault with it. Elizabeth's closest confidante, Isabella had known about her sister's writing from the start, had warned her against it even as she'd kept her secret faithfully.

"He'll soon calm down," Elizabeth said not a little hopefully. "Father has gotten upset with me before and he always forgives me. Remember my season in London, when I wore breeches to the masquerade ball at Kensington? His anger that night was more fierce than a storm, and just as quickly passed."

"Elizabeth! That was nearly seven years ago and he hasn't allowed you to return to London since."

Elizabeth shrugged. "What care I for mincing bucks in powdered wigs and face paint? Father still forgave me that just as he'll forgive me this."

"I'm afraid it isn't as simple this time." Isabella's expression grew suddenly grim. "There is something you should know."

Elizabeth knew a moment of sudden foreboding. "What is it, sister?"

She was close to tears. "Oh, Bess, we are not going to visit Aunt Idonia like Papa said we were. That was only a ruse to get you to agree to leave Drayton Hall willingly. He knew if you were aware of where we were really going, you'd never agree to it."

Elizabeth stared at her. "Isabella . . . where are we going?"

"We're going to the estate of one of his associates, a Lord Purfoyle, in Scotland."

Scotland? Elizabeth was stunned. "Why on earth would Papa send us all the way to Scotland?"

Isabella swallowed hard before responding. "He means for you to wed Lord Purfoyle."

Elizabeth felt the color drain from her face. *Wed him?* "But the man is as old as our father!"

"Papa knew 'twould be your reaction, which is why he misled you into thinking we were going to Aunt Idonia's. Faith, we've already passed the border while you were napping and are well out of England by now. I'm so sorry."

Elizabeth's eyes burned against tears, angry tears at having been betrayed by her own father, a man who, despite their differences, she had always respected and adored. "How could you have kept this from me, Bella? Why did you not tell me before now?"

Whatever might have been Isabella's response was lost on a sudden deafening crack as the carriage lurched perilously forward. They tilted sideways, sending Elizabeth tumbling, lost amid a jumble of voluminous silk petticoats and lace ruffles. The ladies struggled to right themselves as the coach ground to a slow, rough halt.

"Higgins?" Elizabeth called out to the coachman as she pushed back the lopsided brim of her straw bergère. "Whatever has happened?"

" 'Twere a sheep standin' in the middle of the road, my lady. I had to turn us off the road to keep from hitting him, but it looks like we've gotten stuck now. Might've broken a wheel, too."

"Oh, goodness!" said Isabella.

Elizabeth reached for the latch. The door fell open, revealing the back wheels of the carriage utterly mired in what appeared to be a substantial stretch of bog. "Can you repair it?"

"Aye, if I can get to it to fix it, that is," said Higgins, standing aspace a way and scratching his balding head. "It looks hopelessly stuck."

Manfred and Titus, the duke's two men-at-arms, circled around from the other side of the lopsided coach. "We best get you ladies out of there and see what we can do to push the coach free."

"Yes, that is a good idea."

Manfred took a step toward the coach, sinking ankle deep in the mud. When he moved to take another step, his foot slipped clean out of his boot. "Gaw, it's like molasses, it is," he said struggling to get to his boot. A moment later, he lost his balance and fell face first into the mire. When he finally got to his feet, the front of him—his hands, his face, his paunched girth—was hopelessly covered in muck.

Titus was chuckling behind him. Manfred gave his comrade a glare as he removed his soiled coat and waistcoat. "I think I'll be steadier if I were t' carry you on me back, my lady. Can you wrap your arms round me neck?"

Elizabeth was bending over the man in a most indelicate piggyback pose when she heard an unfamiliar voice come suddenly from behind them.

"Och, but you English lassies have a peculiar way of showing a fancy for the lads, you do."

Manfred turned with Elizabeth still draped over his shoulders to see that a man had come unnoticed upon the scene, a man who spoke with a heavy Scottish brogue. He was dressed in the fashion of the Highlands, in a belted tartan plaid that left his legs exposed beneath a loose flowing shirt that he hadn't even bothered to tie at the neck. His hair, dark as soot, hung below his neck and was tied in a queue beneath a bonnet that was decorated with two eagle's feathers. He carried a broadsword at his side and round studded shield strapped to his back that made him look utterly primitive, even feral. The cocksure grin that crossed his face somehow touched a nerve with Elizabeth.

"I suppose you have a better idea?" she said, trying not to think of how ridiculous she must look.

"Aye, I do." He quickly removed his sword and shield, glancing at Manfred. "Put the lass down, man. You can wash yourself off in yon burn."

Then, without another word, the stranger proceeded to walk straight through the mire—shoes, hose and all. In one swift movement, he swept Elizabeth from the carriage step and into his arms. She scarcely had time to react. "How dare you, sir? In England, it is customary to ask a lady's permission before assaulting her person."

"You're no' in England anymore, lass." The man stared at her from behind a scowl. "You want me to put you down then?"

Elizabeth glanced at the sludge that surrounded them, and from which a sour smell had begun to rise. "No, please, do not."

"I dinna think so."

He walked her easily through to drier land, more

dropping her than setting her down, and then turned to retrieve Isabella. It was only then that Elizabeth realized her heart was pounding.

"Have you ever seen such a man?" Isabella whispered as the stranger set to helping Manfred and Titus in pushing the coach free from the bog. "He carried me as if I weighed no more than a feather."

Elizabeth crossed her arms before her. "He is too forward."

"He was just trying to be helpful."

"More likely he was just trying to sneak a hand down your bodice. If Father were here, he would have . . ."

An idea struck Elizabeth then like a lightning bolt, an idea of such ingenuity, such cleverness, she could scarcely contain herself.

Three quarters of an hour later, when the carriage was free and the wheel had been repaired, Elizabeth walked toward the stranger, a much different Elizabeth than she'd been before.

"I wish to thank you, sir, for your kind assistance. I shudder to think what we might have done had you not happened by when you did."

The Highlander looked at her. "Pleased to have been of help, my lady." He turned, pulling on his coat as he readied to leave.

But he couldn't leave. Not yet.

Elizabeth followed him. "I didn't, uh, ask your name. I would at least like to know to whom I owe our debt of gratitude."

"Dùghlas Dùbh MacKinnon fro' the isle of Skye."

Dùghlas Dùbh. It was a fitting name for this un-tamed man.

He stopped at the burn to wash the bog mud from his shoes and hose. As he bent to cup the water in his hands, running his fingers down the length of his calves, Elizabeth found herself staring at the way the muscles in his legs pulled and flexed be-neath the hem of his plaid. There was power in those legs. *Male* power.

When she looked up again, she realized he was staring at her—as she was staring at him. Her skin went hot.

My God, she thought, *I am blushing . . .*

"I am Lady Elizabeth Drayton. The other lady with me is my sister, Lady Isabella Drayton. We are indebted to you for your kindness, Mr. Mac-Kinnon."

Elizabeth held out her hand to him. The High-lander glanced at her a moment, then bowed. "A pleasure, my lady." He turned then and started to walk away. "Good day to you, and Godspeed on your journey."

He hadn't made it more than a couple yards be-fore Elizabeth called to him. "Mr. MacKinnon, may I ask where you are headed?"

"I'm to an inn I know of in Galloway for the night, and then up to the Hielands and home."

She followed him. "You've lost a good amount of daylight in coming to our aid. Please, at least allow us to take you to your Galloway inn. You'll never make it by nightfall and we are headed that way, too."

It was a lie, but he couldn't know that.

The Highlander hesitated, considering her offer. "Thank you, my lady. I've been walking for some time. I would be much obliged for the chance to rest my legs."

"Then you shall." Elizabeth rewarded him with her prettiest smile. Together they returned to the coach and the others. "Please, do sit inside with Isabella and me so we can chat some more along the way. I have never been to Scotland before and would love to hear about it."

As MacKinnon stooped his head to enter the coach, Isabella grabbed Elizabeth's sleeve and gave it a warning tug. "What in the name of heaven are you doing?"

Elizabeth drew a breath of determination. "Nothing, yet, sister, but if I have my wish, this Highlander might just prove very useful in the next few hours."

SIGNET (0451)

"Jaclyn Reding is a rising romance star!"
—*Catherine Coulter*

JACLYN REDING

Other novels in the White Quartet:

❑ **WHITE KNIGHT** 198522/$5.99
Fleeing the cold, cruel knight she was forced to marry, an
unhappy bride takes refuge in a remote castle—and finds a
chance at true love with her mysterious husband....

❑ **WHITE MAGIC** 408551/$5.99
"Charmingly written, witty...sure to please."
—*Romantic Times*

❑ **WHITE HEATHER** 406508/$5.99
"Exciting and passion-filled."—*Rendezvous*

Also Available:

❑ **STEALING HEAVEN** 406494/$5.99

For only $3.99 each, you'll get to surrender to your wildest desires....

LORDS OF DESIRE

A special romance promotion from Signet Books—featuring some of our most popular, award-winning authors...

Arizona Gold by Maggie James
❏ 0-451-40799-7

Bride of Hearts by Janet Lynnford
❏ 0-451-40831-4

Diamonds and Desire by Constance Laux
❏ 0-451-20092-6